THE LAST
POWER WAR

THE LAST POWER WAR

MAGICAL GIRL UNDERGRAD – BOOK 4

Aest Belequa

Podium

Thank you to the Council of the Eternal Hiatus writing group.
They were phenomenal for keeping me rolling and writing on this project,
for holding me accountable, and for helping me grow as an author.

Cover design by Kittra McBriar

ISBN: 978-1-0394-7027-9

Published in 2025 by Podium Publishing
www.podiumentertainment.com

Podium

THE LAST
POWER WAR

PART ONE

1

Meet the Press

Flashbulbs and camera lenses filled the entire quad outside Tokyexico University's Student Union Building. Fans of *Heroics 101*, Dr. Mays, and Mindstorm yelled and shouted behind the media, waving banners. And on the opposite side, APPEAL had assembled, chanting slogans and waving their own flags. It was press conference time.

It'd been a couple of days, and TU's administration had used every trick in the book to keep the reporters off campus and away from students, but finals week was over. So, here I was, on the stage with Mindstorm and Dr. Mays, thinking about how unfair it all was.

They'd had *their* conference earlier, of course. All *they* had to do for finals week was collect papers, proctor exams, and do a little grading. Meanwhile, I'd been attacked by a major-league villain, fought an army of temp heroes to a standstill, cleaned Bianca's nightmare dorm room, *and* managed to at least half-ass my exams—all while both her parents and mine grew ever closer by road and plane.

And now, since they'd had their conferences, all the professors of Superpower Studies had to do was freeze my butt off and wait for the press to eat me alive. At least Bianca was entertaining all the parents, so I didn't have to do *that*, too.

"According to our research team, TU's policy was for little- and minor-league heroes to hole up during the major-league attack," an absolutely gorgeous woman in a bright blue jacket said. "So what was behind your decision to get involved in the Episode?"

I clenched a fist behind the podium. This had been going on for almost ten minutes. "You're mistaken. TU's official policy was for mid-to-low minor- and little-league student supers to avoid contact. However, my partner and I had been moving up the minor leagues, and we considered ourselves qualified to help. We've both worked with the Triad as auxiliary heroes, and we knew how to act in a support role. It also seemed like Lord Destructo and McHammer were using lieutenants, and we wanted to counter them as a threat."

"When the Episode turned into an all-out offensive by 3V1L, how did you continue justifying your presence on the battlefield? There were now two serious threats, and you weren't equipped to handle either of them," another reporter said, smiling a smarmy smile from under his mustache.

"Easy. Once it became clear that 3V1L was involved, it became *our* show. Fursona and I are responsible for dealing with 3V1L, and have been all semester. They're part of our rogues' gallery—honestly, the only part that's been a thorn in our side rather than an annoyance—and this was a direct attack by them on us." I glanced at Mays, who nodded slowly.

He still looked shaken. It'd been days since The Agent shot Dr. Jackson outside of Walnut Tower, and she wasn't out of the hospital yet, but the Ilneats were coming back, and I was confident they'd fix her right up. Dr. Mays didn't seem to share my confidence; he didn't seem to have slept since Tuesday, and I reevaluated whether the professors were having an easy finals week.

I continued, holding up a hand before another reporter could interrupt me. "Look, I get it. You think I made a bad decision. But here's the thing. 3V1L wasn't on campus because they saw an opportunity to help out Lord Destructo and McHammer. They hate those guys—there's even a big rivalry going down in Evergreen that you aren't covering. They came here for me."

Most of the reporters went silent for a moment, but the one in the blue jacket grinned. I winced; I'd seen that smile before. The media reserved it for villains—and when a hero walked into their ambushes.

But she didn't say anything, and after a second or two, the other reporters seemed ready to keep up the bombardment. Another man, this one with a haircut that would've been Agent-like if his hair wasn't so gray, cleared his throat. "How long has 3V1L been after you specifically?"

I could answer this one, but it'd sound funny. "Okay, that's a tough question to answer. Last year, Golden Goose wiped out 3V1L, killed their leadership, and scattered them to the winds. But someone picked up the pieces. I don't know the details, but I think they saw a business opportunity or a chance to diversify their portfolio."

Official policy, passed down from Rocko *and* the Council of Heroes, was *not* to mention The Agent's name. Rocko's reasoning made perfect sense; the Ilneat producer had a perfect plot twist, and they stood to make a lot of money by waiting until the Episode released to make the reveal. The only thing that bugged me was that they *hadn't* released it yet.

The Council of Heroes could only be covering their asses, though.

"So, this mysterious someone took the reins of 3V1L, became the new One *L*, and started recruiting henches and *V*s. This person also did a great job of raiding the Tokyexico Council of Heroes' archives for any information about their identity, tactics, or whereabouts, so there's not much evidence about how long they've been after me, but if I had to put a rough date on it . . . May of this year."

Another reporter shouted, "And you don't know who this One *L* is? How do you propose to deal with 3V1L without a Top Five hero like Golden Goose? Do you have any comments on her death?"

"No comment. Her death's a tragedy, and she'll be mourned," I said stiffly. It was true; plenty of people missed the world's strongest heroine, and even I wished she was back. All this wouldn't be happening if she was around. "I can't speak about the One *L*'s identity, but I do know that, following their assault on Tokyexico University, their organization's a shadow of its former self, which was a . . . shadow . . . of its former . . . self."

I trailed off. The woman in the blue jacket held her hand up, and I nodded at her even though I knew the trap's jaws were closing. She cleared her throat. "Actually, I *can* speak for the One *L*'s identity and his reason for attacking you. The Agent's had a grudge against you ever since you ruined his protege's run at the minor leagues. He's one of the metapowered supers, and if given long enough to snowball, he only has two counters—one of which he put in the hospital. And no one knows where he is. Do you have any comment on that?"

Well, *shit*.

I glanced at Dr. Mays, but he shook his head. Mindstorm, on my other side, wasn't any more helpful. Rocko hadn't given me a briefing on what to do if *this* happened, and I didn't know what the Council of Heroes wanted, either.

So, after an uncomfortable pause stretched a little too long, I cleared my throat and started improvising.

"Yes, The Agent is responsible for all of this. And yes, I was in competition with someone he directly supported last spring. I'm not sure where you're getting your information, but it's very good."

She kept her sharklike smile, and I kept my eyes locked on hers. "So, you're up against a ridiculously powerful hero with no idea how to track him down—"

"Quick correction," I interrupted her, holding up my hand again. Her grin finally slipped briefly, and I pressed my advantage like I was fighting a supervillain. "The Agent is not a hero. Maybe he was at some point in the past, and I understand still wanting him to be one. He looks great on camera, and **[Temp Hero]** lets him set up so many cool storylines by making Extras heroes for an Episode. But the reality is that he's a villain. He's never been a true hero, either. He's always been out for one person, and that's The Agent."

"Okay, you're up against a ridiculously powerful super with no idea how to track him down. How do you intend to beat 3V1L before he rebuilds it?"

Now, it was my turn to smile like a shark. "If I told you that, it wouldn't be a surprise, now would it?"

I landed on Walnut Tower's roof and clomped down the stairs into the green room. Fang Swee's power had been working overtime, and the whole place had changed. I still had my make-up table, but it was off in a corner, and so were the two computer screens that tracked our rogues' gallery. The chaise lounge was off in a corner, too, and so was a very scribbled-on whiteboard.

But *my* couch was gone. It'd been replaced by a full-blown living room set in a conversation pit, with an absolutely massive television that, right now, was playing Bianca's favorite thing to watch over the last four days: Episode footage of her highlights. Luckily, it was muted, and Bee herself was being the good hostess; she'd poured drinks—not alcoholic, even though she wasn't fooling anyone with that—and managed to scrounge together some chips and homemade salsa.

Mom and Dad and Bee's mom and dad filled out the sofa. I'd been apprehensive about letting so many Extras see my workplace, but they'd worn me down, and even though it'd felt a lot like the boundaries between Anika DuPont and Magical Girl Understudy were collapsing even more, Mom and Dad seemed to get it.

They hadn't called me Understudy once, and I wanted to hug them for it every time.

Instead, I got a face full of black hair as Bee hugged me. She pulled me in close, wrapping her arms around me, and whispered a couple of words in my ear.

"Did you call me your sidekick?"

"Of course," I whispered back.

"Good. I don't want to be your partner if it's going to get me in front of the camera."

I burst out laughing. The adults—the adultier adults, that is—were engaged in conversation around the green room's coffee table, and Bee and I slipped away through the door to my apartment. I waved at Dad, and he winked at me. I shot him a thumbs-up.

Then, the maintenance door shut.

"So, it went well, then?" Bee asked.

"Not really. Rocko and the Council are going to be irritated; some reporter figured out who the One *L* is. Other than that, it was fine. I guess. Can we please hang up the Costume for a few days now?" I asked.

"Yeah. Until next year, Fursona and Magical Girl Understudy don't exist." Bee pulled a chair out at the table and opened my laptop. She punched in my password, and I had an all-too-familiar sense of deja vu; Peter had known my passwords, too. Then she opened a web browser and navigated to the "TU Student Organizations" page. "Okay, we've got options. I'd go get the whiteboard, but maybe it's better to make a clean break here."

"Agreed." I untransformed—it felt weird to do that in front of my parents, even though they'd *made me* show them once—and sat down next to Bee. "Oooh, that one."

"Rock climbing club? Really?" Bee poked me in the side. "You know I don't like heights."

"Oh, you're so picky. You can pick, picky!"

She laughed, but then she did. She picked and picked until we had a list of eight clubs to explore in the early weeks of the next semester—from Claymation Club,

Film and History, and Shakespeare, to Fencing, Intramural Indoor Soccer, and Self-Defense. I raised my eyebrow at the last one, and she grinned. "It'd be really easy for us, and it's a great way to get to meet people."

"Okay, we'll meet the helpless Extras, then," I said.

Bianca didn't laugh. "Okay, Anika, I know we've been joking about shop talk a lot, but if we're taking the next couple of weeks off, we really can't talk about our work. At all. I'll talk to the old folks about it and make sure they know we want a regular Christmas."

"That'd be—" My eyes went wide. "Oh fuck."

"Oh, fuck?" Bianca asked.

I nodded, flushing red. Then I leaned in close, just in case someone's parents decided to come on in. "I haven't done my shopping."

2

Shopping

SUNDAY, DECEMBER 20

Bianca wouldn't stop giving me a hard time about my lack of preparation for Christmas, especially when I made her go to the food court for giant pretzels while I bought her a cute top at a shop next to the lingerie shop we'd hidden from Haze-Matt in. Their inventory was all new, and I spent a little time there, just in case something caught my eye, but in the end, regular clothes seemed more appropriate for a family holiday. At least for the part our parents were there for. I'd give her the top at public Christmas, and something more fun later.

She showed up just in time for me to hide the two prewrapped boxes in one of my many bags, and I grinned. "All done. Anything else?"

"Yeah, actually. My dad," Bianca said. "He's a reader, but if he even suspects I've ordered a book for him online, he'll lose his mind. Something something, 'Those internet corporations are ruining this country.' So, a bookstore?"

"Sure," I said. Then I narrowed my eyes theatrically. "Wait a minute! You hadn't finished your shopping, either?!"

"Oh, no, I have something for him, but the book thing's a family tradition, and I hadn't had a chance to get out. Same problem as you, so I don't want to hear it."

"Sure. Uh-huh. After all the ribbing you gave me? Not going to happen."

"Alright, sorry. Let's get going."

The Civic was parked in the oversized parking lot, and we managed to find it after almost ten minutes of wandering. Bee started the engine, I loaded my bags into the back, and we started moving.

"So, what'd you get me?" Bianca asked. When I mimed zipping my lips shut, she laughed. "I'll figure it out, I promise. I always do. Besides, I already know it's clothes, so the question is whether it's sexy clothes or normal ones. Do you know my measurements?"

I laughed as we waited at a red light. "Got them from Pataki."

"That asshole!" Bee mock-gasped.

Traffic finally started moving, and I rattled off my list. "Okay, Mom and Dad covered, Bee covered, something small for Su-Bin and Cam, a package on the way to Grandpa, and . . . a Super Watch login for Collidus. Think that'll work for him?"

"Hopefully. Shop talk."

"Hey, presents aren't shop talk!" I whined, wilting under her glare. "That one's close, though."

"Yep. Get the address for a bookstore near campus."

"On it, babe." She drove, and I navigated through Tokyexico's canyon-like Mid-Town. The whole time, I tried to put anything Understudy-related out of my mind. But I couldn't help thinking about The Agent as we drove past the Council of Heroes building. He was still out there, somewhere, and until we stopped him, he'd be a constant menace. And even though I'd sounded confident with the reporters, I didn't have the first clue as to his whereabouts. I'd been acting the whole time.

Broken Binding Books was a shop just across the main road from Tokyexico University. It occupied a double spot next to an art gallery and a couple of jewelry shops; I thought about letting Bee browse for a book while I checked out the jewelry, but I'd gotten her a necklace she wore sometimes last year, and repeat gifts felt weird. Besides, I'd already dropped a ton of money on her presents. So, even though I wasn't much of a reader outside of plays and schoolbooks, I followed her through the double doors.

It took her less than fifteen seconds to get separated and lost.

The shelves inside were a maze of books, with labels like Pre-Launch Front Range History, Local Authors, and Popular and Academic Fiction. Bianca made a Beeline for the back of the shop, where a sign advertised Westerns and Science Fiction Westerns. I didn't see her again until nearly half an hour later, at the cash register, buying a half dozen books.

I hadn't found anything, but a high school boy *had* attached himself to me, trying desperately to find *something* I'd want to read. "How about geography? We've got a bunch of new and updated travel guides for the Post-Launch, post-cleanup world. Or maybe movie history?"

"No, thanks," I muttered, eyes rolling as Bee grinned sheepishly at me from the door and motioned for me to hurry up and disengage.

"Well, what do you like?" the kid asked.

"Uh, superhero stuff."

"Oh." His face fell, then brightened. "Come back in late January. Toll Publishing made deals with every bookstore in the city. Something about a guaranteed bestseller written by a major superhero. They bought out all our most visible displays—Dad says it cost them a fortune, and we've already hit our second- and third-quarter profit goals from them. But Toll won't tell him what the book's about. Such a cool mystery."

I nodded slowly. "Okay. Late January. Got it." Then I disengaged, headed for Bee, and slipped my hand theatrically into hers. "Let's get going."

We were halfway up the stairs to 1301 Walnut Tower, looking to burn a few extra calories before the future Christmas dinner I had planned, when we ran into a problem. A desk was making its way down to the first floor, with a familiar man holding it up from below. And high above, with her black hair dripping with sweat and her eyes red, was Su-Bin.

When she saw us, she nodded. "Hey, get off the landing for a minute, Annie. Gotta . . . keep our momentum up," she panted, breathing hard as she wrestled the heavy oak desk down the narrow stairs.

"Yep," her dad agreed. Mr. Pak looked like he hadn't slept in a couple of days, but at the same time, he was completely relaxed and triumphant. Mrs. Pak came around the corner high above with the computer chair that went with the desk.

The procession passed, Su-Bin mouthed "My place. I'll explain," at us, and I watched them maneuver the bulky desk around the corner and continue the long, long job of moving furniture.

I looked at Bianca, who shrugged casually. "Guess we drop this off and meet Su-Bin?"

"Yeah, sounds good to me." I started hurrying toward my apartment, letting myself get just a little out of breath, and dropped the wrapped gifts under the tree. With Bee and I staying at her place, I didn't need to worry about her raiding the presents early, and I'd move the lingerie before Christmas so it wouldn't be an embarrassment for both of us.

"Think she's moving somewhere else on campus?" Bee asked.

"Probably not."

Down a floor, outside room 1232, I twiddled my thumbs and waited until the elevator opened and Su-Bin stepped out. She was crying again, fists balled, and she practically spit her words at us. I could feel the hostility, and it wasn't even aimed at Bianca and me—at least, not this time.

Understudy? Fursona? Sure, but not Bianca and me.

"This is bullshit! They want me to move back in with them. They have ever since last year, but last week's attack was too much for them. I've been fighting them all morning, but Dad won't *listen*!"

"The supervillain attack?" I asked.

"What else? That bitch Understudy," Su-Bin said, vitriol dripping from her every word. She took a deep breath, then another. "I made a mistake. I've been so focused on campus safety and crime rates when the key to APPEAL was in front of me the whole time. No one cares about the little things. But Power War? That's a blood sport. And now, I won't be on campus to organize real protests against it."

"I . . ." Bianca trailed off, not sure what to say. Then she started again. "I . . . Your parents have to know how important APPEAL is to you, right? Did you try talking to them about it?"

"Yes, of course I did. They said my club members would understand why I had to be online-only for a while. They said it was only until Power Wars ended, but when will that be, huh? Next year sometime, judging by how things have been going, and whether the 'heroes' win or some villain does, it won't matter. All Power Wars do is entrench super dominance."

"What do you mean by blood sport?" I asked. "And do you have anywhere to sit down?"

"No. Mom took my last chair. They're rearranging the trailer so we can fit the last load in. Look, you two know that supers are just a gimmick for alien TV, right?"

"Yeah," Bianca said before I could disagree. She shot me a *look* that said, "Don't get into shop talk." I nodded along.

"Great. So, do you really think so-called heroes and villains choose when it's time to have a Power War? Maybe the first time, but the second happened when Golden Goose was ready to ascend to number one *and* when superhero ratings were low across Ilneat space." Su-Bin grinned bitterly. "We're seeing a new shuffle in the rankings, or will be soon."

"And you know this how, exactly?" I asked. "Don't you hate superhero shows?"

"Yes. Passionately," Su-Bin's dad said from the stairwell. "Passionately enough to know all the stats behind them, even though she refuses to watch an Episode. She'll be a great general from our apartment, and APPEAL can do everything it's doing now without her putting herself at risk on campus. Isn't that right, Su-Bin?"

"Yeah, Dad, that's right," Su-Bin said, but her eyes rolled almost to the back of her head, and her tone said she didn't believe it and that she was pissed.

"Great. I'll get the last couple of things. Cam's waiting by the truck, and we need to get moving so we can unload all this this afternoon while it's warm out." Mr. Pak nodded. "Anika. Bianca. Good to see you both again. Stay safe on campus, okay?"

"Sure, Mr. Pak," I said halfheartedly.

He paused at the door and turned around, looking at me solemnly. "I know none of you are happy with our decision, but it's what we think is best for Su-Bin, and she's agreed to it. One of the conditions for her stay at Tokyexico University's dorms was that supers wouldn't attack her living space. Since that's happened, it's clear she's not safe here. Even she agrees, and the last thing we want is for her to become a statistic for whoever replaces Golden Goose."

"I understand," Bianca said.

"Thank you." Mr Pak disappeared into the dorm room, which looked shockingly empty.

"I hate this," Su-Bin said, sniffling.

"Yeah, I bet." I gave her a side hug, then let Bee get a hug of her own. "We'll see you, okay? It's not like you're losing all your friends. You're just moving away for a little while. And you'll still be on campus for classes, right?"

"Only the ones that won't let me attend online. It's a commute, and we're not about that," Su-Bin said.

"Oh," I said.

Su-Bin's dad cleared his throat from the door. "Su-Bin, can you help out with a little of this? It's time to go."

She nodded slowly. One more round of goodbyes followed, and a minute later, Su-Bin vanished into the elevator with a stack of books, followed by her father.

"Well, shit," Bianca said.

"Yeah," I agreed, but I had mixed feelings. It'd really suck not to have Su-Bin and Cam at board game nights, and if anything, it felt more isolating to lose her since we didn't have many unpowered friends. But on the other hand, President Pak had been a thorn in Understudy's side for a long time. Clearing the board of an annoyance before we resumed our fight against 3V1L and The Agent could only be—

"Shop talk," Bianca said suddenly.

I did a double take, flushing red. How had she known? Then I nodded slowly. "Shop thoughts, yeah. Think there's anything we can do for her?"

"As Annie and Bianca? Not really. Stay in touch with her, maybe? There could be a good virtual board game setup somewhere that we could play with her. Breaking the shop talk rule for a moment, though, our best bet, if we want her back on campus, is to win the Third Power War. And that means being in top shape, which means a nice, relaxing Christmas with *no shop talk*."

3

No Shop Talk

The dads were getting along well.

Too well.

My dad had brought decorations from our storage unit, and now my apartment looked like the Grinch and Santa had gotten into a drinking contest, both had lost, and they'd vomited lights and garlands onto every surface. Decorations I hadn't seen since middle school festooned my door, and if it weren't for how jealous my few thirteenth-floor neighbors were, it'd be embarrassing. It skirted the line as it was, but leaned closer to endearing. For now.

Worse, they both had the same taste in Christmas music—the kind that was old and outdated when they were kids in the 2010s. I *should* have been gritting my teeth as "Feliz Navidad" rolled into "White Christmas" for what felt like the fiftieth time this morning. Instead, I was loving it.

The only thing I was disappointed about was Bee. She'd volunteered to be Santa, mostly to avoid having either of our dads do it. None of us had seen a problem with it at the time, but she was *obviously* picking on me. Everyone else had gotten two or three presents since the last time I'd opened one, and as much as I understood that the holiday was about giving, I wanted those damn presents.

Plus, my phone kept going off. I kept muting the calls, since they *knew* I was off duty, but Rocko kept right on calling. Whether they had an emergency or not, we were between seasons, and I'd told them I wasn't doing any superhero work until the new year. I needed the break, and they'd agreed after the last Episode that some time off would add to the suspense. So why were they bugging me right now?

I hung up for the fifth time as Bianca finally pulled out a gigantic package from the ever-dwindling pile, flipped the dangly bit of her Santa hat out of her face, and announced, "And one for Annie, from Mom and Dad. Yours, not mine!"

The wrapping paper revealed . . . a box. And inside of that box was another box! After the third box, I started glaring at Dad, who whistled innocently and wouldn't look me in the eye. Mom was too busy trying not to laugh as I opened a fourth box to reveal . . .

"Thanks, you guys," I said, grinning as I held up the soccer shoes. "You must've talked to Bee, then."

"Yeah. The shin guards are in another present, but she said it'd be fine for you to play since there weren't any prizes for the indoor soccer league or anything. You're just going to have fun and get some exercise. We're glad you're getting back into sports and stuff, Anika," Mom said. She smiled. "I think you're doing great at being a super-hero, and I know work/life balance can be hard when you're getting pressured to work more and more. Believe me on that."

I did. I really, really did.

"So, your mom and I are super supportive of anything you want to do that's not your career. I know the superhero thing is a full-time job, but try to separate from the suit when you can. Did I say that right, honey?" Dad asked Mom.

"Yeah, Garret, close enough."

"Bianca, give yourself one, too," Bee's dad shouted, a highly alcoholic mimosa in hand. He'd gone out and bought all the ingredients and some plastic flute glasses since Bee and I "didn't have any booze." That had been a lie, of course. We'd just hidden it all in the Outback Stakeout Zone so our parents wouldn't find it. Not that it had stopped either of us from having a glass or two; Bee was a red-faced, red-nosed Santa, and I could feel the buzz, too.

"Oh, thank god," she mumbled, her face relaxing in relief. I laughed, and so did her parents. Bee was a present hog, and being Santa had to be killing her. She picked the biggest present she had left, which happened to be the top I'd picked out for her.

My phone buzzed again, but it wasn't a call this time. I decided that, what the hell, I'd at least read what Rocko wanted.

<DuPont, pick up. Livestream up to something. Gotta go fast! - Rocko 10:13>

I rolled my eyes and watched Bianca unwrap the top, hold it up to her body, and face the audience. "So, what do you guys think? Did Annie do a good job?"

My face was already warm from the drink, but I turned beet red. The shirt was off-white, with a retro movie poster printed on it—something about a man in a red-and-gold suit of armor fighting aliens. "I've seen what you do to shirts, Bee, and you're only wearing a couple of things instead of your whole ratty wardrobe. This is a start, but you and I need to pick out a style for you. That means more shopping soon."

"I do *not* abuse my clothes," Bee said, faux-outraged, at the same time as she wiped her mouth on her pajama top's sleeve. Everyone laughed, and she narrowed her eyes. "Okay, maybe a little. But sure, more shopping."

She dropped the top into her bag of goodies, dug through the pile, and then handed a book-shaped package to her dad. "Here you go."

As I watched him unwrap his book, my phone buzzed *yet again*, and this time, I didn't bother reading it. Instead, I shut the damn thing off. I was missing out on moments that I hadn't gotten to have last year because my boss couldn't respect that I'd taken leave, and it was time to enforce some boundaries.

The presents were flying now; Bee looked hungry, and more importantly, she was *acting* hungry. Another package flew toward me, this one a pink puffer jacket from Bianca's parents, which I really needed. King Cold had been acting—no. Even ignoring supers, the winter looked to be a cold one.

Rocko could wait. Whatever emergency Livestream had caused, some other superhero could deal with it.

I'd already worked one holiday last year, and I deserved this time off.

The presents were unwrapped. The stockings had been unstuffed. My pile of new clothes, a phone case, headphones for my laptop, and half a dozen other things had been bundled into a bag and placed by my bedroom door so I could deal with them later. Bee's dad and I had made Christmas brunch—I'd put on the Ramsey Fieri Costume since it hardly felt like a superpower—and now, we were all sitting around the green room's conversation pit as Bianca explained the rules of the card game she'd chosen.

I'd already played it—it was a classic one about making your Victorian Gothic family sad before they died—so instead of listening, I let myself zone out on the couch between my parents and pretend I was twelve again.

This was what being a normal nineteen-year-old was like. Parents and girlfriend around, no worrying about some supervillain trying a crazy stunt and you having to go stop it on camera . . . just good food and good times with good people. I could get used to this.

I couldn't, obviously, because in eight days, it'd be the first of the new year, and I'd be back in my Understudy outfit, taking the fight to 3V1L. And, honestly, that *had* to happen. The Agent wanted me, personally, out of the way, and he wouldn't stop until he had his revenge. That meant I couldn't stop, either. But the last week or so had been really nice.

I set up my circus troupe family and nodded, staring at the other three families; Bee had an Addams Family–looking set of cards, Mom and Dad had mad scientists, and Bee's parents had occultists. My hand looked pretty good, with a solid mix of happy cards to play on other people's families and sad ones for mine.

"Okay, let's get this going," Bianca said, grinning.

"This is the least holiday-themed game I've ever played," my dad complained, looking at his clear plastic cards. "But I guess we're going to—"

"Make Anika's ringmaster happy because he just won the lottery and can afford to buy a new elephant!" Mom shouted, stealing a card and slamming it down on my coattail-clad ringmaster.

I rolled my eyes. "Quit picking on me!"

Dad winked at me, struggling to keep a straight face, but Bianca followed up his card with one that doubled the ringmaster's happiness score. I glared daggers at her as everyone else laughed at me.

No, not at me. I hated when my parents told me this as a little girl, but no one was laughing at me. They were laughing *with* me because I was laughing, too.

Bee's mom looked at the cards and decided her cult leader needed to have an accident on the way to work. He broke his leg and had to walk with crutches. The game stopped for a moment as we debated a rule, and then we took another break while Bee went to make more hot chocolate, but even the pauses weren't too frustrating. I was here with my people—most of them, anyway—and that was enough.

"I can't believe you did that to me," Bianca complained, her cheeks even redder. Dinner had been a wine-fueled laugh-fest; after last year, it felt so perfect to have people to celebrate with. But now Bee and I were both a little past tipsy, and she wouldn't let the card game go.

"Yeah, well, it's not like my ringmaster died with a hundred happiness or anything," I fired back.

She keyed open the door to her dorm, and we wobbled our way to her not-quite-as-messy room. The fight to clean it had been . . . a losing battle . . . but we'd managed to make it habitable. Even if three hampers worth of clean laundry were piled up in the corner because neither of us had the energy to fold for an hour, at least it was *clean* now.

Bee collapsed onto her bed, rolled over to a position that would have been sexy if she wasn't so sloshed, and winked dramatically. "Hey, babe."

"You're drunk."

"Sure am. You've got one more present for me, huh?"

"What makes you think that?" I demurred.

"I was counting. You bought me three things, but you only gave me two."

Damn. She was right. *And* she hadn't been digging in the laundry mountain where I'd hidden her present, so I couldn't even be mad.

Or had she?

As I maneuvered my way through the dorm room to the pile and started digging, I caught a glimpse of her doing the same on the far side. I rolled my eyes. "You *didn't.*"

"I did. Best place to hide something in the whole dorm room. Neither of us wants to match my socks." She dove into the pile and came up with a suspicious-looking package. It wasn't my gift to her, though.

"You don't pay much attention, Annie. I got away from you twice at the mall, and now you're going to pay for your . . . lack of . . . paying . . . shut up," Bee trailed off, glaring as I laughed. She threw the package at me, so at least it wasn't breakable. "Open it. Now."

"Yes, ma'am," I replied, sticking my tongue out and lobbing a similarly-sized package her way. "Go to the bathroom and open that one. You'll know exactly what to do with it."

"I bet I will."

Bianca disappeared, and I carefully popped open the wrapping on it. The package inside was all satin and straps, and I rolled my eyes. "Bee, this is gonna take forever to put on!"

"Don't worry. You have time. I'll stay here until you're done, so it'll be a surprise!"

4

Surprise

FRIDAY, JANUARY 1

Bee's parents had left two days ago, but mine doggedly clung to every minute of winter break in Tokyexico. Part of me was thrilled. Having my people here felt great since I'd missed out on last Christmas. But even so, the day had finally come when Mom couldn't take any more time off from the diner, and Dad had to get back to the drill shop.

Now, the station wagon was packed full of the stuff they'd brought—and been given—and I found myself wrapped up in a giant bear hug as Dad said his goodbyes. "Alright, Dot, don't forget to be a kiddo. Work and school are important—"

"Yep," Mom interrupted. "Get your schooling done, focus on your career later, and let yourself be a person, too, Anika."

". . . What your mom said."

"I will," I said.

Bee nodded into her phone. "I'll make sure of it. We've got clubs, and I think we can get away with intramural soccer as long as neither of us gets too competitive."

"Well, then you'd better tone yourself down, Bianca," I said. "You're the most competitive person I know."

Mom glanced at me, raised an eyebrow, and then sighed. "You two be careful, okay? With your work."

"Yes, Mrs. DuPont," Bee said, grinning. She hugged my mom as Dad climbed into the passenger's seat. The station wagon coughed, whirred, and turned over, spewing a quick burst of smog out of its tailpipe. I grabbed Bee's hand as the car backed out of the parking lot, then returned Dad's wave until it disappeared into the cold January morning. Then we were on our own.

And suddenly, we were back on the clock, too. "So, Honeycomb texted you?" I asked quietly.

"Yeah. She wants to meet me outside at Tottergarten, by the playground. She was very clear about that. 'Not inside. Got things to talk about.' Very secret, very serious."

"Okay. So, suit up and get moving?" I asked. If the bee-themed Magical Girl wanted to talk, and she was willing to give up her break at the super daycare to do it, it had to be serious. Did she need more help with a villain? Or maybe she needed someone to act like one at Tottergarten. The whole Anti-Nap League—retired villains—had resigned to take over part of Tokyexico City when the Third Power War started, and as far as I knew, they weren't back yet.

Bee stole the sneakiest kiss as we took the public elevator back to the thirteenth floor. "I'm gonna be glad to have your place back to ourselves," she half whispered, winking.

I nodded and poked her in the side. "What? Not happy with your dorm room?"

"No. Walnut Tower's too nice."

"I agree. It'll be good to be back." I wasn't sure if I was talking about my Costume, apartment, or school. Maybe all three. Was superhero work stressful? Hell yes, it was. But it was also something I'd gotten really good at. The fact that Rocko wanted me to fight a major-league villain this season—and The Agent was all of major league and more—was proof of that. Or maybe it was proof that the Ilneat knew where the ratings were. I couldn't be sure.

Either way, I felt more ready to be Magical Girl Understudy than I had in a long time. Having Mom and Dad around had been great for working through my identity crisis—and it was a full-blown crisis. Had been. Probably would be again. Whatever. Having a plan for maintaining Anika while keeping Understudy going felt good, even if sports still set off my "cheating" senses. Bianca wanted to give it a shot, and if she thought *she* could keep herself under control, so could I, dammit.

I couldn't worry about soccer *or* The Agent right now, though, because I had to worry about Honeycomb. What did she want, anyway? Bianca and I slipped into the green room, which still featured the conversation pit, and started changing into our super Costumes. I watched as she put on the Eagle-sona fursuit, then transformed quickly into Understudy's pink-and-blue Costume. The reddish off-the-shoulder sleeves and comedy and tragedy mask tiara popped into place to a swell of choral music, and a moment later, the wand appeared.

<It's about time you suited up again,> Tails said in my head. *<Looked like a good break, though.>*

"It was. But this isn't a serious Episode. We're just paying a friend a visit."

Fursona and I circled Tottergarten a couple hundred feet up, well above the classic car and block letter sign. Something didn't feel right. Like a trap. Sure, Honeycomb sat on the swing set, her legs pumping slowly as she swung back and forth. And yeah, the Playpen Patrol was nowhere to be seen. But even so, I couldn't help but feel like she was bait.

Bait for Magical Girl Understudy.

"So, are you gonna go talk to her?" Fursona asked through our comms. She banked, slicing in front of my **[Solar Wing's]** path, and I swerved slightly to avoid her eagle fursuit.

"Yeah. Yeah, I'm going." I gulped and dove, heading for the slide. As the wind whipped through my hair, I picked up speed, then stalled out just a foot from the plastic ramp. My wings let go, and I landed on my back, sliding down toward the cold, snow-covered rubber floor.

Honeycomb put her feet down, scraping on the ground until she stopped, and stood up. "Hi, Understudy! Hi, Fursona," she said as my partner landed nearby—much more gracefully but less cool-looking than I had.

"Hi, Honeycomb. How's Tottergarten going?" I asked. "Got enough villains for the Playpen Patrol to deal with?"

"No. But hopefully, the Anti-Nap League will get bored and come back soon. No one's really fighting them, are they?"

"No. They're basically on their own. A couple of minor-league local heroes, but for the most part, they now own the Springs district south of here. It's only a matter of time until they get tired of lording it over the district and decide to leave. That's Tele-Portal's assessment, but she's also too busy to deal with them, and they don't seem interested in expansion," Fursona said. I blinked. When had she had time for updates? And wasn't that breaking the shop talk rule?

"Ah," Honeycomb said. She stuck out her hand, and I shook it. "It's good to see you two. I'm supposed to ask you a couple of things. First, Mrs. N wants to know if you want a job, Understudy."

"A job? Like . . ."

"Like, working at Tottergarten. She's disgustingly powerful—I don't know if you noticed or not, but no one messes with The Narrator."

"Yeah, I kind of figured that out," I said. "But a job? Why?"

"Easy. She's not stupid; the media knows you're getting lined up with a vil who's beyond your skills. That means Mrs. N knows, too. She wants you to be our villain for a while until this whole mess you're in with The Agent blows over. He can hold a grudge, but he won't dare mess with you if you're under Mrs. N's protection."

"Huh. Everyone knows now, huh?" I asked.

"Yeah. Your season finale came out two days ago."

"What?" Fursona asked, surprised. "Rocko didn't say anything."

I shook my head. "They probably did, but we ignored their call. So, Mrs. N wants us somewhere safe? Why does she care so much?"

"I can't really explain that," Honeycomb said. "She's kind of weird about people she knows, and about her kiddos. I think she might think of you two kind of like the Playpen Patrol. Two lost kids out there who need an adult."

Well, that was embarrassing. I flushed red.

"No, not like that!" Honeycomb said, turning crimson herself. "Look, what I mean is . . . The Narrator looks after people. It's what she does. Look at Vigilant Vow and me. And right now, she thinks you need looking after. That you're biting off more than you can chew. She probably doesn't want to see you two get hurt like . . ."

"Jackson," I finished.

That was a fair point, actually. TU had sent an email letting us know that Dr. Jackson's classes would have a substitute professor for the first couple of weeks as she recovered from her bullet wound and pulled herself back into teaching shape. I hadn't been following her recovery, but I was glad she'd make a full one, even if it took a while.

I shook my head. "Honeycomb, tell Mrs. N that I appreciate the offer, but I think we're winning against The Agent. 3V1L's on the run, we know how it's getting so many *V*s together, and Fursona and I are planning an assault at where we think The Agent's hiding. If we're right, we should have this wrapped up soon."

Honeycomb looked at her feet, crestfallen. She pulled out a phone, sent a quick text, and then stared at me. "You're sure? Okay. In that case, I've got another piece of business to take care of."

The door behind us opened, and Vigilant Vow stepped through.

My onetime rival hero looked pretty much the same as always: spiky black hair, hoodie, and scarf familiar. Now he had two crystals over his head, and I tensed, ready for a fight. Neither could be Honeycomb's, not if she was suited up and ready to use her limited powers. That meant . . . what? That he'd found Magical Girls willing to talk to him? To trust him? That didn't seem possible, not after the move he'd pulled last year. He'd *stolen* familiars. He'd *stolen* Tails!

Still, his hands were both where I could see them, and he wasn't holding his wand at the ready, so I didn't spring into action even though his glare would have ripped my heart out if it could have.

"*Vigilant Vow* has something he wants to say to you," Honeycomb said, standing up and putting her hands on her hips. Her eyes narrowed at him.

Vigilant Vow muttered something into his hoodie.

"What was that?" Honeycomb asked. I kept my mouth shut; this wasn't about me, not really. I'd seen Bee make this exact face at me enough times to know what was going on. Vigilant Vow was in trouble. And there wasn't anything I could do to save him from Honeycomb's wrath, even if I wanted to.

Which, I'll admit, I didn't.

Vigilant Vow, however, was a seventeen-year-old boy, and I'd dated enough of them—one—to know what he'd do. So it didn't surprise me when he doubled down, crossing his arms over his chest and refusing to make eye contact with anyone.

I'd dated enough girls to know what'd happen next.

So, when Honeycomb buzzed into action, I wasn't surprised. She grabbed Vigilant Vow's hand and dragged him to the other side of the playground while I stood there awkwardly. Fursona laughed into her mic, and I shot *her* a look that said "Don't you dare." Then I twiddled my thumbs while Honeycomb hissed and whispered at her boyfriend. I caught, "I'll kick your butt myself," which was hilarious, coming from the bee girl.

Then she turned around and marched Vigilant Vow toward me. "Like I was saying, Vigilant Vow has something to *say*."

I nodded, still tense. Behind them, Fursona perched on the play place, ready for . . . something.

"Hi, Understudy. I want to . . . apologize." Vigilant Vow glanced at Honeycomb, who nodded encouragingly, her face softening instantly. Damn, she was good. "I've been talking to Mrs. N about . . . what happened. I don't think I was wrong to compete with you, but I should have seen what Cartman and The Agent were doing. Instead, I just listened to them and did what I was told."

"*And?*" Honeycomb hissed in his ear.

"And it was wrong. I still don't like you—ouch!" He rubbed his side where Honeycomb had poked it. "That stings! Yeah, I don't like you, but . . . thanks. For getting in the way. I owe you."

He reached into his pocket and grabbed a bit of plaid cloth. Then he held it out toward me. "Magical Girl Understudy, please accept my apology. This is part of my familiar's molt, but it should work for you. You can, I don't know, make a Vigilant Vow Costume or something."

I slipped the piece of cloth/centipede molt into my pocket next to my phone and nodded slowly. "I didn't get in the way because you deserved to be protected, but because maybe you'd earn it someday."

"Yeah, I got that. Thanks," Vigilant Vow said. He turned awkwardly, shaking Honeycomb's grip. "Am I done here?"

"Yes, you're done here. Thank you for trying." Honeycomb kissed my former rival's cheek, and he fled back toward Tottergarten's doors.

When he'd left, she turned to me. "Well, that's done. If you're not going to accept Mrs. N's offer, then she has a second one. Information on 3V1L's activities over the last couple of weeks. She'll send it to you. I need to get back inside. It's almost snack time, and you know how Kaiju Kid gets if she gets the wrong snack."

"Thanks, Honeycomb," I said. When she disappeared inside, I took off, heading back toward TU. We'd look over Mrs. N's notes later.

5

Later

Rocko's studio door wouldn't open.

That alone was odd. As far as I could tell, the two Ilneats were always available whenever I'd bugged them. They kept odd hours. So, for their door to be locked when I *knew* they were back on Earth felt wrong. And I needed to get them the scrap of Vigilant Vow's Costume. Would it probably be some redundant Costume I didn't need? Yes. Did I still need to know for sure? Absolutely.

So, it irritated me that I couldn't talk to them.

But Bee and I had been ignoring their calls. Maybe they were still enjoying their Episode-less vacation from *Heroics 101*. Maybe this was some passive-aggressive way of showing that they were annoyed. Or *maybe* they had a big meeting and didn't want us wandering around.

Either way, I needed to get the scarf molt to Pataki, so I taped it to one of the camera drones and pointed it toward the Hot Zone. With the door shut, a manual delivery was my best bet at making things happen reasonably quickly. As the chrome machine disappeared, I took a deep breath. "Okay, what's on the schedule here?"

Bianca smiled. I'd seen that smile before, on Su-Bin when she tutored me in math. And I didn't like it. Then she rolled out my friend, my nemesis: the stolen whiteboard. "The Agent. I've been thinking about him and 3V1L, and I refuse to believe he just vanished like that. So, let's go over what we know, try to put a battle plan together, and take it from there."

She started scribbling on the board, dividing it into three sections. "Okay, let's go over The Agent's retreat during 'Back with Avengeance.' Was he ever under Dr. Mays's effect? If so, when did he break out? And what happened after he shot Dr. Jackson?"

The media and investigating heroes were focused on the murder attempt. It wasn't that supers never killed each other. It was Jackson specifically. She had a disgustingly high win rate, and this might have been her first trip to the hospital—ever—so the powers that be were digging into it. So was the media. That left the rest of the Episode as our problem, not theirs.

"I'm not sure Mays's power ever affected him. He didn't seem to shrug it off. He just ignored it. It reminded me a lot of how Eustace Bagges ignored Monologue's power, but Dr. Mays is a lot stronger. After The Agent shot Dr. Jackson, he said something about an emergency teleport. So, either he has a teleporting villain in his toolkit . . ."

"Which is really likely," Bee said. "We've seen several teleporters. Tele-Portal, Warp Tennyson, and that SSS villain last semester. One of them may have contracted with The Agent. Or the alternative is that he got bailed out for story purposes. But how would he know the bailout was coming?"

We pondered The Agent's new powers for a while, but nothing made sense. Eventually, I shrugged, popping my shoulders pleasantly. "Let's move on. We don't know what's up with The Agent, but we can focus on 3V1L, right? Maybe they'll have a clue about his whereabouts. Are they still doing vil shit?"

Bee nodded. She wrote '3V1L Poudre Operations' and '3V1L Other Operations' on the whiteboard, then set the marker down while I walked to the two screens that had displayed our rogues' gallery. Theseus was still active, and so was Sister Sly, although neither had done much over winter break, and Livestream wasn't anywhere to be found. Had he taken time off? A quick phone search showed no new Episodes on his site, so maybe.

But the biggest change was the Poudre district map, where 3V1L's crimson had a massive gash, splitting it almost in two between North and South Poudre. Only a thin knot of red connected the districts, right where a new chemical plant was being built. "Who's pushing them back?" I asked, staring at it.

"No idea. Could be The Triad, could be the In-You-Endos, could be a local hero making a stand. Either way, they've lost a lot of territory, and from what I can see, they're not retaliating against their attacker." Bee's eyebrow furled. "That's really out of character for them."

"It is. They were hyperaggressive about fighting us whenever we showed up—at least once we proved we couldn't be negotiated with. And they decimated the Mutual Assistance League last year, just before Golden Goose . . ." I trailed off. Without Golden Goose, the whole Power War had gone screwy, and I wished Stella-Lunar was powerful enough to step into that role. But so far, she'd proven to be just a little too inconsistent, her power's phases too unreliable, so the pressure was on local heroes like us.

"Yeah." Bee returned to the whiteboard. "So, we have a mystery attacker who's winning against 3V1L, a surprisingly passive organization, and no known sightings of The Agent. That's ominous."

"Is it? If The Agent's done with 3V1L, would he really stick around and help them?" I asked. "Is 3V1L a dead end now?"

"I don't think so," Bee said. "If it was, they'd be acting tougher and trying to hold on to what they have. I think the One *L* is still giving orders, and they're still following them."

She scribbled 'Poudre districts are a trap?' below '3V1L Poudre Operations,' then kept writing. 'Trigger the trap intentionally,' 'Contact 3V1L's opposition,' and 'Avoid Poudre districts' filled up most of the space, but I erased the last one with my palm. "We're not bailing out on Poudre. 3V1L is our rogue, and we need them defeated."

The planning session ended after almost two hours; we'd start our campaign against 3V1L in earnest in the next couple of days, but today, we needed more information. So, as much as it pained me, Fursona and I were suited up again on my roof. She'd chosen to run the Roo-sona fursuit, which meant I'd fly us to the giant wound in 3V1L's territory. But just to be sure, I sent a quick text before I took off.

<Tele-Portal, where are In-You-Endos operating? - Understudy 2:35>

I didn't expect to hear from her right away, so I wasn't surprised when she didn't message me back that exact second. Instead, I passed my phone to Fursona, who pocketed it. "If that goes off, let me know what it says. We'll be careful in our approach, just in case it's them or Stella-Lunar."

"Got it," Fursona said.

I summoned my sailboard with **[Solar Wing]** and took off, Fursona tense between my arms. She still didn't love flying, so I made sure to give her a calm, relaxing ride. That is to say, I stayed relatively steady and didn't throw any loop the loops. The University District's brick-facade apartments and businesses gave way to the industrial wasteland of South Poudre—3V1L's home territory—and I felt my own stress levels rising.

We slowly circled the district, looking for 3V1L activity in the fuel plants and warehouses, but couldn't find a thing. Had they gone this far to ground? I needed more answers, and an aerial flyover from three hundred feet up wouldn't be enough. So, after twenty minutes, I ducked down toward the street that marked the easternmost point in the gash.

Two heroes stood there, talking to each other and staring at a chemical plant. I hadn't seen either of them since the job fair two Octobers ago, but the angelic one turned and waved like we were old friends. "Hello! Are you the reinforcements we asked the Council of Heroes for?"

"Uh, no. Magical Girl Understudy and Fursona. We're getting back to our rogues' gallery after winter break and noticed that 3V1L's had some setbacks in the last couple of weeks. So, we thought we'd come down and see what was happening."

"Oh." She looked dejected for a moment—almost Honeycomb-like—but pulled herself together. Her halo seemed to glow brighter, and her wings spread for a moment. "But if you're fighting 3V1L, too, maybe we can make an alliance. I'm—"

"Tranquility, right?" Fursona asked. "We met at the job fair."

"Yeah. The Mutual Assistance League is back in business and pushing 3V1L hard. Or at least, what's left of us is." She pointed at the armored, bear-skin-wearing gunslinger next to her. "War Bear and I survived 3V1L's counterattack against us last winter, and we're finally rebuilt enough to fight back."

"What? They killed your teammates?" I asked.

"Not quite. They did convince a bunch of us that the Poudre districts were the wrong place to make a stand, though, and then the Power War set War Bear and me back even more. But listen. You want 3V1L gone, too, right?"

I nodded.

War Bear cleared his throat and spoke, his voice soft and rumbling at the same time. The gigantic gun over his shoulder looked like something a hero shouldn't be using, but here he was, with the Mutual Assistance League. "One or two of the *Vs* are holed up in the chemical plant and the construction around it. We're trying to split the district and take South Poudre, but we can't do that as long as their fortress here's in the way. And the MAL doesn't have the firepower to root them out anymore."

"So you asked for reinforcements, and we showed up?" Fursona asked. She shivered in the January cold, and I copied her. It was psychosomatic, like yawning. But also, it was cold!

"Yeah. There aren't reinforcements available—not with how the Power War's going—so War Bear and I tried ourselves yesterday. We thought that with the holiday, the henches would be at home getting drunk, but we had no luck. And they've been reinforcing since then."

I nodded slowly. "Tranquility, what's your plan for the district?"

"Oh, the five-point plan!" Tranquility looked thrilled, though War Bear rolled his eyes. "Okay, first. Housing. Gotta fix the housing situation here and get it price stabilized. Then, green spaces. I don't know if you noticed, but it stinks here. Plants would help, but we need a lot of them—city parks, vegetable gardens, and so on. Once we've got that, diversify the local economy with different, new jobs. It'll be—"

I held up a hand. She had a better long-term plan for South Poudre than I did for finishing school. "I'm sure you've put a lot of thought into it, and it sounds good. Why so much investment in Poudre, though?"

"I grew up here, and in real life, I have a degree in urban planning. It seemed like the right place to fight that battle after we win the superpowered one." Tranquility smiled brightly below her halo and mask. "It's one thing to win, but it's another to make the world better."

The angel hero had a point, and I nodded. "Okay. This is perfect. Fursona and I have the firepower to clear that plant, and they're not expecting us. We'll get them out, you two can take over the district, and we'll support you while you get your five-point plan running. Agreed?" I stuck my hand out.

Tranquility grasped it firmly, and I felt her energy flowing through me like an electrical shock. My muscles relaxed, and I felt less tense than I had in months. She said, "Agreed. We'll provide support and make sure 3V1L doesn't retreat west or south. They'll have to leave through the east side. What was it that Sun Tzu said?" That last bit was aimed at War Bear.

The gunslinger clipped his weapon onto his armor and held out his hands, T-posing. As Tranquility picked him up and flew toward the nearest roof overlooking the construction, he said, "Always leave your enemies a way out. A cornered rat is a desperate rat."

[Casting Call]
[Episode: Power War: The Righteous Cause - PG-13]
[Role: Heroic Helping Hand! Do you accept the role? (Yes/No)]
[Role Focus: Grit + Flamboyance]

6

Desperate Rats

[Power War: The Righteous Cause: Act One in Progress]

Fursona and I walked toward the construction zone, on alert for the ubiquitous 3V1L henches and maybe even a *V* or two. This was it—hopefully, there'd be someone who knew *something* about The Agent's whereabouts, and we could get started on tracking him down.

"Plan?" I asked my partner.

"I don't have one. We'll just hit fast and hard. We're both fresh and ready for this, right?"

"Right."

The MoonTech chemical plant wasn't the biggest one in South Poudre—at least, not yet. But the sprawling construction around the existing tanks and pipework left no doubt about the company's intentions. A sign on the broken chain-link fence said that MoonTech was striving to be North America's biggest supplier of industrial lubricants and cleaning supplies, and that this construction would bring up to one thousand jobs to the Poudre districts.

The plant itself was still operational; either that, or the whole area around it was permanently acid-scented now. I pointed toward its tangle of smokestacks, tanks, and pipes. "I bet we'll find whoever's in charge there. The Mutual Assistance League should be nearby, but they'll just hold the line and keep anyone from getting behind us."

BANG!

Before I could keep strategizing, a gun fired. It sounded louder than the pistols 3V1L's henches used and came from behind us. A window exploded at the chemical plant's office. "That's our cue!" Fursona yelled, hopping into the active construction zone.

I followed her, and a chrome camera drone followed me, but I hadn't even gotten halfway in when a whole crane-load of steel I-beams plummeted from the sky and crashed into the ground, knocking me aside even though they missed.

[HP 12/13]

I whirled as rumbling sounds filled the construction yard. "They're in the machines!" I yelled as a bulldozer crested a hill and lurched toward Fursona. She hopped its blade and landed on top of the machine's cab; I saw her swing into it feetfirst, but then a backhoe's bucket spun toward me, and I had to duck. I fired a **[Starlance]**, which punched into the machine's windshield, cracking it.

[Dramatic Damage! +1 Drama Point]

The driver stopped the massive machine and leaped free just before it could fall into an exposed foundation pit. I was already running toward the steel skeleton of a new warehouse, firing another **[Starlance]** at a hench with a welding torch. The pink-and-blue bolt of energy hit the man in the chest. A moment later, *he* fell into the foundation.

[Dramatic Damage! +1 Drama Point]

But the whole battlefield was chaos already. There were a dozen yellow-painted construction machines. The whole place was a maze of wet concrete, exposed rebar, and open trenches half filled with wires and pipes, and the henches—

Something hit me in the shoulder and knocked me to the ground. I rolled into the foundation, following the already surrendering henchman.

[HP 11/13]

But I didn't have time to deal with him. I used **[Solar Wing]** and threw myself back into the air, where the tower crane was already picking up another load of steel girders. The camera drone followed me, and I reached the huge machine's cockpit in just a moment. I landed above it, magical wings retracting, and pulled the door open.

The familiar mask of a *V* greeted me, along with the swirl of a red cape. A moment later, he was outside the tower crane, on top of its huge metal arm, with a crossbow in one hand and a metal shield in the other.

I looped around and joined him. "You're copying Crossbow?"

"I don't even know who that is," the *V* shot back. "I'm the Second *V*."

"Never mind. Of course you don't know." I leaped toward him, then froze mid-air, spinning and firing a **[Limelight Barrage]** toward him.

[Dramatic Damage! +2 Drama Points]

The first ray missed. So did the second, and he ate the third with his shield. But the last two punched into him one after the other, and I was already dodging the expected crossbow bolt. I didn't expect a second one right after it, though, and only **[Quick-Time Change]** and **[Freeze-Frame]** saved me. I landed, already shifted into Copy Cat; if he wanted to play the ranged villain, I'd be melee.

[Flashy Fitting-Room! +1 Flamboyance Point]
[Steel Yourself! +1 Grit Point]

The mind-meld between Tails and I finished, and my two tails flicked out to help me balance as I charged toward the Second *V*, a hundred fifty feet in the air. Below me, Fursona was kicking ass—literally. She booted a hench out of a dump truck, tail-slammed another, and leaped out of the way of a slow-moving steamroller.

Then I hit the Second *V*. I immediately **[Doom Balled]**, clamping my limbs around him and scratching through his cloak and Costume until little lines of blood appeared. He slammed me with his shield, but I was a cat—and also protected by **[Fursonal Furcefield]**—and the blow didn't knock me completely off the crane.

[Badass Damage! +4 Badass Points]
[Tough Kitty! +1 Grit Point]

He backed off and fired another bolt; this one punched into my chest, and the armor didn't stop it. I stepped back half a foot to absorb the blow, and my foot slipped. And just like that, I was hanging above the battlefield, scrambling for purchase as the *V* walked confidently toward me. "I guess this is where the One *L*'s thirst for revenge ends," he gloated, looming over me.

[HP 9/13]

I reached up and slashed his foot with **[Cat-Scratch Fever]**.

[Dramatic Damage! +1 Drama Point]

He recoiled, staggering away from me as I pulled myself back up onto the crane. His shield dropped onto the crane, then bounced away toward the construction zone below as he clutched his eyes, shouting something I couldn't understand. For a second, I thought about pressing my advantage. Now was the time, after all. But instead, I lunged forward and grabbed his stupid cape.

He struggled, but I had a few uninterrupted seconds without his vision. I tripped him, slamming him shoulder-first onto the crane, and kicked out at his crossbow until he dropped it. Then I started yelling at him. "Crossbow? Seriously?"

"I still don't know who that is!" he yelled back.

"Goddammit, stay here. I'll be back for you!" I stepped away, running to the other side of the crane. **[Cat-Scratch Fever's]** damage over time and status effect would keep him down, and he didn't have his weapons, either. Then I slow-transformed back to Understudy.

The rest of the fight was down below.

As soon as I finished my transformation sequence, I leaped off the crane, trusting **[Solar Wing]** to catch me on the way down. I landed on a hench with my full weight, using **[Spotlight Strike]** to smash through his point of superhero damage before he could pull the trigger on his cheap-looking pistol. It still went off when it hit the ground, burying its bullet in wet concrete.

[Stylish Strike! +1 Flamboyance Point]

Then there was a whirlwind of henches with construction tools.

I punched one in the face, took a shovel to the shoulder, and **[Starlanced]** one who came at me with a goddamn jackhammer. What he thought he'd accomplish staggering toward me with that heavy thing, I couldn't say, but luckily, the heavy power tool's engine landed on him when he hit the ground, not the chisel.

[Dramatic Damage! +1 Drama Point]
[Badass Takedown! +1 Badass Point]

Then Fursona erupted from a pile of henches. I hadn't even seen her under there, but when the first hench went flying a dozen feet in the air and hit the ground next to me, I realized that not only was she swarmed, but she was handling it just fine.

I launched myself back into the air, strafing the battlefield with **[Starlance]** and taking out one hench who'd taken a position up high in the construction's metal frame with a gun. He screamed on the way down to the ground, just like in the movies.

[Dramatic Damage! +1 Drama Point]

The battlefield was quiet-ish for a second; machines' engines were still rumbling, but no one was fighting. Fursona breathed heavily enough that I could hear it without my earpiece, and her suit was covered in dirt, wet concrete, and water. She grinned. "Good to be back at it, huh?"

"Yeah. Yeah, it's good."

Something hit the ground below me and lunged toward the crossbow. His red cape was stretched out like a parachute, and as he hit the ground, he rolled toward me, reloaded in one smooth motion, and fired.

As the bolt zipped toward me, I had just enough time to realize that I hadn't *seen* any notifications about the damage-over-time part of **[Cat-Scratch Fever]**.

Then it exploded.

A dozen darts slammed into me, knocking me out of the air before I could dodge or transform. I hit the ground, rolling as tiny strings wrapped around me, pinning my arms to my sides. When the rolls stopped, I started pulling against the tiny strings. They were parting, yes, but not fast enough.

[HP 6/13]

Ten strings left. Five. Too late. The Second *V* loomed over me, but this time, from farther away. He loaded his crossbow and pulled the string back. Then he took aim—

WHAM!

The full weight of a Bianca-sized plushie kangaroo smashed him into a patch of wet concrete. His crossbow bolt launched and clattered into the unfinished building, then exploded, this time in a fiery blast. I freed myself and launched back into the air with **[Solar Wing]**. Fursona had the Second *V* in hand, but interference from the henches could tip the balance.

So, as his minions surged toward the fight, I landed between my partner and the oncoming construction henches.

I blasted the first two with **[Starlances]**, but they were moving fast, and I needed something with more stopping power, so as the first shovel headed for my . . . head . . . I used **[Quick-Time Change]** and **[Freeze-Frame]**. As the blade passed through my skull like it wasn't there, I did the Itsy Bitsy Spider. Rainy Day's weather-themed Costume formed around my sixth-grade self, and I opened my eyes with a flash of lightning.

[**Flashy Fitting-Room!** +1 Flamboyance Point]
[**Steel Yourself!** +1 Grit Point]

I was already building up a storm with **[Thunderhead]**, but it wouldn't finish fast enough, so I pushed the whole group of burly, masked construction workers with **[Wind Front]**. They tumbled backward, and I bought myself and Fursona a few seconds.

[**Pause for Effect!** +1 Drama Point]
[**Badass Move!** +1 Badass Point]

They were already picking themselves up, though, and the storm wasn't done forming. It crackled overhead, but was I going to have enough time? I wasn't sure. I had one more transformation, but no real powerhouse moves left. So I backed up, all five foot zero inches of me, as the towering construction henches rushed me again.

They'd almost reached me when I **[Rode the Lightning]**.

[**Thunderstruck!** +1 Drama Point]
[**Electric Lightshow!** +1 Flamboyance Point]

As the tendril of lightning ripped through the first hench, the others paused for a moment. Then one in the back turned and ran, and I smiled, already **[Quick-Time Changing]** into Understudy.

[Flashy Fitting-Room! +1 Flamboyance Point]
[Rejuvenation Activated: HP 11/13]

Fursona was wrapping up her fight with the Second *V*, I only had a half dozen henches left to deal with, and the whole battlefield was under control except for the water leaks, idling machines, and—

CRASH!

—something that hit me like a truck.

It wasn't a truck, though. As I folded around the machine's engine block, conflicting emotions went through my head: anger, disbelief, and a little bit of fear.

Then my head tried—and failed—to go through the white van's windshield at the same time as its brakes squealed. I hit the ground and, thankfully, rolled down into a pit that was half filled with water. The van lurched to a stop, hazards flashing.

[HP 9/13]

7

Hazards Flashing

The van's engine revved again, this time right at the edge of the pit. At the same time, its doors opened, cutting off the construction company's name on its side, and a clown car's worth of henches ran out. I sighed dramatically, picked myself up from the muddy filth I'd landed in, and squared off against my true rival.

I hadn't seen a white van in a while, and I'd started to think that maybe their reign of terror had ended. Clearly, that wasn't true. Was S—Jumper's hench from last year—in the driver's seat? It revved again, but I was pretty sure I was safe in the pit.

Then it reversed like a missile, swerving back and forth as its horn blared over the beeping chime. Henches leaped out of the way, cursing and swearing, as it headed toward Fursona and the Second *V*. So, yeah. That wasn't ideal. And I definitely couldn't stay in my nice, safe mud pit. Fursona was good, but she couldn't handle a *V* *and* a van. So it was up to me to distract one of them.

My hopes that we could swap and she could fight the maniac driver were dashed, though. The moment I started out of the hole, the van flipped back into drive, gears grinding, and accelerated back at me. I climbed out and fired a **[Starlance]** toward the truck. It hit the grill, which *had* been a kill shot before.

[Dramatic Damage! +1 Drama Point]

But instead, it bounced off. A bit of the black plastic fell off, too, but the damn thing was still driving toward me! As its back tires slipped in the mud, I threw myself sideways, landing in a gravel pile. The brakes squealed again—I could *smell* them burning as the reverse lights went on while the van kept moving forward—and I picked myself up. I fired another **[Starlance]** into the rear windshield. It crumpled into the van's cargo bay with a shattering sound.

[Dramatic Damage! +1 Drama Point]

But the driver didn't stop. The lights flickered as I pumped another shot into it, then a shot rang out, and a bullet slammed into my chest—right in the sternum.

[Dramatic Damage! +1 Drama Point]
[HP 8/13]

I spun off-balance, and the van's driver took advantage, slamming into me with wheels churning in the dirt. *That* knocked me onto my butt and pressed the air out of my lungs.

[HP 7/13]

This driver wasn't just playing to knock me out of the fight, either. He was driving to take me out *permanently*. I needed a change of tactics. But that wasn't easy, not with the van and a half dozen henches on me. I blasted another one with a **[Starlance]**, but I just didn't have the firepower to take out all of them. I couldn't get airborne, either. It'd take too long.

I needed a new plan. And I had one, but it was stupid.

Of course, I'd survived being stupider than this.

At least, I had a couple of times.

As the van bore down on me again, I fired another **[Starlance]** at a hench. It knocked him down, but I hardly cared. Both my eyes were on the van charging at me. Its tires were screaming, but I didn't move as its blinking hazards bore down on me. Then, at the last second, I spun to the side.

[Dramatic Damage! +1 Drama Point]

The driver's face stared at mine as he desperately tried to change the van's angle to get another hit in, but it was too late. As it flashed past me, I grabbed the shattered back window's frame and let the van's momentum swing me around.

The van's speed jerked me off my feet and wrenched at my shoulders. Then, I slammed into the back of the van with a thudding sound—trying to avoid the shattered glass—and quickly pulled myself inside.

It wasn't the same layout as S's van. This one featured a wide back with seats but no barrier between the driver's cab and the big space in the back.

Perfect.

I pulled myself forward, hands gripping headrests as the driver fishtailed the huge vehicle back and forth. Ten feet. Eight feet. Six.

Close enough. I used **[Spotlight Strike]**, highlighting the driver's head, and punched him in the temple a second later.

[Stylish Strike! +1 Flamboyance Point]

The brakes slammed on again, and I catapulted against his seat back as he looked at me incredulously. "You crazy bitch, you hit me in the ear!"

I blinked. "Sorry," I said reflexively, at the same time as I brandished my wand and fired a **[Starlance]** into the steering wheel.

[Dramatic Damage! +1 Drama Point]

The van's dashboard exploded. Shards of plastic and speedometer caromed around the cab, showering us both with dials and fragments of numbers. At the same time, the engine sputtered and chugged, then began to squeal loudly before steam erupted from under the hood. As the steam and smoke vented into the cab, the driver kicked open his door and fell out onto the now rutted dirt road.

I followed him, wand held high. "They made you do it?" I asked sarcastically.

He nodded.

"Great. Stay there." I pointed at the skeletal building's frame. "If you move, I'll be back."

It took a minute to mop up the last couple of minions, but when the fighting ended, I stood atop my fallen, van-shaped foe, surrounded by whining, defeated henches, watching Fursona accept the Second *V*'s surrender. The chrome drones hovered around us, taking in the aftermath of the fighting, and even though I heard a gunshot—another high-powered one, probably War Bear—I couldn't help but feel great!

[End of Act One: Act Two in Three Minutes]

I was back in the saddle again. "Well, that went well," I said, nodding as Fursona hopped over.

"Yeah, I thought you were in trouble. Do you have some belt on your Costume that attracts those things?" Fursona pointed at the van.

"Har har. It's good to stretch my legs again."

"You got hit by a van going forty-five."

"And it'll be even better to stretch them tomorrow. I'm going to be *so* sore." I really was. My superhero damage had, as always, taken the worst of it. Still, I'd have a hard time walking around in the morning—but at least classes weren't until next week. "Plenty of time to recover, but for now, we need to keep pushing."

"Yeah. Chem plant time?"

"Chem plant time." I took a minute to stretch out and take in the massive building. The MoonTech plant loomed over the whole construction yard; all the new buildings represented a quarter of the company's property, and it was the only part that hadn't been covered in warehouses, massive tanks, and hedges made of steel pipes. If this had been Act One, I couldn't wait for—

[Power War: The Righteous Cause: Act Two in Progress]

—that.

I didn't know much about chemical plants, but I was willing to bet that the henches swarming the tanks between us and the building weren't there to sell Girl Scout cookies or anything nice. I used **[Solar Wing]** to cut the gap while Fursona hopped behind me. She'd gotten so fast I almost couldn't keep up with her, and before the henches could open fire, we'd covered half of the distance.

Then the bullets started zipping past. "Split Ends, form one!" I said through the comms.

"Got it!"

I peeled up and to the right. At the same time, Fursona slid on her knees to the left, using her cybertronic tail and hands to steer. We'd practiced this move for a while, of course, but the chaos of our campaign against 3V1L hadn't given us many opportunities to use any called strategies. Bullets whizzed under me, and I spun mid-air to make myself a harder target, then dove hard for the nearest tank.

It was massive, a curved steel wall fifty feet long, and I stopped my dive halfway down its rusty-looking face. The air stank this close, like gasoline and acid, and I realized I was still a good thirty feet off the ground.

A hench was aiming their cheap pistol at me from the stairs circling the huge steel container. I blasted her with a **[Starlance]**, then a second one when her construction helmet took the hit.

[Dramatic Damage! +1 Drama Point]

That one knocked her off the catwalk, and she hit the ground with a crunch. I winced but didn't have time to check on her.

BANG!

Another gun went off. This bullet slammed into me, and I cartwheeled through the air to land on the steel, diamond-grid stairs. As I rolled, the serrated diamonds ripped into my Costume and skin. Superhero damage really was amazing, though. Instead of being hamburgered, I'd have some small cuts and bruises. No biggie.

[HP 5/13]

I recovered onto one knee, firing a [**Limelight Barrage**] into the massed henches descending the stairs toward me. As [**Starlances**] scattered them like bowling pins, I was already looking up for the next threat.

[**Dramatic Damage! +5 Drama Points**]

It came from below.

Something popped, and the tank opened from the bottom a moment later. Some sort of solvent—thousands of gallons of it—poured from the ruptured metal. Someone shot into it, but instead of a massive fireball, the bullet splashed into the foul-smelling chemicals. All around, henches were screaming and running from the solvent tsunami.

I joined them, climbing the safety stairs as quickly as my legs would carry me. The tank wobbled, threatening to collapse under me. So I ran faster.

I was at the top, already using [**Solar Wing**], when a hench ran toward me. I readied my wand, but his hands were already up in surrender. "They made me, I swear!"

"Sure." I returned to summoning my [**Solar Wing**], then stopped as the whole tank shook again. "Do you have a way off this thing?"

"No."

"Shit. Okay, listen, stand in front of me." I pointed at the exact spot I wanted him to be, then summoned my sailboard underneath us. One hand wrapped around his waist—I was going to save his life, but dammit, he'd be the damsel for a second.

Then we took off.

Luckily, I was used to flying with the person who was the most scared of heights, because this guy had to be the second-most. I practically had to fight him every time I wanted to turn, and our flight only lasted a handful of seconds before the sailboard crash-landed on the plant's delivery bays. He rolled away, screaming as he faceplanted into the concrete.

[**Badass Takedown! +1 Badass Point**]

I rolled my eyes. That wasn't even an intentional move. But all around me, guns were going off. I had no idea where Fursona was. "Hey, babe," I said over the comms. "I've secured the doors. Ready to go in?"

"Just—" A horrific crunching sound filled my headset, and I winced. Someone had just gotten their nose kicked in. "—Just a minute! *Some* of us are busy here!"

"Anything I can do to help?"

"Sure! Get your butt over here and *help!*"

She sounded annoyed, and it wasn't even like I'd been doing nothing. I picked myself up and brushed off the dust. [**Solar Wing**] activated, and I took to the air, looking for the Justice-Roo. She had to be somewhere nearby, and if I followed the sounds of henches screaming, I was sure I'd find her sooner or later.

As I banked right to circle the main building, though, something hit me.

It wasn't like a gunshot. The closest I'd experienced to it was the white van attack, but this was worse, even though it didn't hurt. It felt like a solid wall of heat, pressure, and hatred. Then, the shock wave hit.

Every window in the area shattered. The pressure waves buffeted me back and forth, sending me spiraling downward, and I fought my wings to keep airborne. One tank after another ruptured, sending gouts of flame sky-high.

8

Sky-High

Last semester, when Sister Sly and 3V1L had been at war, the media had focused on the worst fires and danger spots. It had given me the impression that the entire district was on fire, and even though that was clearly a lie, Fursona and I had gotten suited up and out there as fast as we could.

This time, there was no way to exaggerate.

The entire district wasn't on fire, but it felt that way. And the west half of MoonTech's grounds definitely was. Tank after massive tank went up, some sputtering as they exploded and filled the air with toxic chemicals, others erupting in gigantic balls of fire that sent shock waves rippling across the district. Then came the sound.

It was nothing like an explosion on TV, and it wasn't even anything like Sister Sly's grenades. I'd never experienced anything like it before. It sounded—and felt—like a giant had slapped me out of the sky and stomped on the whole city. The whump and the shock wave toppled the half-finished building's frame. Fursona and I were on our way to a property damage record, and we'd leveled the Grant Building!

My ears wouldn't stop ringing, but I heard Fursona yelling from my comms through the tinnitus. "Building building building! Go!"

That seemed like good advice. As another fuel tank filled the air with blazing crude oil, I decided to take it. I aimed for the windows in what I *hoped* was the administrative part of the plant, zipped through the recently de-glassed window frame, and rolled to a stop on linoleum tiles.

The building's walls blocked the worst of the shock waves, but I still wished I'd built my mom's Costume. She probably had something to make this kind of thing less awful. Tanks kept exploding for the next thirty seconds, and a thick black smoke started rolling through the window, so I got up to get a move on. "Hey, babe, I'm inside. Second floor, in some offices."

"Got it. We're downstairs, heading toward the building's far side," Fursona said.

"We?"

"Yeah. I've got a few henches who didn't want to hang around while the whole place exploded. They're . . . kind of weird, in an 'I didn't want this to happen' way. Meet us in the back and you'll see."

"Got it. I'm on my way." The office I'd landed in wasn't anything special. It was filthy, with grime and dust everywhere, and a dirty computer screen was powered on. I stopped to check it out; the screen was on a pressure relief system, and the words *Critical Failure* blinked across it.

So that explained what had happened outside. I stared at the diagram of the building's complex pipe network; I could try to relieve some of the pressure and stop the rest of the tanks from bursting, but honestly, this was Su-Bin's wheelhouse. It was all numbers and blinking lights, and anything I did would probably just make it worse.

Besides, the camera drone was following me. I wiped some ash smudges off its lens and ducked out of the office into a long hallway. And that's when I noticed that something had gone very, very wrong.

A pair of henches were on one knee, firing pistols, but not at me. A yellow hazmat suit filled the far side of the hall—one with an 3V1L mask covering its plastic face shield. I had this sudden, horrific thought: The Agent had contracted with *Haze-Matt*?! Then, two jets of yellow-brown gas filled the hall, blowing toward the two stunned-looking henches.

I stepped into the hall, spinning into a **[Quick-Time Change]**/**[Freeze-Frame]** move, and after a quick Itsy Bitsy Spider dance, fired a **[Wind Front]** right into the offending, mustard-colored gas.

[Flashy Fitting-Room! +1 Flamboyance Point]
[Steel Yourself! +1 Grit Point]
[Badass Move! +1 Badass Point]

The cloud billowed, filling the office I'd just been in as the wannabe Haze-Matt's wrist-mounted gas guns slowed. The tank on their back—the suit wasn't exactly formfitting—blinked red, then started a spinning yellow-green pattern as it recharged. "Magical Girl Understudy," the fake Haze-Matt said.

"Listen, First *V*, or whoever you are, if you keep this up, you'll be killing your allies. Surrender, we'll get that power away from you, and you can claim that they made you do it!" I said, facing off against the hulking yellow suit.

"Ah, that's where you're wrong. I don't *want* to be the Third *V*. I've got such phenomenal power, and the One *L* isn't around to stop me. Once I deal with you, I'll be unstoppable, and even *he* won't want to fight me." The voice from inside the suit had a sinister, half-crazed tone.

"Are you breathing that crap?" I asked.

"No. I'm *thriving* in it." The Haze-Matt Temp Villain's tank blinked blue, and another wave of sulfur-scented gas gusted toward us.

In the end, I kept all three of us out of the gas.

I hit it with another **[Wind Front]**, then with a **[Virga]** when the gust wasn't enough. The Cunning points I received from the power were negated by the part where I healed two henches, and when the last of the green-brown particles fell out of the sky, I couldn't see Fake Haze-Matt anywhere.

[Badass Move! +1 Badass Point]

I called it in. "Fursona, be aware that the Third *V* is here. They're rogue. The Agent powered them up with Haze-Matt's powers, but it looks like that came with some . . . problems. I'm not sure where they went, but I've got two surrendered henches. You two *did* surrender, right?"

One of the henches hastily dropped his handgun while the other held her hands in the air, whistling and kicking her weapon away from her like she was totally innocent. "Yeah, yeah, they made me do it, et cetera, and so on," I said, waving them over to a bathroom. "Hide in here or come with me. Your choice."

"Okay. I have a half dozen henches with me. We're on the production floor, which is . . . probably not ideal," Fursona said. "You have no idea where the Third *V* is?"

"No idea."

"We're coming with you," the lady hench said.

"Great," I muttered. "Just great."

[End of Act Two: Act Three in Three Minutes]

At least we had an intermission to get moving, but all the henches were complicating things. Now that they'd surrendered, I was supposed to keep them safe—but how was I supposed to do that with Temp Haze-Matt out there? They clearly didn't care about anyone else's safety; if they had, they'd never have rigged the tanks to overpressurize and blow, and they certainly wouldn't be using chemical weapons by their allies.

So, with a mixture of relief and apprehension, I pointed at a door. "Does this one lead to the work floor?"

The guy nodded. "Yeah. Through there. You'll want a mask, though."

I almost pointed at the domino mask on my face, then thought better of it. Instead, I followed him to a locker room where a handful of gigantic, thick-lensed gas masks sat around. He helped me fit one to my face, and I stared at him through the thick plastic lenses. "Why are you helping me?" I asked.

"Because I didn't sign up for this. I thought the One *L* would use the plant for weapons or something, not destroy it. This is my job, and it's the only work I can find in South Poudre. Now I've got nothing. Henching's not a career for me—just a way to make ends meet for a couple of months. That's all."

"Well, shit," I muttered. "Fursona, I'm going to send the henches toward Tranquility. She's not likely to shoot them on sight, and they seem like the kind of project she'd want to deal with. You good with that?"

I was halfway to the production floor when Fursona answered. "Yeah, makes sense. We're looking for a way out. Most of mine are construction, with one manager type. No one knows what's what down here, and it *stinks*."

"Okay, hold your position. I've got a plant worker hench here. We'll come get you, and I'll have him lead the others to Tranquility. Is she still holed up across the way?"

"Yes. I think so. She could have moved to deal with the explosions."

I nodded. "Got it."

We stepped out onto the production floor, and I winced under my mask. "Has this place ever gotten a safety inspection?!" It reeked of acid, even through the gas mask.

"What's a safety inspector?" the man asked, shrugging at the rickety-looking catwalk over three huge tanks. Unlike the ones outside, they hadn't exploded. Also unlike the ones outside, fumes billowed from their open tops. The cavernous metal room's girders and beams were exposed, with a thin metal wall separating it from the outside; I could probably punch a hole in it with **[Limelight Barrage]**, but that came with risks. How stable was the building after the multiple explosions? I didn't know.

[Power War: The Righteous Cause: Act Three in Progress]

"Magical Girl Understudy, I know that's not your name." Temp Haze-Matt's voice echoed over a loudspeaker. "Why don't you take off that mask and give the world a look at the girl in the car?"

I tensed, looking up at the ceiling. How did *they* know that? And where were they? On the catwalk or behind a tank? I couldn't tell, and that scared the hell out of me. The employee-turned-henchman-turned-guide pointed at the wall, and I nodded. "Let's go," I whispered.

We crept along the wall, closer and closer to the back wall. I kept glancing behind us. How could someone in a bright yellow suit be so sneaky?

Something clinked off a steel pipe, then exploded with a tiny bang, and the passage we'd just come through filled with bright green smoke. "I'm going to find you, and I'm going to let everyone know you're nothing, Understudy. Then I'll find that car."

How the *fuck* did he know about that? I pointed toward the back, then made a walking motion with my fingers. The two former henches nodded and started moving, and I used a **[Quick-Time Change]** to switch back to Understudy and **[Solar Wing]** to get some altitude over the slowly expanding gas. The brilliant wings expanded from my shoulder, and I leaped into the air over the emerald smog.

I circled. My two henches were dashing ahead, not bothering with stealth, and another gas grenade exploded behind them. This time, the chemical mix was red-brown and descended quickly onto the steel braces and concrete floor. Spots of rust exploded across the room.

I had to find Temp Haze-Matt before they found my henches—or Fursona. She wasn't equipped for this, and neither were the henches with her. So, the next time a gas grenade rattled against the floor, I looked around.

And there they were. Their bright yellow suit flashed as they dashed along one of the catwalks below me, and I dove. I fired a **[Starlance]**, which hit them square in the back, right next to the gas tank. They turned, looking at me with a shocked posture as I landed on the far side of the catwalk. "You hurt me," they muttered incredulously.

[Dramatic Damage! +1 Drama Point]

"Yeah, I did. Listen, we'll get you out of that suit and get you some help, but you need to come quietly. Haze-Matt's not someone you want to be—trust me. I wish he hadn't died, but it has to be torture being him." I didn't want to think that Fake Haze-Matt was as bad as the original. Maybe Dr. Ayers could put their brain back in order, or someone else could. But I also wasn't equipped to talk a villain like this down.

"You *hurt* me!" Fake Haze-Matt's posture changed, and my heart dropped. They aimed their chemical sprayers at me, clearly getting ready for battle. "No one's hurt me before, not since I made this my lair. You'll pay for that!"

Their sprayers started spinning, and a trio of grenades fell from the tank contraption on their back onto a feeding device on their belt. I raised my wand.

I'd have to do this the hard way. They weren't going to come quietly.

9

Come Quietly

The catwalk was quiet, but behind me, I could hear henches—and hopefully, Fursona—heading for the door. Below me, the three massive tanks of industrial solvent bubbled and popped away as they cooked, and tendrils of fumes filled the air. I didn't want to stack up against Haze-Matt. Even a minor-league version of him could easily be trouble.

But I didn't want Fake Haze-Matt to get away, either. And they *knew* something about The Agent. So I had to win this one.

Fake Haze-Matt moved first. The two gas fans on their wrists vomited pale yellow smog at me as they stomped across the catwalk. It stuck to the metal, dripping onto the grate and hissing when it hit the solvent tanks below. I took a step back, then another.

But soon, there weren't any more steps back to take.

So, instead of retreating, I fired a **[Limelight Barrage]** toward the villain. The shots exploded against the hazmat suit and staggered against the railings. I pressed the attack with **[Starlance]**, but they threw a grenade that exploded midair, filling the space between us with gray dust. It hung there as my lance zoomed toward it.

[Dramatic Damage! +5 Drama Points]
[Dramatic Damage! +1 Drama Point]

BOOM!
When my **[Starlance]** hit the dust cloud, it exploded in a blinding flash. The whole catwalk rocked, and Fake Haze-Matt had to hold the railing to avoid falling. I wasn't so lucky.

[HP 3/13]

The explosion threw me into the air, and I barely got my [**Solar Wing**] under me in time to avoid the boiling solvent tub. I banked, dipping down between the huge tanks and angling back up as another grenade exploded midair. The wings caught my forward motion, stopping me just out of the blast zone.

But the villain was already throwing another one, which wasn't aimed my way. It was heading for the ground.

For Fursona and the henches.

I dove again, this time as hard as I could. And, just before the grenade hit the ground for its first bounce, I used [**Quick-Time Change**]. As Tails and I mind-merged, I had a brief second to make sure the angles were good.

[**Flashy Fitting-Room! +1 Flamboyance Point**]

[**Freeze-Frame**] was running, but I let my plushie cat's instincts take over. We hit the ground. My legs coiled, and Tails lunged us toward the grenade.

[**Steel Yourself! +1 Grit Point**]

We batted the grenade. Time started again, and it bounced under one of the solvent tanks even as Fursona and the henches ran for the door. I used [**Leaping Leopards**] to hop back onto the catwalk—now a literal one, too! Tails wanted me to arch my back and hiss, but I wasn't giving her *that* much control.

[**Badass Move! +1 Badass Point**]

But I did need to do *something* about Fake Haze-Matt. And I didn't want to knock them out. I wanted to talk to them and get the info I needed.

It was time for a change of plans.

I ran toward the villain, whose grenades were all reloading. They sprayed fog my way, filling the catwalk with an orange and red mixture of gasses that stung my throat and forced me to cough, but then I was in range.

[**Tough Kitty! +1 Grit Point**]
[**HP 2/13**]

I used [**Doom Ball**]. My claws ripped into Fake Haze-Matt's yellow suit, and though they didn't catch any skin, the suit ruptured in a half dozen places, leaking air with a deflating balloon sound. I leaped away before it could get in my nose.

[**Badass Damage! +4 Badass Points**]

The suit was deflating around Fake Haze-Matt as foul-smelling gas erupted from the half dozen openings I'd created. But their grenades refilled, and the villain dumped all three onto the catwalk at once.

BOOM!

The whole platform shook. Then, metal shrieking, it tore itself apart right between us. Fake Haze-Matt clung to their railing as the whole thing swayed toward a solvent tank, splashing cleaning solution that hissed when it touched the floor. The burning smell in my nose overwrote all my instincts, replacing them with one Tails thought.

Climb.

I climbed, even as my half of the catwalk twisted free from its brackets and plunged into a boiling, bubbling tub below. "This place really *doesn't* have safety inspectors, does it?" I asked, throwing myself toward the relative safety of the floor.

[Tough Kitty! +1 Grit Point]

I hit the ground rolling, and popped up just in time to see the catwalk pry open the grenade-damaged tank and send a wave of acrid concentrated cleaner my way. The greenish wave washed toward me, and I leaped for a pile of crates.

I didn't quite make it—it was too far—and ten thousand gallons of acid rushed toward me.

Then, a hand closed on the scruff of my neck, and Fursona jerked me up onto what was left of the catwalk. "I got you, Understudy!"

I let her pull me up to safety, twisting to avoid the worst of the razor-sharp steel where it had broken off. The whole working floor was trashed; acid had torn pockmarks in the metal walls, and the floor was pitted where it wasn't still covered with stinking, sizzling cleaner.

But more importantly, Fake Haze-Matt was still clinging to their perch on a slowly dissolving bit of catwalk.

"Thanks, babe, but we've gotta get them before they get away!" I said, pointing.

"I've got you on this, too!" Fursona said. She pointed back a couple of steps. "I'll toss you."

"What?"

"I'll toss you. Neither of us can jump that gap and get him."

"Alright," I said, staring at the gap. It *was* farther than I'd ever jumped, but I didn't have time to switch to Understudy for the flight. The villain was already running out of time.

I used **[Leaping Leopard]** again. This wouldn't be so bad, right?

We'd never practiced this. Ever. So, I wasn't quite ready for her to jump *herself* as my foot made contact with her paws. I went flying through the air, Tails yowling in my head the whole time, and barely caught Fake Haze-Matt with my extended paws, ripping them off the catwalk and slamming them into the ground.

[Badass Move! +1 Badass Point]

We rolled, and I ended up on top of them, pinning their gas fans to their sides with my legs while I straddled their stomach. Their mask fell off, and I suddenly realized I was straddling a very pretty-looking boy. "*V*, surrender, or I'll finish the fight!" I shouted in his face, not expecting a response.

But shockingly, I got one. "I surrender," the villain said.

The Third *V* was blonde, with longish hair that reeked of sweat and chemicals. He stared up at me with terrified-looking eyes. "What's going on?" he asked, looking around stupidly.

I almost hit him right there. He couldn't possibly believe that I bought his bullshit, could he? But when the camera drone dipped in close, and he flinched, I realized that he wasn't a supervillain. He might not even have been a henchman. After all, he hadn't told me anyone had made him do it.

So, if he wasn't a *V*, and he wasn't a hench, what *was* he?

"Could you get off me?" he asked, wincing.

"Not until you explain yourself."

"I will, I will." When I didn't move, he turned even more petulant. "Please? I promise I'm done—really, I am. I'm just a really big fan of Haze-Matt's shows, and when the opportunity presented itself to *be* him for a day or two, I couldn't say no."

"Wait." I sat there, keeping the kid pinned. He couldn't be much younger than me—maybe eighteen—and he looked genuine. But even so, I wasn't about to let someone with Haze-Matt's powers get up without backup.

Then he started wiggling, trying to squirm free. And he *wouldn't* shut up. "Listen, Understudy, I know you're not going to hurt me, and I know my rights. I'm a villain fan, and I know even Haze-Matt had to be treated with respect. So come on, let me up!"

He wouldn't. Stop. Struggling. Not even when I threatened him with a faceful of claws like Tails suggested. So, as Fursona walked over, I relented, climbing off him and offering him a paw up. He took it, flushed red from his efforts—and maybe from our position, which Fursona clearly noticed by the way her plastic eyes lingered on me for a moment. "What?"

"Nothing," she said quickly. "So, this is the villain?"

"I'm not a villain," the boy insisted.

"Then what are you?"

"I'm . . ." He flushed even redder. "I'm a cosplayer."

I stared at him incredulously. Fursona burst into laughter. "Understudy, you almost got beaten by a *cosplayer*? You'll never live this one down, and it's *all* on camera."

"Shut up, babe," I whispered. Then I cleared my throat. "So that's why you had Haze-Matt's mannerisms, then. Explains some things. Okay, how does a cosplayer get involved with 3V1L?"

"Uh, it's not that complicated, really. The Agent had Haze-Matt's power contracted for a while, but the problem with Haze-Matt is that his powers make you go crazy when you're suited up. So, he couldn't exactly give that power out. But I'm Haze-Matt's biggest fan. After he died, I was devastated."

I couldn't relate. There were a lot of villains the world could live with. McHammer and Lord Destructo. Jumper. Even Mindstorm wasn't *so* bad. But Haze-Matt was a *problem*, and as much as I hated to admit it, the world was better off without him. I regretted his death, but I hadn't killed him, and he wouldn't kill any more Extras. Besides, I'd had therapy for that whole mess.

The kid kept going. "But two days ago, I got a knock on my apartment door, and when I opened it? Bang, The Agent, right in *my* entryway. I invited him in, he took one look at my Haze-Matt cosplay, and just like that, a deal popped into my head. I'd get to *be* Haze-Matt, not just play him at conventions and stuff. He'd get to use the power. It was a win-win."

"But you lost," I said.

"I did. But before I did, I got to live my dream." The kid's face fell. "I'm just disappointed that my suit's wrecked. This thing cost me over five thousand to make."

"And do you know where The Agent is now?" I asked, ignoring his whining.

"Kind of." When the kid didn't say anything else, I glared at him. "Okay, okay, listen. He didn't give me an address to visit him, but I've got a location I was supposed to go to. I'd get to talk to an 3V1L member there, and he'd get a message to The Agent for me. The guy's playing a high-secrecy game. Not surprising. He's probably got half the city after him."

I didn't think so. The other heroes' hands were full with the villains still active for the Third Power War. The Agent was my problem, at least according to Rocko.

"Okay. Give us the address, and we'll take it from here," I said. He handed it over, and the Episode ended. Hopefully, Rocko would cut this whole conversation out.

[Episode Finished!]
[Episode: Power War: The Righteous Cause – PG-13]
[Penalties: N/A]
[Episode Finished! +3 of each Style Point]
[Winner Winner! +3 of each Style Point]
[Role Focus: Flamboyance + Grit - Goal Unmet]
[Alias - Understudy] [Archetype - Magical Girl] [Community Rank - 163/523]
[HP 7/13]
[Styles and Skills]
▶ Archetype Skill - Transformation Sequence
▶ Combo Skills - Power-Weaving
▶ Badass (53) (Skill Roll Available)
▶ Cunning (52) (Skill Roll Available)
▶ Drama (72) (Skill Roll Available)

▶ Bit-Part Barrage 2
▶ Starlance 1
▶ Flamboyance (63) (Skill Roll Available)
▶ Signature Skill - Adaptive Armoire 3
▶ Stored Costumes: (Rainy Day, Copy Cat, Lab Assistant Panic)
▶ Solar Wing 1
▶ Quick-Time Change 3
▶ Improvised Ovation 1
▶ Grit (53) (Skill Roll Available)
▶ Freeze-Frame 1

As the stats message appeared, I blinked. "Wow! All five styles?"

10

Five Styles

[Rank-Up! Freeze-Frame 2: The time-stop lasts two seconds instead of one]
[Rank-Up! Starlance 3: Starlance tracks better, offering increased cornering]
[Rank-Up! Virga 3: Rain produces additional healing for allies only]
[Rank-Up! Solar Wing 2: Automatically deploy glide-wings even when not in use]
[Skill Upgrade! Leaping Leopards 1 to Pouncing Panther 1: Gain invisibility for a moment before leaping, hitting the target's weak spots]

I had a lot of skills to deal with, and as the rolls came in, I stopped to think about each of them. **[Freeze-Frame's]** increased time stop was powerful; the extra second would be an eternity for making better choices and dodging even more attacks, and I was a little shocked it was a Grit power. Sure, it'd help defensively, but it had big-time offensive applications if I used it right.

The rank-up on **[Starlance]** could help a lot, too, but my bet was on it being a minor change that'd help it hit more but not change its usage. I was more excited about the **[Solar Wing]** change, which was a nice safety net—literally. And **[Virga's]** upgrade—which finally made it the asymmetrical power I wanted it to be—had the potential to turn it into a game-changer. I had to keep in mind that it still healed my enemies, just not as much as friends.

But the skill upgrade from **[Leaping Leopards]** to **[Pouncing Panther]** looked disgustingly solid. Not only did it keep the original power's two hops, but stealth for a second or two would leave my opponents even more off-balance. Would it be worth it to completely retool Copy Cat into a stealth and ambush Costume? Maybe. I'd put some thought into setting that up soon, but it definitely had the tools now.

But more pressing than that were our newfound allies. I needed to talk with them and debrief them on what we'd found—especially Tranquility. She seemed like the brains of the operation.

The Mutual Assistance League, such as it was, had moved in as soon as Fake Haze-Matt went down, and within a minute, the henches were disarmed, sitting against an outbuilding and chatting quietly about how "he made me." When one of them asked another what she'd do with her pay, I couldn't take it anymore.

I stalked away from where War Bear and Fursona loomed over our prisoners—an intimidating duo for sure—and joined the angelic-looking Tranquility near the epicenter of our fight with Fake Haze-Matt. The chemical plant had taken a beating from our battle, and it didn't look like it'd be open anytime soon, but I had to ask her something.

When I caught up to her, Tranquility was clearing the work floor with a golden wind that slowly blew the chemical fumes—and the solvent soaking the concrete floor—into one corner. "Hey . . . so, that's done," I said.

"Thank you. Did you figure out what you needed from it?" she asked, not bothering to look at me.

"Yes, I think so. The Third *V* was a shocker, though. Did you know he was in there? He almost felt like a trap specifically for me, and he was out of control."

Tranquility stopped the wind with a wave of her hand, and the towering chemical spill she'd piled into the corner wiggled like Jell-O. It *didn't* slide down and recover the floor, and I stared at it briefly while she talked. "No. We'd only seen henches and the Second *V*. And you say he was just attacking everyone?"

"No. He had Haze-Matt's powers." I explained The Agent's role in everything, since if the press knew, there wasn't any need to keep it from potential allies.

As I talked, she nodded thoughtfully and continued touch-up cleaning, adding gallons of liquid to the already towering pile of undulating water. "That should do until a proper cleanup crew can get here. It'll be a mess if it lets go early, though. I'll ask War Bear to put in an emergency cleanup request. Maybe we can MIRACLE this area or something."

"Yeah. One of the mooks said something about this being the only job he could get in-district."

"That's a pretty common reason these poor people go hench," Tranquility said sadly. "Some of the districts got left behind. The Poudre districts aren't Thornton levels of bad, but they're not doing well, and that's part of why War Bear and I decided to start the Mutual Assistance League here."

This all sounded like an elevator pitch she'd given a dozen times—or a hundred—but I let her roll through it. I'd met a lot of superheroes in my career, but she seemed like one of the first who really truly cared about the people she was supposedly fighting for, and as she talked about economic depression, revitalization, and how most henches weren't the problem but the symptoms of one, I started to realize she really believed what she was saying. She sounded a lot like The Narrator did when she talked about her kids.

After a minute, I nodded slowly. "We should catch up sometime when I've finished dealing with The Agent, Tranquility. But right now, I've got to get back to my hideout and start planning my next move."

"Your next move. I see a problem with that, though," she said as sirens screamed into the night. She flapped her wings and hopped up to the top of the building, then waited while I flew up. She pointed down at the police, then at the cars following them, and I groaned. Were they media, APPEAL, or something else?

"The police won't be able to hold Fake Haze-Matt, and when they let him go, he'll talk to 3V1L about what happened. Do you have a plan for that? Because if you don't, you'd better act quickly on whatever information he gave you."

I shook my head. "No. I'll go talk to the cops and see if they'll take him to Almhurst for a while. They did that with my . . . old rival, a sort of protective custody until they could move him home."

"Okay." The sirens were closing in, and Tranquility nodded and held out her hand. I shook it, and she continued. "You'd better go manage the police, then. And your fans."

With a groan, I took off and landed near the first blue-and-red set of lights. Sure enough, it wasn't just the police or the media; how my fans had found me, I had no idea, but it was going to be a long afternoon.

SATURDAY, JANUARY 2

I stood in Almhurst Penitentiary's entry, staring at the green-caped, goggle-clad hero behind the desk with an incredulous look on my face. "What do you mean you can't hold him?"

"What we mean is that your hench in a suit doesn't meet the legal definition of a superhero anymore now that his powers are gone, and he's got connections with lawyers who represent some *very* powerful villains and know how to play the game," he said. He flipped through some paperwork, obviously trying to end the conversation. "So we can't hold him."

Fursona wouldn't take no for an answer, though. "Listen, we're trying to hunt a serious-business villain and get him off the streets before he kills again, and—"

"Blah, blah, blah," the hero said. "Listen, someone like Haze-Matt? Sure, we could keep him. He was a danger to himself and everyone around him. Someone like that kid we had in here last year? Yeah, he wouldn't survive a trip back to his hometown, so it's easy to hold him here. But this guy's a mook. He wouldn't last three days in here."

"So give us two."

"No."

The industrial orange smell was oppressive—probably something the chemical plant had made—and I could hardly think as the desk hero's goggles slowly moved from me to the monitors he was . . . monitoring. "If that's all your business here, I'm going to have to ask you to leave. Almhurst doesn't typically do guest visits, and especially not on release days."

I groaned, rubbing my eyes. "Please help us. We need twenty-four hours. Can you give us that, at least?"

His gaze shifted to me, and he fiddled with his keyboard, sighing. "I can send you to see The Warden, but that's all I can do. If anyone has a solution, it's him. But he won't be happy to see you, and he won't bend the rules. He never does."

"We'll see about that," Fursona grumbled.

"Thank you," I said, nodding. "Which way?"

"Upstairs, two rights, then a left. Follow the arrow. The remote will only get you into the doors you need. Don't try anything else, or you'll see The Warden in a way you don't want."

"Thanks," I said again.

He nodded and went back to staring at his computer. Was he playing a game or monitoring the building's security? I couldn't tell, and I didn't care. All I cared about was getting to our meeting with The Warden.

We climbed the steel stairs, following the desk hero's directions very carefully. The arrow on our remote led us through a maze of white, corporate-looking hallways, and we eventually arrived at an office door. My hand had almost touched the steel handle when it sprang open, revealing a room filled with computer screens. Almost all of them showed different angles of Almhurst's obviously extensive security network, and they flicked through loops so quickly I could barely see each camera angle.

But the biggest monitor displayed a digital face. Its lips moved uncannily like a person's, and its green-gray eyes pierced mine unblinkingly. "Magical Girl Understudy and Fursona, here about Prisoner 8343563, formerly the Third *V*," it said in a digital drawl.

I nodded. "Are you The Warden?"

"I am. You're trying to extend a prisoner's incarceration extralegally. Why?"

Fursona cleared her throat. "Because he's given us information that only helps us hunt down The Agent if he doesn't know he's given it to us. If the hench confesses, our fight in South Poudre will have been for nothing."

"Not nothing. Your fight removed several henches from the streets for a couple of days and gave the Mutual Assistance League help when they needed it," the electronic voice interrupted. "The Mutual Assistance League has a history of excellent post conflict action, but lacks the firepower to win the battle first."

Some of the screens flicked through old news stories about the Mutual Assistance League's best efforts in the Poudre district, mostly against old 3V1L, and their post-Episode actions. The attempts at bettering the district, their work finding employment for former henches, and so on—they'd been busy, but they'd rarely outright won, even when they had a whole league.

The voice continued over them. "Thanks to you, they can focus on what they do best: fixing the district. And if I'm lucky, there will be fewer henches from the Poudre districts filling my temporary holding cells."

"So, will you help us?"

"No."

I wanted to cry. I *needed* to get moving, though, because if The Warden couldn't—or wouldn't—help us, we had hours before Fake Haze-Matt got released and tipped off the rest of 3V1L. But I couldn't move. The TV-screen face stared at me piercingly.

"However, I will tell you that he's due to be released in two hours, so if you want to do something, now is the time."

I nodded as the door popped open, and all the screens went blank. Then, I headed for the door. It wasn't much. We'd have to go today, and go quickly. But already a plan was forming in my head. We'd run an Investigative Episode, then try to parlay that into a real one—one that'd end with us squaring off against The Agent. Hopefully, he wouldn't have henches with him, but that seemed unlikely.

As we stepped through the door and back into Almhurst's quiet administrative hallways, The Warden spoke again.

"Thank you for helping Tranquility. She means the world to me. And thank you for your super service."

11

Thank You for Your Super Service

Bee's Honda's gauges and meters were all redlining as she pulled into the Walnut Tower parking lot and slammed the brakes with a grinding, squealing cacophony. I already had my seatbelt off and the door open before she'd fully stopped, and we sprinted the stairs like a pair of madwomen; there wasn't time to take the elevator.

"Okay, when we get up there, we'll get changed, then what?" Bianca asked breathlessly.

I sucked down some air as we rested on the eighth-floor landing for a second. "We head over to the address, try to do some digging, and see what we can see. It'll be easy."

"You say so."

"I do."

We kept running past the door to Su-Bin's floor. I winced but kept going; I'd call her later when there was time, but right now, we needed to get to the green room, get changed, and get airborne. I even pushed—gently—past Avan, who eyed Bee and me with curiosity. "Hey, Anika, how was your—"

"No time right now. We'll catch up later. Coffee tomorrow?" I asked, then grimaced as Bee looked at me with a raised eyebrow. "The three of us, I mean."

"Sure, but I'll hold you to it this time," Avan said.

I nodded breathlessly and kept moving until we disappeared into Room 1301 at the very top of the tower. "I'm going Eagle-sona for this one," Bianca said. She tossed her backpack aside, pulled off her jacket and pants, and changed into shorts and a tank top even though it was January. I stared at her jealously for a second, still in my winter clothes, then started my own transformation.

As the light show ended and the music stopped, I tucked away my wand and let Tails hop onto my shoulders so I could have two free hands to get Bee all strapped into her suit. "That'll be a good move for this one. I'll head in on the ground, but if you can cover me from above and let me know if 3V1L's making a move, that'll help a lot."

"That's the plan." Bee put the eagle mask over her head, and my girlfriend disappeared, replaced by my partner again.

I quickly rebuilt Copy Cat into the stealth suit it could totally be—complete with **[Set Dressing]** and **[Pouncing Panther]** for maximum invisibility, but also dropping **[Doom Ball]** and **[Hometown Heroine]** to make room. Without them, I'd be missing a ton of firepower: hopefully, we wouldn't have to fight until I could shift out of the recon and infiltration build. After another moment's thought, I dropped **[Fursonal Furcefield]**, too; I needed investigative powers, and **[Check the Script]** looked perfect.

Then we headed to the rooftop and took off, me on **[Solar Wing]** and Fursona under her suit's power.

I'd only been to Thornton a couple of times; before the Power War, it wasn't somewhere you went unless you had to, and after, the In-You-Endos had kept it more or less under control—but all that meant was that there weren't a lot of villains. If anything, the derelict buildings and shattered sidewalks that'd never quite recovered even before the Bear Lord rampaged through it were even less inviting now.

It wasn't somewhere I'd choose to live, that was for sure.

But the second we crossed into the district, the Investigative Episode popped up.

[Investigative Casting Call]
[Investigative Episode: Thornton on the Outs - PG]
[Role: Amateur Sleuth! Do you accept the role? (Yes/No)]
[Role Focus: Cunning + Drama]

We accepted the call and flew in toward the broken district.

[Thornton on the Outs: Act One in Progress]

"Okay," I said over the comms. "We've got three goals. First, find the address. Second, see if we can find evidence of The Agent or a *V*. And third—"

"Avoid the In-You-Endos," Fursona said. "Definitely avoid the In-You-Endos."

"Yep."

We had to hurry, because it had taken almost an hour to get home—even with Bee's reckless driving—and we only had a little while to stake the place out. If we couldn't find any evidence by the time the sun set, we'd have to call it, and we'd be back to square one.

So, there wasn't much time for subtlety.

Still, that didn't mean we'd be careless. "I'll loop around above and let you know what's going on," Fursona said. "You hit the ground, get shifted over, and move in—but be careful. I can be wherever you are in five seconds until you go inside. After that, it'll get more complicated."

"Got it." I dove hard for the street a block away from the target building, landing in a vacant lot whose weeds were poking through the dirty-looking snow. I quickly shifted into Copy Cat, using **[Quick-Time Change]** to merge minds with Tails, and moved into a nearby alley.

[Flashy Fitting-Room! +1 Flamboyance Point]

"Okay, you're half a block south of the target," Fursona said. "You should go stealth here. There's no way The Agent doesn't have guards outside, whether it's his lair or not."

"Agreed," I murmured—muttering carried less far than whispering—and used **[Set Dressing]**. I could still see my paws, but no one else could, in theory. But I still couldn't waltz right in. "Any sign of the In-You-Endos?"

[Dastardly Plan! +1 Cunning Point]

"Negative. Keep moving," Fursona said. Was she *enjoying* the pseudomilitary operation we had going on? I liked the air support, but what I wouldn't give for some Theseus missiles for extra cover.

I stepped out onto the street, counting on **[Set Dressing]** to keep my presence masked. The old, abandoned house could have been Su-Bin's parents' place for all I knew; even with winter covering the worst of it, it clearly hadn't been maintained in a decade or more. But the downstairs windows were still intact, and the front door was locked. I started making my way around. "Do you see a way in?"

"No. I'm doing a wider pass to check the sides." Fursona went quiet, and I saw her shadow zip by on the snow-covered yard. I waited nearby, counting on the camouflage. Someone walked by ten feet from me. Then they kept right on walking, even as I stared at them.

"Okay," Fursona said after a minute. "The second floor's all boarded up, except for one window that looks like they tried and failed to do it. This place has to be miserably cold."

"I'm on it." I moved into the yard, feeling snow crunch under my feet. When I looked behind me, a line of prints marked my passage. I stared at them, but I didn't have any way to deal with them. "Think they'll decide my prints are a mountain lion's?"

"What? Like Snagglemaw? No way. You're too small."

"That's what she said," I said.

"That *is* what I said."

That was weird. I didn't usually make jokes like that; they'd seemed on the immature side since I was Collidus's age. But I used **[Check the Script]**, which highlighted not only the target window but a fence that, with a little work, I could use as a launch pad—or a second push-off point for my double jump.

[Good Thinking! +1 Cunning Point]

Then, gathering my legs under me, I let Tails aim us. **[Pouncing Panther]** went off, and we flew through the air, bouncing off the rotten wooden fence. We landed halfway into the window, and our claws scrabbled for purchase. *<Sorry, I'm nya-t very good at aiming a body this big,>* Tails said.

[Badass Move! +1 Badass Point]

After a moment, I took over and dragged us into the attic. "We're in. Infiltration successful."

"That's . . ." Fursona trailed off.

"That's what?" I asked, moving through the attic and looking for ways to see what was going on below.

"That's . . . great. I'm going to do a wide, high patrol. Something's not right here," Fursona said. "You won't have air support for a bit, but you're inside anyway, so it'll be fine."

"Okay. I'm moving in."

The attic boards creaked slightly under my feet, but so did the whole house. More importantly, I couldn't hear another sound, and neither could Tails. Plus, I was invisible, so it wasn't like anyone would find me even if they tried. I still tried to move quietly, though.

Eventually, I found a place right over the door where I could see—barely—down into the dust-covered entryway. It certainly looked like no one had been here in months. Then, at Tails's urging, I lay down and closed one eye. The other watched.

And I waited.

And waited.

And waited.

And then, for variety, I waited a little more. It had to have been an hour, and we were running out of time. Maybe it'd even been longer; I couldn't check because the light from my phone might give me away.

Fursona hadn't been in range in a while; I had no idea what was keeping her, but I'd sent her a signal for comm silence, so she wasn't expecting to hear from me unless something went wrong. She'd sent a busy signal back.

And I'd learned something about Tails.

She got bored easily, and when she did, she started whining about wanting to *do* something, or at least sleep. The emphasis on the *do* was a little odd, too, but I ignored it for now.

So, honestly, when the door opened with a piercing screech, and a man in a tattered Haze-Matt suit stepped through, I almost screamed. I did jump a little, and he looked up toward the ceiling for a second before continuing into the hall. He walked to a pad on the wall, typed in a code, and opened a door.

"Fursona," I muttered as soon as the door closed. "Our friend just showed up."

'Great, I'm a little busy," Fursona yelled over the comms. "How about you do the spying, and I'll just keep getting screwed here?"

"What?"

"Nothing," she said. In the background, something that sounded like an electric sander howled. "I'll fill you up—*in, Jesus fucking Christ!*—later."

"Ooookay." I turned my attention to Fake Haze-Matt, who'd slipped through the door. The attic boards were probably creaky, so I made sure to move as lightly as I could, testing each board under my paw and trying desperately to follow him. I also used **[Check the Script]** to see if it'd highlight where the temp villain was going.

It did.

[Good Thinking! +1 Cunning Point]

He hurried through the hallway toward a bedroom—or at least, something the right size to be one—and opened the door. There, in a spiked 3V1L helmet, sat an Extra.

She sat in a rickety-looking wooden chair and nodded when Fake Haze-Matt pushed through the door. "About time you got here. The boss wants a debrief."

"Of course he does. And you're recording it, I assume?"

"You assume correctly. So, you were tasked with stopping the Mutual Assistance League and taking back their section of Poudre. And that failed, obviously."

"Obviously."

I stared down as the Extra interrogated the temp vil like he couldn't fill the whole room with toxic smog in a half-second. He couldn't anymore, but it was still shocking to see her lay into the man who'd once been Fake-Haze-Matt. She pushed hard, ignoring his frustrated responses and pressing him with a list of pre-built questions that felt like nothing a chaotic mess of an organization like 3V1L would use.

And the whole time, I listened for anything—anything—that I could use. But it wasn't until the end that I finally got something.

"Alright, *V* Number Three, this concludes our meeting. You are to report to 3V1L headquarters back in North Poudre and return your helmet. Consider your employment with 3V1L terminated, effective immediately. You can collect your final paycheck when you return your helmet, and the organization will pay you 60% of your wages via mailed check for the next month while you search for alternative employment."

The Third *V*—Fake Haze-Matt—sputtered, the chemical tank on his back chattering and hissing as it filled up. I tensed, ready to use my catlike reflexes to stop him or flee. But the hench didn't flinch, and after a moment, his shoulders slumped.

"Wait, I'm being fired after going up against four heroes? Of course I lost. The whole situation was unbalanced, even with Haze-Matt's powers."

The hench stared at him, and I could almost *see* the smile under her mask. She held out a slip of paper, and he snatched it as she kept talking. "That is correct. The date and time of your offboarding is on your notice. Your services are no longer needed."

12

Your Services Are No Longer Needed

My friend, the temp vil cosplayer, glared at the hench for another moment, then stomped toward the door. At the same time, I crept along behind him, listening to his litany of under-the-breath complaints. He grumbled about everything, from Fursona and me to the whole 3V1L organization, all the way to Golden Goose's attack last year.

It was honestly annoying, but it *did* cover up the time I stepped on a loose floorboard and knocked a bit of plaster off the ceiling. And it *did* keep him distracted all the way to the door and onto the cracked sidewalk.

So that was nice.

"Fuck you," Fake Haze-Matt muttered the whole way out of the house and across the snow-and-weed-covered path. "Fuck this. I'm done. I put my life on the line, and for what? A fucking pink slip?"

As he stomped down the sidewalk toward a beater of an old motorcycle, he read the paper, then balled it up into a tight, crumpled sphere. He threw it into the gutter, where it started soaking up melted snow, and climbed onto the motorcycle.

"Fursona, I've got a possible lead." As the bike took off, roaring down the road, I used **[Pouncing Panther]** to get down from the attic and landed near the paper. Its soaking wet text was almost unreadable, but I unfolded it and held it flat, then hurried away from the 3V1L outpost before the henchwoman could come out and spot me. That'd be a disaster at this point.

[Badass Move! +1 Badass Point]

"Great." It didn't *sound* great. It sounded like she had her hands full.

"Do you need help?" I asked.

"*No!*" She paused, took a breath, and continued. "Look, we're not the only super-heroes in Thornton, and I got caught up in some shit. These villains are getting pounded, but you *don't* need to get involved. It's way, way better if you slip out of here."

"You're sure you're okay?"

"Yes," she said through clenched teeth. "Do not get involved. Just go back to the green room, and I'll meet you there in, say, an hour."

"Got it, babe. Be careful out there."

"Har har."

So, back at the green room, I spread the soaking wet paper on the conversation pit's table and sprayed it down with my hair dryer until it started to curl at the edges. Then I peered over it until I found what I was looking for: a date, time, and address.

[Good Thinking! +1 Cunning Point]
[Episode Finished!]
[Investigative Episode: Thornton on the Outs - PG]
[Penalties: N/A]
[Episode Finished! +3 of each Style Point]
[Winner Winner! +3 of each Style Point]
[Role Focus: Cunning + Drama - Goal Partially Met: +5 Cunning Points]
[Alias - Understudy] [Archetype - Magical Girl] [Community Rank - 160/523]
[HP 13/13]
[Styles and Skills]
▶ Archetype Skill - Transformation Sequence
▶ Combo Skills - Power-Weaving
▶ Badass (11)
▶ Cunning (17)
▶ Drama (28)
▶ Bit-Part Barrage 2
▶ Starlance 1
▶ Flamboyance (20)
▶ Signature Skill - Adaptive Armoire 3
▶ Stored Costumes: (Rainy Day, Copy Cat, Lab Assistant Panic)
▶ Solar Wing 2
▶ Quick-Time Change 3
▶ Improvised Ovation 2
▶ Grit (9)
▶ Freeze-Frame 2

It was . . . perfect! We had everything we needed. Everything. The Agent was going down, and if not, we'd be able to find where he was from their headquarters. I found it hard to believe they had just handed out that address, and yet . . . there the paper was, sitting there on my coffee table. I stared at it, trying to figure out where I'd seen it before. 25679 Madrid. 25679 Madrid . . .

It just wouldn't click, no matter what I did or how I turned it over in my head. After a minute, I gave up, leaving it on the table. The Episode was over, and it was time to put away Understudy and become Anika again. I untransformed and headed to my kitchen for a snack. One granola bar for myself and microwaved pizza pockets for Bianca. She'd love that. I set them up, ready to heat the second she walked through the door.

After fifteen minutes, I ate my granola bar.

After another ten, I sent her a text and got the automatic "I'm in a fight" response we'd programmed in.

After an hour, I was starting to get worried. She'd never left me hanging like this before. I'd done it to her on occasion, but I'd tried to communicate what was happening. What *was* happening, anyway?

She finally came home two hours later, just before I finished cooking a quick dinner. The pizza pockets were long since put away, and I'd almost finished the lemon pepper chicken and veggies, when I heard her in the green room. She groaned, moaned, and struggled with her suit for a minute. "Hey, babe, I hear you. I can't leave the stove, but if you come here, I'll help you!"

"Oh, thank fuck." A half-unsuited eagle pushed through the door and staggered toward me. I blinked; she reeked. Of sweat and violence, yes, but also of . . . perfume? Really, *really* stinky perfume—and not green apples. She stopped at the edge of the kitchen, turned around, and raised her arms. "Help?"

"Okay, babe," I said, laughing a little as my tension bled off. As I got closer, the . . . unique . . . smell wafting off her got all but unbearable. "What did you run into out there?"

"The In-You-Endos."

I stopped, trying not to laugh. But she looked over her shoulder, and I couldn't see an ounce of humor in her eyes. My smile fell. "Oh shit, you're serious. And I bet . . ."

"Yeah. Captain Yiff for four hours. Solid. The only ones who didn't call me that were Magical Girl [Censored] and A Cat Who Can Talk. The damn cat didn't say *anything*, either. Captain Vibration insisted it could talk, but it just looked at me and licked itself. The whole Episode."

"Jeez." I unbuckled her, then turned the chicken and veggies down so they'd stay warm without drying out. "Go take a shower. The food will be here when you're done."

She sniffed an armpit, nodded, and started pulling off her top right there in the kitchen. I glared at her and shook my head. "No. Make sure they get right in the laundry before the whole place smells like a Macy's exploded."

"Okay, Mom."

"And make sure you get *clean*."

"Jeez." Bianca stalked off to the shower, and a few moments later, the water started running.

I turned everything down to the lowest it'd go and pulled up a chair to make sure nothing burned. The Triad had warned us about the In-You-Endos. If it was their zone for the Third Power War, why weren't they on top of 3V1L there? I almost wanted to contact them and ask, but Tele-Portal had been pretty clear: do not mess with the In-You-Endos.

Wherever their cartoon dick was on the map was theirs and theirs alone. We should have known better. Then again, we'd needed this Episode. And we *had* gotten what we needed.

By the time Bee finished her quick but thorough shower, I had the table set. I'd even found a candle in hopes of a romantic evening. But my hopes were dashed when Bee came out in sweats and a hoodie, glued to her phone. She sat down across from me, looked at the candle, and smiled. "That's adorable, babe."

"Thanks. What's got your attention?"

"Classes. Same setup as last semester; the teachers are supplying the books and stuff, and our schedules are locked in. We've got Episode Manipulation, Power Balancing, Building for Success, and First Aid."

"Nothing fun, huh?" I served the chicken, and she dug into it gratefully. We ate for a while; she was starving, and one thing I could count on her for was putting away whatever I served. Then, I grabbed my own phone and checked my emails.

Subject: Spring 2044 Schedule

To Magical Girl Understudy,

For your final semester in the Associate's Degree in Superpower Studies program at Tokyexico University, we've assigned you to the following classes:

MWF 8:00–8:50 - Episode Manipulation

MWF 9:00–9:50 - Building for Success

MWF 11:00–11:50 - First Aid

MWF 2:00–2:50 - Power Builds and Role Optimization

These classes will complement your current knowledge and skills, and prepare you for your future postgraduation. They offer an interesting mix of in-Episode flexibility, powerset optimization, and skills to use with Extras both inside and outside of Episodes.

Supplies for all four courses will be provided by the Department of Superpower Studies or, in the case of First Aid, Tokyexico University in general. You don't need to purchase anything in order to attend.

Thank you,

Dr. Mays

Head of Superpower Studies

Tokyexico University

Dr. Mays's email was shockingly terse, without any of the goofy jokes he'd filled previous ones with. I understood; he had to be hurting after The Agent had broken his power and shot Dr. Jackson. As far as I could tell, no one knew how he'd done it yet. Mays's lockdown advertising power was supposed to be unstoppable, with only Jackson able to break it—and maybe The Narrator by narrating him away. Other than that, no hero had ever broken out before.

So that had to be a source of worry for him. Plus, his partner was in the hospital. Or, I hoped, she was in rehab. Taking a shot or two wasn't something you recovered from quickly, and even a superhero would need some help if they *actually* got shot without superhero damage.

"Do you think she'll be okay?" I asked Bee.

"Who, Jackson?" She swallowed, then nodded. "She's a tough lady. Sure, she hasn't taken as many hits as you or me, most likely, and she didn't seem to have super-hero damage, either. But Tokyexico General's solid, and the other hospitals aren't exactly poor quality, either. Honestly, I'm surprised the Ilneats didn't just hit her with a healing patch and call it good."

"Yeah. That *is* a little odd." I was quiet for a minute—the food was just too good—before clearing my throat. "Okay. Tomorrow's the beginning of a new school year. Are you ready for it?"

"You're hiding something." Bee's eyes sparkled, and she looked at me intensely. I shifted, because for a moment, I wasn't sure what I was hiding.

Then, slowly, I nodded. "Does the address '25679 Madrid' mean anything to you?"

"Yes. That's Fred Callahan's address. He was a 3V1L member last semester, and we found all that stuff in his place."

"You're right!" I slapped my forehead, then stood up. Bee followed me into the green room, where the parts of her Eagle-sona suit she *hadn't* waited for me to help her with lay scattered around the room. I showed her the crumpled, mangled paper with the ink-bled letters.

She took one look at it and raised her eyebrow. "Really? They built their base *under* that guy's house?"

"I mean, it makes sense," I said. "We found all that stuff and stopped digging. It's like a weird camouflage. If you're obviously bad, maybe the heroes won't look deeper."

"Yeah. But that's super high risk. Most detectives and police wouldn't stop," Bee said.

"But we're not most detectives and police. We're superheroes, and unless the Episode ended there, we wouldn't bother checking it out further. We'd be off to the next problem—or in this case, to find our sidekick."

"So they took advantage of our stupidity?"

"Precisely." I sent a quick text Rocko's way.

<Hey. Got a lead. Going after The Agent - Annie 6:31>

We cleaned up, waited for a text, and played a board game for a while. Then, when Bee got a message that the Episode she'd just been in was airing, we watched that until she couldn't handle it anymore. When she was dying of embarrassment as

Magical Girl [Censored] and Madame Drench fought McHammer to a standstill, I finally shut it off—much to her relief. Then, as we got ready for bed, I received a text from Rocko.

<Great. Wait a bit, though. He won't get tipped off - Rocko 9:45>
<Come see us in three days - Rocko 9:45>
<I have something for you - Rocko 9:46>

PART TWO

13

Wardrobe

TUESDAY, JANUARY 5

[Welcome to Rocko's Studio. System Disabled. Now arriving Backstage.]

I hadn't seen heads or tails of Rocko since Golden Goose's death, and had only talked to them a couple of times in the months following it; in a way, it had been nice, but having *some* idea of what the studio wanted from me helped. Rocko was always there, ready to greet us with a big gorilla-toothed smile and a lack of personal space. So, as Bianca and I stepped into the Hot Zone and Rocko's Studio, only to be greeted by an empty heat, I could only look around in confusion.

There weren't even any water bottles for us.

"Rocko? Rocko, you there?" Bee called into the office.

It felt . . . off. They'd always greeted us, and now they were nowhere to be seen. I sat in an uncomfortably warm plastic chair and waited for the gorilla/otter alien to show up. I sort of regretted hanging up on them over winter break. Were they pissed at me, or was this something else?

Eventually, though, a door opened, and a harried-looking Rocko appeared. I could usually tell how stressed the four-armed Ilneat was by how many cigars they were smoking. Today was the first four-alarm-fire day I'd ever seen.

It took the Ilneat almost three seconds to notice us. When they did, they blinked, put one cigar out on their desk ashtray, and grinned a toothy grin. "DuPont! Marino! What are you doing here?"

"You . . . asked us to come half an hour ago?" Bee answered. "You said you and Pataki had something for—"

"Oh! Oh yes, we definitely have something for you." They sat down heavily at their desk, rubbing their black eyes. "Pataki. They're here."

The second Ilneat shouted something from Costuming. Rocko grumbled, pushed themselves out of their chair, and stomped away. "You two stay here. Don't move."

The moment the door slammed shut behind my producer, I looked at Bee. "Something's funny here."

"Agreed. Should we investigate?"

I thought about it. I really did. But in the end, Rocko's business was their business, not mine. They'd made it pretty clear that I kicked butt for the camera drones and they did the business side of things. Right now, that meant my priority was on beating 3V1L, tracking down The Agent, and ending his plotting—not on figuring out what had Rocko's nonexistent underwear in a twist.

Instead, I let myself be excited for a moment. Whatever Pataki had been working on, it had required some of Vigilant Vow's Costume, plus a Costume scrap they wouldn't even tell me about, it was so high-secrecy. It had to be cool. Really cool!

A mannequin on wheels rolled out into the lobby. Even covered by a sheet, I could see it was massive; Rocko pushed it with all four arms, huffing and puffing. "Marino, you're out here. Yours is easy to adjust with straps. DuPont, you're with Pataki in Costuming. Let's get going, girls!"

"Alright, DuPont, let's talk shop. I've been watching your Episodes, and you've got all the powers you'll ever need to dominate. Anything else you get is just an added bonus."

I didn't agree with Pataki at all. Compared to someone like Stella-Lunar, I was hopelessly outmatched. I opened my mouth to say as much, but the Ilneat pulled the cigarette out of their mouth and held up their hand. Their raspy drawl continued almost without pause. "What you need is raw numerical power. Unfortunately, most heroes can only get that by spending time in Episodes. But you—and Marino—are special, and I've been working on a way around that little problem.

"So, let me start by getting you in the machine. Feet on the *X*s, hands out from your body, and so on. We'll start with the dummy Costume, then give you an explanation once I've introduced it."

"Got it," I said, climbing onto the scanning machine, where the hard-light me appeared after a long, drawn-out process.

"Your biggest problem is that, yeah, you're flexible, and that lets you win fights against equally-powered enemies. That's a good thing, but you're not dealing with an *equally-powered* enemy, are you? You're dealing with major-league vils more and more frequently, and you remember what happened with Stella-Lunar, right?"

"Yeah, I remember I survived for a few minutes."

"Sure, sure. That's not gonna cut it against The Agent. That's barely cutting it against his minions, and he's got a few tricks up his sleeve that he hasn't revealed yet. So."

"So?"

Pataki didn't say much more, just mumbled and fiddled with the controls. Then, after what seemed like an eternity, an outfit appeared over my body. It fit the mannequin me perfectly, but it felt completely off at the same time. Like Pataki was trying to hide something about it. I pushed that thought to the back of my mind and stared.

"Introducing Super Girl Spotlight Star," Pataki drawled. They smiled predatorily—an odd look with their gorilla teeth—and ran their free hand through their fur. "This one was my magnum opus until Marino's Costume. Might still be, in fact. It combines powers from your former rival, Vigilant Vow, and a top-ranked superhero who will remain anonymous but doesn't need her Costume anymore. Don't ask how I got that Costume fragment, by the way. It's complicated."

I wasn't about to ask. I was too busy staring.

The Spotlight Star Costume wasn't like anything I'd worn before. I was used to showing a little leg, and to having a lightweight outfit, but the skirts on this thing felt more Victorian than ballet. They poofed out and then draped down to my calves. I couldn't decide whether they were armored or just ridiculous, though the gauntlets and vambraces made me think armor. Not the sleek, futuristic armor of Stella-Lunar, though; no, this felt positively medieval.

The hood was more proof that Pataki had been inspired by a faux–Middle Ages aesthetic. It, like the whole dress, was white with red-pink and sky-blue highlights, comedy and tragedy masks, and entirely too many stars. It looked a lot like my little-league outfit—if someone had decided to armor it, add even more bows and frills, and give it an ominous-looking hood.

I reached out to touch it, but Pataki cleared their throat. "Powers first. You need to understand its restrictions. I had to bend a lot of rules to get the Style System to even acknowledge what we *wanted* the Costume to do." They tapped on their computer screen for a moment, and a system message popped up. "Come look."

I looked. The Costume was nothing like anything I'd seen before, with the possible exception of Rescue Girl Lucky Star, which had two Signature Skills. But instead of two, this one had four—and no powers I could see. "Okay, you've got me. How does this work?"

[**Costume - Super Girl Spotlight Star**]
[**HP 14/14**]
[**Styles and Skills**]
▶**Archetype Skill - Transformation Sequence**
▶**Badass**
▶**Cunning**
▶**Signature Skill - Advanced Accessories**
▶**Signature Skill - Style Siphon**
▶**Drama**
▶**Signature Skill - Meter's Running (8/8)**
▶**Flamboyance**

▶ Signature Skill - Adaptive Armoire 1
▶ Stored Costumes: (Understudy)
▶ Grit

"Well, that's where I came in," Pataki said proudly. "Rocko wanted this done last year, but it wasn't a realistic timeline. But with the right combination of system prompts, a good box of Costume scraps, and some time, I came up with three Signature Skills that, together, did the jobs we were looking for. First up is **[Advanced Accessories]**."

The screen shifted, the words flipping like a Skill Roll until the first of three Signature Skills' descriptions appeared.

[New Signature Skill! Advanced Accessories: Gain access to all equipped Costumes' non-Signature powers at maximum power. Reset all uses/Act]

I cracked my knuckles, smiling. If I had my way, I'd spend the rest of my career in this suit, just based on this one power. It completely neutralized every weakness I had, like a dream come true. In fact . . .

"Could I stand up to Stella-Lunar with this power?" I asked, dreams of the fight in Vigilant Vow's lair filling my mind. It wouldn't ever end that way again. If we ran into each other and she wanted to fight me, I'd show her. Maybe a friendly spar?

"No. If this was the only power Spotlight Star had, you could probably beat her." Pataki let me fantasize for another three seconds before crushing my dreams. "This was the initial power I designed the Costume around, but the Style System refused to allow it. Didn't give me a reason for the refusal. Just wouldn't let it happen. It worked perfectly on the basic sims, but actually putting it together? No way!"

The computer screen changed again.

[New Signature Skill! Style Siphon: Using powers in this Costume does not generate Style Points]

"So, I had to slap a couple of restrictions on its power level. Sorry."
I winced. "So, using this Costume slows down my growth?"
"Yeah. Sorry."
"It's fine. What's the last Signature Skill?" I asked.

[New Signature Skill! Meter's Running: Only eight power-uses per use of the Spotlight Star Costume. Can only use one/Episode]

"Ouch," I said. "That's pretty bad."
"Honestly, it's not," Pataki said. "After the first restriction, I spent some time tinkering with restrictions that the Style System would see as keeping its power in line with a minor-league hero's power, but that wouldn't play out that way in

reality. This was the best option because it negates the first drawback. You don't gain Style Points, but since you only get eight powers as Spotlight Star in an Episode, you'll still use your regular Costumes enough that you won't fall behind too much."

"No, I get it," I said, rubbing my eyes and stepping off the machine's *X*. "But look, you sold this as the solution to my Agent problem. I'm not seeing it."

Pataki glanced away for a moment, then looked back, but wouldn't meet my eyes. "How about this, then? You've got a lead on The Agent. Follow up on it, take Spotlight Star with you, and give it a test run. Then decide how you feel about my super-suit."

I opened my mouth to say something, but held my tongue. Instead, I nodded slowly. "Thanks, Pataki. I'm sure it's a good Costume. I'm just trying to work through the restrictions and figure out how to use it."

"That's what test drives are for."

"DuPont, get out here! Time for you two to go." Rocko's voice pushed into the room, followed by Rocko themselves. They looked over me and the virtual Costume. "Well? Will it work?"

"Yes," I said. And it would. It'd give me a huge power spike on demand, and if I could use it against The Agent before he knew about it, maybe I could catch him off guard. The restrictions were rough, though. Still, I plastered a smile on my face. "It's great."

"Don't sound so enthusiastic. Marino's done packing her new suit up, so you two need to get out there and get to work. You've wasted enough time playing around with 3V1L. We need a decisive victory that forces The Agent out of hiding and into a battle you two can win, and these Costumes are your key to that."

"Thanks, Rocko. Thanks, Pataki," I said and headed for the door.

[System Enabled]

The moment the door to the green room closed, Bianca sat in the conversation pit, bouncing on the sofa. Her backpack was absolutely stuffed full, and I raised an eyebrow at the yellow-green croc tail sticking out of it. But her question hit first. "So, what'd you get?"

"Super Girl Spotlight Star." I ran through the description, and Bianca grinned the whole time. She nodded as I explained the restrictions, asking questions as I talked.

Then she dropped one I wasn't expecting. "What's the definition of maximum power?"

"What do you mean?" I asked.

"Well, if maximum power is the biggest power anyone's ever gotten, that's one thing. But if it's the biggest the System's capable of granting, that could be a very, very different scale. I'm honestly scared if it's that, so hopefully it's not."

"Yeah, I bet it's max based on anyone who has gotten my powers, or the biggest anyone's gotten a power. Something like that. Otherwise, it *would* be broken." I stretched and pointed at the backpack. "What'd you get?"

Bianca's smile grew wider until it looked like her face was about to split in two. "Remember the Playpen Patrol's new kid last Christmas?"

"Yeah. Why?"

If anything, her smile grew even brighter. I shivered as she pulled the green-and-yellow plushie monster Costume out of her backpack, taking her time to stand up and hold it upright. Then she said one word. "Kaiju-sona."

I couldn't stop laughing—a little of the funny kind, but mostly the kind villains did when they went mad with power. That was a bad sign, but all the same. Between bursts of giggles, I thought about The Agent. He wouldn't know what hit him.

14

Team Building

As I pulled off my warm clothes and shoved them into a locker in the Roth Arena women's locker room, I did a quick mental recap of my spring semester's first couple of days. Classes were going to be a lot.

Episode Manipulation with Dr. Mindstorm focused on pushing the Episode structure to its limits and using the rating system to your advantage. According to her, a powerful hero could play down—I'd seen that before, of course, but she said we could do it without messing with the rating system. I'd seen that, too. The difference was that she'd be teaching techniques to bring more firepower into weaker Episodes, prevent other powerful supers from realizing the Episode was more power-hungry than it appeared, and create imbalances using that technique, among others.

It felt like cheating. But on the other hand, if it could keep top-tier vils out of our Episodes with 3V1L or let us punch up, I was okay with it.

Then there was Power Builds and Role Optimization with Dr. Mays. Part of it felt like something I already understood; I'd been build-oriented for a while, while Fursona only had so much experience with Eagle-sona. But with Super Girl Spotlight Star in the picture, making sure my builds were optimal felt more important, and I needed to understand every role as well as possible to do that. So, without playing favorites too much, this one was shaping up to be the most important class.

The biggest problem with it was Dr. Mays himself.

He didn't seem focused; he was barely his usual jokey self for a couple of minutes each class period. And he wasn't teaching with enthusiasm. That was a *problem*, because despite the material being important, it was also pretty dry. Fursona was obviously bored out of her mind—and she *needed* this class, too.

Building for Success's first two class periods had been canceled due to the substitute instructor needing extra time to prepare. Understandable, really. Dr. Jackson was supposed to teach it, but she was out of commission for a while. No one begrudged her that at all. And to be honest, it sounded a lot like a second Extra Relations. The syllabus that'd been emailed to us included units on brand management, social media presence, and understanding marketing deals—odd, since the Studios took care of most of that.

And First Aid was . . . First Aid. I had powers for that.

The whole schedule landing on Monday, Wednesday, and Friday did make for a hectic day, but it also freed up two school days for Episodes. We hadn't pressed on Tuesday because whatever Rocko had for us, we wanted it before we went after The Agent. But this evening, we'd make it happen.

First, though, we had soccer.

"Are you sure about this?" I asked Bianca.

"Why wouldn't I be? We want a normal experience. This is a normal thing to do. And we'll make sure we're on the same team. It'll be great."

"I've never played soccer, that's all."

"Oh. Really? Not even magnet ball as a kid?"

"That doesn't count." I laced up my shoes and stood up. Bianca showed me how the shin guards went on; since I hadn't seen a pair since I was seven, I was grateful for the help. Then we paraded out onto the court.

A wall of padding surrounded the basketball court. Every possible way in was walled, exactly at the soccer court's out-of-bounds lines. On either side, a pair of smallish goals sat facing each other, and in the center, a gaggle of college kids stood around, waiting for something.

"What's going on?" Bee asked, stalking toward the crowd in her volleyball-style shorts and white workout top.

"Team building," someone muttered. "Go put your names in. Teams are randomly selected one person at a time to make sure they're not stacked with friend groups or anything, and that there's a good mix of men and women on each one."

"Ah." I stared at the sign-in sheet, suddenly even more apprehensive. The odds of Bee and me being on the same team were . . . low.

Sure enough, Bee got picked for the yellow team, while I got stuck on orange. She looked apologetic but stalked over to the far court, where yellow and blue were set up. I hurried toward orange's camp by the far goal.

A brown-haired boy cleared his throat once the orange team was completely assembled. "Has anyone here played indoor before? I haven't, but I've been watching videos during workouts for a few weeks to fake my way through coaching."

A chorus of noes washed softly over our end of the field. Then a tiny girl with blonde hair cleared her throat. "Yeah. I was varsity on our soccer team at school, and I played a little indoor during the winters. Just don't call me coach."

"Got it," the big, brown-haired boy said. "I'm Adam. My brother's on the green team over there, so we *need* to beat them. Let's all work hard, play to win, and—"

"Nah," the tiny girl said. "I'm here to have fun. I'd have tried out for the college team if I wanted to play that hard. Let's start with some basic passing drills. Ball control's critical, especially in indoor, since there's not an out-of-bounds."

"What?" I asked.

"You can bounce the ball off the pad barriers. At least, you could at home."

"Yep," Adam said.

We grabbed soccer balls from the rack in the court's center and then broke into pairs. And as the tiny girl and I kicked the ball back and forth, then stopped while she pulled my foot into different positions until the ball *actually* went where I wanted it to, I started to feel surprisingly comfortable.

It was easy. Not the soccer thing. That was really hard; kicking with different parts of my shoe gave totally different results, and making the ball go where I wanted it to was shockingly challenging. But not using my powers? That was easy. Not being a superhero? Also easy. Maybe clubs and casual sports *were* the way to let Annie be a separate person from Understudy.

We stopped after a few minutes, already sweating a little in the huge, heated arena, and assembled by the goal. "Okay, I'm Sierra," the blonde said. "We're going over positions because it's obvious that most of us haven't played much. The rules say we have to rotate people and that everyone has to play at least three positions during the season. So, we need a keeper, two defenders, two midfielders, and two forwards."

I raised my hand. "I'll play midfield first."

"Really?" Adam cleared his throat. "That's a pass-heavy position, and you're pretty new. You're tall, though. You could be a good keeper."

Sierra glared at him. "We're here to learn how to play and have fun, not be competitive. What's your name?"

"Uh, Annie."

"Okay, Annie. You want to play midfield? Why?"

"Because I'll get good at everything that way. Sure, it'll be rough at first, but I've dealt with bumpy roads before. I'm a fast learner, as long as it's not math."

"Ha. Alright, fair enough. So you're a midfielder now. Who else wants a position? If you don't pick, I'll assign them." For someone who didn't want to be called coach, Sierra sure was acting like one.

Adam ended up as the other midfielder, and when we broke back into partner pairs to practice dribbling and passing more, we ended up together. As we paced off and set up cones, I took a look at him. The dude was massive; almost built like a tank, his muscles weren't just bulky. He reminded me a lot of Su-Bin's boyfriend, Cam. Someone with real muscles, not just show ones. Someone who worked out hard to *be* strong, not just look like it. So when he stuck his hand out to shake, I squeezed it firmly, then increased my grip to match his.

He stared at me for a moment, eyes narrowing slightly. "What?" I asked. Then he pushed a little harder, too.

"Nothing. You reminded me of someone, that's all. So, we're doing dribbling drills, kicking around either side of the cones, then passing the ball back to the other person so they can go. I've seen these before. I'll go first," Adam said. He started down the court, taking small kicks and moving slowly but in control. There was something hesitant about him, like he wasn't trying too hard.

Or like he was.

I pushed it out of my head as the ball bounced across the polished wooden floor. My whole brain went into getting a foot in front of it; when it bounced off my arch and stopped in front of me, I couldn't help but smile.

Then I started jogging through the cones, weaving and kicking, weaving and kicking. The wind in my hair felt great, even though I wasn't moving anywhere near as fast as I did with [**Solar Wing**]. And yeah, I missed the ball a few times and had to go back for it, but it wasn't like anyone else was nailing it, either—at least, not most people.

Bianca was casually bouncing a ball over and over using only her feet, not letting it touch the ground as she walked slowly through *her* cone maze. And Sierra obviously knew exactly what she was doing. She navigated hers at a dead sprint.

Still, I could feel myself improving, and doing it without the Style System having any say in it. And, somehow, that felt good.

When practice ended, I was sweat-drenched, red-faced, and completely exhausted. "Don't call me coach" Sierra had put us through our paces, and my legs felt like Jell-O. But I'd gotten way, *way* better at indoor soccer. In a couple more practices, I might actually be ready for a game. Maybe not against Bee—she was really good—but maybe the green team, or the purple, red, pink, and black teams. They were waiting for the court as we finished, so there'd be more than four teams total.

"So, what'd you think?" I asked Bee as we filed back into the locker room and changed into warm clothes.

"My team's fine. We'll be competitive against everyone."

"No, I mean about the club. Can we do it? If you're too competitive, that's going to be a problem," I said.

Bianca was quiet as she pulled a sweatshirt on over her activewear. Then she cleared her throat. "Let's see how a game goes. We can decide after."

"Fair enough."

We walked home across the snow-covered campus; the sky was clear, and it'd be a cold night, but even so, we had a lot to prep for. Homework, yes, but that was taking a backseat tonight. The wind was blowing from the north—a stale, chemical smell—and we hurried along the sidewalk toward Walnut Tower.

The moment we got inside, Bee disappeared into the shower. I waited my turn, rinsed off, and changed into fresh, warm clothes. Bianca was already halfway into her Kaiju-sona suit when I emerged, and I transformed into Understudy. "Let me guess. I'm flying today?"

"Yeah. This suit's not the most mobile outside of one *large* feature, but I can only use it for a little while at a time. It's a big drain on my energy reserves. Now, are you ready?"

"I am." I took a deep breath and headed for the roof. Tonight was the night. Tonight, we were taking down The Agent. And there was no stopping us. Not this time.

15

Not This Time

[Casting Call]
[Episode: Power War: Free Agency - R]
[Role: Avenger! Do you accept the role? (Yes/No)]
[Role Focus: Drama + Flamboyance]
[Power War: Free Agency: Act One in Progress]

The plan was simple.

Show up at Fred Callahan's place, make sure there weren't any Extras around, and tear it apart until we found the entrance to 3V1L's lair. Fursona had gone Kaiju-sona, though she was still her normal size. She hadn't said whether she got big like Kaiju Kid, but she'd insinuated it. And I couldn't roll up in Super Girl Spotlight Star and waste my time in it.

So, instead, I was in Copy Cat. "I'm in position," I murmured. "Checking windows."

<You should jump through one,> Tails interrupted in my head.

"No, I shouldn't. Not yet," I said. Then I cleared my throat. "Okay, I'm getting a pretty similar setup to last time. Lots of 3V1L junk everywhere. The place looks filthier than before. I'm not convinced Fred's been back—there's dust everywhere."

"Okay. I'm breaching the front door in three . . . two . . ."

"One," I said and used [Pouncing Panther] to propel myself through the window, just like my stuffed cat familiar wanted me to. Glass shattered around me, but superhero damage dealt with the impact. She yowled something in my head as we hit the ground next to a pile of horned henchman helmets.

[Badass Move! +1 Badass Point]
[HP 13/14]

A half-second later, something crashed near the entrance. It repeated, and a roar echoed through the building as Kaiju-sona tore the front door off its hinges. An alarm started wailing.

"That's new," Fursona quipped.

I blasted the nearest blaring speaker with a **[Starlance]** and rolled my eyes. "If I were an evil organization's secret door, where would I be?"

[Dramatic Damage! +1 Drama Point]

"Somewhere the supers checked last time the place got raided," Fursona said. She pointed at the bedroom. "In there, under the bed."

"Of course. Move the entrance around every time a hero shows up." I rushed into the bedroom where, sure enough, the bed's back feet didn't *quite* touch the floor. "Good thinking, Fursona."

"I know. The System just told me, too."

The bed opened when I pushed on it, revealing a flight of stairs lit by greenish LED strips that bathed a concrete tunnel in a pallid glow. I transformed into Understudy; the only thing tankier-looking than Roo-sona was Kaiju-sona, so I'd be better off providing ranged support.

Ahead, I heard footsteps rushing toward us. I readied my wand for a **[Starlance]**. This was it. The Agent had to be down here. He *had* to be. I was going to finish this, put the murderous villain where he belonged, and move on after a year of struggle.

A dark-haired man in a *V*'s mask poked his head around the corner. "Attention, Magical Girl Understudy, we are the Second *V*, and you're trespassing on private property! Please leave."

That sounded like weakness to me. I cleared my throat, but before I could respond, Fursona yelled, "We have a warrant, and that warrant is *justice*," and rushed the villain.

They scattered before the spike-covered plushie kaiju and her fire breath, and I followed up with a **[Starlance]**. It caught one of the villains, who screamed and threw himself on the ground.

But he then also turned and rushed me. And at the same time, he dodged into a closet, ducking the ray altogether.

[Dramatic Damage! +1 Drama Point]

Two of the three new villains disappeared, but the third split into three again. Was he copying Bud Lightbeam? There was no way *he'd* sold his power, too! One of them swung a baseball bat toward Fursona, who caught it with a scale-covered shoulder. Another fired a gun at me; the bullet hit me dead in the chest, driving the air out of my lungs even as superhero damage did its job.

[HP 10/14]

I whirled and fired a room-clearing [**Limelight Barrage**] into the hall. Two of the three villains winked out as rays crashed into them, but the third took two hits, then split into three again. "Nice try, but I can do this all day."

[**Dramatic Damage! +3 Drama Points**]

"I'm sure you can!" Fursona said. She roared and filled the concrete hall with fire. As the blast traveled down the hall and the Second *V*s retreated, she turned toward me. "A cloner! Got any ideas?"

"Yeah. I go Super Girl and sweep him out of the way." I was excited to try it. More than excited—I couldn't wait. But then I shook my head. "But if I do, I won't have it for later, and I doubt this guy's the toughest opponent we'll see today."

"And I can't go big here. Too small, won't have an impact. So we do this the hard way?"

A bullet ricocheted off the wall over my head. "Yeah. The hard way. Awestruck?"

"Awestruck." Fursona nodded.

Before the next bullet hit, I used [**Power-Weaving**] and [**Quick-Time Change**]. As time froze and I shrank down to the early teenage Magical Girl Rainy Day, I rushed forward, taking advantage of [**Freeze-Frame**] to get under the clone *V*s' shots.

[**Flashy Fitting-Room! +1 Flamboyance Point**]
[**Steel Yourself! +1 Grit Point**]
[**Floating Points: 1 Flamboyance**]

[**Thunderhead**] crackled out a moment later, its shock wave punching into the clone *V*s. As they slammed back into the wall, they vanished. Fursona took advantage and closed the gap between the *V*s and us. But before she could make contact, two more clones appeared out of nowhere, and the *V* grinned as he backpedaled.

[**Pause for Effect! +1 Drama Point**]
[**Floating Points: 3 Flamboyance, 1 Grit**]

The *V* and his clones lashed out at Fursona, pummeling her with fists and firing a pistol at her. I didn't panic—the bullets wouldn't put her in the hospital through her superhero damage—but my gut did churn as I remembered the shot hitting Dr. Jackson. Something had to give, and I rushed forward as the vil backed away through the tunnel. The storm built overhead—and inside me.

Fursona kicked one gigantic, stumpy leg out, slamming it into a clone *V*. Then, as I closed the gap, her tail thrashed, and the other clone winked out. Her plushie hide had scarred where a bullet's impact had crashed into her, but she looked fine.

I **[Rode the Lightning]** as I got in range of the *V*. Lightning lashed out at him, surging from the storm overhead to power my combo. The thunder crashed. A dozen half-formed shadow clones appeared and vanished. Then, the lightning stopped.

[Electric Lightshow! +1 Flamboyance Point]
[Thunderstruck! +1 Drama Point]
[Power-Weaving! +6 Flamboyance, +3 Grit, +1 Drama Point]

The *V* stepped back through a doorframe as the thunder echoed and quieted. Fursona coughed up another gout of flame, but it didn't quite reach. The *V* dropped into a martial arts stance, splitting off a pair of clones as he did.

I rolled my eyes. "You're outmatched. Surrender, *V*!"

"I don't think so. Your attacks are shocking, but I'm not stirred."

"That makes no sense!"

Fursona stared at me; I could feel her eyes rolling beneath her Kaiju-sona helmet. I blushed. "No, you're right. Kick ass, talk to the prisoners after."

"Yep," she said.

The shadow clones opened fire with their pistols as the Second *V* ducked back. Pistol shots bounced off Fursona, but I used **[Virga]** to heal the superhero damage as quickly as it came in—or almost as quickly. The shadow clones didn't count as enemies, either, and the healing picked up my superhero damage, too, leaving me nearly full.

[Medic! +2 Cunning Points]
[HP 13/14]
[Doctors Without Borders! -1 Cunning Point]

But even though Kaiju-sona could handle the shadow clones, she wasn't making any progress toward the *V* himself. He kept retreating, summoning more copies whenever he lost one. "I'm going to slow-transform," I said over the comms. "Can you keep the pressure up?"

"Yeah, but that's all I can do," Fursona said. She sounded out of breath—unusual for her. "This suit takes a lot more to fight in than it should."

Huh. Pataki hadn't said anything about extra strain in Spotlight Star, but Kaiju-sona must've been different. "Okay. Back in a minute!"

"Got it."

As Fursona lumbered down the hall toward the Second *V*, I started a full-blown **[Transformation Sequence]**. The music swelled, the lights went wild, and Fursona had to switch from offense to defense as the Second *V* turned and tried to attack me with everything he had. But it was too late. As the music finally cut off, I switched back to Understudy and swiped a **[Starlance]** into the battle.

[Dramatic Damage! +1 Drama Point]

The *V* stepped back, breathing heavily, and the fight paused. I went over my options.

I could probably link together a second combo. Maybe something with Copy Cat. If I did, it'd probably be enough to break the cloner's stalling, and if Fursona could get to him, I didn't think anyone could handle a close-range Kaiju.

But if it didn't work, I'd be stuck in an infiltration-built Copy Cat and need another slow-transform. That'd leave Fursona fighting the stall without support again.

So, my other option was to try machine-gunning down clones so my partner could make headway.

I went with that.

[Starlance] after **[Starlance]** ripped down the hall, and the Second *V* spawned clones to catch them. But I wasn't aiming for him, and the clones played right into my goals. With every clone I blasted, Fursona got closer and closer to the *V*.

[Dramatic Damage! +1 Drama Point]
[Dramatic Damage! +1 Drama Point]

He glanced at the hulking, wide-shouldered T-Rex, backpedaling, but missed a beat. One of my **[Starlances]** targeted him, catching him in the shoulder. He staggered. Fursona tore through a clone, loomed over the Second *V*, and roared. Flames rippled out from her plushie mouth.

[Dramatic Damage! +1 Drama Point]

And the *V* vanished.

I looked from side to side, trying to find him. Where had he gone? Did he have teleportation, too? And why hadn't he used it earlier to flank us with his clones? But Fursona just laughed. She burped smoke and pushed down with her clawed arms. "Too little, too late, *V*. You're mine!"

As smoke swirled around her, I could see a man's silhouette. He hadn't teleported; he'd gone invisible. But Fursona already had him grappled. I winced as fire blazed out from her mouth, filling the hall.

Then, both suddenly and very expectedly, I got a notification.

[End of Act One: Act Two in Three Minutes]

The *V* winked back into sight, looking worse for wear. This close, I could actually see his uniform: the 3V1L helmet smoking from Fursona's attack, the cloak smoldering away, and the armor seared black from the attack. He coughed—his didn't include fire, but did have a little smoke in it—and raised his hands. "You two are nuts! The alarm's already fired, and backup's on the way!"

I cracked my knuckles. "Backup? More *V*s, then? Don't worry, we'll be in and out as soon as we find The Agent."

"The One *L*?" The villain's face whitened under his helmet. He laughed nervously. "You're in the wrong place."

"That sounds like a lie," Fursona said. Her eyes wobbled on thin plush stalks as she laughed.

The *V* shook his head. "He only visits every so often. He arrives out of nowhere and then disappears. He's hiding out somewhere else and only comes by to empower *V*s."

Why was he telling me this? I rolled my eyes; it had to be misdirection. Then I laughed, putting as much disbelief and scorn into it as possible. "Let me guess. 'The princess is in another castle'?"

16

Castle

[**Power War: Free Agency: Act Two in Progress**]

Something felt off as we pushed down the hall and into the 3V1L base below Fred Callahan's house. Yeah, the Second *V* was behind us, looking beaten. And yeah, Fursona's Kaiju-sona outfit had been *performing*. But I couldn't shake the tightness in my shoulder blades.

What if the *V* wasn't lying?

What would Fursona and I do if he was telling the truth and The Agent wasn't here? We didn't have any other leads, so we'd be back to checking random Episodes and hoping for a hint. The Council of Heroes' archive wouldn't give us anything new; there was no way The Agent would leave a trail there—or in his own Episodes. So we'd be back to square . . . not one, but pretty early on the board. Helping the Mutual Assistance League people, maybe, or trying patrols like the one we'd made with Tractor-Beam-Girl.

Neither was a good option. Neither was one I wanted to think about. And it didn't matter. The moment I shoved the door at the end of the hall and revealed a wide, chrome-lined hallway that felt like something Theseus would have in his industrial-corporate base, I knew that even if The Agent wasn't here now, he had been recently.

That'd be enough. "Fursona, Split Ends?"

"Yeah." She ducked left, hugging the chrome walls, and I glued myself to the right side of the wide room. There were doors everywhere; one had to lead to The Agent or evidence that he was around.

I put my hand on a doorknob.

The moment I did, the door slammed open and I pulled myself back as a *V* slammed into the room. She was stocky and built like a tank—she had to be well-acquainted with the weight room. I fired a [**Starlance**] her way to kick off the fighting, but before it could hit, a shimmering golden barrier consumed the whole attack with a hum. Her wand flashed out, and another shield appeared, this one locked onto her free arm. "I'm afraid you're not welcome here! Dark Girl First *V* is here to kick your butt!"

"Oh, god," I muttered under my breath. How many cosplayers had The Agent hired?! Then I squared up. "3V1L, time to exit stage left!"

Then the **[Starlances]** started flying. One after another crashed into her barriers as she manifested another shield. I couldn't punch through her defenses, but I could lock her attention on me. That way Fursona could—

Another door half disappeared for a moment as a tall, thin man stepped through. His tightly curled black hair peeked over his 3V1L mask, and as the door rematerialized behind him, he warped through space and landed between Fursona and the First *V*.

"Let me guess. Third *V*?" Fursona asked. Then, without waiting for a response, she roared flames and juggernauted toward him.

So, Shield *V* was mine, then.

And so was *another* supervillain in an 3V1L mask. This one threw himself over the First *V*'s shield, hanging midair for too long and changing directions to catapult toward me. It wasn't flight—not quite—but it was all I could do to get out of the way. "So, three *V*s in here, one beaten out there. Still want to tell me your boss isn't home?"

The Second *V*—the flier—looped around, seeming to stretch in place before catching a point in midair with his gloved hand. He orbited the hand once, slingshotting up to a breakneck speed. Then, in a streak of blue that reminded me of Springlock's power, he surged toward me.

[HP 11/14]

I couldn't dodge fast enough, and the impact drove me into the chrome wall. As stars briefly filled my eyes, I watched the First *V* rush me, her gold-and-blue shields glowing. They formed a box of energy ready to close on me like a Venus flytrap. She was trying to lock me down; if she did that, the three *V*s might be able to beat Fursona even in their weakened, too-many-*V*s state. As the walls rocketed toward me, I used **[Quick-Time Change]** to activate **[Freeze-Frame]**, letting my mind merge with Tails's, and dashed for the gap between barriers.

[Flashy Fitting-Room! +1 Flamboyance Point]
[True Grit! +1 Grit Point]

The world started moving again while I was still ten feet from the gap. Was I going to make it? I was totally going to make it!

I wasn't going to make it!

I used [**Pouncing Panther**], going invisible for a moment and throwing myself toward the ever-shrinking gap in the barriers. The shields nicked my whiskers as I flew by, and Tails hissed in fury in my mind. Then I landed safely on the other side and used [**Set Dressing**]. The current Copy Cat build wasn't built for a brawl; I'd need to be careful.

[Badass Move! +1 Badass Point]
[Dastardly Plan! +1 Cunning Point]

The Springlock wannabe *V* threw a giant potted fern my way as I went invisible; it shattered on my superhero damage, knocking me back a step. I responded with a well-planned second [**Pouncing Panther**] that landed me on top of him, scratching the hell out of his shoulders before finishing with a [**Cat-Scratch Fever**] that left him blinded, bleary-eyed, and stunned by the fury of my cat-based attack!

[HP 9/14]
[Badass Move! +1 Badass Point]
[Dramatic Damage! +1 Drama Point]

Fursona's Kaiju form crashed into the phasing *V* on the far side of the hall, who stepped through her massive frame like she wasn't there. He punched twice, fist reaching into her fursuit, and she reeled back and breathed a solid wall of flame. As the flames chased him, the Third *V* fled.

Shield *V* was using her shields to cut the room into smaller and smaller pieces, and the Springlock wannabe kept forcing me into tinier sections. If we kept up this dance, I'd be in serious trouble. And more importantly, The Agent—the One *L*—was *here*. I couldn't miss out on my chance. And luckily, I didn't have to.

As shields closed in around me, I started a [**Transformation Sequence**] out of Copy Cat . . .

. . . and into Super Girl Spotlight Star.

My vision narrowed to a single point of impossibly bright light. Around me, choral music swelled—but if the music for Understudy had been dramatic, this was over-the-top. Hundreds of voices sang it all at once; the pressure felt deafening until Super Girl Spotlight Star's hood rose to cover my head. Then, the last point of light faded, and everything was dark.

My feet touched the ground. I opened my eyes.

A series of Style System messages appeared.

[**Advanced Accessories: Magical Girl Understudy, Magical Girl Rainy Day, Copy Cat**]

[Skill Siphon Activated: Style Points Disabled]
[Meter's Running: 7/8]

Shields. Three of them. Frozen in place. It took me a second to realize that I'd activated **[Freeze-Frame]** when I transformed. Another second went by while I made a plan. Then, three more. When time finally started again, I stood behind Fursona, my back to her plushie-spiked tail. One of her eyestalks lolled over, staring at me. "Hi," I said.

"You're using your new suit?"

"Yeah. This is it," I said. "Cover me?"

"Sure. Still too tight in here to get good use out of mine," Fursona said. She roared fire at the stunned-looking phasing *V*, who didn't dodge fast enough; I could practically see his superhero damage going down.

Then I had other things to deal with—two of them. The shield *V* barreled in from the right, while farther back, the Springlock wannabe got ready to catapult himself toward me.

I couldn't allow that. I was the strongest hero in this Episode—at least for now—and I'd be dictating the pace. As the shield *V* closed the gap, barriers flaring colors, I whirled midair and used **[Limelight Barrage]**. But instead of a single wave of **[Starlances]**, a quartet of **[Maximum Starlances]**—the move Stella-Lunar used, thanks to the Spotlight Star Costume—flashed out from my wand. Shield *V* blocked one of them, but it took two of her shields to stop it. The second closed in on her, turning impossibly quickly as the bright silver-gold spear homed in. Then it impacted. She went flying and hit a door, slumped against it, and crashed to the ground.

The other two rushed toward the Springlock wannabe. Before he could dodge, they made contact, knocking him across the chrome-plated hall and toppling a potted palm over him.

[Dramatic Damage!]
[Meter's Running: 6/8]

This wasn't working. It was too slow. I used **[Thunderhead]**, wincing as my meter dropped again. The storm flashed pink and blue overhead, a mirror of my flaring Victorian-inspired skirts. The Springlock wannabe threw the entire palm my way. I used **[Quick-Time Change]** for **[Freeze-Frame]**; there wasn't a Costume to change into, but the five seconds of movement let me position behind the *V*.

[Pause for Effect!]
[Flashy Fitting-Room!]
[Steel Yourself!]
[Meter's Running: 2/8]

Then, the moment I dropped [**Freeze-Frame**], I [**Rode the Lightning**].

It felt like being the goddess of thunder. Lightning rippled across my Costume, filling the blue cloth with a glowing, pulsing sapphire-white light. Tendril after tendril of electricity pulsed out toward the Springlock wannabe, and he couldn't dodge fast enough. His body lit up like a cartoon getting electrocuted. Power surged through the room. Every lightbulb overhead exploded, throwing us all into darkness except for Fursona's flame breath and my still-glowing Costume.

[**Electric Lightshow!**]
[**Meter's Running: 1/8**]

I was already almost out of moves? How could I possibly take the fight to The Agent without Spotlight Star? I pushed the thought to the back of my head. Fursona still had some tricks up her sleeve; that'd be enough.

Speaking of Fursona, her flame breath rippled out toward the last remaining *V*, but he phased through a wall into one of the side rooms. A moment later, he opened the door and ran back out, punching through Kaiju-sona's plushie hide like it was nothing. Her eyestalk flopped back and forth with each blow.

I used my last power—[**Pouncing Panther**]—but instead of going invisible, a massive roar echoed in my mind as Tails filled it. She was so big. So striped. So . . . orange. She took over, and the roar ripped out of my throat. Fursona froze. So did the phasing *V*. It wasn't a time-stop; they both looked stunned, not truly frozen, and the plants' leaves still moved as I flew through the air propelled on my temporary tiger legs.

[**Badass Damage!**]
[**Meter's Running: 0/8**]

I hit the last *V* like a truck; he didn't have time to phase between the stun and my impact. His neck snapped back, and his head bounced off the concrete floor like someone whose lights had just been put out.

The darkness pressed in as a single singer's voice chanted the same choral chant, but in a sad minor key. As the boy's high-pitched voice faded to nothing, the hood vanished, and my body glowed midair. The standard light show whirled around me, gathering into a point above my head and then vanishing.

I opened my eyes. My feet hit the ground. And a moment later, the emergency lights flickered on.

I was back in my minor-league Understudy Costume. Around me, three *V*s lay on the ground; I rushed toward the phasing one, hand on his throat. His heart was beating, and I could see his chest rising and falling. Relief washed over me; I'd hit him hard enough to kill him, but even though he was an enemy, I was glad I hadn't.

[**End of Act Two: Act Three in Three Minutes**]

"Wow, Understudy, that was cool!" Fursona said. She cracked her neck; the lizard suit's googly eyestalks wobbled back and forth as she did, and I grinned for a second.

"Yeah. But now I won't have it for The Agent."

"That's okay. I've got a trick that's a lot like that. Did you pack juice boxes?"

I stared at her like she was a madwoman. "Juice boxes?"

17

Juice Boxes

Fursona was just kidding. I hoped. If her power really relied on sugar like Kaiju Kid's, that could be a challenge to work around. Hopefully, she'd packed some of her own. "Did you bring enough for everyone?" I asked hopefully.

"No. Rocko said the suit would need a fuel source, so until I know how much it'll burn, they're all mine," she said. "Delicious, nutritious Hi-C!"

I winced. Damn, she was serious. Then I composed myself, looking at the door to what I hoped would be The Agent's lair. This was it. The big win. "Ready?"

"Battle plan?"

"No. We'll call it when we see what's inside the room." I didn't want to commit to something that wouldn't work—flexibility was a virtue.

"Got it."

My hand snaked out to the door, and Fursona coiled her considerable bulk into a sprinter's pose. I nodded. She nodded back. The handle turned, and I jerked the door open.

As the Kaiju-sona suit filled the door, I got a quick glimpse into the room. And I was *thrilled*.

The room was round, lined in futuristic chrome and potted ferns like the hallway. In the middle, a half dozen *V*s—looking newly empowered—milled around a smarmy, oily-looking man in a three-piece suit. The Agent took one look at the fursuit-clad heroine filling his entryway, flipped his wallet open, and smiled winningly. The grin didn't reach his eyes. "Hello, Fursona. I'm assuming you're here to license that fantastic suit? I'm willing to offer you twice what I did at the job fair."

I pushed past her, wand out. I scanned him; he didn't have a briefcase, and I couldn't see a gun in plain sight—but he could be wearing a harness under his suit. If he didn't have one, we could end this right here. "Agent, surrender, and I'll make sure you get to Almhurst Penitentiary safely. You're hurting people, and it has to stop."

The Agent laughed. His name tag—I couldn't read it from here—glowed slightly even in the well-lit room. Had his facade slipped at all? Maybe a touch, but I couldn't tell. He pointed at me. "*Vs*, this is Magical Girl Understudy. She's a problem for us. Get rid of her."

Before any of them could move, I used [**Power-Weaving**] and fired a [**Limelight Barrage**] into the crowd. Right away, I could tell not being in Spotlight Star would always be a letdown—a half dozen [**Starlances**] scattered across the *Vs*, but they didn't pack the same punch Stella-Lunar's empowered ones did. Still, I got some hits in; a couple of *Vs* staggered back.

[Dramatic Damage! +4 Drama Points]

Fursona crashed into the temp villains a moment later; they scattered like bowling pins—except for one guy in a 3V1L mask whose muscles rippled as he grabbed my partner in a wrestling hold. He slid back a few feet, dug in his heels, and stopped.

And the whole time The Agent backed away, keeping his temp vils between him and me.

I needed a breach—a big one. So I used [**Quick-Time Change**] and [**Freeze-Frame**], building my combo and getting ready to shred some temp vils. The Itsy Bitsy Spider played, and I spent my couple of free seconds rotating around the pile of vils.

[Flashy Fitting-Room! +1 Flamboyance Point]
[Steel Yourself! +1 Grit Point]
[Floating Points: 3 Drama, 1 Flamboyance]

There. I had a line directly to The Agent! I used [**Thunderhead**], letting the shock wave component knock a hammer-wielding *V* who looked a lot like Candi Crush aside.

[Pause for Effect! +1 Drama Point]
[Power-Weaving! +6 Drama, +3 Flamboyance, +1 Grit Point]

The storm cloud overhead filled the entire top half of the room. I ducked under a laser beam as it reflected off the chrome walls, sawing ferns into pieces. Fursona's roar filled the room; it echoed off the round walls, giving the impression of a hundred Kaiju-sonas.

I used [**Ride the Lightning**]. Surely, The Agent wouldn't survive an empowered-[**Thunderhead**]-boosted [**Ride the Lightning**]. The tendril of electricity arced into him, splitting to zap a couple of nearby vils.

[Electric Lightshow! +1 Flamboyance Point]

And he shimmered for a moment as the lightning broke on him. His body glowed for half a second, then flicked red. "Wow, you hit hard nowadays. You're sure you don't want to let bygones be bygones? I'd offer you a new deal if I could license your Rainy Day setup. It'd be a real shocker for the Mutual Assistance League."

"You don't . . . you don't even care that I'm here to fight you, do you?" I asked. My fists clenched. My heart pounded—I could feel it in my temples, under my domino mask.

"I'll be honest with you," The Agent said, "there's nothing you can do to stop me."

Kaiju-sona smashed the muscle-bound temp villain into the tile floor. He bounced awkwardly, half stood, and took a T-Rex tail to the chest for his trouble. I grinned. "I bet Kaiju-sona can, though."

"I don't think so." The Agent put his hands behind his head and smiled winningly. His white teeth flashed in the fluorescent lights, and I grimaced. He was such a douchebag! And I knew just how to wipe the smile off his face.

"Want to bet? Fursona, have a juice box!"

A lot could happen in ten seconds.

Fursona started laughing. She'd sounded a little scary while fighting the cloning *V* in the hall, but this sounded downright uncontrollable. She managed to stop for a second, then continued to laugh a moment later.

Then, her fursuit started to grow. She rose quickly, towering over the three *V*s who'd been trying to fight her. The muscle-bound grappler fell off her as her eyestalks swung around her head like morning stars. They touched the ceiling.

And she didn't stop there. As her laughs grew more and more roar-like, the plaster cracked under her plushie pressure. Then it gave, buckling and folding like an upside-down taco. Plaster and chrome showered down around us, beams splintering and tumbling to the ground. I dodged left.

The Agent ducked right.

"Emergency Teleport, Thornberry, now," The Agent said, staring at the fifty-foot-tall and growing Kaiju-sona. He shimmered and vanished as I tried to **[Wind Front]** him off his feet. The hurricane-force wind passed through the spot he'd just been and knocked a temp *V* onto the cracked, sharp tiles.

[Badass Move! +1 Badass Point]

Fursona's tail thrashed. Ferns and chrome plating flew everywhere. The setting sun over North Poudre silhouetted her perfectly as she roared over the remains of Fred Callahan's house—one thing was for sure: we didn't need to worry about *this* base anymore.

One tree trunk of a leg slammed into the tile, buckling it as water poured down in a torrent from broken pipes. The air smelled like electricity and smoke as Fursona waded through the rubble and erupted toward the sky.

Five *Vs* remained; the super-strength one had gotten back up, but another—the laser-beamer, maybe?—was down for the count. I watched as she stomped another into the tile before he could so much as use a power. Then her tail split the air as it whistled toward me.

I used **[Quick-Time Change]** and **[Freeze-Frame]**, switching back to Understudy and dodging her accidental attack. "Watch where you're aiming, Fursona!"

She didn't say anything. She roared, a long, guttural half-shriek that I swore people could hear in Mid-Town. Then her flame breath washed over Fred Callahan's former house, setting the wooden frame ablaze.

As she stomped out of the wreckage, four *Vs* arrayed in front of her, I used **[Solar Wing]** and got into the air around her head. "You lead, I'll cover," I said.

The massive head nodded, eyestalks flopping through the air like boulders, and I pulled up a little higher. The Agent was gone—we didn't know where he'd gone, and as far as I could tell, neither did the *Vs*. So, we couldn't win, not really.

But Fursona seemed determined to make sure 3V1L paid the price. A gout of pinkish-red fire burst from her mouth toward one of the *Vs*. As it engulfed her and her superhero damage ticked down, I fired a **[Starlance]** toward the laser *V*, trying to suppress him.

[Dramatic Damage! +1 Drama Point]

It hit. He hit the ground a moment later, holding his hands up. "Glass cannons, they're all the same," I said.

Fursona laughed a gravelly, roared laugh as she knocked yet another *V* to the side. Her movements looked sloppier than they had just a few seconds ago; her timer had to be running low, too. But we only had one *V* left. I zipped toward the plant-conjuring *V*—who hadn't accomplished anything in the fight. "You want to just not?"

He glared at me, face turned up toward the sunset. His mouth opened to say something, but before he could, something massive eclipsed the pale-yellow winter sun. Fursona loomed behind me—I couldn't turn to see her, but it couldn't be anyone else. Her roar split the air, and the flames leaking from her plushie mouth lit up the evening sky in pink.

The *V*'s mouth snapped closed, and he raised his hands.

"Good choice."

[Episode Finished!]
[Episode: Power War: Free Agency - R]
[Penalties: N/A]
[Episode Finished! +3 of each Style Point]
[Call It a Draw! +2 of each Style Point]
[Role Focus: Drama + Flamboyance - Goal Met: +10 to Focused Styles]
[Alias - Understudy] [Archetype - Magical Girl] [Community Rank - 155/523]

[HP 14/14]
[Styles and Skills]
▶ Archetype Skill - Transformation Sequence
▶ Combo Skills - Power-Weaving
▶ Badass (20)
▶ Cunning (24)
▶ Drama (61) (Skill Roll Available)
▶ Limelight Barrage 2
▶ Starlance 2
▶ Flamboyance (46)
▶ Signature Skill - Adaptive Armoire 3
▶ Stored Costumes: (Rainy Day, Copy Cat, Lab Assistant Panic)
▶ Solar Wing 2
▶ Quick-Time Change 3
▶ Improvised Ovation 2
▶ Grit (29)
▶ Freeze-Frame 2
[Rank-Up! Starlance 3: Starlance fires a Stellar Ray at a secondary target 10% of the time]

Bee held it together inside the Kaiju-sona suit until we got back to the green room. She shrank down—thank god—after the Episode ended, and I loaded her onto my **[Solar Wing]** sailboard. I could feel her shivering the whole time, but that was pretty normal. If she didn't have control, flight was still rough for her.

But then she didn't stop when we landed, either. *That* was worrying; she usually pulled it together pretty quickly. But this time, she didn't stop as we worked our way down the stairs or when I unzipped the Kaiju-sona suit. Her lips chattered as she stuttered a quick "Sorry" my way, but I ignored her. She looked pale, and while she didn't feel cold, something was definitely off.

"We're okay." I tried to make myself seem as peppy as possible because she looked so defeated. She'd been crushed after losses before, but we'd at least tied. I tried to give her a warm hug, but she shrugged it off and flopped onto the conversation pit's sofa.

"We're not. Rocko didn't . . . didn't tell me that it'd take that much out of me. I need . . ."

"Need what?" I stood up, ready to get my girlfriend whatever she needed.

"Citrus. Do we have any oranges? It worked for other size-increasing heroes in the movies."

Oh. Oh! It wasn't a problem with the fight. It was just . . . she'd said the furzilla mode or whatever needed fuel. It had probably burned through the juice box in a matter of seconds. I stood up and headed to the kitchen. There had to be oranges there. How could there not be oranges there?

I checked the fridge, the pantry, and everywhere else, but couldn't track any down. Had we been to the store recently? Or had I just forgotten to buy them the last couple of trips? I couldn't remember. But I did have one ace up my sleeve.

I grabbed the tube of concentrated juice from the freezer and put it in the microwave. Deep inside me, Ramsey Fieri was rolling in her metaphorical grave, but I didn't care. Bee was going to hate the flavor, but sometimes it wasn't really about whether you liked it. It was about taking your medicine.

The microwave beeped, and I poured the melted pinkish-orange concentrate into a pitcher, filled it with water, and stirred. When it looked mixed enough, I poured a single glass—I wanted nothing to do with the sour abomination I'd created—and brought it to Bee.

She stared at it, blinked, and then gulped it down. The shaking slowed down over the next minute or two, and she looked up at me from the couch, a mix of revulsion and gratefulness on her face. "Really? Grapefruit juice?"

18

Grapefruit Juice

MONDAY, JANUARY 11

Rocko had been busy; they'd locked their studio door and wouldn't answer their phone for days. But I'd finally gotten them to pick up, and now the four of us—Pataki, Rocko, Bee, and I—were video-chatting and debating the new suits' problems and whether they were fixable.

"So, the biggest issue for me is metabolism. I need a better source of sugar if I'm going to pilot the Kaiju-sona suit," Bianca said. "That suit takes way too much out of me."

She wasn't lying. It had taken her almost a day to recover from less than two minutes of Kaiju mode. That wouldn't be a problem most of the time, but if 3V1L realized it was a weakness, they could start a couple of must-fight Episodes and wear her down. Just because she was now the biggest hero in Tokyexico City by mass didn't mean she was unbeatable.

"Alright, alright," Pataki drawled around their cigarette. "Maybe an IV drip system or a bladder hydration system with cleaning ports to keep the sugar buildup from getting overwhelming. Those are both easy fixes."

"I'd rather have the hydration system. Better than getting stuck with a needle whenever I want to do superhero stuff."

"You got it. DuPont, you said you have problems with the Spotlight Star Costume?" Rocko had a pair of cigars going; their eyes flashed toward another door in the back, then back to me.

"I burn through eight powers too quickly," I said. "I'd already used a power just transforming into Spotlight Star thanks to [**Freeze-Frame**], and [**Meter's Running**] is super-unforgiving. Is there a way to give me more powers while in Spotlight Star? Or, I don't know? Make powers that activate independently not count against the eight-power restriction?"

Rocko raised an eyebrow and glanced at Pataki. The Ilneat tailor shook her head slowly. "I'm not sure how to fix it, DuPont. The Style System didn't want the suit to exist as it is, and any improvements could make the whole thing stop working."

"Huh." I sat there quietly. Something felt off about this. "So, you Ilneats really don't have control over the Style System?"

"That's classified information," Rocko interrupted.

"What you need to know is that the Spotlight Star Costume is probably as good as it gets until you're a major-league hero. We might be able to tweak one or two powers, and it's possible that you'll level it," Pataki said.

I took a good look at their background—a spaceship window with a familiar-looking blue-and-green planet in the distance. It was time for a subject change. "So, with you up there, how am I supposed to get the quick intel I need to beat The Agent?"

Rocko's tone shifted. They'd been a little grumpy, but they'd just turned down-right prickly. "DuPont, how about you focus on getting a few other Episodes under your belt? Let us worry about getting you and The Agent into an Episode together later, but for now, figure out how to make Spotlight Star work. That's your job. Our job is to ensure the *Heroics 101* season has all the highs and lows it needs. Stick to your job, and we'll stick to ours."

The Ilneats hung up shortly after, citing a meeting with the Network. I wasn't sure how much I believed them. Finding time to talk to Rocko was getting frustrating, and when I'd finally pinned them down, Rocko had told me not to worry about The Agent, then squirmed away. That felt . . .

That felt really weird.

Rocko had been so hyperaggressive last year and even some of last semester. They'd pushed hard to get one more Episode in or to stick to impossibly demanding schedules. And their door had always been open for me, my whole career. Now, it felt like they were trying to avoid us. They certainly weren't engaged in *Heroics 101* like they had been; it'd been four days since the fight at 3V1L's secret lair, and the Episode hadn't aired yet.

"None of this is like Rocko," I said from the conversation pit's couch. Bee had her arms around my waist and was cuddling me like a stuffed animal; I'd given up on breaking free and accepted my horrible fate. "They're usually more . . ."

"More of a jerk?" Bee said. She snuggled against my back, warming me up nicely. "Yeah, I agree with you. They've been so focused on *Heroics 101*, and now it's like an endless line of meetings with no time for us. What do you think's going on?"

"Well, without starting an Investigative Episode?"

She nodded.

"It could be that Rocko's moving up in the world. If they've gotten a promotion, maybe they have to spend more time with the Network, which leaves less time and energy for Earth and us. But something about that feels off. They wouldn't always be so annoyed, especially not over nothing."

"Unless the promotion's not something they wanted," Bee said.

We both paused, looked at each other, and burst into laughter. That couldn't be true. Everything we knew about Rocko said they'd do whatever it took to move up in the ranks. A promotion they didn't want was too hard to believe. But it did break the tension; after a ridiculous statement like Bee's, neither of us could stay focused—or mad.

"How about food?" Bee asked once we'd both calmed down. She pushed me toward the couch's edge, then climbed over me to stand up.

I sighed and started a [**Transformation Sequence**] into Ramsey Fieri, but Bee pulled me out of it before I could finish it. "Not your food. It's good, but I was thinking about going somewhere?"

"Oh?"

"Yeah. The food court."

My eyes rolled before I could stop them. "We can do better than that. Come on, find the dress you wore to MacBeth and be ready in half an hour."

"Half an hour? There's no way you'll make it in time," Bee said. She was already running for the bedroom as I pushed myself off the couch and toward my bathroom. I needed a shower. And make-up. And to pick the right outfit to complement hers.

"Fifty-three minutes, twenty-eight seconds," Bee pronounced triumphantly as I flounced into her passenger's seat. She started the Civic and backed out while I buckled up. "Slow, slow, slow!"

"I can't believe you were timing me. So unfair."

"Oh, come on, you knew there was no way you'd be ready in time." As we pulled onto University Street, I saw her white dress under the oversized puffer jacket she had on. The car smelled like green apples, too, and I found myself relaxing and melting into the cracked faux leather seat as the heater slowly warmed it up.

"What are we eating?" Bee asked.

"The sushi place?" I suggested, but Bee's face told me that wasn't going to fly. "Or . . . something more filling?"

"Yeah."

"Italian?"

"Been there, done that." Bee pointed the car toward Mid-Town. "I'm driving toward Broadway Mall, and if we haven't picked something I want by the time I get there, we're going to the food court. So you better think fast."

"Hamburgers," I blurted without thinking about it. "Mexican? Thai? Chinese? Steaks?"

"Steaks it is."

I searched for a place, gave Bee the directions, and returned to melting into her passenger seat. We pulled up to a nearly empty parking lot near Mid-Town a few minutes later. The restaurant still had Christmas lights out, and a half dozen fake electric candles illuminated the entry.

The maitre d' guided us to a booth in the back, deployed the menus, and left us mercifully alone. "Brittany" would be our waitress, and she'd be by soon. I continued melting into the booth, enjoying the aroma of the restaurant and the green apple smell that lingered close by.

"Okay, let's talk shop for three minutes, then no business for the rest of the night. Deal?"

"Deal." I cleared my throat and looked around. The restaurant was completely empty, but even so, I dropped my voice to a murmur. "I think we should target Episodes in our rogues' gallery. If we keep the pressure up on 3V1L, we might force The Agent to make a mistake. Once he does, we can capitalize on it."

"That doesn't sound like the go go go Understudy who's been pushing hard to corner him and finish 3V1L."

"Well, that hasn't worked as well as I'd hoped. We can push against 3V1L, make Episodes for Rocko, and bide our time." It hurt me to suggest it. I wanted the big win. I *needed* to bring The Agent in; he'd shot Dr. Jackson! But we didn't have any leads. 3V1L had abandoned their lair under Callahan's, and the Mutual Assistance League had almost cut the two Poudre districts in half.

"Okay. So, Sister Sly?"

"Hasn't been seen in weeks."

"Theseus?"

"He's an option, but I think Alkirk's been keeping him on a short leash for the last couple of months. We could contact him to see if he wants a rematch."

Bee went quiet for a bit, poring over the menu. When Brittany showed up, I ordered salmon—I was really in the mood for fish—and Bee got a steak, potatoes, and veggies. Then, an alarm went off on her phone, and she cleared her throat. "Shop talk over. We can talk about work again when we're in the car."

"Okay."

Bread and butter arrived a minute later, distracting us even more, and I got to watch Bee devour roll after roll. She really was a bottomless pit—almost as much as Gourmet. When she'd eaten her three, and I'd had my one, I asked the big question—the one I knew was on her mind. "Do you think your soccer team can beat mine?"

"Absolutely. Your midfielders are weak."

"Hey, now!" I glared at her, then turned it into a fake pout. "I'm doing my best!"

"I'm sure you are, but midfielders are the glue that holds a soccer team together. That's why I demanded the spot. When we play each other, we'll be lining up in the same positions. I'll show you how the game's *really* played."

I grinned impishly. "Oh, touched a competitive nerve there, huh? And what if we win?"

"You won't," Bee said with the supreme confidence of someone telling the absolute truth.

"But what if we do?"

"Oh." Her cheeks reddened a little. Then she returned my grin. "I'd be very surprised and also in awe of my amazing partner and her team of oranges. It'd be superhot."

"Aw, you flatterer." I kicked her under the table.

Our food showed up a little after that, cutting off the public displays of affection. I hadn't realized how hungry I was, and the salmon on rice had the exact right flavor. Bee was completely silent the whole time we ate, except when I tried to steal a bite of her steak. She growled at me ferally enough that I decided the meat wasn't worth it.

The ride home was quiet, too. So was the trip up the stairs, and we both flopped into bed in a mutual, unspoken tiredness. I pulled out my phone and checked my emails while Bianca tried to distract me; I'd gotten a message from another student, and I had to know what it said.

Subject: Film History Meeting 1/21

Film History Members,

A reminder that our first meeting is scheduled for Thursday, January 21. We'll be doing our semiannual watch of Braveheart—and yes, I know there are flaws all over it. That's what makes it such a great opening film to dissect. It also matches our second semester's theme. Please meet at the Alder Building, Room 237. Bring an open mind and a working knowledge of political trends in Europe in the early twenty-first century. If you don't have one, that's okay, too!

Carl Fairplay

Bee stole the phone. When she saw the movie we'd be watching, her brow furled. "What's *Braveheart*?"

19

Braveheart

Alder Building, Room 237 was where the Tokyexico University APPEAL chapter had met the one time Bianca and I had attended a meeting. Last January, it had felt like walking into a den of scytheteeth, even with the script that said "Shut up and stay quiet." This time, showing up for the Film History club, I couldn't help but have that same feeling.

Still, the smell of pizza sauce mixed with bagpipe music in the air outside, and there wasn't an official greeter or anything, so Bianca and I ducked inside.

"Hello," someone said, and a couple of history students glanced our way, but no one ran over to introduce us to the crowd. Which, honestly, was probably for the best. We slipped away to the middle seats, where we wouldn't intrude on any cliques that had formed throughout the year.

I looked around the room while Bee got in line for pizza. No one looked familiar. I half expected to see Avan here, or someone else from my Post–Launch Day North American History class. But no, most of the students here were either older—juniors or seniors—or freshmen. Part of the goal was to meet other people. Still, a lot of the people at the other tables were already engrossed in discussions about India, the Australians' lost war against the emus, or a dozen other topics I wasn't familiar with.

Instead of mingling, I decided to wait for pizza. I didn't have to wait long, either. Bee sat down with four pepperoni slices, then disappeared, only to return with drinks. "You should have come with me. I could have used the hands."

I shrugged. "Hey, someone has to hold the seats. Gotta have a good view for the movie."

"Yeah, yeah, whatever you tell yourself to justify not helping me," Bee said, winking. She sat down and started eating.

We hadn't even gotten through our first slice when a woman a couple of years older than me stood up and cleared her throat at the podium. "Hello. I'm Catherine, the unofficial president of Film History. This semester's theme is resistance against overwhelming foes—we've got a couple of members who are also part of APPEAL, and they put together the only voting bloc when we were deciding on a theme. Before we get started, is there any business for the good of the order? No? Okay, great."

I sighed. Bee shot me a look, and I pulled myself together. It wasn't just that the club seemed fly-by-night compared to APPEAL or even TUSSA. It was that APPEAL had their fingers here, too. What did they think they were resisting? Me?

Catherine clapped her hands. "Now, here's the deal with Braveheart. We pick this movie every year for the first movie of the second semester because it doesn't do a good job of being historically accurate, but it's a game-changing movie in history in a lot of ways. I'll give bonus points to any *new* table that comes up with *both* a historical fail—costuming, order of events, anachronistic language or accents, and so on—*and* a plausible or proven real-world impact the movie had. Right now, Knights of the Square Table's in the lead. Anyone brave enough to take them down?"

I blinked. What the hell was she talking about? Bee raised her hand. "Hey, is this competitive? How do the points work?"

Catherine nodded, staring Bee in the eye. "You're new, huh? Welcome. Yeah, it's semicompetitive, unofficially. Some of the groups treat movie nights like trivia games, and since it gets more people engaged with how we want to approach movies, I'm all for it. So, Knights of the Square Table's got a lead going into the second semester. Let's do this thing. You can register your team after the movie if you want."

"But what do you get for winning?" Bee asked. I could see her mind turning over—how she could pull off a win here. My eyes rolled before I could stop myself, and I buried myself in my pizza so she wouldn't see.

"Bragging rights." Catherine pressed play, and the movie started.

As the narrator described the final battle after Wallace's execution, the eye-rolls in the Alder Building were practically palpable. I looked around; I'd thought it was pretty good. A little—okay, a lot—dated, but I could see why people liked it. What I couldn't see were the historical fails that the Knights of the Square Table were already rattling off one after another—flawed music, poor costuming, and, of course, entire battles out of order.

Catherine let them talk, scribbling on a notepad as they went. Then, she listened to the other groups speak for a while. Finally, she cleared her throat. "Okay, so obviously, the movie's not historically accurate. Why do we show it when we could be showing a dozen other, better films instead? What's so important about it?"

Silence. Dead silence. If it weren't for Bianca eating a fourth slice of pizza, I'd have been able to hear Catherine breathe. The Knights of the Square Table looked around, almost daring someone to answer.

A rival table did. A boy with dark, curly hair stood up. "Okay, so, Pre-Launch Day, the Scottish part of the United Kingdom had a series of referendums on becoming independent. They'd been tied to England for hundreds of years—long enough that people had gotten used to it. They held a vote in 2014 and didn't vote for independence, but it was close."

"And why do we care?" Catherine asked.

"Because the vote took place on the 700th anniversary of the Battle of Bannockburn."

"Partial points there. Open for cleanup."

Now, one of the Knights stood up. "I'll clean up the answer. I've heard there was a divide between people in their twenties and younger when Braveheart came out, who generally voted yes, and older voters who tended to vote no. So, Braveheart's historically significant not because it's a historically accurate movie—go watch *The Return of Martin Guerre* if you want that—but because it influenced history after it."

"Points awarded." Catherine nodded. "So, do we call it a historically useful movie?"

"No," the Knight responded. "It messed with history too much to be anything but a propaganda piece."

"I disagree." The black-haired boy wasn't ready to give up. He breathed in and set himself like he was going to battle. "Just because something's not real doesn't mean it doesn't create beliefs or influence behavior. And that's really what we're talking about. Besides, to say that Braveheart is just a propaganda piece devalues the historical significance of propaganda. Half the films we watched last semester qualify as propaganda, but that doesn't mean they're not important."

"Okay, point conceded," the Knight said, sitting back down.

The discussion raged about whether films had that much influence or not, but eventually, the lights in the Alder Building flickered, signaling the Film History Club members that it was time to leave. Catherine cleared her throat again. "Okay. One month until we dig into a weird one that's never come up before. Next time, we'll be watching a movie called *The Counterfeiters*, about resistance against the Nazis in World War II. I'm excited to explore a lesser-known story, so thanks to Jeremy for bringing it up.

"Remember, our theme this year is resistance against overwhelming foes. Come ready to discuss how small actions can influence massive events. Thanks for attending, and I'll see you in February."

By the time I got back to Walnut Tower, Room 1301, I thought that maybe, just *maybe*, I understood what Su-Bun thought she was fighting for and what the Film History class thought Wallace had been fighting for. And, from a certain point of view, they were similar. If you put the Ilneats in the role of England and APPEAL as the Scots, at least. I wasn't sure where that left me, though.

I needed to make a phone call.

As the phone sat on my coffee table, ringing, and Bianca and I stared at it, I tried to compose myself for the conversation I was about to have. Su-Bin's name appeared on the phone, and her voice came through a moment later.

"Hey, Annie."

"Hi. Bee's here with me. Do you have a couple of minutes?"

"Sure, what's up?" Su-Bin sounded stressed.

I looked Bee's way, and she picked up the thread. "Before we jump into that, obligatory small talk time. How's living at home going?"

Su-Bin went quiet for a minute. "It's fine. Mom and Dad mostly leave me alone, and they have some good ideas for APPEAL. But it's so much harder to focus on my schoolwork, and I've been missing meetings."

"Ouch." I paused, and the pause went from pregnant to awkward quickly. "Are you still seeing Cam?"

"Yeah. I've gotten to 'see him' see him twice, and it's not really enough. But we're making it work. Sort of get what my roommate was about now, though, with always having her boyfriend over."

Bee grinned at me, winked, and said, "Yeah, it's nice to have your partner nearby."

The silence stretched a little awkwardly before Su-Bin picked up the conversation. "So, do you need something, or are you just catching up?"

I nodded. "Actually, yeah, I've got questions. I haven't been 'getting' APPEAL, and I want to know what you think you're fighting for."

"We want to go back to when people weren't reliant on superheroes to protect them from supervillains," Su-Bin rattled off.

"And what about the Ilneats?" I asked.

"Well, they're a core part of the problem, right? They've got this whole TV show thing going on, and they're focused on ratings, but they're not actually worried about the consequences of what they're doing. By using superheroes and supervillains, they can get away with a bunch of stuff Earth wouldn't put up with—and we're grateful because they saved us from ourselves. They keep the spotlight on the fighting and the devastation, and that keeps us busy."

I nodded slowly. "That's a change from last year, huh?"

"It's a change from last semester. I've been doing a lot of reading up on anti-Ilneat schools of thought. I realized that making a conflict with Magical Girl Understudy wasn't solving the real problem. It happened around the time Golden Goose died. Whatever happened with her, I'm not convinced she's solely responsible. A monster and a danger, yeah."

I waited for the "but," but it didn't come. That was okay; Su-Bin obviously hadn't fully formed the thought in her head, and maybe she hadn't even talked with APPEAL about it yet. Besides, I'd gotten what I wanted out of the conversation. "So, what game would you like to play when we get a virtual tabletop going?"

"There's a superhero card game I've been looking at," Su-Bin said.

I stared at the phone, dumbfounded, and then burst into laughter.

"What?"

"You've never been a fan of superheroes," Bee responded, suppressing laughter of her own, "and you run the antisuper club."

"So? I can enjoy the fiction and not like the reality." Su-Bin stopped. "I'll try to find it online and see if we can play it. I think you two would like it a lot; it skips over the bad stuff and focuses only on the enjoyable fantasy of being a Speedster or a Magical Girl."

We talked about the rest of the game for fifteen minutes, then Su-Bin yawned. "I hate to do this to you girls, but I'm about done for the night. If you want, I'd love to talk more about supers and Ilneats tomorrow—or any time, once I've fully wrapped my head around what I'm thinking."

"Sure. Sleep well," I said. Bee said her goodbyes, and we hung up.

Right away, Bee looked at me. "What are you thinking?"

"I'm not." And it was true. For all that Su-Bin had sounded exhausted, I was just as beat—maybe more so, even. The movie had lasted way too late, and all I wanted to do now was sleep.

But after changing into my pajamas and crawling into bed, as I waited for sleep with Bee's arms around me, I couldn't stop hearing bagpipe music.

PART THREE

20

Book Store

Hell Friday was over.

My classes all had presentations or essays due, and Power Builds and Role Optimization had thrown a nasty pop quiz my way. I hadn't expected it out of Dr. Mays. Mindstorm? Sure. But Mays seemed so relaxed most of the time. I thought I'd done well, but I couldn't be sure. We were learning about synergies—which apparently were different from combos and involved powersets that worked smoothly together to do a specific job, like [**Thunderhead**] and [**Ride the Lightning**]. Except instead of two powers, it was the whole build.

Only a few supers did that. It was a fast track to being a one-trick pony, which meant getting countered by a clever rival. But I saw some potential in it. I had so many powers that I could optimize a single build as a silver bullet option and still cover other bases.

Building for Success's substitute was finally rolling; sure enough, he was focused on superhero life's brand management and marketing aspects. There was a lot to learn there. Rocko had always covered that, but knowing what was going on could only help Bee and me out in dealing with the Ilneats. I missed Dr. Jackson, though. The sub was kind of boring.

Bee and I had been trying to learn about Episode manipulation, playing down, and bringing our full power to lower-league Episodes without getting flagged. It felt scummy, but Mindstorm assured us that both heroes and villains did it all the time.

In all, it had truly been a Hell Friday. And there were only like sixteen more this semester.

I couldn't wait for May.

Still, we'd managed to escape campus just after Power Builds and Role Optimization. I found myself hanging out at the mall in a sporting goods store. I'd already bought all the sports bras and soccer shorts I needed, but Bianca was being all serious about getting the *perfect* indoor soccer shoes. I had a bad feeling that she'd be too competitive for the club soccer league.

She came out with a box featuring a red-and-white shoe that screamed speed. "This is the one. What's next?"

"Book store?" I asked. I hadn't been able to get the kid at Broken Binding Books out of my head, and the idea that a superhero had written—or ghostwritten—a memoir or something was really exciting. It was one thing to watch Stella-Lunar on the screen, but to get inside her head and know what she was thinking? Most minor-league heroes didn't have that kind of opportunity—except after she kicked in their teeth.

"Sure, why not?" Bianca headed for the door. "Got something in mind, huh? That's exciting!"

"Yeah. There's a book that should be out, and I want to read it."

"Got it."

After a bit of searching, we found the Civic, and Bee threw it into gear. Broken Binding Books awaited!

Bianca stopped outside the double spot, and I stared at the larger-than-life cardboard figures standing next to the door. A girl stared back. She couldn't be older than thirteen, and her wide, beaming mouth only accentuated her joy-filled eyes. The undercut blonde hairstyle didn't quite match her sundress; she looked like the kind of kid who'd be happier in overalls and covered in dirt—a frog-catching girl.

Behind her loomed Golden Goose—almost realistic if you could believe her muscles and curves. She smiled just like the girl, but the grin didn't reach her eyes. Something felt off in that cardboard figure. Like they'd gotten Golden Goose's blood-lust and violent attitude perfect. I shivered and unbuckled my seatbelt.

If Golden Goose had written a memoir, why hadn't anyone heard anything? This kind of thing would've absolutely blown up; any publisher would've been thrilled to have a scoop like it.

"Well, this is what you wanted, right?" Bianca asked. "I'm not sure how I feel about someone profiting from her death."

"Yeah, I get that. I'm not sure I'm on board with that either." I got out of the car. Bee followed me. "But I do want to read it."

"Okay. Let's do this. I'll go explore the shelves. Text me when you're ready to go home, and I'll meet you at the checkout counter."

I waved goodbye as Bianca dove into the crowd of people at the door, then followed her. Half of the people crowded into the maze of shelves weren't there for the smiling girl and Golden Goose, but the half that were had inserted themselves in a blobby line halfway down the central aisle. I took my place at the back, staring at another cardboard cutout of Golden Goose. The line inched forward slowly, one person at a time, until I could see the book's title under Golden Goose's muscular form: *The Diary of Golden Goose: An Exposé into the Dark Side of Superheroes.*

I shivered, but the high school kid popped up next to me before I could think too much about it. "Hey, you did come back. I figured you might not, but I'm glad you did. The book's selling like crazy. You interested?"

It weirded me out a little that he recognized me, but the boy seemed so earnest that I couldn't help but nod. "I've been interested in superheroes since, like, thirteen-ish. The whole thing's fascinating to me."

"Okay. How about this? I'm awesome, and I work here, so I can grab you a copy without making you wait in line. I've been doing it for a lot of people to try to keep the line moving. There's a meet-and-greet with one of the book's editors, but that's not the same as meeting the author. Unfortunately, that's not an option for you."

"Sure, that'd be great," I said. As I stared at the smiling girl, I couldn't help but wonder who she'd been. She looked carefree, like I'd been when I floated in a tube down the Winter River before the Style System grabbed me. What had her life been like? Who was she before she put on the mask? The book that boy was grabbing offered me a rare chance—one I'd only had twice—to get to know a superhero's secret identity.

And not just any superhero. I'd get to see what Golden Goose herself had thought about her life. The scariest superhero, with a body count higher than most villains before her still-unsolved death—and I'd get to see behind the curtain. The world had gotten more dangerous after her death, but even so, this was the first time I'd thought about her as a person instead of . . . a force of nature.

Reading the diary crept up my priority list until I had to have it. I could hardly wait for the kid to come back. And the line kept creeping forward.

"Okay, got it. I'll get you checked out," the kid said. He'd appeared out of nowhere with the thin book in one hand.

I shook my head. "My girlfriend's in here shopping for herself. I'll collect her and then wait in line like everyone else."

"Suit yourself. Oh, and thanks for swinging by Broken Binding Books." He disappeared into the crowd to help someone else, and I tucked the book under my arm to find Bee. Now that I had it, the next step was getting out of here and back to Walnut Tower, where I could react to whatever was in it like a superhero instead of an Extra.

So, of course, I caught Bianca browsing the books on soccer.

"Hey, you ready?" I asked, even though I *knew* she wasn't. The book was burning a metaphorical hole in my pocket, and I wanted to *leave*.

"No. We just got here. How did you get through the line so quickly?" Bee asked. She didn't look my way. Her head was buried in a book on coaching strategies. I almost felt guilty for not thinking about soccer outside of my team's practices.

"Uh, the kid working here got a copy for me, so I hardly had to wait at all."

"Well, now you have to wait. I'm browsing."

So I sat and I stared at Bee as she painstakingly looked through *Soccer for Dummies*, checked out an autobiography by some soccer player who only went by one name, and slowly filled a basket with sports books. As I watched, I couldn't help but realize that being a superhero had changed her life an awful lot. It wasn't so bad for me; I'd been a kid, and it had been something new and exciting—plus, I got to do it with Peter.

But Bianca had had a whole high school experience without the mask. She'd developed into who she wanted to be—a sports star on her high school team, messy about a lot of stuff but the kind of person who recorded her classes, and so on. She'd had a girlfriend back home and everything. And then the Style System picked her.

And yeah, she had an awesome life with me, of course. But watching her dig into the sports shelves and thinking back to how *hard* she practiced for the yellow team, I realized that *this* was who Bee had been before.

So, after a minute of staring at her to make her feel awkward so she'd move, I decided to let her do her thing. Instead, I flipped *The Diary of Golden Goose* over and skimmed the back.

The explosive diary of the world's most powerful superhero!

Golden Goose was a goddess even among superheroes. Her power level eclipsed every other super, and she ruled North America's shows with an iron fist and no-nonsense attitude.

Now, for the first time, Toll Publishing brings you an edited, uncensored look into the life of Jasmine Saxton. In her own words, she describes the challenges and struggles of working with the Ilneat Studios as a star, her challenges keeping herself separate from the suit, and a detailed look into the last few months of her life.

The synopsis didn't give much information, and I almost opened it up to start reading. But I couldn't—not here. Instead, I stood up and joined Bee at the bookshelf. "Found anything good?"

"Yeah. The Yellowjackets need a coach, and they think I'm the best bet. We're meeting tonight to talk about basic soccer strategy and maybe have a little drinky drink." Bee gathered her half dozen books and turned toward the busy checkout counter. "So you're just getting the one?"

"Yep."

Checkout happened quickly; they had two people running registers and moved the dozens of people ahead of us through as fast as they could. All our books went into a plastic bag with a flying hardcover logo, and Bee led us back to her Civic.

"Okay, any other stops?" she asked.

"I don't think so." I was itching to dig into the book—it seemed like Golden Goose might have dealt with the same problems I was having with Rocko, and even if she didn't, I wanted to see what she was thinking. To get inside her mass-murdering head. Not because I thought I'd like what I found, but because the pressure of being the best had to change her in all sorts of ways.

Bee dropped me off at Walnut Tower with her books, then set off for the Student Union Building. I rode the elevator up, put some coffee on, and set Bee's books on her shelf next to the school books she hadn't cracked open all semester. Then, flopping onto my bed, I pulled out *The Diary of Golden Goose*.

21

The Diary of Golden Goose

The girl on the book cover had undercut blonde hair, a chipped tooth, and green eyes; she couldn't have been over thirteen, in her tank top and baggy shorts, and she looked happy. No, not happy. She looked innocent. It wasn't the same picture as the cardboard figure at the store, but it *was* the same girl. The frog-catching girl.

I cracked the cover, opened to page one, and started reading. But the first part wasn't Golden Goose at all. Instead, I was greeted by a picture of a toddler with a shock of dark hair and a blue toy train in his hand. He smiled at the camera, just like Golden Goose did on the cover. Below the picture, the first sentence of the diary started, but *that* wasn't Golden Goose, either.

You. Supers. Powereds. Whatever you call yourselves.

You all think you're so powerful. So untouchable. That your alien overlords are so advanced that there's no point in resisting. If they're so advanced, then why is my son Petro dead?

He liked trains. He wanted to be an engineer or a conductor, just like his dad here in Tokyexico and his grandfather back in the old country, before the fucking aliens shuffled us all up. He was three years old. He'll always be three years old in my head. He and my beautiful wife, Sarina, had a whole life ahead of them. There's a picture of her, too, in case they publish this with the rest of the journal.

The aliens said it was painless, but I'm not so sure. How can it be painless when it's all I've felt for months? I never found his favorite engine. Their deaths didn't mean anything, either. The next day, everyone went to work, just like they always fucking did. I got two weeks off. That's all their deaths meant to anyone but me. I got a payout. A couple million dollars. And the aliens called it good. But I've paid the price for their deaths every day for the last seven months, and money won't change that.

Now, Golden Goose is dead. That was supposed to be the end of it. My revenge was supposed to be complete. But after I killed Golden Goose, I found this diary.

And now I have something much more violent in mind for you so-called heroes and villains. Because as much as I hate you—and I fucking hate you—I hate the system that killed my family more.

You all know the trap you're in. You all see its flaws, its weaknesses. How it abuses people and spits them out. But you all think it's someone else's problem. I'm talking to you too, "Extras." You don't care if Tapdance wipes out a city. It's not your city, after all. And if Stella-Lunar blows up someone's Thanksgiving dinner and Grandma gets hurt? That's the cost of having supers. That's the cost of Launch Day. That's life.

No more.

It's time you all find out who's behind the mask. How close you all are to a super snapping on any given day.

Jasmine Saxton would have wanted this. Petro and Sarina would have, too. My son and wife were worth more than a couple million dollars. I'll never forgive the aliens for that. And now, thanks to their deaths, the whole mess those bastards have created is about to be exposed.

Enjoy your read. And supers?
Fuck you,
The Extras you've killed

Had the cops known about this? Toll Publishing had to have told them and shared the letter with them, right? It could just be another case of the police not revealing their evidence. And what horrific evidence it was.

I'd *watched* that Episode. I couldn't prove it, but last spring, during my stakeout, I'd watched Golden Goose pick something up on my phone. It had to have been the train. That meant I'd watched someone's family die.

If I'd been smart, I would have stopped reading right there. It would have been easier to wait for Bee because we both knew that whatever was inside the rest of the book wouldn't be an easy read. But I couldn't stop. I turned the page and now *finally* started reading Golden Goose's words. Maybe she'd have an explanation, but right now, I felt the unnamed man's anger pulsing through me.

My name is Jasmine Saxton. I am twenty-nine years old, and I've been Golden Goose since I was thirteen.

And recently, I've been staring at a little blue train engine. It's not much of anything, but I can't stop looking. Snowball doesn't know. If they knew, they'd take it away.

I've got a penthouse suite in Yorkston. The wall's covered in framed newspaper articles about all the great things Golden Goose has done. The people she's saved from villains. The villains she's put away. And until two months ago, that was me.

But I don't want it to be anymore.

So I'm going to write in this journal whenever I can. It'll be my little secret, because if Snowball doesn't want me to have a train from a little boy in Tokyexico, they won't want me to keep this journal, either. And when I've written down everything, I'll take it and get it published. Why? Because there are a thousand little girls across North America who wish they could be me, or Stella-Lunar, or any of the other superheroines, and they need to know what it's like.

It's not all fun and games.

It's not fun and games at all.

I laughed. She was right about that. Did I love what I did? Absolutely. But did it suck watching The Agent slip through your fingers despite your best preparations, leaving you with a destroyed factory and a thousand angry Extras who all wanted to know where they'd live and work now? *Yeah*, it did.

I hadn't killed anyone yet, either, and certainly not a kid. Dealing with that would be brutal. Dealing with as many kills as she had? Impossible.

I was fourteen years old the first time I wore the earpiece.

It was Snowball's idea. They knew all the hero things to say, and I didn't. I'd always wanted to be a star, and I had no idea what to say. Not a good combination. Snowball kept getting more and more angry with me. I remember that really well because they'd say, "Saxton, you have the powerset to be the best, but you're the most tongue-tied hero in North America." And then, one day, they came up with the earpiece as a solution.

And it was perfect.

I didn't have to think about what to say or do anymore. I just had to follow orders. To do what Snowball told me through the earpiece, and to say what they wanted me to say.

It wasn't until I'd killed my first Extra that I realized the earpiece was a trap, and by then, I couldn't stop.

The covers were up around me, even though sweat covered me. I reached for a glass of water, but it was empty. I'd turned to the next page at least a hundred times; how long had I been reading? A while. Yeah, a while. But Bianca wasn't home yet, and she wouldn't be for most of the evening. She'd said not to wait up for her or to worry, and that she might crash at the other girls' place off campus if she had too much to drink.

I was cool with it—more time to read this. Rocko had never been that horrible. Sure, they'd been annoying, but not beyond what any employer would be like with a deadline approaching that'd make or break their business.

Right?

By the time I hit the Major Leagues at fifteen, Jasmine Saxton didn't exist anymore. I was Golden Goose, whether the mask was on or not.

I'd see my parents a couple of times a year, and I'd send them part of my paycheck. It kept them out of debt, but didn't move them into a new house or any of the dreams I'd had for them. "Just a little more," Snowball would say. "Just a little more, and we'll get that mansion for them."

I'd nod, but I knew it wasn't going to happen. And when I went to see them, I went as Golden Goose, not Jasmine.

It wasn't until I picked up that goddamned train engine that Jasmine resurfaced, and she was a scared fifteen-year-old girl in a twenty-nine-year-old superhero's body.

The hours ticked by. One. Two. Three. I wasn't usually a big reader. I'd been bouncing off textbooks my whole school career, and reading for fun just wasn't something I had time for. But even though I wanted to sleep, I couldn't pull myself away from the diary. Before I knew it, I was on the last page, shaking as I sobbed under the blanket, with my cell phone lighting the last paragraph in *The Diary of Golden Goose.*

I can't write down all the things I've had to do. All the people I've hurt. It'd be too much. All I can do is write this and hope it keeps some little girl out of Snowball's hands. Or the others. Because it's too late for Jasmine, but maybe not for Olivia, or Sam, or some other kid who wants to be a superhero and doesn't know what it's really like.

~~*Golden Goose*~~

Jasmine Saxton

I stood on my rooftop balcony, the cold night wind whipping through my hair and blowing tears across my face. The diary sat on my bed, open to the last page. I couldn't move—my muscles shook too much. I could hardly breathe. My throat felt like it was as narrow as a coffee straw. All I could do was stare off into the night. Golden Goose had always been a monster. A legendary hero, yes, but someone I'd have paid every dollar I'd had to never see up close again. And when she'd died, that had thrown the entire Power War into chaos. I'd thought that was bad.

The man who'd killed her was right. This would be worse.

I couldn't stop thinking about Rocko, though. Had they been playing the same game with me? There hadn't been an earpiece, but had there been something else? Was I expendable, just another movie star to chew up and spit out when my show stopped being popular?

I refused to believe it. But I couldn't deny it, either. And those thoughts wouldn't reconcile in my head.

Then something snapped. I couldn't do this anymore. Something had to give. Something had to *break*. And I only had one option.

I raced down to my closet and tore into it, clothes flying every which way. The book had released today. If Rocko *was* fucking with my head, I'd know tomorrow for sure, when they clamped down on Fursona and me. And if they *were* fucking with my head, tonight might be my only night to think about this before The Agent or Theseus or Lord Destructo did something, and I was right back in the Power Wars meat grinder without any time to stop and think clearly—just like last semester, but worse.

So, this snap that was happening? I couldn't put it off. Not for another minute. I had to *destroy* something. Or at least make a plan to. Then maybe I could think straight again.

I pulled off my pajamas and stepped into my mom's supervillain Costume. What I was about to do couldn't be traced back to me, and that meant only one option—if it even worked. I'd never tried making a Costume of my own without Pataki's help. But then again, this was a complete Costume. It'd work. It had to.

The tight outfit's yellow and green colors looked strange on me, and sparks wove across it as I zipped it up and fastened it shut. I peered smugly from behind the domino mask, and this time, with Tails looking at me worriedly, I said, "Transform."

Truthfully, I didn't think it would work. I hoped, but I didn't believe. But the sparks started arcing farther and farther away, a storm built around me, and when it finished, someone who looked kind of like Madame Shockwave stood in front of my mirror, staring back at me. Tails hid under the bed as I whispered, "Time to make some waves."

Tails looked at me, a lightning pattern to her fur, and shook her head sadly. *<Time for a full villainous breakdown?>*

No. It wasn't one of those. I had to do *something* about this, though. I was a superhero, and I couldn't let what had happened to Golden Goose—and Mom, and all of us—slide. But I wasn't breaking down, either. I needed a plan. Even though the snap was happening, I *couldn't* just push.

"Not yet. But soon."

[Costume - Dark Girl Shock and Awe]
[HP 14/14]
[Styles and Skills]
▶ Archetype Skill - Transformation Sequence
▶ Badass
▶ Blitz 3
▶ Cunning
▶ Live-Wire Limit Break 3
▶ Drama
▶ Shock and Awww 3
▶ Flamboyance
▶ Signature Skill - Adaptive Armoire 1
▶ Stored Costumes: (None)
▶ Wallshocker 3
▶ Grit
▶ Grounding 3

22

Not Yet, But Soon

Bianca would be back any minute. I couldn't let her catch me mid-villainous break-down. Who knew how she'd react? So I did the only thing I could do; I took off Mom's suit, hung it back up, and pushed a few outfits I never wore in front of it so she wouldn't be able to see it. Then, I walked slowly toward the green room and slipped inside.

The moment I did, I started a **[Transformation Sequence]**, then slowly trans-formed into Lab Assistant Panic. I'd definitely snapped. Something was *wrong* here. But just because something was wrong with Snowball didn't mean I could just barrel into the Hot Zone as Dark Girl Shock and Awe. I needed a plan, and Lab Assistant Panic was probably my smartest build—if I could resist the breakdown.

And I did need to resist the breakdown.

The whiteboard called, but I couldn't use it; Bee might see. I needed to go some-where else. Somewhere Bee would never find my plans. I looked around, but nowhere in the green room would work. Neither would my apartment unless I got weird about stuff. Since she'd moved in, Bianca spent almost all her time there, and I hadn't estab-lished a "me" space. So where could I go?

My key ring jingled in TA-1LZ's mouth, and I stared at it—and at the one key that we hadn't used since Christmas.

"TA-1LZ, you're a genius." Bianca's secret base—the Outback Stakeout Zone—would be perfect. I packed a bag with the supplies Lab Assistant Panic thought I'd need. The Shock and Awe Costume, a few markers, some red string, and a map of Tokyexico went into it, along with some instant coffee packets that Ramsey Fieri almost vomited from. Then I stowed it by the door and sent a quick text.

<Hey, how long are you out for? - Annie 11:22>

As I waited for a response, I couldn't help but think about the poor kid who'd become Golden Goose. How could Snowball have messed Jasmine up so much? And in the name of a little—okay, a lot—of profit? And what was I going to do about it? I had some ideas but, without a plan, nothing concrete.

APPEAL was in my thoughts, too, and I couldn't clear them. For months now, I'd been starting to wonder about whether they were right. Not about everything. Superheroes and supervillains were a fact of life now, and nothing was changing that. But about whether superhero shows were safe for other people. All the way from our first class period in Superpower Ethics, we'd been exposed to villains—and heroes— putting Extras in harm's way in the name of their shows. That couldn't be right.

Everywhere I looked, I kept finding examples. Stella-Lunar's attack on the Thanksgiving dinner. Tele-Portal's nonchalance about calling people Extras—and how I'd just done it, too. My Episodes on campus that had destroyed buildings in the name of ratings. And especially my therapist, Dr. Ayers, who'd suggested that kills happened and that Extras dying sometimes was just business as usual.

<Another hour or so. I'll walk back w/ friends - Bianca 11:26>
<Okay. Great. I'll be up. Can't sleep after that book - Annie 11:27>
<You read the whole thing? - Bianca 11:27>
<Yeah. You should too - Annie 11:27>
<Okay. Talk to you later tonight. Sleep if you need to - Bianca 11:28>

Perfect. I transformed back to Anika DuPont, grabbed the backpack, and hit the regular old elevator for the first floor. It stopped a few floors down, only for Avan to get on. "Hey," I said politely, making sure my backpack was secure. It wouldn't do to let him see what was in it.

"Hey. Are we ever going to get that coffee?" Avan asked.

"I don't know. Not right now. I'm heading to a friend's place for some studying," I lied smoothly. "I'm drowning in classes right now."

"Yeah, I get that. Me too."

The elevator crept down slower than I'd have liked until, at last, it dinged on the first floor. I headed for the door, but Avan cleared his throat. "Where are you heading? I could walk you over."

"Thanks." I accepted Avan's offer. "I'm heading over to Bee's—Bianca's."

"Great. Lead the way."

As I wove my way across campus, Avan and I caught up. His radio show, "Smooth Talk with DJ Smooth," was midway through its second year running, and he was feeling pretty good about his choice to major in telecommunications. He was still—unfortunately, from his perspective—single, but there were a few people who might be possibilities. I rolled my eyes at that; he'd tried to get a coffee date with me for over a year, so if I was one of the people on his list, he had no chance.

I told him about Su-Bin leaving campus, and he nodded slowly. "Yeah, Cam's a workout buddy. I figure he's pretty down about it, but he doesn't say much. We mostly just lift."

"I bet."

Eventually, we arrived at Bee's building, and I slipped inside. "Thanks for the talk and walk. How about Monday at four for coffee? I'll make sure Bee's cool with it and text you."

He nodded again. "Sure. Let me see your phone." I handed it over, and he punched in his number. With a wave, he disappeared into the cold January night.

I shed my jacket as I hurried toward Bee's room, the backpack hanging from one hand, then the other. The Outback Stakeout Zone was so close. I unlocked Bee's door, then slipped through her maintenance door and into the Stakeout Zone.

Dust coated *everything*. Bee and I hadn't bothered cleaning it for our parents' visit since her mom and dad knew she was a mess, and mine knew enough to respect her secret identity—at least a little, at least while other people were around. But it was obvious that Fursona hadn't operated out of here in . . . a while. Probably since last spring semester, when we'd gone through that rocky patch after the window incident.

But other than the dust, it was exactly what I needed. A quiet space no one would expect Dark Girl Shock and Awe and Lab Assistant Panic to collaborate in. It had wide open walls I could use to make my plans and a space where another white-board *could* go if I wanted to risk Mindstorm's wrath by stealing it. There was only one problem.

At some point, I'd have to tell Bianca. She'd get it, but I couldn't just hide it from her—not even if she decided to fight against me. I had to tell her. But when?

I took a deep breath.

What if I just . . . didn't?

No, that'd be the wrong call. I'd tell her before Shock and Awe did anything. I'd tell her as soon as I had a plan. That'd be best; maybe she'd talk me down from it, or maybe by then, Bee would have read *The Diary of Golden Goose*. Then she'd understand. She'd get it. I could even incorporate her into my plans. That'd make her happy.

<This isn't a good idea,> Tails said from the backpack the moment I opened it up. A notepad came out, and she pushed it toward me with her button nose. *<You're going to hurt someone or get hurt yourself.>*

"I know." I started scribbling in the book, putting together a plan. The next two days would be busy, but if I made the right contacts, they'd work out exactly how I needed them to, freeing Shock and Awe to make a play.

After almost twenty minutes, I had the rough outlines of a plan. There was just one step to take.

I got my phone out and sent a quick text.

<Theseus, I need a favor - Understudy 12:10>

There was no way he'd text me back tonight, so I didn't even bother waiting—
My phone buzzed.

<You want to fight? When? - Theseus 12:11>

Haha! The plan was coming together!

The Outback Stakeout Zone's painted landscape walls were covered in red string, notes, and a few sketches I'd made. The notepad sat on a table in the room's center. And, most damningly, my vil Costumes' names were all over everything. If Bee were to check here any time in the next day, I'd be *so* busted, but I doubted that'd happen. She never came here anymore. It really was the perfect evil lair for my villainous Costumes—especially since I was planning villainy!

I changed into Magical Girl Understudy and took the elevator down into the tunnel network under Tokyexico University. If I hurried, I could make it home before Bee and set the next stage of my trap. If not, I'd have to come up with an explanation for where I'd been.

As it turned out, I needn't have worried.

I was half-asleep when Bee came home, changed into a nightie, and looked at the book on her pillow. She picked it up and skimmed the back. "Interesting."

The smile on my face had to look predatory, but I was facing the wall, not her, and I waited while she read the first page, then set it on her nightstand. I had her! She was as good as on board for my plan.

The bed creaked a little as she climbed under the covers and wrapped her freezing hands around me. I shivered and rolled over to look at her. "Hi."

She pulled me in for a sleepy cuddle. Her body felt cold, and I couldn't help but wonder how long she'd been out and about. I also couldn't help but smell the booze on her breath, but I sleepily kissed her anyway.

"Hey, babe," she whispered in my ear.

"Theseus texted while you were out," I mumbled back. It wasn't quite a lie.

She stiffened a little. "Really?"

"Yeah. He wants to fight tomorrow. I guess Alkirk's on the move again, and he needs a couple heroes to put on a good show. He figured we were the most qualified."

"Great. Super Girl and Kaiju? Actually, no. I'm too tired and too drinky-drunk for this. We'll deal with it tomorrow." Bee's arms tightened around me, and I let her start drifting off.

The next hour was a whirlwind of thoughts as I struggled to get the rest of the way to sleep. Phase One was up and running. And, honestly, it was the perfect Phase One, because if I decided to abandon Lab Assistant Panic's plan and stop trying to set up Shock and Awe, it'd still line up perfectly with my other goal: beating The Agent. We needed to fight some other rogues and let 3V1L relax for a bit. That way, he'd become complacent, and we could catch him off guard.

I didn't want to abandon the plan, though. I *wanted* to let my villains run loose for a little bit, and to put pressure on the Networks to deal with . . . everything. Rocko and the others . . . especially Snowball, but all of them . . . they all had to know that what they were doing was hurting people. The man in the diary's foreword was right. Something had to change. The other heroes just needed a wake-up call. Maybe the diary could be it. Or maybe my plan would be.

What did I really want? What were my goals after my little snap earlier? I'd let Lab Assistant Panic take the reins, but without any oversight from the rest of me, she could cause a lot of unfocused chaos.

And how did APPEAL fit into this? How could I use them, and what did I owe Su-Bin? After all, *The Diary of Golden Goose* showed just how right she'd been about so much. I definitely needed to make things up to her, but I couldn't. She didn't know I was Understudy. She *couldn't ever* know I was Understudy.

This whole mess was way too complicated, but eventually, Bee's arms loosened as she drifted off, and I let myself sleep a moment later.

23

Later

SATURDAY, JANUARY 30

[Casting Call]
[Episode: Short: The Hand of Fate - PG-13]
[Role: Heroine! Do you accept the role? (Yes/No)]
[Role Focus: Cunning + Flamboyance]
[The Hand of Fate: Act One in Progress]

By the time Fursona—in her Kaiju suit, thank god—and I left Walnut Tower and headed for Mid-Town, the nerves were really getting to me, and I had regrets. Not about the plan. The plan was fine. Or, more accurately, I couldn't *do* any better with the resources I had, and I couldn't trust any other heroes or villains except Fursona. I wasn't sure about getting Fursona to use her Kaiju mode so she'd be tired tonight. A whole Episode just to get her to lay down and read.

But my frustration . . . that was the wrong word, but I couldn't think of a better one . . . toward Snowball, Cartman, and all the other Ilneats had only grown, and I was *committed*. The more I thought about it, the more I saw flashes of Snowball in Rocko, and I hadn't even dug back further than a year in my head. I had to do something, and this was what I could do.

So we rocketed through the air on my sailboard, heading for the Alkirk building. Not that I expected to find Theseus there; I'd told him to find a suitable arena and start making chaos, and that we'd be there pretty quickly.

The first explosion at the old football stadium clued us in on how literally he'd taken that, and we dove for the stands. Snow covered the yard markers and clung to the uprights on the goalposts, and coming out of the locker room with a funny-looking machine tucked in his six arms was Theseus. The machine had parts that could—loosely—be described as limbs, so that had to be why he was here. At least, it was his excuse.

"He's been upgrading," Fursona said.

I nodded. "Sure has."

All six of the supervillain's arms connected improbably at his shoulders, giving him a thrashing mess of different weapons; I saw a chainsaw, two harpoon-launcher-looking things, a machine gun of some type, a crab claw—not a metal one, but a giant crab's claw—and the expected rocket launcher. I sighed in relief, turning it into a gasp for Fursona's benefit. "He's loaded for bear."

"But not for Kaiju," she replied.

"No, not for that." I landed, hopping off the board as it disappeared.

Kaiju-sona stomped toward the villain. "Theseus, we've already beaten you once! Surrender!"

"Oh, I'm wringing my hands in worry! Listen, Fursona, you two may have been powering up, but so have I. I've got the best tech Alkirk can afford to kick your butts with." Theseus fired a harpoon at Fursona, who ducked it.

The fight was on!

I leaped to the side to get a **[Starlance]** off around Fursona's wide plushie suit. It zipped toward Theseus, slamming into him and firing a ray off toward the sky. I blinked, but it made sense; there wasn't a secondary target to hit yet.

[Dramatic Damage! +1 Drama Point]

Theseus turned toward me. "Trying to give yourself a leg up? It won't help!" I dodged as the machine gun started opening fire on me. Its shells bounced off the crossbar and buried themselves in the snow, but a few crashed into me, throwing me into a drift. My head rang, but before I could get up, Theseus was rushing toward me.

[HP 10/14]

I backpedaled as the chainsaw arm whooshed through the air toward me. Its elbow joint sparked—a weak point? As the blade roared, I ducked, and it made contact with the solid steel goalpost. It dug in, more sparks flying, and I used **[Spotlight Strike]** to slam the joint. A loud creaking filled the air as the arm disconnected, the blade kicking up snow and thrashing around.

[Stylish Strike! +1 Flamboyance Point]

But the many-armed villain only laughed and fired another harpoon at me. It crashed into the snow, and I laughed. "That's your best sho—ooof!"

[HP 9/14]

Theseus retracted the harpoon, pulling his many-armed frame toward me. As he collided, the impact drove me into the ground—and pushed some air from my lungs.

I tried to suck in a breath, but the crab claw clamped shut around my neck, cutting off the air. I kicked and flailed dramatically but couldn't even reach the villain. Was there a weak point on this arm? No? It was too soon for this!

"Guess we're not neck and neck anymore," Theseus quipped.

[HP 8/14]

Something slammed into him and roared. A wave of fire ripped over him, and he let go. I hit the snow, gasping for breath, as Fursona said, "No, I'm head and shoulders over you!"

I sucked in air, massaging my neck; even through superhero damage, it still hurt. But the plan was coming together. Theseus fired a long volley from the machine gun arm and retracted both of his harpoons, forcing Fursona to disengage before she could do more than damage the crab arm's connection point. And in the distance, I could hear the first drone humming its way in.

My wand stuck out. I took aim. "[Starlance]!" I shouted, and the ray ripped into the cold January air. It made contact with the Alkirk drone but only clipped it. A secondary ray shot from the impact hit Theseus in the back of the head, and he winced.

[Dramatic Damage! +2 Drama Points]

As the drone started a controlled fall toward the snowy midfield, I fired another [Starlance] toward it. But this time, I missed. I tried for another shot, but a harpoon sliced the air over my head, and a moment later, the machine gun arm rattled back to life. "No laser, Theseus?" I asked as I dodged.

"Not yet," he replied.

"Well, that's going to be a problem for you! [Limelight Barrage]!" A half dozen [Starlances] took off toward the villain, who tried to dodge—and failed. The first impact clipped one of the harpoon launchers, and the rest crashed into his center of mass, right where I'd aimed.

[Dramatic Damage! +5 Drama Points]

He snarled, rushing toward the downed drone and detaching his broken crab claw. The new arm socketed in a moment later—an electrically charged Tesla coil. It whined loudly, sending a lightning bolt across the battlefield toward me. I used [Quick-Time Change] and [Freeze-Frame] to dodge this time, finishing my Itsy Bitsy Spider dance and rushing to a new position.

[Flashy Fitting-Room! +1 Flamboyance Point]
[Steel Yourself! +1 Grit Point]

As time picked up, the electrical arm went into the most obvious "charging" state I'd ever seen. Panels opened on its sides, revealing glowing-hot heat sinks. Theseus waved them through the frigid air, leaving steam in the arm's wake. "Guess you're catching me red-handed!"

"Goddammit, Theseus, stop with the puns!" Fursona slammed into him, tail thrashing and massive plushie jaws biting. They wrestled for a bit, but the electrical arm's heat sinks retracted, and another electrical blast ripped into her, knocking her away as sparks coursed dramatically across her suit.

"Hey, leave Fursona alone!" I shouted, using **[Power-Weaving]** and **[Wind Front]** to shove the villain away from my partner. Then I followed it up by putting a **[Thunderhead]** up, knocking him even farther away. As the clouds overhead went from white-gray to an angry near-black, I smiled. "You're in trouble now!"

[Badass Move! +1 Badass Point]
[Pause for Effect! +1 Drama Point]
[Floating Points: 1 Badass]

Theseus responded with a laugh and a burst of machine gun fire that caught me unprepared. Pain flared across my stomach and chest, and I hit the ground. But it wasn't a **[Combo-Breaker]**, so I popped back up and kept fighting.

[HP 4/14]

His lightning arm was almost recharged. Now was the moment. I used **[Ride the Lightning]**, letting the electricity pour through me. It rushed toward him in a familiar tendril, ripping into the heat sinks on his arm. They popped and crackled, then exploded in a rippling boom that tore his entire arm off his shoulder.

[Ride the Lightning! +1 Flamboyance Point]
[Floating Points: 3 Badass, 1 Drama]

As he reeled from the blow, I followed it up with a **[Thunderhead]**-empowered **[Wind Front]** and threw the villain across the field and into the visitor's entrance tunnel. The blast kicked up a massive amount of snow, too, and I lost sight of him for a moment, but I could hear another drone overhead.

[Badass Move! +1 Badass Point]
[Thunderstruck! +1 Drama Point]
[Power-Weaving! +6 Badass, +3 Drama, +1 Flamboyance Point]

With the combo landed and the drone getting closer, I quickly used **[Quick-Time Change]** and flipped back to Magical Girl Understudy. Technically, Lab Assistant Panic would be the best suit against Theseus's current weapons, but I couldn't risk it. The plan had to go off perfectly, and an early villainous breakdown could mess everything up.

[Flashy Fitting-Room! +1 Flamboyance Point]
[Rejuvenation Activated! HP 9/14]

But I hadn't even fully finished the choral music and lights when Theseus erupted from the locker room.

According to plan.

I used [Solar Wing] to take to the air and fired a [Starlance] toward the villain as Fursona roared and sent another gout of flame his way. He couldn't dodge both, and he didn't try. Instead, he tanked the damage with one of the harpoon launchers and the smoking stub of his Tesla coil, then aimed the machine gun up toward me.

[Dramatic Damage! +1 Drama Point]

My damage wasn't enough to stop Theseus—not even close—and he fired a harpoon that punched through Kaiju-sona's tail and pinned her to the ground. As she struggled to free herself, the villain turned toward me again. "Time to fall back to Earth, Magical Girl Understudy!"

The machine gun rippled out a barrage of gunfire, and I ducked and dodged through the air on my [Solar Wing]. But every burst forced me lower to the ground, and one sliced across my back and clipped one of the wings.

[HP 5/14]

I was at critical HP. Another burst could easily take me out. But at the same time, I had to do something. Fursona wasn't free yet; the harpoon's reversed teeth gripped the frozen ground too tightly. So I stopped midair and started another [Quick-Time Change]—this time to Super Girl Spotlight Star.

The music swelled as the hood covered my head, and I took my [Freeze-Frame] seconds to get off to the side, away from Theseus's machine gun. If we wanted to win this, we needed to do something about *that*.

[Advanced Accessories: Magical Girl Understudy, Magical Girl Rainy Day, Copy Cat]
[Skill Siphon Activated: Style Points Disabled]
[Meter's Running: 7/8]

I set up a shot with [Limelight Barrage]. Four massive [Maximum Starlances] slammed into Theseus, sending arms tumbling to the ground, but missing both the harpoon pinning Fursona and the rocket launcher. More drones buzzed toward the battlefield, but I couldn't be bothered with them right now.

[Dramatic Damage!]
[Meter's Running: 5/8]

My entire attention was on Theseus.

The harpoon snapped; Fursona had given up on pulling it out and just broke it instead. She roared toward the villain, but another arm dropped next to him before she could get there. The wreckage of his electricity cannon fell off, and a moment later, a glowing shield covered the new arm in a blue semisphere. She slammed into it, bounced off, and ate a laser ray to the face for her trouble.

That did it.

As she popped up, plush smoking, her roaring doubled in volume. She'd drank the juice box. And that meant . . .

It was time.

As she doubled in size, then doubled again, I used another **[Quick-Time Change]** to switch back to Understudy. At the same time, a dozen rockets zoomed toward me, and I **[Freeze-Framed]** to the edge of the blast zone. The explosion rippled across me, even though I wasn't *in* it, and the shock knocked me off my **[Solar Wing]**.

[HP 2/14]

Would that be enough? I'd see in . . . one second.
WHAM!

[HP 0/14]

I hit the snow and tried to push myself up, but as Theseus rushed toward the ever-growing Kaiju-sona, he lashed out with a wrecked arm, hitting me with the ruined chainsaw's bulky gas motor. As darkness rushed around me, I had one last thought: this was all going according to plan.

24

According to Plan

[Episode Finished!]
[Episode: Short: The Hand of Fate - PG-13]
[Penalties: N/A]
[Episode Finished! +3 of each Style Point]
[Call It a Draw! +2 of each Style Point]
[Role Focus: Cunning + Flamboyance - Goal Met: +10 to Focused Styles]
[Alias - Understudy] [Archetype - Magical Girl] [Community Rank - 155/523]
[HP 0/14]
[Styles and Skills]
▶ Archetype Skill - Transformation Sequence
▶ Combo Skills - Power-Weaving
▶ Badass (31)
▶ Cunning (29)
▶ Drama (28)
▶ Limelight Barrage 2
▶ Starlance 3
▶ Flamboyance (55) (Skill Roll Available)
▶ Signature Skill - Adaptive Armoire 3
▶ Stored Costumes: (Rainy Day, Copy Cat, Lab Assistant Panic)
▶ Solar Wing 2
▶ Quick-Time Change 3
▶ Improvised Ovation 2
▶ Grit (35)
▶ Freeze-Frame 2
[50 Flamboyance Credits Used. Rolling Skill!]
[Rank-Up! Wallshocker 4: Damage to buildings extends farther from the epi-center]

Kaiju-sona had lugged me all the way from Mile Tall Arena to Walnut Tower via the secret tunnel below campus, but it had taxed the hell out of her, so now we had a choice to make. She was exhausted, I probably had a minor concussion, and that wasn't ideal for either of us.

Worse, through my headache, I had to listen to her excited yet exhausted babble about how she'd beaten Theseus and stopped him from getting the . . . whatever he was after. I nodded along, a bit unfocused, and concentrated on pulling myself together as she rambled on and on. But eventually, we got to my bedroom, and I tucked her in. It wouldn't be a good idea for me to sleep, but *she* needed the rest.

Plus, *The Diary of Golden Goose* was strategically placed nearby.

"I want my phone," Bee whined. "And citrus. So much citrus. Please."

I nodded. "I'll go find it. Where did you leave it?"

"My pocket in the Kaiju suit. Thanks."

"No problem. While I'm looking, here. It'll keep you occupied." I handed her the diary and disappeared from the bedroom before she could protest or give me any more whined orders. Not that I *minded* doing things for her. I'd gladly find all the orange juice and buy her a new phone if I had to. But Phase Two of the plan was in progress, and now, I needed to stall. And also, my head felt fuzzy.

So, the first thing I did was head to the green room. Sure enough, Bee's phone was right where she'd said it was. I pocketed it before stomping around for a while, burning time and—hopefully—giving her a chance to read a little of Jasmine Saxton's book before I got back. By then, also hopefully, she'd be hooked, and I could pretty much let her go.

So I stalled for a few crucial minutes during the orange juice pour, then went to the bathroom before delivering the drink and phone.

By the time I got back, Bee's nose was buried in the book. I set the drink and phone down on her table, letting her ignore them as she flipped a page, and climbed across her to my side of the bed. My head rested on her stomach, and I closed my eyes, but she brought one hand down and started playing with my hair.

Perfect, I thought, as she twirled it around one finger mindlessly, eyes glued to the page. I didn't want to sleep anyway.

I woke up to Bee shaking.

Not shaking me. Just shaking.

That got my eyes open, and I sat upright. She looked pale, but at first, I couldn't figure out if she was shaking from crying or from the lack of sugar in her system. Eventually, I looked at the still-full orange juice and the dent on our comforter where my head had been. "You didn't drink anything," I accused.

"Guilty," she whispered back. "Sorry."

I stood up and handed her the orange juice. It wasn't cold anymore, but she sucked it down through the straw, looking grateful. Her eyes were red, though. She *had* been crying.

Which meant the plan was working. "How's the book? Did you really read the whole thing?" I asked.

"It's so *sad*. And I keep thinking back to your mom and Vigilant Vow while I'm reading it. I'm almost done, so give me a few minutes."

"Got it." I curled up next to her and let myself zone out. Not sleep. The moment was too important for sleeping, but letting my mind drift to all the other things happening felt right.

I couldn't focus on anything, though, and after a few minutes, I gave up and let Bee return to playing with my hair.

Eventually, the book snapped shut.

I waited while Bianca composed herself. When she stood up and wandered down the hall with her empty cup, I kept waiting. And I was still waiting when she came back. "We need to do something about this," she said.

"Us?"

"Yeah. Us. There has to be something we can do. This feels way more important than The Agent. So what do we do?" Bianca still looked distraught as she sat on the foot of the bed.

I cleared my throat. "I have an idea. But you've got to trust me. A lot. Like, a *lot*, a lot."

"Okay. I trust you."

"Great. Follow me." I headed for the door. "Oh, and, uh . . . don't get mad."

"You broke into my apartment?" Bee asked, eyes narrowing just the slightest bit.

I shrugged. "No. I used the key you gave me to get into your apartment and then the *other* key to get into the Outback Stakeout Zone. I was busy last night, but I didn't break in."

Bee rolled her eyes. She still looked a little annoyed, but she *had* given me the keys and told me her place was mine. The painted walls were covered with my red strings and notes, and she strolled up to them. "You did all this last night?"

"You were gone for a long time," I said.

She was quiet for a while, reading all my notes and seeing how they connected. I watched her brow furrow as she read the section on doing the first-ever Episode in the Hot Zone. I thought it was pretty clever to start something next to the Ilneat enclave, but I'd modified the plan a little since my initial ideas. Now, it relied on getting a hero who'd be willing to not pull punches—or one who knew what was going on.

Finding someone willing to crush an upstart, independent villain like Dark Girl Shock and Awe would be easy. It'd be a lot harder to find one who'd do the kind of collateral damage I needed during the fight, and I couldn't toy with most of the heroes who'd respond to my threat.

So, Fursona would be ideal as the good guy to my bad.

But she shook her head. "Annie, this isn't going to work."

My face fell as I stared at my hour and a half of work. She wasn't in. I'd have to rely on some other hero to help, and worse; if she could see weak spots in my strategy, so could Stella-Lunar, The Triad, or any other heroes who responded. "What's wrong with it?"

"A couple of things. First, I assume your goal is to make the Ilneats pay a little for what's in that book?"

"And Mom, and Vigilant Vow, and . . . yeah."

"Okay. Do you actually know where their studio buildings are? I'd be willing to bet that most of the Hot Zone's full of utility for the Ilneats who work there, and as great as it'd be to knock out a Costuming building, I don't think Pataki's the real problem, are they?"

I shook my head. The Ilneat Costume designer hadn't ever been anything but business-focused, but they hadn't pushed like Rocko had. If I had to guess, they were probably an employee, not part of the Network's decision-making. So no, Pataki wasn't my target, and neither were the Ilneats like them.

"So, you want your chaotic spillover to hit the Ilneats' studios, not the support buildings. That means you don't want to start near Mid-Town. There's no way they'd put their studios that close to the Tokyexico Council of Heroes building. It's a lamp to heroes' and villains' moths, and they'd want some space between a place where open fighting happens a lot and their studio buildings. So, you need to start from somewhere with no value." Bianca quickly glanced around the room. "No whiteboard, huh?"

"No. So, I need to start the Episode from . . ." I looked at the map of Tokyexico I'd tacked to the wall over a painting of some koalas. "Thornton? It's close."

"Yeah. I'd go with Thornton. It's low-population, too, so you can get some big destruction without putting anyone in danger. We'll check and find a completely abandoned block or two. If we start on the outskirts, we can quickly spill over into the Hot Zone. There's just one problem."

"The In-You-Endos?"

"Okay, there's just two problems." Bianca sighed. "The In-You-Endos might be easier to deal with than you'd expect. I'll work on that. But the bigger issue is that you're going to get big shot heroes on you the second you cross into the Hot Zone. They'll call in any available major-leaguers to mop you up, then stick you in Almhurst. Do you have a plan for *that*?"

I had to admit that I didn't.

"Okay. There's a way to handle it. It should peel the In-You-Endos off, too. Let me make a phone call or two real quick." Bianca stepped out into her dorm room, and I waited anxiously. Now that I had new eyes on my plan, it was obvious how many issues there were. The minutes ticked by, and I had to resist the urge to check on Bee—or to find a red marker to cross out parts of the plan and add others.

By the time Bee finished her phone call and returned, I'd given up resisting, and I was already making changes. She cleared her throat. "Hey, Annie. Check this out. And give me the marker."

I handed it over, and she grinned. "I've put together a strike force to deal with Madame Shock's—"

"Dark Girl Shock and Awe," I interrupted.

"Sure. With Dark Girl Shock and Awe's bold attack. You'll love your enemies for this Episode. I think it'll be a fun time."

"Who?"

"Me, plus a couple of surprises. If I tell you, it'll look too artificial. So, that takes care of who you're fighting. I have an idea for dealing with the major-leaguers, possibly including the In-You-Endos. But it's risky. I've never contacted them before, and they're not exactly a controllable variable, if you know what I mean."

"No. I barely passed math." I laughed. "But seriously, who are you thinking?"

"Fanfic. We used them once to set up the major-leaguers on campus so we could do your series finale." Bianca started fiddling on her phone. I got behind her so I could watch, and she went through the complicated login process for the Super Watch site, involving visiting an online storefront, clicking on an out-of-stock model, and navigating a complicated portal. But then she was in.

"So you're going to try to find Fanfic on Super Watch?" I asked, rolling my eyes.

"No. I'm going to make a bait post, and they're going to fall right into my trap. It'll be easy. I hope." Bee got to work while I watched over her shoulder. When she'd finished, she handed me the phone.

Possible Sighting: Is Fanfic active in Parker?

Hello, superhero watchers. I heard a rumor that Fanfic was planning on making a move in the Parker district. Something about a horror Episode? Does anyone know much about that? I've always wanted to get involved in one of their Episodes as an Extra, and this would fulfill that dream, but I've never heard of them advertising their location. Still, it'd be so exciting! I'm thinking about heading there, just in case.

Thoughts?

"That'll never work," I said.

"It doesn't have to. Not perfectly, at least. If I can get four or five people to roll with it, the major-leaguers will have to at least pay attention to it. That'd be enough to keep them off our backs—and Fanfic's weird. They *sometimes* strike right where the major-leaguers are, and in a Power War, there's a chance that the vils won't help the heroes deal with them."

"So you set a false flag, hope the heroes go for it, and then hope that Fanfic decides to challenge themselves?" I nodded appreciatively. "It could work. When do we launch this Episode?"

"Tomorrow morning." Bee paused. "Actually, maybe tonight, right after soccer."

"Oh shit. Who are you playing?" I asked.

"You." Bianca smiled evilly.

25

Evilly

The good thing about indoor intramural soccer was that there weren't many fans.

The bad thing was that with only a few of us on the court, I was solely responsible for stopping Bianca.

And the worst thing was that her eyes had gone all hypercompetitive. She didn't even act like she recognized me. I didn't think I'd *ever* seen her like this—maybe under her Fursona Costume, but not outside of it. Board game nights were nothing compared to this. If I couldn't stop her, she looked like she'd put the entire team on her back. Maybe Sierra could handle her—she'd chosen to play defense—but I wasn't sure about that, either.

But, as Coach Sierra had said, I didn't have to stop her from scoring. I just had to stop her from touching the ball.

From the opening whistle and kickoff, I could tell that'd be a tall order.

The black-and-white ball flew through the air, over my head, and our other defender got it. He dashed forward, aiming straight for Bee, then kicked the ball my way as she jogged toward him. But it had been a trap; as I got control of the ball, she turned and surged toward me with what felt like superspeed. I turned and tried to bounce it off the sidewall toward my team's forwards. But Bee's foot wormed between my legs and flicked my pass off course before I could.

Bee gave me a smug grin as she ran by, and I pouted back. "Hey, now. Pick on someone with your own experience!"

"I will!" She ran by as I hurried to keep up, pressuring Sierra on defense. I lowered my head and sprinted toward her, only to shoot off course as Sierra's hand went up. She was pointing at the other team's forward, who was uncovered. I tried to get there.

But the ball flew by first, and a moment later, he kicked it into our goal.

1-0.

I reset, switching sides with Adam as Bianca moved toward his side of the field. Sierra yelled something about sticking to Bee like glue, and I nodded. My chest was already pumping as I sucked in air, and we'd only been playing for like five minutes.

Most of the rest of the game flowed through either Bianca or Sierra, and I couldn't figure out which one was more important. Bianca had basically locked down the game at half-court, and every time the ball got past her, she went into overdrive. I couldn't believe how fast she was; I'd be shocked if she wasn't using superpowers. Fursona was a hybrid Speedster/Bruiser, so it was within her powerset.

But Sierra matched her. Every attack broke on her or went around her, and I started thinking about the game a little differently. She was back there, along with our other defender. Even Bee would struggle to score on her as long as she held firm. Therefore, what we needed was a chance to score ourselves.

I cheated a little into the yellow team's territory, pushing my own forward . . . forward. All I needed was two passes. One from Sierra up to me and one from me to our forward. If I could get them—

The ball zoomed toward me.

I bounced it off my chest and started running. Bee had to be close, and I had to beat her to it. I could practically feel her on my back as I kicked the ball, dribbling it forward. Once. Twice. Three times. Then I reeled back and launched it toward the forward.

A moment later, he'd scored.

1–1.

I turned toward my girlfriend, grinning. But when I saw her sweat-covered face, something had changed. Her eyes weren't hypercompetitive anymore. They were pissed. If they could speak, they'd scream "How could you embarrass me like that?" at me.

Then she stilled her expression. "Good job, Annie. That'll be the last time, though."

"Not if I have anything to say about it," I replied. I wanted to win as badly as she did, and I'd found a strategy that just might work.

The final score was a blowout.

12–4.

We'd lost.

So, obviously, that hurt. I hadn't *really* expected anything else—losing to my girlfriend and partner was always going to suck, and the reality was that I'd gotten beaten so badly at midfield that it was entirely my fault. But at the same time, everyone knew I'd been outmatched. Sierra had even said as much as I moped after the game. A couple of orange slices weren't going to make it better.

But they did help.

It sucked losing to Bianca. She was a good sport about it, and she was more than willing to talk about how she'd beaten me and how I could counter it. But the real reason it sucked was that it was the first time I'd lost to her when something was at stake.

Still, after a while, I shrugged it off. The soccer match was important to her, but to me, it was just a thing Annie did. And even losing, it'd been nice to be Annie and lose as her. Besides, I'd have to get used to losing to Bianca—and quickly, because this wasn't my only scheduled loss today.

I suited up, pulling on Mom's slightly too tight Madame Shockwave Costume. Bee was already ready to go; she'd jammed Kaiju-sona into her backpack. I had a tougher task. As I pulled my warm clothes over Mom's spandex Costume, I stretched out. Things didn't move quite right, and I couldn't wait to get out of my warm stuff and transform.

But I also couldn't travel around as either Magical Girl Understudy or Madame Shockwave. The former might implicate me in the crimes Dark Girl Shock and Awe was about to commit, and the latter didn't have a good movement power for getting me across town.

So, as Bee took off in her Civic, I called a Ride-Plus.

The car showed up a minute later, and I wormed my way into the back. The driver—a big dark-haired guy—smiled at me and tapped on a convenient sign listing my options for the ride. I picked #1: The Quiet Ride. He nodded. "Where are you going?"

"Thornton. Near the south side," I replied, pulling out my phone.

"Got it. Half an hour."

"Thanks."

The silence pressed in like a comfortable blanket; he was obviously used to it, and I had stuff to do. I pulled out my phone and navigated to the Super Watch site again. The post had a dozen comments on it. Most were speculation about Fanfic's where-abouts. Two people thought the poster was crazy for wanting to be anywhere near a villain who acted like that. And one . . . one *might* have been from the villain themself.

It was cryptic. Nothing definitive. But if I read it right, it sounded like they might've been taking the bait. They definitely knew it was bait, but they might've been taking it anyway.

It'd be great for us if they did. Fursona and her team wouldn't get called up to deal with a Fanfic incursion, but every major-leaguer would be. That'd leave the field of battle completely clear for us.

I'd said that I shrugged off the orange team's loss to yellow. That was a lie. I couldn't help but dwell on it as my Ride-Plus drove through Mid-Town and into the wreckage of Thornton. We were at the bottom of the bragging rights standings now. I'd have to play way harder against green next week.

But even so, Bianca was a great girlfriend and an awesome partner, and I was lucky to have her. She'd set this up so that, even though I'd probably lose to her team, we'd get to complete our secret objective. We'd be able to take the fight into Ilneat territory and give them a taste of what they did to us. What we'd been doing to Extras. Something like that; I couldn't quite figure out why I was mad. I just was. The damn *Diary of Golden Goose* had been the final straw. I hoped it was for other supers, too.

I thought about checking, but the Ride-Plus's brakes squealed, and a moment later, the driver stopped. "Here you are. When you're ready to leave, you have my number in your texts."

"Thanks. And thanks for the ride menu."

"No problem. I saw it in a meme, and it seemed like a good idea. Good luck . . . here." He gestured at the surrounding slums.

"Thanks again." I exited the car and walked away, and his burgundy four-door took off, heading back into Mid-Town—and carefully bypassing the Hot Zone that sprawled out in front of me.

"Okay." I pulled Tails out of my jacket, where she'd been tucked in safely, and headed for the nearest abandoned building. "Okay. It's time to make Dark Girl Shock and Awe's debut."

<Are you sure this is a good idea right meow?> Tails asked.

I rolled my eyes. "This is the only idea I have, so it's the best one." Then I slipped through a broken window and into the cover of the abandoned apartment building. A few doors were open; I checked each of them, closing them to ensure a little bit of privacy. Then, satisfied, I sent a quick text.

<Hi Fursona. Go time. See you soon - Shocks 4:14>
<Got it. We're on our way. 10 minutes - Fursona 4:15>

Ten minutes. That'd be enough time. I started up a [**Transformation Sequence**]. The air filled with static, and sparks hopped off my spandex-clad body as I spun midair. My hair stood upright; when I looked at Tails, her plush had poofed out like someone had rubbed her with a balloon. She hissed angrily but didn't try to stop me.

A moment later, a thought crashed into my brain. *She couldn't stop me!* Nothing *could stop me! I was an unknown villain with the perfect plan for my debut! All I had to do was stick to my script!*

The static in the air turned into a pulsing Tesla coil of energy around me, then stopped. Tails's lightning pattern became more and more defined. And when I hit the ground, I wore a pair of black-, green-, and yellow-colored tights, a similarly shaded skirt and top that left my navel slightly exposed, and retro-style shoulder pads.

"Let's make it sparky," I said, trying out a catchphrase.

<Nyo. Absolutely not.>

I glowered at the electro-cat. "Okay. Nine minutes. Let's go." I fired up the [**Casting Call**].

A menu popped up, and for the first time, I got to see what a villain saw when they initiated an Episode. The **[Casting Call]** looked almost like the others, but every variable had a dial except for the rating. Heroes didn't get anything like this—not even for Investigative Episodes. I changed stuff and fiddled around, typing in the air until it looked right. I checked all the optional options, including one called 'System Updates' that looked like it had some sort of penalty associated with it.

Then I accepted it.

[Casting Call]
[Episode: Power War: Shock Value - PG-13]
[Role: Shocking Betrayer! Do you accept the role? (Yes/No)]
[Role Focus: Badass + Cunning]
[Power War: Shock Value: Act One in Progress]

I'd done a lot of Episodes. I'd even been a villain in a couple. But I'd never run an Episode as a villain before. So, as I strode out and started knocking down abandoned buildings with **[Blitz]** and **[Shock and Awww]**, sending electricity and sonic booms into already rickety foundations I left in my wake, I was surprised to get a trio of new pop-ups.

[A Vigilante is Joining the Fight]
[Name: Unknown]
[Heroes are Joining the Fight]
[Name: Unknown]
[Name: Unknown]

Villains got to see basic information about whether heroes were joining? I grinned, bracing myself for Fursona and the team she'd put together. She'd be in for a shock!

26

In for a Shock

Fursona had brought two other heroes. I ran through a mental list of who they could be. They'd have to be experienced and tough enough to fight Madame Shockwave—who'd *killed* someone on her first outing—but also weak enough to not win against me. As I thought through the heroes she could have conscripted, the two she'd picked became obvious. The system update had given me a hint, and the buzzing in the air only confirmed it.

"Magical Girl Honeycomb, you can't stop me!" I shouted into the evening haze over Thornton.

The bee-themed Magical Girl strode around the corner, a confidence to her that shouldn't have been there. Didn't she know who she was up against? I'd mop the floor with her—but at the same time, I was glad for my domino mask hiding my identity.

"Maybe not," Honeycomb said, cracking a single knuckle and wincing. "Maybe I'm unable to stop you, but I am able to ask you to stop."

I blinked. That sounded a lot like—

Before I could finish my thought, a purple flash filled the air, and I whirled as Vigilant Vow summoned a gigantic pink rabbit. "I swear to fight evil, uphold justice, and look damn cute doing it!" he said.

I winced. "I don't recognize that one. New Magical Girl?"

"Yes. Magical Girl Battle Bun. Now, let's go." His dark, spiky hair and reddening face peeked out from under his hoodie as he dropped into a fighting stance, two more crystals overhead.

"Sure. [**Shock and Awww**]!" A sparking shock wave rippled out from around me, electricity and force surging toward my enemies. Honeycomb's gossamer wings threw her over it, and the rabbit hopped toward me, but it threw Vigilant Vow across the street and into a snowdrift.

[**Dramatic Damage! +1 Drama Point**]

A chrome camera drone with a slightly different look than Rocko's captured the whole fight; I'd said that whoever's studio showed up could have this one, and it looked like . . . *someone* had grabbed it. "Not so fast, huh?" I asked Vigilant Vow, only to catch a splash of warm, sticky honey across my back. I tried to move but couldn't.

"Stick around!" Honeycomb yelled triumphantly. The rabbit slammed into me a moment later, kicking and biting with its hilariously sharp plastic teeth. I used **[Grounding]** and took the hits, letting the cables from my feet dissipate the pain into the ground.

[True Grit! +1 Grit Point]
[HP 13/14]

Then, before the plushie bunny could escape, I fired up **[Blitz]**. The Badass move acted more like a Speedster's than a Bruiser's, propelling me across the street and toward Honeycomb, breaking her honey spray. I slammed into the surprised Magical Girl before she could react, driving the air from her lungs in a surprised "Ooof!"

[Badass Damage! +1 Badass Point]

A voice in the back of my head said I needed to retreat. This had to be Fursona's Phase One, and the plan wasn't to wreck Thornton. It was to move the fight into the Hot Zone. But these upstart heroes thought they could stand against me. Against *me*! I had to show them!

So, as Vigilant Vow summoned a massive bird with a deep red pouch under its beak, I used **[Live-Wire Limit Break]**. Sparking, crackling wires surrounded my arms and legs, electricity snapping as they augmented my arms and legs. More importantly, my mind sped up to keep up with my enhanced body. It felt like I had a million new synapses firing up there! I dashed toward Vigilant Vow—but it was too late!

[Good Thinking! +1 Cunning Point]

The bird threw itself into my path, its red pouch expanding until it filled my vision. I bounced off it, caroming through a nearby store's boarded window and the glass behind it.

[HP 12/14]

Okay. Okay. I shook my head to clear it as my lightning-bolt-patterned cat peered over me. A tangle of shattered shelves surrounded me, and for a moment, I only wanted to beat these two upstart little-leaguers to within an inch of their lives. *<Hey, remember what your girlfriend says about sticking to the script? You should do that meow!>*

Tails was right. I needed to make it a good show *while* retreating toward the Hot Zone. A quick, **[Live-Wire Limit Break]**-empowered shove cleared the shelves, and I slipped out the store's back door as Vigilant Vow's pair of familiars pushed through the broken window. I'd reset the fight and do things on my—

"**[Honey Spray]**!"

Honeycomb fell from the sky like a thunderbolt, and I couldn't aim one of my own at her before the sticky substance landed all around me. It didn't hurt—I didn't know if Honeycomb *had* any powers that hurt. But it did slow me down, and before I could escape the alleyway, Vigilant Vow and his two familiars crashed through the door. The rabbit hopped, spinning midair, and lashed out with both feet. I should have been able to dodge, but all the honey slowed me down.

"Oof!" I said as its feet hit my stomach. Then "Oof!" again as I bounced off a dumpster.

[HP 10/14]

I couldn't afford to take this kind of damage. We were still in Act One, and I needed superhero damage to fight against Fursona—and to cause chaos once we got into the Hot Zone.

So, as Honeycomb took to the air again and Vigilant Vow's familiars advanced toward me, I used **[Blitz]** again. But this time, I was leaving.

[**Badass Move! +1 Badass Point**]

[Live-Wire Limit Break] was still running, too, and I easily outpaced most of my pursuers. Honeycomb was tough to shake; she'd gotten airborne, and I couldn't evade her. But I didn't really want to. She needed to know where I was heading so she could tell the others. We had to make a fight out of it.

The red-throated bird landed in front of me, and I slowed down to avoid its ridiculous crimson air sack. As I did, Vigilant Vow jogged around the corner. "What are you trying to accomplish?"

I paused. The heroes wouldn't stop, and I couldn't shake them. But I'd seen this scene a hundred times and played it out a dozen or more times myself. Plus, Bianca and I had worked on this line. "I'm trying to deliver a shock to the whole system, be a spark of change, and wave goodbye to the current, corrupt order."

"And you're fine with destroying a whole district to get what you want?" Honeycomb asked. She landed in front of me, completing my encirclement. No matter which way I went, I had a fight on my hands.

"No. If it wakes people up, I'm fine with destroying the whole *city*." The camera drone was eating this up; that wasn't right. Bianca and I had planned on the cameras cutting off at some point, and I'd been willing to bet that it'd happen right here. But

I had to keep going. "You have to feel it, right? The tides changing? We can't keep doing what we've been doing. None of us can anymore. We have to fight for what we believe in."

"And what do you believe in?" Honeycomb asked loudly. Too loudly; I could hear Vigilant Vow and his familiars closing in while she tried to distract me.

"Justice."

As the bird and rabbit both lunged toward me, I used **[Shock and Awww]**. It threw all four assailants away, slamming them into walls and dumpsters just like I'd been a second ago.

[Dramatic Damage! +4 Drama Points]

I winced. That wasn't supposed to hit quite that hard. But as Honeycomb and the bird recovered, I started running, getting ready to fight a running battle against two less-powered heroes. The first corner gave me an opportunity, and as the funny-looking bird came around it, I fired off an uncharged **[Wallshocker]**. The shock wave rippled off a wall on the far side of the narrow street, a boom echoing as the air superheated at the impact point. Sparks flew through the air, chips cracked off the concrete wall, and the bird was down a moment later!

[Stylish Strike! +1 Flamboyance Point]

That left . . . Vigilant Vow, his rabbit, one unknown familiar, and Honeycomb. I could draw this out. And the Hot Zone's border was only a few blocks away.

My feet beat the pavement as **[Live-Wire Limit Break]** faded for the first time. I could hear Vigilant Vow's shoes echoing my steps, and I piled on as much speed as I could without using the power again. The small park Fursona and I had identified as the best breakthrough point was close. I just had to get—

WHAM!

Something slammed into me. I rolled across the pavement, a tangle of limbs and wings flailing as Honeycomb's fists pounded my back. She swung fast and hard, and it was all I could do for a moment to keep my head sheltered. I had to get some distance—what was *with* her?

[HP 9/14]

I used **[Blitz]** again. Instead of trying to hit her this time, I surged down the block, leaving Honeycomb on the sidewalk behind me. She hit the ground with a thump.

[Badass Move! +1 Badass Point]

As Vigilant Vow ran past into the street behind me, I used **[Live-Wire Limit Break]** again. These two didn't have a chance against me. My mind sped up to keep up with my wire-enhanced body, and I rushed the vigilante before he could summon another familiar. "The trouble with your power is that it's slow," I said conversationally as I punched him and grabbed his wand hand. The black wand stopped inches from his crystal.

[Good Thinking! +1 Cunning Point]

He swung at me, but I blocked it casually, letting the sparking wires shock him for his trouble. As he recoiled, I let him go. He hit the pavement—hard. Almost as hard as his girlfriend had.

[Good Thinking! +1 Cunning Point]

Both heroes pushed themselves to their feet. I stared at them and laughed. "You're really going to keep trying, huh? I said you couldn't stop me, and I meant it."

"And I said I was able to ask you to stop, and I . . . I meant it, too." Honeycomb couldn't stop panting. The poor girl was completely out of her league. So was Vigilant Vow now that he didn't have his Agent-granted familiar army.

But I didn't have time for mercy. I needed to handle this *before* Fursona showed up, because with only this Costume, I couldn't handle her and them together. Heck, I wasn't sure I could handle her alone. I used **[Blitz]**, this time aiming for the vigilante who'd been my rival. Then, as I slammed into him faster than he could see, I used another weak **[Wallshocker]**. The electrical explosion echoed off the nearby buildings and slammed into him. Then he slammed into the ground.

[Badass Damage! +1 Badass Point]
[Stylish Strike! +1 Flamboyance Point]

Honeycomb fired a glob of honey my way, leaping into the air to avoid my next **[Blitz]**. I let her go—partially because I didn't have a great antiair option in this build. I'd been lucky. The bird had chosen to fight me on the ground, and Honeycomb was . . . less relevant than I'm sure she'd hoped to be.

After a few moments of strafing, she seemed to realize it, too. She dipped toward me, firing another **[Honey Spray]**, but as I dodged, she switched focus to the down-but-not-out Vigilant Vow. She hoisted him over her shoulder and took off, bumble-beeing through the air with his extra weight. "We'll be back, evildoer!"

"I'm looking forward to it." I laughed. "Why don't you bring some extra firepower?"

[End of Act One: Act Two in Three Minutes]

27

Firepower

[Power War: Shock Value: Act Two in Progress]

Fursona hadn't shown herself by the time the second act started. I wasn't sure where she was, but that didn't worry me at all. Part of the plan was to make it look as real as possible, from the fight with Honeycomb and Vigilant Vow to my facial expressions when my partner-turned-foil attacked me.

So, instead of looking around trying to find her, I decided to cause some mayhem.

The first building was about a block from the Hot Zone's border—conveniently, the fight with the little-league heroes had pushed me right to an abandoned apartment complex. The building towered over me, four stories of broken windows and chipped, faded paint over cinderblocks. A few dead plants clung to its sides, and browned weeds poked through the thin layer of snow.

It'd be perfect.

I started charging **[Wallshocker]**. This was the move that had blown up the bank in my mom's first Episode. I'd read it and immediately realized that a weakly charged version would be fine, but a bigger one could very easily level a building. That was what had happened to her unintentionally.

That was what I was trying to do now.

As power coursed through me, I couldn't help but start laughing. Tails stared at me, and I could tell that if she was TA-1LZ, she'd be warning me about an impending villainous breakdown. But I didn't care. This was the way—the first step in . . . something. I hadn't fully decided what, and right now, all I could focus on was the blue-white lightning building in me.

I had to let it go. I had to hang on another couple of seconds. I couldn't.

The lightning ripped out of me and blasted into the wall. The fragmented glass and plywood covering empty window frames gave out first, bursting into the building like they'd been hit by a three-ton hammer. The destruction was incredible; even

[Limelight Barrage] didn't usually hit this hard. I couldn't stop laughing, holding my hands up like a mad scientist.

But it was only starting. The electricity poured out of me, and the lowest row of cinderblocks began glowing. *<Understudy, duck!>* Tails shouted in my head, sprinting for cover with her stubby legs whirling like a cartoon.

I decided I'd listen, just this once. But I also wanted to see the building go up, so I took cover behind a nearby car that sat on its rims, tires long since rotted away.

The building seemed to collapse outward. Cinderblocks started falling into the street, and I stared at the countless tons of weight hovering overhead as Tails kept running. Then, blue-white light filled the air, and the whole thing collapsed inward. Shattering blocks filled the air with sharp fragments that bounced off the car and blew out windows all along the block; it sounded like Theseus's machine gun going off, combined with the roar of MoonTech's fuel tanks exploding.

And it didn't stop for almost a minute. When it finally tapered off, my chest hurt from laughing, and I was covered in dust that I brushed casually off my shoulder. "That was fun!" I said. And it was. I'd rarely been a villain, and only for a little while at a time. The only other time had been helping Gourmet out, and Ramsey Fieri barely counted.

But this? Giving myself willingly to a full breakdown? This was *fun*.

[Devastating Demolition! +5 Flamboyance Points]

And it paid? This was—

"Never fear! The Justice-Lizard's here! Throw down your arms, evildoer, and surrender!"

Fursona's Kaiju Costume stomped out of the dust, eyestalks bobbing up and down as she squared up. I grinned. "You're right on time, hero! Right on time . . . to lose!"

I used **[Blitz]** to close the distance before the bulky suit could react, slamming into her at full speed and knocking her backward. Then, as her tail whipped toward me, I ducked, sliding across the rubble-strewn asphalt and letting it shred my tights around the knees.

[Badass Damage! +1 Badass Point]

I'd hit her, sure, but she looked like she'd barely even noticed. Her flame breath washed over me, and I felt the heat sizzling my superhero damage away. I backpedaled, wishing I had a better ranged damage loadout for handling her.

[HP 7/14]

"Hey, don't forget the goal," she said over my earpiece. I'd forgotten I was even wearing that; honestly, I wasn't sure I cared about the goal anymore. A superhero was trying to stop me from my rightful reign of terror over this district. This was *mine*; Power War rules said so!

Her arm went up, and I followed its outstretched claw as it pointed over my shoulder. There, far away to the south, a reddish haze was slowly filling the air. "Everything's working. Make this look good."

"Oh, so you're going to try to trick me!" I shouted, using [**Shock and Awww**] to send a brutal shock wave across the ground. It knocked her off her feet, but not anywhere near as far as the little-leaguers and their familiars. Not anywhere near as far away as I needed her, either.

[**Dramatic Damage! +1 Drama Point**]

Worse, I'd only gotten one point. As she recovered and slammed her clawed fists into the ground—sending her *own* shock wave my way—I used [**Live-Wire Limit Break**]. The extra speed in my wire-wrapped limbs and my brain gave me one way out from the slow-motion pulse.

[**Good Thinking! +1 Cunning Point**]

I jumped. High. And backward. My feet hit the still-shaking ground, and I recovered, then backed away from the dinosaur filling my vision. She hadn't even used the juice box yet—I knew, because she was supposed to use it at a specific point in the fight—but she was still kicking my butt. A claw slammed into me. Then another. The impacts threw me south toward the open lot next to the Hot Zone.

[**HP 5/14**]

I was almost there. But I couldn't take these kinds of hits.

As Kaiju-sona charged, I kept up the [**Live-Wire Limit Break**], using it to escape from the furious, fursuited superhero. A pair of camera drones—one of hers, one I didn't recognize—followed her. And the moment I had enough distance, I started charging another [**Wallshocker**].

The power charged.

So did Kaiju-sona.

I wasn't sure what she was even trying to do. Was she trying to *stop* me? Or just make a show of things? From my perspective as a villain, I couldn't be sure. But what I could be sure of was that the three abandoned buildings nearby would put a stop to any real aggression she had.

The [**Wallshocker**] fired.

[**Devastating Demolition! +5 Flamboyance Points**]

For a moment—one brief, empty moment filled only with the ecstasy of victory and the agony of loss—I thought I'd killed Fursona. The abandoned apartments fell on her, burying her under a hundred tons of bricks and concrete, and it was all I could do to **[Blitz]** away from the chaos.

The dust cleared. The sounds of shattering walls stopped. And all I could see along Fitch Street was a pile of rubble that had to be five feet thick, or maybe ten.

Then, something started rumbling in the midst of the devastation.

The rumbling turned into a roar, and I took a step back. Then another. The ruins swelled like a bubble. Then . . .

The bubble popped.

Kaiju-sona's full form erupted from the ground, roaring a jet of flame that lit up the entire district and almost—almost—rivaled whatever Fanfic was doing across the city. I took three more steps back; she wouldn't stop growing! And then, as her massive, googly-eyed head turned toward me, I turned tail and ran.

There was no way I could take her. I'd just used my most powerful move. And I hadn't gotten three steps when the rhythmic stomping of her chase filled me with horror. I glanced over my shoulder.

She wasn't fast. Her legs churned so much slower than mine. But one lumbering stride covered the same distance for every ten steps I took. I couldn't extend my lead even with **[Live-Wire Limit Break]** going.

"Hey, don't forget, run toward the Hot Zone!" Fursona shouted in my earpiece. "We need to stick to the script!"

Right. The script. Control flooded over me. I wasn't a villain—not really. I was just playing one on TV. And now that Fursona had used her giant form, we had a limited time to execute the plan. So I kept running but turned toward the Ilneats' enclave within Tokyexico.

Not that I stopped fighting, though.

As Fursona's massive tail thrashed through the air, I used **[Grounding]** and allowed the impact to disperse across the network of wires enclosing my body. It *hurt*, but not like it should have. I could totally tank like . . . two more of those hits. Maybe three, if I didn't mind losing all my superhero damage!

[True Grit! +1 Grit Point]
[HP 3/14]

I **[Blitzed]** away from my partner, bouncing off her leg as I dashed. The impact knocked her aside—by a couple of millimeters, maybe. Then I was out of range again, flames licking at my Costume's backside.

[Badass Damage! +1 Badass Point]

Then, there it was.

The Hot Zone.

I'd been in it dozens of times, meeting with Rocko, and I'd seen it from the pinnacle of the Tokyexico Council of Heroes' building. But this close, and on the ground, it gave off an entirely different feeling.

The snow had melted all around it in a massive circle extending fifty feet around the border. The buildings on the other side were also different: low warehouses and the occasional spikelike, windowless skyscraper. And, of course, the heat beat down on me, made worse by Fursona's flame breath, which she still hadn't shut off.

I backpedaled yet again. "Okay, 'hero,' time for my stand!"

"If you're making a stand, stand still!" Fursona yelled in my earpiece. "We need to make an impact here, and I can't do that if you're running away!"

I complied. It hurt to comply with a hero, but if I had to cooperate with one, at least it was *her*. But that didn't mean I was going down without a fight. I used **[Grounding]** to root myself in place and take the inevitable hit, then started charging my last **[Wallshocker]** of the second act.

Fursona's massive bulk slammed down into me, her foot trying to crush me like a bug, and I resisted the urge to scream. Everything went clear through the villainous breakdown. This was the moment we'd set up the entire Episode for.

[True Grit! +1 Grit Point]
[HP 1/14]

In the distance, I could see Vigilant Vow's familiars returning to the fight, and overhead, Honeycomb buzzed her way toward me. I was going to lose. And that was okay because I was also going to win. The goal was in sight.

[Wallshocker] went off, the rippling blue-white lightning coursing through Fursona and disintegrating the two familiars. Buildings tumbled around the empty lot we'd meticulously chosen as our entry point into the Hot Zone. An alarm blared in the distance, and dust filled the air.

[Devastating Damage! +5 Flamboyance Points]

When it cleared, devastation surrounded us. Between Fursona's rampage and my **[Wallshocker]**, we'd hit the Hot Zone's border as hard as we could. Electricity still coursed through the air overhead.

But we'd missed something.

The Hot Zone was intact.

28

Intact

The Hot Zone hadn't even noticed my [**Wallshocker**].

The blue-white lightning from the power rippled up an invisible barrier along the border, less than a foot away from me. It surged back and forth, and it was disgustingly clear that our plan had failed to consider one crucial detail. I thought back to the "Eustace Holds the Bagge!" Episode, and Professor Eustace Bagges, the Ilneat professor Monologue had tried to kidnap last year.

He'd ignored most powers that Episode.

So, of course—*of course*—we'd failed to remember that. And we hadn't even considered that the Hot Zone might have some crazy alien forcefield. But if that was the case, how did Extras get in and out to do the maintenance work and stuff the Ilneats needed? I'd watched them go in and out from the Council of Heroes building after my first fight with Stella-Lunar. Was the shield down sometimes? Maybe we'd just timed this badly.

Everything was quiet outside of the Hot Zone for a moment, though I could hear the alarm howling away inside. A brick overbalanced and tipped, clattering down a wall of rubble. I stared at Fursona.

"I think we've lost this one," Fursona said in my earpiece. I couldn't respond verbally, so I nodded. "Play along. We'll reset and try again after we figure out what to do about *that*."

I nodded again.

"Evildoer, it's time to face the music!" Kaiju-Fursona shouted. Then she roared a flaming breath my way and stomped forward.

I was getting really tired of taking falls, though. I'd lost to Theseus specifically to force her to use all her power to beat him, but that didn't mean I had to lose *this* Episode. So, as the flames ripped toward me, I used [**Blitz**] and ducked between the massive Kaiju's legs.

[Badass Move! +1 Badass Point]

"I can't win," I yelled back, echoing Honeycomb's battle cry earlier, "but I can not lose!"

A glob of honey hit the ground next to me, and I spun, activating **[Live-Wire Limit Break]** to get more speed. My plan at this point was pretty simple. I needed to get rid of either Vigilant Vow or Honeycomb, then draw out the fight against Kaiju-sona until she burned all her sugar fuel. And to do that, I'd need to slow her down.

[Good Thinking! +1 Cunning Point]

So, as Honeycomb dove toward me with her flower skirt fluttering in the wind behind her, I used a fast **[Shock and Awww]**. The burst wasn't as powerful as a partially charged **[Wallshocker]**, but it tossed her through a boarded-up window, and I followed a moment later.

[Dramatic Damage! +1 Drama Point]

She was just getting up and turning when I used **[Blitz]** to quickly knock her back down, then pummeled her into submission with a series of speedy blows. The moment her hands went over her head, I stopped; just because she didn't know who I was didn't mean I wanted to be responsible for breaking her. But I needed her down and out. "Sorry about this," I said.

[Badass Damage! +3 Badass Points]

"Sorry about what?"

I punched her in the nose. Hard. She went limp. Then I shouted out toward the hulking Kaiju and three familiars that Vigilant Vow had summoned. "Your ally's down and is now my hostage."

Kaiju-sona roared, and for a moment, I thought I'd lose the Episode right there. But then she shrank down with an almost deafening yawn, returning to her normal size to stand next to a furious-looking Vigilant Vow. "What are your terms, then?"

I'd already gotten what I wanted; it was unlikely Fursona had the juice to keep fighting after being Full Kaiju for so long, and with Honeycomb down, I could negotiate this into a draw. "Simple. I hand the bee girl to your ally, he leaves with her, and we keep fighting."

The kaiju's googly eyes bobbed as Fursona nodded. I almost sighed in relief, but one of the camera drones had its lens on me. Instead, I laughed a little for show. "Good choice, 'heroes.' I'll bring her to the window. You wait one minute and then take her."

The second I had her propped up against the wall for Vigilant Vow to grab, I retreated into the building. Abandoned armchairs lined the walls, and the carpet had long since rotted away, but clearly this had once been a decent place to live. Still, I needed some space, and I needed to make sure I wasn't being followed. Not by either of the heroes and definitely not by any camera drones.

Once I was finally far enough away that I figured it'd be safe, I started a [**Transformation Sequence**] and switched over to Magical Girl Understudy. It hurt to throw away a possible win, but control was coming back, and right now, the priority was getting clear before someone investigated the alarm and the attack on the Hot Zone's shield generator. And, unfortunately, that meant taking the L.

It didn't take long to fly back over with [**Solar Wing**] and land next to the exhausted-looking plushie Kaiju. "Sorry I'm late. It took me a while to get across town. Did you beat the vil you were after?"

"No. No, she, uh, got away," Fursona said, *not* looking at the camera drones.

"Oh." I made a show of disappointment, thankful for my high school acting career. "Do you think you can help hunt her down?"

"No. I'm drained. I *had* her, though. It was the craziest fight I've been in in . . . a week or two, I guess? Probably on par with "Grant Building Dogpile" for destruction, and for her to survive a three vs. one? That's one tough vil. I hope I don't have to fight *her* again."

There was subtext there, which meant that there'd be more than just subtext later. I wasn't getting a lecture, but I already knew what Fursona would say once her suit was off. That Shock and Awe was dangerous. That her powers shouldn't be used without a lot of thought. "Come on, then. Let's get you home. Some other hero will have to deal with her."

"Are you sure? I could figure out a way . . ." Fursona yawned, and I raised my eyebrow at her below my mask. ". . . to get home myself so you could take the fight to her. You're fresh. If you found her, she'd be finished."

"No, you're beat. Let's go." I pulled her in front of me and took off on my magical sailboard, leaving pink and blue contrails behind in the evening sky.

[Episode Canceled: Power War: Shock Value]
[Alias - Understudy] [Archetype - Magical Girl] [Community Rank - 155/523]
[HP 1/14]
[**Styles and Skills**]
▶ Archetype Skill - Transformation Sequence
▶ Combo Skills - Power-Weaving
▶ Badass (41)
▶ Cunning (44)
▶ Drama (35)
▶ Limelight Barrage 2
▶ Starlance 3

▶ Flamboyance (22)
▶ Signature Skill - Adaptive Armoire 3
▶ Stored Costumes: (Rainy Day, Copy Cat, Lab Assistant Panic)
▶ Solar Wing 2
▶ Quick-Time Change 3
▶ Improvised Ovation 2
▶ Grit (38)
▶ Freeze-Frame 2

"Fuck!" I swore as we flopped onto the green room's couch. The TV was off, and neither of us went for the remote. Over in the corner, the computer monitors had been turned off; they'd been off for over a day because neither of us wanted to work on 3V1L right now.

Maybe that had been a mistake.

Maybe we should have stayed on target. If we'd just kept working on tracking down The Agent, we'd probably have made progress. Maybe we'd even have pinned him down by now, somewhere where he couldn't just vanish into thin air. It was just so damn frustrating; we couldn't make progress on *anything*. I wanted to scream. I wanted to cry.

Part of the crying was the growing headache, which was why I *wasn't* screaming. It had started building as we flew home, hitting like a hurricane before I could get to the ibuprofen. And now that I was here, it had me fully in its grip. I was supposed to be making phone calls. Instead, I sat on the couch, looking dejectedly at the turned-off monitors over my shoulder. "So, that went pretty badly."

"Yeah. Do we want to do a postmortem on it? Could be helpful," Bee asked. She was mostly out of her Kaiju-sona suit and looking exhausted, but unlike her last two Full Kaiju appearances, we'd taken precautions, and she had a glass of juice in her hands—and the whole pitcher on the conversation pit's coffee table. She looked a strange combination of sad, tired, and relieved as she sipped her orange juice.

I nodded slowly, holding back frustrated tears and shutting my eyes to keep even the green room's well-balanced light out. "We didn't do the right research. We should have known what the Hot Zone's defenses were like, but we assumed we'd be able to waltz right in. That was a mistake. If we try again, we need to be better informed."

"Okay, sure, but what went well?" Bee asked. "I haven't psychologized you in a while, but it seems like you need it here. Positive thinking and growth. So, what did we do well that we could capitalize on later?"

"Uh," I said, stalling. From my perspective, the whole thing had been a disaster right from the time . . .

"Oh, right. Bringing in Vigilant Vow and Honeycomb helped set up the stakes, and made Shock and Awe feel like a serious threat." Once I'd gotten started, I found other positives. "The finish let me not lose to Kaiju-sona, which was good for me emotionally. We picked a great place to bring Shock and Awe; she's too destructive to use anywhere else, but Thornton being almost completely empty was perfect. You got to win a solo-ish Episode. Kind of."

"Yeah, those are all good, but even the finish wasn't a complete waste of time. We learned something useful about the Hot Zone. Now, we just have to figure out how to use it."

"Or if we even want to use it." I massaged my face. "Look, we took a shot. It didn't work. Now, we need to cover our butts for a bit. That means not putting ourselves out there as enemies to the studios, at least not any more than we already are."

Bee's hand rested on my knee, and I cracked open my eyes to look at her. She had a worried expression on her face. "Costume got you whooped? I get that, believe me. Kaiju-sona does it to me every time."

"No, I don't think so. I probably just need to sleep it off. Feels like a hangover." I stood up. "It hurts behind my eyes."

"I hate that. Yeah, go to bed. I'll take care of any evidence in the green room. We can go deal with the Outback Stakeout Zone tomorrow."

"No, there's one thing we need to take care of before I can go to bed, and that's Rocko. We need to make sure they know our story, and it'd be best coming from me," I said.

"Yeah, the part of the plan where you have an alibi for not being there. You were at, what? Shakespeare Club?"

"That's right." I pulled out my phone, turned it on, and winced. The bright blue light hurt to look at, and I could feel a tear working its way down my face.

Then Bee's hand closed over it. "Go. To. Bed. I'll make the call."

"Thanks," I whispered as she kissed my forehead. I turned to head for my bed, with Bee following me as I went, orange juice in one hand and my phone in the other. She watched as I stripped down, changed into pajamas, and brushed my teeth, wincing the whole time. Then she tucked me into bed—for a moment, it irritated me, but then I remembered I'd done the same thing to her when she'd been exhausted after being Full Kaiju the first time.

"If you need anything, let me know. Otherwise, I'll be back here in a minute or two," Bianca said from the door. Then it clicked shut, leaving me in blissful darkness. I barely even thought about the canceled Episode. Instead, my eyes squeezed shut, and by the time Bee joined me, I was too asleep to notice.

PART FOUR

29

Headaches

"Annie, your phone's been going off for the last twenty minutes," Bianca said from my bedroom door. "It's Rocko."

I buried my head deeper under the covers where I'd been hiding. The migraine I'd been fighting wouldn't fade—if anything, it was worse. I squeezed my eyes shut, crossed my fingers, and silently wished she'd go away.

She didn't. She pulled on my blankets instead, and we had a brief tug-of-war before they slid off the bed and onto the floor with a whump. I blinked at the sudden light and the exhausted-looking Bianca looming over me. Then I shut my eyes again. If I pretended I wasn't awake, maybe she'd leave. It was worth a shot.

Then something thumped down on the end table. I cracked an eye and smiled. "Bee, you're the best." A trio of ibuprofen and a glass of water sat there, and I struggled upright, popped the pills, and drained the glass in one long pull.

She handed me a slice of bread. "If you get crumbs on my side, I'm gonna kick your ass worse than yesterday."

"Oh, yeah . . . sorry, I thought it'd work."

"Don't be sorry. It was a good idea, but we didn't execute it correctly. We'll talk more about it later. For now, bread, water, drugs."

"Thanks." I chewed the white bread, swallowed, and took my pills.

"Honeycomb and Vigilant Vow both got pretty beat up last night. I've been texting her, and she says they got in over their heads—and it wasn't my fault. Guess who they're blaming?"

"Me?" I groaned.

Bianca grinned. "No, dumbass," she teased. "The villain in the Episode, who probably won't ever appear again, right?"

I flushed red. My first thought was to push back. I needed Dark Girl Shock and Awe; she'd already made a statement about seeking justice and trying to wake people up, and she was necessary for . . . whatever our little rebellion had been and would turn into. But when I told Bee as much, she laughed. "I don't think so. Your mom was right. That powerset's just not practical in a place with any population at all."

I set down the water cup and slowly pulled myself out of bed. "Thanks again," I said, smiling weakly.

"No problem. Now that that's taken care of, you should probably check your phone," Bee said. "Rocko's been blowing up our lines. They want us back out there. No mention of last night. Nothing. Zero."

I grimaced at the wall of text messages.

<DuPont, get yourself together. Get here, and get to work - Rocko 9:23>
<DuPont, I'm serious. 3V1L's on the move - Rocko 10:01>
<If you don't get out there, *Heroics 101* is in trouble - Rocko 10:04>
<Don't throw away everything we've worked for - Rocko 10:09>

And on and on. I finally read the last one, blood boiling.

<DuPont, you don't know what you're doing. Come in as soon as possible - Rocko 1:14>

Bianca flicked on the TV; we hadn't watched anything in a couple of days, and it was time to catch up. Still in my nightie, I padded out to the couch, found *The Diary of Golden Goose* on the coffee table, and opened it to a random page. But before I could focus on the words, the muted news story on the TV caught my eye. Bianca unmuted while I stared at Dr. Mindstorm. She stood at a TU podium, flashbulbs going off around her.

". . . my immediate resignation from Tokyexico University's faculty. I've been suspicious of the Ilneats for a long time, and with Golden Goose's diary, those suspicions have been reinforced. I am also declaring my . . . contract . . . with the Ilneat Network void, as well as the terms of my treaty with Mister Felsic. As of noon today . . . Mindstorm is back in business."

The news anchor took over. "Mindstorm's statement yesterday, while initially unique, has been followed up by a dozen other superheroes and villains in the minor and major leagues over the last eighteen hours. Golden Goose's diary seems to have changed the entire superpowered landscape, with powerful heroes and villains coming out in support of their Ilneat production studios and against them. The biggest heroes in Tokyexico seem inclined to stay with their studios, including Stella-Lunar and The Triad. However, a couple of big-name villains have followed Mindstorm and declared their contracts void.

"It remains to be seen how this shake-up will play out, both in terms of the Third Power War and the future of the studio system in general. However, TCNN will be there to cover these world-shaking events as they happen."

The screen went blue on one side and red on the other, and pictures of Stella-Lunar and The Triad appeared on one side. I shut the TV off as Mindstorm and McHammer's portraits appeared on the other side. This was what Golden Goose's killer meant by the whole mess being exposed.

I stalked into the green room. Bianca followed me, a tray with cereal on it in her hands. She set it down on the conversation pit's coffee table and went to the two computer screens. "So, uh, what's going on?"

I stared at the two screens; where they'd once featured our rogues' gallery, they now showed the same two lists I'd seen on TV. As I watched, two names appeared on the first one, right below McHammer's: Gourmet and The Crumb. Then another popped up under The Triad's: Dr. Mays.

"They're picking sides," I whispered.

As the rosters filled out, with heroes and villains from across Tokyexico City and North America choosing their sides, I stared at Rocko's door. The star on it didn't look quite as shiny as it had a couple of days ago, and I had a sudden thought.

I'd go talk to them. They'd explain everything, how the abuse Snowball had heaped on Jasmine Saxton was just one bad apple. It'd make sense, and I could go back to doing what I'd been doing. But would it be the truth?

No, it wouldn't be.

To say nothing of the Extras the Network had put in harm's way, Honeycomb's career had been sidelined by Ed because her powers weren't adequate. They hadn't tried to find a different job for her. They'd just focused on Jumper since the villain was at least capable and crafty. And Cartman had broken my mom, kept their job, and turned around to manipulate Vigilant Vow. I wished I could talk to Gourmet, but she'd already made her choice. Her name was under Mindstorm's, on the side that was against the Network. So was Theseus's.

I paused at that. Theseus and Gourmet had both taken career paths that pushed them away from the Ilneat studios. As I watched, three more names appeared on the 'Against' list: Honeycomb's, Vigilant Vow's, and The Narrator's. None of them worked well with the Network, either.

That was a headscratcher. All three of them had antistudio feelings, but Mrs. N stayed out of these kinds of fights. If it didn't involve her daycare, she just . . . didn't engage. For her to pick sides and put herself out there, risking the daycare, meant something. I had to figure out what, though.

"What are we going to do?" Bianca asked.

"I don't know yet. What do you think we should do?" My hand still hovered over Rocko's studio door, and I pulled it away to join her on the couch.

"I don't know."

"Me either." But that wasn't entirely true. There were two choices. Just two. And they both had pros and cons.

The obvious choice was to join Stella-Lunar's team. She was the best; I'd grown up practically worshiping her, and there was no telling what the Network would do to the supers who were against them.

I didn't want to linger on that last thought. So, instead, I stood up and walked to the roof.

Really, it was simple. One side had all the power. They already had the best hero in North America, the strongest team in Tokyexico, and a lockdown metapowered hero in Mays. Against them, the other side had an assortment of minor-league heroes and villains, a couple of powerhouses, and The Narrator. The right call was to join up with Stella-Lunar. But even so, I lingered on the roof and watched the snow fall.

It wasn't a whiteout. The news had called for a blizzard, but instead, all we were getting was flakes swirling in a light breeze. The air smelled crisp, and I took one deep breath, then another.

"Hey, Annie, you need to see this," Bianca called from the stairs.

I groaned. My mind was made up, and all I had to do was make a decision and get my name on the prostudio list. Rocko had given me everything, and I owed them my career, some of my best friends, and both of my relationships. Besides, they'd never treated me like Golden Goose. I'd always been a partner in their studio.

When I went downstairs, the news was blaring again.

"Pennyworth, the financial crime-based villain currently controlling Yorkston's stock market, has joined the opposition to the Ilneat Network," the talking head was saying. "According to him, the Ilneat Network made the equivalent of eight trillion dollars from superhero shows last year, but the overall share given to Earth's heroes was less than a tenth of a percent. In his statement, he apologized for not noticing the lack of pay sooner, saying that he assumed his compensation matched that of other heroes' and villains'.

"Okay," I said, "that could just be a coincidence, right?"

"You have no idea how much you make, do you?" Bianca asked.

"Uh, no. Rocko paid me, and I always felt like it was fair. But . . ." I pulled out my phone and dialed the Ilneat's number. As it rang and rang, I thought about what I was going to ask, what I was going to say. But it just kept ringing, and eventually, I hung up. Instead, I stomped to the door and pushed down on the handle.

Or at least, I tried to.

But it wouldn't move. I was locked out of Rocko's studio.

Instead, a text message appeared on my phone.

<DuPont, make the right choice here. Heads I win, tails you lose - Rocko 1:45>

I screamed in frustration and tossed the phone onto the couch where it bounced onto the floor. I didn't even bother checking it for damage. The bastard wasn't helping me make a decision. And it was such a permanent decision. My name would be on a *list* of other rebelling heroes. No, rebelling *supers*. Half of each team was vils. But this choice would be permanent, unlike our attempt to wreck the Hot Zone. We couldn't walk this back.

"Mindstorm has put out a call for any supers who believe they've been mistreated by the Ilneat Network to meet her at her lair if they're in the Tokyexico City area. If not, she'll be in touch," the talking head said. "Is this the beginning of a new phase in the Third Power War? TCNN recommends all unpowered citizens take shelter, just in case!"

I glanced at the two computer screens. My head spun; could I walk away from Rocko and *Heroics 101*? It and *Small-Town Super* had been my whole life, and it'd be easiest to keep working wi—

A new name popped onto the prostudio list, and my hands balled into fists.

The Agent.

My throat tightened, and I glared so hard my eyes hurt. He'd chosen his side, and I couldn't work with him. No way. He was slimy enough that if he was on one side, he knew it was the wrong one, but he'd come out ahead if it won. And that made up my mind. I started my **[Transformation Sequence]**, nodding at the antistudio list. Was it the weaker side? Absolutely. But that didn't matter right now.

What did matter was that, as Magical Girl Understudy and Fursona's names appeared on the list a minute later, I felt good. *Right*, even. My phone buzzed. I ignored it, though. My contract was void.

30

Void

MONDAY, FEBRUARY 1

As far as I was concerned, classes were canceled.

Fursona and I flew hard toward the address that Mindstorm had sent us; she'd only told us where the meeting was happening ten minutes ago, and said that anyone who didn't show up was ". . . unserious . . . about this whole thing. Be there or be neutral."

I knew a lot of supers who wouldn't be there, not because they didn't want to be, but because they weren't fast enough to make it.

Mindstorm's house sat in a single-family neighborhood south of Tokyexico University; she'd drained her pool for the winter, but just like she'd said, a corner of the cover was unfolded, and below it, I could see a door. I punched in the code she'd texted, and a moment later, a metallic eye popped out of the wall. It beeped at us a couple of times, took flash photos of our faces, then withdrew.

A screeching sound filled the air as an entire side of the pool opened, revealing a long, dark hallway.

"Think it's a trap?" Bee asked.

"No." I shook my head and headed in. "We're not in an Episode, and Mindstorm's been suspicious of them for a while. She wouldn't actively oppose them before, but she wasn't afraid to come out against them here—and in a public way. She's not here to trap a couple of minor-leaguers."

But the farther we walked down the hall, the more worried I got. Mindstorm had obviously spared no expense to make her lair an impossible-to-assault fortress. Every corner seemed to be defended by the best weapons a Genius could install, and there wasn't ten feet between each airlock. All the doors were open, though, and the guns, flamethrowers, and pressure plates were offline.

"See, nothing to worry about," I said. I reached for a door handle, but it flew open before I could open it.

"Welcome, welcome," a hulking man with a hammer said. He wasn't quite as big as Lord Destructo, but he was *big*. Punch and Grapple were big—heck, Cam was big, too—but this guy looked like he ate barbells. The only part that wasn't a walking wall of muscle was his legs, and it wasn't because he was skipping leg day; it was the parachute pants his Costume featured. He stuck out a hand, and I shook it reflexively.

"Who are you two?" McHammer asked, crushing my ego almost as much as he'd crushed my hand.

"Magical Girl Understudy and Fursona. Mid-minor leagues. We did an attempted raid on the Hot Zone two days ago," Fursona said. She was in her kangaroo fursuit, but even with her extra strength, she couldn't match his grip. "We're all in on this . . . whatever it is."

"It's a rebellion, kiddo," McHammer said. "Come inside."

He got out of the way, and we squeezed past him.

The room was a vast, round dome; a holographic brain hovered high in the air, with glass tubes running to and from its supercomputer-looking projector. The stainless steel walls glistened in the murky bluish light, and tiny sparks flashed from exposed wiring. But closer to the floor, I couldn't see anything. There were so many people.

There had to be forty of us. Maybe fifty. I recognized a bunch of heroes and villains: Gourmet, Tearjerker, and Lady Lockless from the SSS; Springlock and Milo from TUSSA; and The Narrator. She smiled and waved when she saw us, but her eyebrows furrowed in worry. I remembered what Honeycomb had said about her thinking of us as her kids and that she'd wanted us to back off against The Agent.

There were others, of course, but the hulking form of McHammer walked through the crowd toward a balcony. He stopped under it, face shifting from the somewhat jovial man who'd greeted us to a severe and villainous look. "Alright, I'm calling this meeting to order!"

As Livestream and a familiar-looking fox-nun villain stopped near us, I shivered. It suddenly occurred to me that if someone started something, this entire room was a massive explosion waiting to happen. How had I thought this was a good idea? And more importantly, how could I get out if I had to?

We were too far from the exit for a clean break. That meant fighting. I'd have to go Super Girl Spotlight Star and blow all my most powerful attacks to clear a path, then hope that Mindstorm didn't shut her doors or—

"Welcome . . . to my lair," Mindstorm said dramatically, and I whirled.

She stood on her balcony, well above McHammer and the crowd. Her smile looked like a combination of relief and smugness; I'd had a dozen office hours meetings with her, but I'd only seen her in her element like this twice. Once, she'd kicked our teeth in as part of a lesson, and once, when she'd fought McHammer *and* Lord Destructo. Clearly, she hadn't minded the challenge, and she hadn't held it against McHammer, either, if they were allies now.

"I'm happy to see so many of . . . us," she continued, and I shivered. "You all know who I am, and I'm not . . . wasting time . . . with an introduction session. As of right now, we're all in this . . . rebellion . . . together. If you have rivals or enemies in this group, put aside your grudges. You'll have time later, after we . . . win. After the Ilneats are gone."

Something about how Mindstorm said what we all seemed to want, but said it so casually, sent more shivers up my spine. I glanced around as she kept talking; Sister Sly kept shooting *looks* at Fursona, and my partner wasn't exactly chill about being in the same room as her, either. I didn't have as many *true* enemies in the room, but Theseus had arrived a touch late, and in the back, I could see the neon-helmeted Roadrage.

Mindstorm didn't seem worried about the room's increasingly tense atmosphere, though. She kept going as if it wasn't an issue. "Since we're all hanging together or separately, I want to . . . reassure . . . you all about a few important things.

"First, I believe the Ilneats won't reveal your identities to the masses unless they start losing . . . hard. I've studied them for a long time, and I believe that they'll view even this as a chance at higher ratings. That means you should be safe from reveals . . . on that front. But be cautious. You may want to . . . take steps to mitigate any reveals that could happen. I'll leave that to you to decide how best to take care of yourselves . . . except for student supers. See me after . . . class. You have additional challenges on that front."

The crowd laughed nervously at Mindstorm's joke. I did, too. She might be a bitch, and she definitely was a villain, but even I grudgingly admitted that she'd helped me in my year and a half of college. And, even though it was a dumb joke, it seemed to help. I could feel some of the tension melting off . . . a little.

"Next . . . we need to discuss the reality of our situation. We are outgunned and outmatched—and that's before the . . . Ilneats . . . get involved. Stella-Lunar, The Agent, and The Triad are all top-tier supers, and so is Lord Destructo. Worse, they have Dr. Mays. We can't fight them in a straight-up fight and expect to . . . win."

I could hear disgruntled heroes and villains murmuring in the crowd at that. McHammer cleared his throat. "Everyone, shut up and listen. The boss is talking about how we win, not how we're going to lose."

"Thank you, McHammer. Now . . . if I thought we couldn't win, I wouldn't . . . fight. This isn't going to be easy, though. We need to spread out their bigs and . . . defeat them one at a time. But unlike in Episodes, we can't just . . . win. Villains, this part is on you.

"That means ethical combat. You need to change your tactics. No hostages. No destruction unless it's unavoidable. None of that. We aren't villains anymore. We're the heroes, and we need to win the Extras over. Otherwise . . . this won't work."

I nodded. That all made sense. Mindstorm went on and on about the tactics we'd have to use: the strategies she had for pinning down Stella-Lunar and The Triad, for cornering Lord Destructo, and for removing Dr. Mays from the board without actually fighting him. I listened intently, even as some of the more impulsive supers started to grow bored. She was right; we couldn't handle them in a real fight. We had to fight them like we were the weaker side.

We had to be villains.

But we had to *act* like heroes.

Then, Mindstorm turned to the bigger problem. "A . . . rogue element . . . attempted an assault on the Hot Zone two nights ago. They discovered that the whole district is protected. Additionally, all movement in and out of our studio doors is cut off. That leaves us with a major problem; we can beat Stella-Lunar all we want, but if we don't take her producer off the table, we haven't won. I'm working on solutions to that . . . problem.

"In that regard, I want all major-leaguers and upper-tier minor-leaguers to go with McHammer. He'll be laying out the first stage of our plan to take the Tokyexico Council of Heroes off the table. It'll be . . . counterintuitive, but necessary."

I blinked. That was an odd choice, since the Council of Heroes hadn't officially chosen sides in the upcoming conflict. Then I started walking toward McHammer. But before I could get there, Mindstorm stopped me. "If you've had any conversations with APPEAL or similar groups, I want to see you near the door. You're going to engage in our hearts and . . . minds . . . program. Welcome to Psychological Operations 101 with Dr. Mindstorm."

Fursona and I joined Mindstorm and a handful of others by the door. None of the heavy hitters were there, but I could see that Acid Burn had joined us, along with a few other mid-tier heroes and villains. I cleared my throat. "So, hearts and minds, huh?"

"Yes. You're the most important front in our . . . war. The Extras should be sympathetic to our cause, but I can't promise that. If they decide the status quo is better than the war we're about to fight, we can't . . . win. So, at the very least, I need APPEAL and the others off the table. It would be better to . . . convert them into allies, but I'll . . . accept neutrality."

"What do you want us to do?" Livestream asked.

"You, specifically, have a platform that's not controlled by the studios. So do you, Gourmet, but yours is a little . . . different. So you two will work on public relations. Grab Foamy Flash and The Crumb, work together, and figure out how to message that we may have been villains, but we're the . . . good guys now," Mindstorm said. "When you've figured out your messaging, report back to me. Livestream, you're the liaison. *Not* in charge, just reporting back to me. Work together, not for someone."

"Got it," Gourmet said. "See you later, Snack." She waved at me and stalked off, following the streaming villain toward another corner of the crowded room. I sort of wanted to ask why she was here; she'd never gotten along with her studio, but she had a pretty good gig going on with her cooking show.

"Next, Earth governments. We don't need . . . a lot of them. But we do need a couple. Any volunteers to deal with them? Well-known heroes, ideally."

A couple of hands shot up, and Mindstorm directed them to the side. "I'll work directly with you in a minute. Let me line everyone else out on their jobs."

She cleared her throat. "The rest of you are here because you've interacted with antisuper groups. Your job is to turn them into anti-Ilneat groups. Convince them that we're on the same side."

I winced; I'd known it was coming, but I couldn't see how we could possibly convert Su-Bin into a super-loving president. The chances seemed null.

31

Null

TUESDAY, FEBRUARY 2

The good news was that I had Tuesdays off from school—not that either Bianca or I
cared much about our classes with everything else happening. That meant it was easy
to call Su-Bin, ask if I could come over, and schedule a time. Bee wasn't coming; we'd
agreed to stay separated on this mission, since there were . . . consequences . . . if it
went poorly. Not just fighting, but worse.

The bad news was that I had no idea how to maneuver Su-Bin into aligning the
local APPEAL chapter with the Pro-Earth League.

Sure, I had options. We were pretty good friends, and there was a chance I'd be
able to do things subtly. But I didn't exactly have a lot of faith in my ability to stick to
the script. What seemed more likely was that I'd make suggestions and Su-Bin would
push back, digging in even more heavily. That was especially true given the list of
villains who'd joined up with the Pro-Earth League. Most of our roster were former
villains, current villains, or heroes who could easily have been villains.

I could hardly move through Mindstorm's lair without running into one.

So, really, the only chance I had was to shake up Su-Bin's entire worldview. And
I *did* have an option to do that, but it wasn't a *good* one. It was also why Bianca wasn't
with me; she was protecting herself and providing a possible outlet if everything went
wrong, then and possibly right after.

I stopped outside the apartment door and sent a quick text.

<Hey, I'm here - Annie 1:15>

She didn't respond, and I was left to twiddle my thumbs for a minute while I
stared at the wooden barrier in front of me. If I was Understudy, I could find a window and crash in. If I let Shock and Awe take over, I could just flatten it. But as Anika
DuPont, I was completely reliant on the girl inside to—

The door opened. "Hi, Annie," Su-Bin said.

She looked bad. Angry, depressed, with half done makeup she'd definitely slept in. Now wasn't the time for this. For a moment, I debated leaving. I could fake a call from Bee and get out of here. This was a bad idea. But then she moved out of the way and made a "come in" gesture, and I had no choice. I was committed.

Instead of running, I ignored the butterflies trying to escape my stomach and hurried over to Su-Bin's couch. A different strategy was in order.

When I sat down, her face shifted to relief, and she flopped onto the couch next to me. "Thank god. I haven't seen anyone in person except Cam all January."

"So, your parents are keeping you cooped up here?" I asked. "Where are they?"

"Oh, both at work. I'm *supposed* to be studying, or in class, or something, but you try staying motivated for a math degree when you can't get any fresh air. They're convinced the entire world's going crazy. I almost had them convinced I could attend classes one or two days a week, but then that book came out, and they clamped down again." She slumped down even farther, then perked up just slightly. "You said you'd borrowed a game from the library?"

"Yeah. I picked it out just for you, and I think it'll be perfect given your . . . situation. It's about pattern-making, quilts, and cats." As I explained the rules, she seemed to get a little happier, and when I gave her a board, she quickly laid out her starting tiles. I could already tell I'd be losing by our second game. "Yeah, that looks about right."

"It's a math game, even though it doesn't look like it." Su-Bin smiled for the first time, confirming what I'd dreaded: I didn't have a chance.

By the fourth game, we'd both agreed not to treat it as a competition. For one thing, Su-Bin was already setting up double reward bonuses, and I could barely even get the single rewards. For another, she had more cats than I did every round. The only thing I had going for me was the color streaks, and that just wasn't enough.

More importantly, though, her mood had shifted, and I felt like maybe . . . just maybe . . . I could try bringing up APPEAL and the Pro-Earth League. "So, you and your club must have an opinion on everything that's going on with Golden Goose and the supers on TV?"

"Yeah. I think it's all a gimmick. It's part of the Third Power War, and we're not convinced it's going to change anything about the balance of power. It's kind of like, uh, professional wrestling earlier this century, where they had their CEO or whatever play the role of a villain. The Ilneats are just doing it for ratings, and it'll work. People love this kind of drama," Su-Bin rattled off almost breathlessly. She grabbed a dark blue tile with flowers and put it on her quilt, then reached for a gray cat. "Triple score for that one."

I winced and set out a piece to replace the one she'd taken. "Okay. But what if it's *not* that?"

"It definitely is that. But sure, let's play that game. Suppose it's real. Suppose everything I've heard about that diary is true, and the reaction of all these supers is genuine. Let's even pretend that the 'good guys'—" she made air quotes for emphasis, "—win somehow, in spite of what looks like overwhelming odds. They've got a few good tacticians and some ridiculous powers, so they might be able to. What then?"

I shrugged and grabbed a yellow fern for another color streak, along with a banana to mark it. "I don't know. Probably try to work out a post-Ilneat future?"

"And what does that look like? A constant Power War, or just a massive one that ends with some sort of new world order? Neither is good for you and me."

"That's something we'd have to figure out, but I doubt we can do that while the Ilneats control all the supers. There are, what, a million of them?" I asked.

"Way less. Probably less than a hundred thousand, mostly concentrated in big cities. They look powerful because the media portrays them as powerful, but they're not any stronger than you or me." Su-Bin glared at her choices and grabbed a piece almost at random. I relaxed; she'd given up on one of her double bonus objectives. And, at the same time, she clearly still had no idea I was Magical Girl Understudy.

Speaking of which . . .

"Su-Bin, honestly, how much of your skepticism is because of Magical Girl Understudy?"

She paused at that, a scowl returning to her face. I watched her turn the question over in her head, staying quiet even while she picked her piece and placed it on the board. "Setting aside that she's on the Pro-Earth League's side, I still don't think they have a good plan for postconflict. And I don't see the conflict going well for regular folks. I mean, look at the fallout from Golden Goose's death."

"What do you mean?"

"Power Wars aren't good for Extras in the best of times. When Golden Goose got killed, it caused a huge flare-up of violence in most cities, especially those nearest to Yorkston. Extras took the worst of it. That'll happen again when the postdiary war pops off."

"Oh." I thought about that. She wasn't wrong, which sent a shiver down my spine. Unless the Pro-Earth League made a play directly into the Hot Zone and forced the Ilneats to the table fast, it *would* turn into a protracted fight. It probably would boil over into residential areas, and there were some supers who were nukes. Tapdance came to mind, along with a few others. They *would* hurt Extras. They couldn't help it.

"So, the Pro-Earthers have to prove they're on the Extras' side before they can have any sort of conversation with *my* chapter of APPEAL," Su-Bin continued. "I get that we're not exactly important, but I think the national organization's in agreement with that, and many other groups probably are, too. Ideally—and I know I'm just a college kid, but we're speculating today, right? Ideally, I'd like to see a post-Ilneat plan, the dismantling of the Episode system, and a commitment to ending the conflict as bloodlessly as possible."

That was something—an opening. But I couldn't press too hard. It might be enough; I'd bring it back to Mindstorm and let her mull it over. Maybe it'd help inform our strategic needs.

It also meant I wouldn't have to use my ace in the hole, and that was, in all honesty, a really big deal. Revealing myself would have killed our friendship, among other problems, and I was happy to have avoided it. I cleared my throat and placed another tile. "Okay. How's Cam doing?"

"Oh, he's fine." She placed her tile, looking sad. "We were going to meet tomorrow, but with all this, I doubt I'll get out the door anytime soon. Speaking of Cam, though, can you do me a favor?"

"Sure, anything you need." I meant it, too. If it didn't involve outing myself—which I'd been prepared to do if I thought it might flip her attitude toward the Pro-Earth League—I'd do whatever I could to make her happy.

"Thanks." She paused. "I want to play some games, the four of us, on Saturday. Can you and Bee get that virtual tabletop set up?"

I nodded, placed another piece, and raised an eyebrow at her. "That's it? Definitely."

We played for another hour or so, but then it was time to head back to the green room. I had messages to send to Mindstorm, a plan to talk over with Bee, and—unfortunately—classes to study for unless I wanted to repeat all this next year. So, I said my goodbyes, quickly called Bee, and waited for her to show up.

The moment she pulled up, I was in the car, buckling my seatbelt. "So, how'd it go?" Bianca asked.

"It went well. We didn't get what Mindstorm wanted, but I also didn't have to use the nuclear option. Instead, we've got a way for APPEAL and the Pro-Earth League to start coming to terms, and some insight into what her club's thinking."

"I still think it's wild that Mindstorm cares so much about the local chapter. She barely mentioned the national APPEAL group as being important," Bee said.

I paused at that. It *was* strange; even Su-Bin had invoked the larger APPEAL organization to give her argument more weight. Why hadn't Mindstorm put any thought into the bigger picture? A thought struck me, and I grabbed my phone to pull up the lists of supers who'd joined each faction. The progalaxy faction, as they were calling themselves, had almost triple the members we did—and they looked stronger, overall.

That didn't bode well, and there was no way Mindstorm was unaware of that. So, if she knew what was happening, what was her plan? I asked Bee, but she didn't have any idea, either.

When we finally pulled into the Walnut Tower parking lot and headed up to the green room, I could tell that Bee had been busy. The door with the star and Rocko's studio name was boarded up in such a haphazard way I couldn't help but laugh. When I did, she glared at me. "Mindstorm put out a message asking us to secure our hideouts. I spent most of my time back in the Outback Stakeout Zone, tearing down all your plans and making sure they were thrown away."

"And then I called you before you could finish . . . this?"

"Yeah. We're at war, so we can't have a way for the enemy to get directly into our fortress."

"Not that it'll matter if Tapdance joins their side and levels Tokyexico," I muttered.

Bianca nodded. Then she grabbed my laptop, and I started composing an email. Mindstorm had to know what we'd learned.

32

What We'd Learned

"Thank you for rejoining me," Mindstorm said. Fursona, Lady Lockless, and a few other college heroes and villains, along with me, had reconvened in Mindstorm's lair. The complete absence of any super more powerful than mid-minor league was glaringly obvious, though; only Mindstorm and McHammer were still here. "I have come up with . . . a plan."

Sara-N-Dipity stared at her professor stonily. Mindstorm's lip lifted just slightly in what might be interpreted as a smile, or maybe a sneer. I shivered a little. We'd entered a new room—a dark one with two digital maps covered in red and green dots. As I watched, two more green dots crossed North America and arrived in Yorkston. It was the only city where the numbers were even close.

Everywhere else, red outnumbered green two to one, three to one, or by even more.

"You think this plan will work?" Sara-N-Dipity asked.

"I . . . don't know," Mindstorm admitted. "That's the only reason you're still here, Sara. Otherwise, I'd have moved you to Yorkston. If you're still . . . in this room, you're essential to the plan. Everyone else is in Yorkston, trying to put pressure on the pro-Ilneat supers and force them to defend there. Or . . . they're The Narrator and cannot be moved. Regardless, that is a feint. The real battle will happen here, in Tokyexico City."

"Really?" I asked.

Mindstorm nodded. "We've learned a few things in the last couple of days. One is that every connecting point between the Ilneats' Hot Zone and the rest of Earth has been severed, with no . . . exceptions. They have holed up in their Hot Zones, and normally, that would be the end of it. If we cannot reach them, we cannot hurt them. However . . . we have an ace in the hole."

"Who?" Fursona asked.

Lady Lockless cleared her throat. "I've been trying like you asked, Mindstorm, but the Ilneats have their base blockaded, not just locked up, and every time I try to break in, the fuzz shows up out of nowhere. I can't jimmy those locks."

"That's not . . . surprising. It does tell us what we need to know, though. I still believe you can do this." Mindstorm told her, staring at the ballgown-clad woman. "We simply need to find the correct door. I believe I . . . know where one is. Now, as for the public support, what I'm about to . . . lay out for you must be executed cleanly, in such a way that no Extras are hurt. Do you understand, everyone? It must be done perfectly, or I fear the . . . APPEAL-oriented Extras won't come around."

She took a bite of delivery noodles—cold, and obviously from the night before— while we nodded slowly.

Things were moving fast all of a sudden. I didn't like it.

I had no idea what our odds were. Sara said we had a 30% chance of success, and as Fursona, the rest of the Pro-Earth League's minor- and little-league ladies, and I changed into our Costumes in a bathroom we'd conveniently blocked off with Lady Lockless's power for just that purpose, I was shocked it was that high. To make this work, even Mindstorm had left for Yorkston, making it super obvious she was going.

I shivered and finished my transformation. Without her, our only backup with any firepower was McHammer—well, him, Kaiju-sona, and Super Girl Spotlight Star. But our major-league modes were limited, and I wasn't sure how well we'd be able to do against heroes like Stella-Lunar or The Triad, who *hadn't* left. We had a plan for them, but Stella was . . . powerful.

"Bee, you ready for this?" I asked.

"No. You?"

I hesitated, because the truth was that even though the odds were not in our favor no matter who was calling it, I was. This was a better plan than trying to crash the Hot Zone with a giant lizard and a walking demolition crew. It had subtlety, fore-thought, and, most importantly, speed. The only part I didn't like was our first target, but Mindstorm had insisted, and Sara agreed.

The Tokyexico Council of Heroes building gave us our best shot at a door into a Hot Zone.

So, once Gourmet, Tractor-Beam-Girl, and the four other Magical Girls had finished in their stalls, I put my hand on the door. Sara sent a quick text to the boys across the street, and we waited. Things had to be executed perfectly for this to work.

"Three," Sara said.

My eyes narrowed. Who knew what we'd be fighting when that door opened? It depended on how quickly we could take the tower and turn its defenses toward keeping the pro-Ilneat supers out, but one thing was certain. Without the tower, we couldn't execute any further phases of the plan.

"Two."

I could feel sweat below my impeccably clean glove. Behind me, Kaiju-sona smacked one clawed fist into the other, ready for battle. Magical Girls Candi Crush, Foamy Flash, Sugar, and Chili Powder had formed an impromptu team, and they'd be the first out since they had the most challenging job. We'd move out behind a shield of bubbles and spice, but after that, it'd be mayhem. But all we had to do was get McHammer to the Council of Heroes. He was pretty confident he could do the rest.

"One."

I opened the door and, as the rest of the Pro-Earth League rushed out into the street, accepted a **[Casting Call]** without thinking about it.

[Casting Call]
[Episode: Power War: The Battle of Mid-Town - R]
[Role: Rebellious Raider! Do you accept the role? (Yes/No)]
[Role Focus: Drama + Flamboyance]
[Power War: The Battle of Mid-Town: Act One in Progress]

Things went wrong almost immediately.

"Attention, villains," a familiar voice shouted out. I recognized it immediately; I'd first heard it in an Episode, and I had her poster on my wall back at home, but more importantly, Stella-Lunar had clobbered me last year when I tried to defend a wrecked, helpless Vigilant Vow. "I swore to defend Tokyexico in starlight and under new moon. To stand against evil and corruption. And, above all, to remain true to what's right and just. So witness star, so witness moon."

I shivered, getting ready to **[Quick-Time Change]** into Super Girl Spotlight Star just to try to have a chance. But before I could, the other Magical Girls stepped up. "Mindstorm said this might happen. The four of us can take her," Foamy Flash said. Her voice wasn't exactly filled with confidence.

"Okay." I nodded. "You've got this."

As the four little- and minor-league Magical Girls squared off against Earth's mightiest hero, I took a deep breath and tried to put that fight behind me. All around, other supers were already fighting with each other. Lord Destructo stood in the middle of the street, with Theseus, Gourmet, and The Crumb all engaging him. Despite hating each other, Tractor-Beam-Girl and Flare were fighting with Grapple and Tearjerker.

As Fursona and I headed toward the Council of Heroes building, every step we took unattacked felt both nerve-wracking and exhilarating. Could we really make it? The door was fifty feet away. Thirty. Ten. We crashed through the glass, sending shattered shards across the first floor's tile as a super caromed off the asphalt behind us.

Three heroes stood in the lobby, and I cursed. "Shit. Hi, Tele-Portal."

"Hi. Guess this is happening." My old mentor stood on her stilts, bouncing slightly. Slightly ahead of her and to the left, The Underdelver revved his mech's drills. And hovering slightly behind both, I could see Bud Lightbeam, Bud Lightbeam, and Bud Lightbeam, ready for battle.

I decided to fire first. **[Limelight Barrage]** picked me up, spun me around, and sent a volley of beams across the hall toward Tele-Portal. Fursona had declared her the team's leader—or as close to one as they had. She was a force multiplier, and if we could take her—

"Oh shit!" I said, throwing myself to the floor as the hero's portal cannon opened a gate in front of her and another next to me. All five **[Starlances]** ripped out of the portal and surged toward me, then, at the last second, swerved back toward The Triad. Tele-Portal shifted her portal, and I hit the tile again. I'd just gotten up!

Kaiju-sona roared, her fursuit's arms over her head, and vomited flame toward The Underdelver as she rushed him. They clashed like a pair of titans, the shock wave almost visible. And Bud Lightbeam fired a trio of lasers across the room—which I dodged. Barely.

"**[Starlance]**! **[Starlance]**!" I shouted, adding two more beams to Tele-Portal's portal juggling. The improved handling on them was keeping a ton of lances in play, and if I could just add a few more, maybe Tele-Portal would be too busy keeping them out of the fight to help her teammates.

It was the best plan I had. From what I could hear outside, we weren't getting any help in here. Beams, bubbles, and explosions had filled the air even before we made it in.

It took almost twenty seconds of dodging and overloading Tele-Portal, and I ate a Bud Lightbeam laser trying, but eventually, I *thought* I'd gotten Tele-Portal out of the fight. She was spawning new portals faster than I could see, and the incredible lightshow in the Council of Heroes' lobby almost felt like a strobe light. One of my rays hit The Underdelver, then another. His mech hardly seemed to notice, though.

[Dramatic Damage! +1 Drama Point]
[Dramatic Damage! +1 Drama Point]

"Attack Pattern Three!" Tele-Portal shouted, and The Triad disengaged. As she juggled my **[Starlances]**, they formed up differently; this time with Bud Lightbeam and his clones in the lead.

"Tele-Portal, you can't really think you're on the right side, here?" I asked, getting ready to fire another **[Starlance]**.

She didn't reply. Instead, she yawned and snapped a finger, opening a massive portal in front of her team. Another opened above us, and it was all I could do to avoid the three lasers that cut across us from overhead. But at the same time, all the [**Starlances**] I'd launched *finally* started hitting things.

[Dramatic Damage! +9 Drama Points]

Tele-Portal staggered, and even The Underdelver's mech seemed to rock slightly from the barrage that hit him as he covered her. For a moment, I let myself hope that I'd done some meaningful damage.

But another portal opened, and another, and suddenly, Fursona and I were cut off by a constant line of lasers. I'd said Tele-Portal was a force multiplier before. But I'd never seen her do anything like this. As she and Bud Lightbeam sliced the lobby's tile and fake plants to pieces, their barrage pushed Fursona into a smaller and smaller space for her continued duel with The Underdelver.

At the same time, I realized Tele-Portal wasn't grabbing all the lasers. The three Bud Lightbeams were pressuring me, and she was only redirecting the attacks that threatened her team. As another beam sliced across my superhero damage shield and left my shoulder blade burning, I realized that something had to change.

[HP 8/14]

Actually, one thing specifically had to change. Me.
Otherwise, we were going to lose.
So I started up a [**Power-Weaving**] combo and used [**Quick-Time Change**], freezing the lasers. We had to take out *someone*, and I had an idea for beating the Genius piloting the mech suit. I couldn't beat him as a Genius, but I *could* overload his systems. So, with an Itsy Bitsy Spider and a quick dodge through the lasers during [**Freeze-Frame**], I ducked toward my girlfriend and her opponent.

[Flashy Fitting-Room! +1 Flamboyance Point]
[Steel Yourself! +1 Grit Point]
[Floating Points: 1 Flamboyance]

If I could overload his mech, The Underdelver wouldn't be a threat anymore. It was the fastest way to even the odds. So, as I rushed forward and used [**Thunder-head**] to knock the Bud Lightbeams away and start powering up my attack, all my focus was on the Genius.

[Pause for Effect! +1 Drama Point]
[Floating Points: 3 Flamboyance, 1 Grit]

And that's why I didn't see another portal open right behind me. As the storm cloud overhead darkened, I started using [**Ride the Lightning**]. But even as the storm charged around me, a fist reached out and slammed into my back. My lightning burst stopped charging and melted away. The blow itself hadn't hurt, but Tele-Portal had turned the tables on me. "You broke my combo!"

[Combo Broken! Floating Points Lost. Power Lost.]

33

Broken Combo

"Yep," Tele-Portal said, stepping out of her portal toward me. The Underdelver was all caught up fighting with Kaiju-sona, but that left me with Tele-Portal and Bud Lightbeam, who was closing in. I'd missed my window to even our odds.

Bud's lasers ripped across me, dropping my superhero damage precipitously even as I whirled and used **[Wind Front]** to buffet Tele-Portal away. She took the hit, and so did I, but my blow barely hurt her. I *couldn't* take another Bud Lightbeam hit.

[HP 2/14]
[**Badass Move! +1 Badass Point**]
[**Thunderstruck! +1 Drama Point**]

And luckily for me, I didn't have to.

A heartbeat later—maybe two, since mine was redlining—something heavy crashed through the atrium's doors. It hit the Bud Lightbeams, scattering them like bowling pins as Tele-Portal opened a portal and dove through it. Whoever or whatever it was didn't matter. What mattered was that this was my window; I used **[Quick-Time Change]** and switched to Copy Cat. "Let's get moving!"

[**Flashy Fitting-Room! +1 Flamboyance Point**]
[**Rejuvenation Activated: HP 7/14**]

"Got it!" Kaiju-sona didn't look great; she definitely hadn't been winning her one-on-one with The Underdelver. But even so, we got moving, heading for the stairs. The mech suit stomped after us until we got to the stairs. Then it stopped.

It couldn't fit—or maybe The Underdelver knew the stairs couldn't handle the machine's weight. Either way, we had a second or two to escape and regroup.

A portal opened right in front of us, and Bud Lightbeam stepped through it, along with his clones. Kaiju-sona didn't waste any time, throwing herself right at the superhero and driving two of them into the ground. One stayed up—for another second or so before I used **[Pouncing Panther]** to hit him, bounce off a wall, and hit him again.

[Badass Damage! +1 Badass Point]

We had to pump out as much damage as possible, then leave. I didn't need to tell Fursona that, and she didn't say anything to me. We both knew we were finished if the whole Triad caught up. In melee, though, Bud Lightbeam wasn't as much of a threat.

So I used **[Doom Ball]** before he could fire another laser. My claws ripped into his suit, opening wounds across his body. He might be able to fly, and he might have laser vision, but he wasn't tougher than normal.

[Badass Damage! +4 Badass Points]

Fursona was ripping into her Buds, too, but one fought his way free and threw himself back into the portal. I thought about taking another leap and finishing him off, but he'd almost certainly landed near the rest of The Triad. I couldn't risk it. Instead, I grabbed Fursona's clawed hand and started running. We hauled ass down the . . . hall . . . only stopping to duck into a men's restroom nearby. Hopefully, The Triad wouldn't look there.

Even more hopefully, they wouldn't pull the security footage.

[End of Act One: Act Two in Three Minutes]

"Well, I hope the other teams are having better luck than we are," Fursona said quietly from our hiding place in one of the stalls.

I nodded. "This is going . . . well."

"Uh-huh? How do you figure this is fine?"

"Well, we've got one of the two biggest threats in here, and the other is fighting a four-on-one outside. Hopefully, the other battles will go in our favor, and we'll get some reinforcements. Plus, The Triad's probably dealing with whoever got thrown through the first floor earlier. That gives us some time to make a plan."

Fursona shook her head, sending her googly eyestalks bouncing wildly. Under other circumstances, it would have been funny. But as it stood, I wasn't in a laughing mood. I might think we could win this, but I wasn't pretending it'd be easy. I shifted back to Magical Girl Understudy. "We need to capitalize on this distraction and plan for a big fight. Hopefully, one at the top of the tower."

"Uh, Understudy, you know I won't be able to use Full Kaiju up there, right?"

"No," I said, rolling my eyes. "I don't know that. I *do* know it'll be really destructive when you use Full Kaiju up there. So, our prep needs to be clearing the building. Any ideas?"

"Yeah. Get Tele-Portal to do it for us. That's what her power's best for." Fursona stretched, shoulders popping under her suit. "But how to do that?"

"I have . . . an idea. But it's not a good one."

[Power War: The Battle of Mid-Town: Act Two in Progress]

"You were right," Fursona shouted as we sprinted toward one of the stairwells, "this is a bad idea!"

"Well, I'm open to other ones!" I shouted back.

The moment we left the bathroom heading for the stairwell, Bud Lightbeam appeared. This time, though, he was outside the building, firing his lasers in and turning the hall we had to traverse into a death trap. Worse, Tele-Portal had opened some gates, and was doubling the number of beams—and aiming them from the far side.

It only took a second longer to see Fursona's point. "Yeah, you're right. We won't make it all the way. Do it here!"

"You're sure?"

"Yeah. We'll get what we want either way! Just do it!"

Fursona nodded. She sucked in a deep breath, then vomited fire straight up—right at a smoke detector. As alarms rippled across the building and sprinklers started soaking the dark blue and green carpets on the second floor, I nodded. "Now, we keep the fighting away from the stairs. Keep evacuation routes open as best we can. And keep moving up!"

One of Bud Lightbeam's lasers ripped across me, but with all the water in the air, it . . . I wouldn't say tickled, but it didn't hurt anywhere near as badly as it had earlier. It was like the concentrated light had dissipated instead of hitting at full strength. I grinned; neutralizing Bud Lightbeam hadn't been my plan—in fact, I hadn't realized he even had this weakness. Then again, I'd never seen a Triad Episode in the rain, so . . .

[HP 5/14]

It wasn't like I could take a lot of those hits, though. We needed to keep moving, so I sprinted toward the elevator shaft. Fursona's claws worked their way into the gap between the closed doors, and she hissed from the effort of prying them open.

At the same time, the floor collapsed behind us, and The Underdelver pulled himself up through a gap between I-beams, framed by the fire behind him. "ATTEN-TION, VILLAINS! SURRENDER NOW!" an automated voice blasted from the machine's speakers as its drills revved.

Something told me a little water wasn't going to stop this guy.

So I gave him a full **[Limelight Barrage]** at nearly point-blank. The **[Starlances]** peppered his mech, bouncing off steel and ripping into rubber joints. He raised a drill to block the ones aimed for his face plate, and I followed up the attack with a **[Starlance]** by itself that he managed to swat out of the air with his arm.

[Dramatic Damage! +3 Drama Points]

I hadn't dealt critical damage, but as far as I could tell, The Triad's biggest weakness wasn't mobility or firepower, but healing. If I could get chip damage now, maybe we could pull something off later.

The door screeched open behind me even as The Underdelver's drill punched toward my shoulder. I ducked, summoned my sailboard with **[Solar Wing]**, and took off, grabbing Kaiju-sona. We tore up the elevator shaft, aiming for the very top.

Fursona clung to my steering bar and leaned back into me, treating me like a safety harness. I could hardly blame her; we rocketed up through a narrow, but perfectly vertical, tube that happened to be nearly pitch-black. If it wasn't for my neon contrails, we wouldn't have any light at all.

That was the only thing that warned us about the oncoming elevator.

It caught us from behind; as it zoomed toward us, I dropped **[Solar Wing]**, landing as elegantly as possible on the speeding steel box. Fursona's own landing wasn't so graceful, but I didn't have time to deal with it. Neither of us did; this thing was overclocking its speed. "Find the door and open it!" I snapped.

"Way ahead of you!" Fursona's claws scrabbled for purchase on the maintenance door in the elevator's ceiling, and she dribbled fire from her mouth like a toddler to light her work. Suddenly the door popped free, and I dropped through the hole. Fursona followed a moment later.

Not that the impact wouldn't *hurt* when this thing reached its stopping point. It definitely would, but at least we wouldn't be crushed quite as badly.

"Brace!" I yelled, **[Quick-Time Changing]** into Copy Cat again.

The entire world devolved into shrieking metal and plush as I finished the transformation.

Fursona threw herself over me as the ceiling stopped and the floor kept moving. The elevator's doors gave first, bending violently outward into the . . . whichever floor we'd stopped on. The other three walls crumpled, collapsing inward and squeezing Fursona and me into an increasingly tight space. Dust filled the air, and a few alarms went off.

But when it was over, Fursona and I were more or less okay.

I went invisible with **[Set Dressing]**. Then I wormed my way out from the wreckage while Fursona started freeing her bigger, bulkier form. "I'll see where we are," I whispered.

[Dastardly Plan! +1 Cunning Point]

"Got it," she replied, trying—and failing—to be quiet.

The hall was familiar. But then again, the Council of Heroes building was corporate as hell, so it could just be reminding me of the first floor—or the second. Or the hospital wing; I'd been *there* before. But it only took one look at the nameplates next to nearby doors to know exactly where I was. I hurried through the hall, heading toward an office I *knew* would be nearby. "Fursona, this is Dr. Ayers's floor. I'm making sure she's on her way out before you start your growth cycle."

"Got it. I'm almost out, and I don't think The Triad knows exactly where we are."

"Okay. I think we're two floors below the Council of Heroes."

"I'll see you in a couple of minutes, then. Lots of junk to move here."

I kept moving. Dr. Ayers's office was just a few doors down, and I jerked the door open without knocking.

And there she was. Curly black hair, streaks of gray, and a coffee cup. But what struck me was the headset she was wearing—and that she looked right at me.

"Hello, Understudy. I'm sorry, but counseling is closed due to an emergency," she said.

"You're a . . . super?" I asked, dumbfounded. Had she lied to me? And how had she known I was Understudy? Actually, that second one was a dumb question. She'd probably watched some of my Episodes, after all.

"No, but a therapist is always prepared, and with all the chaos outside, I wanted to be ready before I evacuated. The device is Genius-made, and it helps me see the unseen. Like you."

I relaxed. "So, now what?"

"Now, I head for the elevator and leave," she said.

"I wouldn't. It crashed on its way up, and definitely won't make it back down." As if to punctuate my words, I heard it screech and start tumbling back down the shaft. My heart pounded. Had Fursona gotten clear?

Then I felt something looming behind me. "Hi, Fursona," I said. "Meet Dr. Ayers."

"Hello, Fursona, nice to meet you. I'm Understudy's therapist. She's told me so much about you," Dr. Ayers said, sticking her hand out for a shake.

Fursona did not shake. "Understudy, we need to keep moving. Dr. Ayers, we'll talk later. I'm not convinced you're doing what's best for my partner, and that bothers me, but now's not the time. Stairs are past the . . . wreckage."

Dr. Ayers nodded stiffly. "Of course. I hope you two lose, of course, but either way, we'll meet later. I'll call you."

And just like that, my therapist disappeared.

"Think that's everyone?" I asked.

"Probably not, but—"

Before I could finish, the building shook. "What was that?" Fursona asked.

I didn't know. But I had a bad feeling I was about to find out.

34

Find Out

Staring down through the wall-to-wall glass windows on the upper half of the Tokyexico Council of Heroes building, I could see the fight raging below.

I couldn't tell who was winning.

Three Magical Girls were airborne, while Foamy Flash surfed a massive wave of suds with Bubble-Bill. Explosions of bubbles and beam weapons filled the air, punctuated by huge bursts of light as Stella-Lunar used her powers. I couldn't find Chili Powder, and Candi Crush had been grounded.

Farther down the road, Flare was playing more conservatively than I'd ever seen him fight while Tractor-Beam-Girl cried on the asphalt. Tearjerker must have gotten her, leaving Flare to handle both her and Grapple. He couldn't get in close against the wrestling-themed hero, so that left strafing and harassing the two progalaxy supers.

And, as I peered down, I saw a man in parachute pants wielding a hammer finish crushing some vil I didn't know. He sprinted toward the Council of Heroes building, and I smiled as he got inside. "Okay, Fursona, we need to keep pushing. McHammer's inside. Let's keep his path clear."

The Council of Heroes' room was only a couple floors up. If we could get there, we could checkmate them or force them onto the battlefield. Either was a win.

There were only three things standing in our way, and they stepped out of a portal as we headed toward the next flight of stairs.

"Magical Girl Understudy, you were supposed to be better than this," Tele-Portal said. She sounded bored, but I knew she was just burning the candle at every possible end by using her power. "I *taught* you better than this."

"You did. That's why I have to stand up for what I think is right," I retorted. "Why aren't you fighting for the right side?"

"I am. You're too young to remember anything about pre-Launch Day, but things are better now. They're more peaceful. You know that other than Man vs. Nature and

Power Wars, we haven't had a single war in the last twenty years? Do you know the last time there wasn't a war on Earth before that?"

"No."

"Basically never. So sometimes Extras get hurt? It sucks, and it shouldn't happen, but it's an acceptable price for peace."

I pondered that. Then I shook my head. "It's not worth the cost. Heroes should be doing better than this, and I think the Ilneats are making us worse."

"I disagree," Tele-Portal said. "Are we going to fight about it?"

"Yes. [**Starlance**]!" I fired a bolt at my former mentor, expecting her to juggle it like she had before. Instead, she took the blow right to her face, reacting like she'd been slapped.

[**Dramatic Damage! +1 Drama Point**]

Then, before I could see what had happened, I was outside the tower, falling. I used [**Solar Wing**] and caught myself midair, staring at the portal I'd been thrown out of. It disappeared from the side of the building, and I realized that Tele-Portal had set up a trap. I'd need to move quickly if I wanted to get back to Fursona before—

[HP 2/14]

A massive beam of solid white light filled the air, and even though it only clipped me, it was enough to tell that Stella-Lunar had gained some power since the last time we'd fought. A quick spin through the air broke my fall toward the tower's sloping side, and also let me see that Stella-Lunar wasn't focused on me. I was collateral damage in this case.

That didn't fill me with confidence in handling The Triad, but I didn't have a choice. If I didn't hurry, they'd kick Fursona's butt, then turn on me. I rocketed toward the building, heedless of whether or not Stella had seen me. "Fursona, now's the time!"

"You're sure?" Bee's voice came over my earbud. "Now?"

"Yeah! Three! Two! One!"

The entire side of the Tokyexico Council of Heroes building erupted in a shower of glass, steel, and concrete as Kaiju-sona surged to her full size.

The Council of Heroes building disintegrated into a cloud of glass fragments that rained down on the fighting below us. Heroes and villains alike scattered, running for cover. And over the sounds of twisting, screaming steel, and shattering windows, Full Kaiju roared.

I stopped midair. She was clinging to the skyscraper's frame like a gorilla, gushing a spout of flame straight up. But even as she did, The Triad was already moving to counter her, and the damage wasn't enough for me to break into the Council of Heroes' room and try for the checkmate.

The only play was to force multiply off her, so I used **[Quick-Time Change]**, let the choral music wash over me as a hood covered my face, and used my seconds of **[Freeze-Frame]** to get through the still-flying rubble and duck into the building—behind The Triad.

[Advanced Accessories: Magical Girl Understudy, Magical Girl Rainy Day, Copy Cat]
[Skill Siphon Activated: Style Points Disabled]
[Meter's Running: 7/8]

The plan was refreshingly simple from here. Fursona and I had been over it a dozen times; she'd soak damage while I tried to wipe out two members of the major-league team. I had *no idea* if I had that kind of firepower, and that's why I couldn't start with The Underdelver.

Instead, I used **[Power-Weaving]** before anyone could turn to see me and fired my **[Limelight Barrage]** on Bud Lightbeam. The four **[Maximum Starlances]** rocketed into his back and another Bud's back, popping both clones instantly. At the same time, extra **[Stellar Rays]** jumped from the impacts to spread damage all around The Triad.

[Dramatic Damage!]
[Meter's Running: 6/8]

Before they could turn, I was already shifting to my next heavy hitting power. **[Doom Ball]** activated as I hit the last Bud Lightbeam, and before he could clone again, I had my nails ripping into his Costume and opening skin. At this range, he couldn't use his flight or cloning, and I was behind him, so he couldn't laser me in the face, either. The wounds I opened were bigger than anything I'd ever caused.

[Badass Damage!]
[Meter's Running: 5/8]
[Floating Points]

I didn't even get combo points in Spotlight Star? That was disappointing.

He hit the ground, and a moment later, a massive set of claws crashed down on him as I jumped free. Fursona hadn't targeted him, but in her attempts to keep The Underdelver off me, she'd accidentally crushed him.

Or not.

As her arm lifted, I could tell he'd been portaled to safety before the blow could land. But even so, he was out of the fight—at least for now. That was all I could ask for.

The next move was more of a puzzle: how best to crack The Underdelver's armor? I'd wanted to do this earlier, but Tele-Portal had interfered. This time, though? She didn't know I was comboing. In fact, she probably had no idea what I *was* doing.

I [**Rode the Lightning**] and let the goddess of thunder take over. The white light and flaring tendrils of electricity filled the air, all pointing toward The Underdelver. As I moved, the big fluorescent lights cracked overhead, and sparks danced across the mech suit's drills.

[**Electric Lightshow!**]
[**Meter's Running: 4/8**]
[**Floating Points**]

I was halfway done. Once I'd tapped out Super Girl Spotlight Star, it'd just be me, and I *needed* to knock out at least one more member of The Triad. So, as The Underdelver's mech slowly turned toward me, creaking and sparking, I used [**Starlance**].

[**Dramatic Damage!**]
[**Meter's Running: 3/8**]
[**Power-Weaving!**]

The single [**Maximum Starlance**] hit The Underdelver, boring a hole right through the weakened steel plates and into his body. Acrid smoke poured from the rig, and a moment later, the machine let out a loud "EJECT EJECT EJECT!" The man who'd been piloting it flew out the top and right into a portal before vanishing. The extra [**Stellar Ray**] caught Tele-Portal, knocking her into a wall on her stilts.

At the same moment, the Bud Lightbeams returned. He was airborne, firing his lasers at Full Kaiju Fursona for all he was worth. I could hear her sucking down juice boxes through my headphones, but she couldn't quite return fire.

So, with The Underdelver's mech a smoking ruin behind me, I turned toward the only other super who could stop us. Bud Lightbeam had made a mistake; out there in the air, Tele-Portal couldn't help him anywhere near as much. And I was going to capitalize on it.

I used [**Solar Wing**], very, *very* aware that I was almost out of moves and that I couldn't hit all three clones. But I *did* have a play in mind—one that could let Fursona deal the finishing blow.

[**Meter's Running: 2/8**]

I looped around behind the cloning superhero, got in close, and used [**Thunderhead**]. The storm started brewing, but that wasn't the part of the power I'd cared about. Even as the first knockback hit the three clones and pushed them closer to the massive lizard clinging to the Council of Heroes building, I was already using [**Wind Front**] to follow up.

[**Pause for Effect!**]
[**Badass Move!**]
[**Meter's Running: 0/8**]

The hurricane-force wind threw the Buds right into Fursona, who wrapped them up in a one-armed bear hug and breathed fire right into them. The clones vanished, and a moment later, she tossed the last one into the building. He rolled, arms flailing, and stopped right in front of Tele-Portal.

At the same time, I transformed back into Understudy. I'd only had eight moves, and I'd capitalized on them perfectly this time. And now, all we had to do was beat one support hero.

As I landed next to Fursona's lizard leg, Tele-Portal shook her head at me. "Understudy, you've grown a lot. That was pretty impressive. It'll take Bud and Underdelver a few minutes to recover, even back at base. But I can't let you go up those stairs. You're not ready for the Council of Heroes."

I shook my head at my former mentor. "We've beaten you, Tele-Portal. Whatever they're hiding up there for, Fursona and I have proven we've got the right to fight them. And we're not alone. McHammer's on his way."

She nodded slowly, trying not to yawn. "Fine. Don't say I didn't warn you." Then, before I could say anything else, she vanished.

[**End of Act Two: Act Three in Three Minutes**]

"Okay, I think it's over. You can come down now," I said, patting Fursona's ankle. It was as high on her Full Kaiju form as I could reach. "We won."

Fursona shrank, worming through the twisted metal she'd created as she returned to her normal size. The sound of furious straw-sucking filled my ear for a second. Then she cleared her throat. "What did she mean by that last bit?"

"I have no idea. Let's find out." I walked toward the stairwell just as our parachute pants–wearing, villainous ally stepped out the door.

He took one look at the missing side of the building and whistled. "Damn, you two make a mess. Did you evacuate people first, as per the plan?"

"Yeah. Started a little fire, then checked the offices up here. There shouldn't be any Extras around," Fursona said.

"Good. Let's keep moving."

The Council of Heroes was only two stories up from where we'd fought The Triad, but a solid steel door was in our way. "No problem," McHammer said. His hammer crashed into the lock once. Twice. Three times.

As he worked on breaking in, I steeled myself. I didn't have much left in the tank, not for a room full of major-leaguers. Whatever we found inside, it was going to be one hell of a fight. But we had to win. There wasn't a choice; Mindstorm and the rest of the Pro-Earth League were counting on us.

As the sixth hammer blow landed, the door buckled. McHammer pushed it open, and we rushed into a wide, circular room with blacked-out windows. Arrayed against us were five heroes. One woman wore power armor, while another looked more dressed for a ski race. A man in spandex stood at the head of a table. Another was dressed in a white suit, with white hair and white skin. And, last but not least, an archer held a glowing crossbow at his shoulder.

[Power War: The Battle of Mid-Town: Act Three in Progress]

McHammer didn't waste any time. Before the door even finished hitting the ground, he gave a berserker roar and rushed the nearest hero—the woman in the power armor. His hammer swung back, then slammed into her torso.

She shattered.

35

Shattered

The power armor folded like paper as McHammer's . . . hammer . . . smashed through it. I froze halfway through my mad dash into the room, a **[Limelight Barrage]** dying on my lips. I'd expected the blow to break bones and reveal bruised skin, but instead, under the flimsy power armor, there was . . . nothing. A delicate metal spine. Some intricate-looking mechanical bits that had fanned across the floor. And . . . empty space. She wasn't human. She was . . . a bot?

I froze as Crossbow raised his bow. "Back off, villains. We won't ask twice." The other council members dropped into fighting stances as McHammer finished smashing the power-armored robot. But none of them moved—not to help their fallen, fake comrade, and not to attack McHammer, either. The bow pointed at me, then at Fursona, moving between us almost too fast to follow.

What was going on?

None of this made sense. The rough pile of gears and struts that had, ten seconds ago, been one of the council members sparked and popped as a small fire broke out in her . . . heart? I'd thought . . . I don't know what I'd thought. That the Council was working with the Ilneats, maybe? Or that they were retired heroes from before my time. But not this.

McHammer hefted his maul. "You don't even have to ask once," he replied. And, just like that, he rushed the remaining four council members.

Crossbow's bolt took him in the chest, knocking him aside for a moment, but he recovered almost instantly as the hero backpedaled and reloaded. A moment later, Fursona roared into battle; she had to be tired out after being Full Kaiju, but she doggedly slammed into the ski racer. A second later, something crashed into *her*, knocking her back a foot or two.

I blasted the man in the white suit with a **[Starlance]**. Even as the bolt of energy left my wand, I prepared for a bigger **[Limelight Barrage]** in case the first attack wasn't enough. After all, we had four major-league heroes to deal with—assuming they weren't robots, too.

[Dramatic Damage! +1 Drama Point]

They were.

Suddenly, there were two. The white-suited man went down with a smoking hole in his chest, while Crossbow—or whatever he was—wouldn't be getting up anytime soon. The one Fursona was in the process of mauling wasn't looking so good, though the spandex-clad man hadn't been hit yet.

I raised my wand and started blasting.

The "fight," if you could call it that, only lasted fifteen seconds. When it had finished, digital voice boxes and chunks of motherboards littered the oval-shaped room's floor, every camera we could find had been smashed, and a thin electric-smelling smoke hung in the air.

We'd taken the Tokyexico Council of Heroes building.

But the Episode still wasn't over.

"What's next?" I asked McHammer. The plan hadn't accounted for such a quick victory—or at least, the version I'd heard hadn't. I was both relieved that we'd pulled it off and apprehensive about what came next, especially when my phone buzzed. I blocked the call without thinking more about it. Rocko wasn't someone I wanted to talk to today. Or at all, probably.

"Next, we sit tight for a bit, ladies," McHammer said. He walked to the bucket seat the Crossbow bot had been in, plopped down in it, and started fiddling with his watch. "Reinforcements are going to be a few minutes. We need to get ready for their arrival; once they're here, we can consolidate and plan our next move."

That sounded . . . reasonable. Surprisingly reasonable, especially coming from a villain I'd always figured was more the berserker type. I nodded and settled into the ski-racer's seat. Fursona stood near the door, no doubt not wanting to bend her tail trying to wriggle into a chair of her own. "So we just hold it for a couple of minutes? That's it?"

"Yeah, pretty much. She'll either show up herself or send reinforcements. From there, even Stella won't be a threat. Don't want to say it'll be easy, because—"

An explosion from below interrupted McHammer before he could finish.

"That, huh?" I asked, popping to my feet and running to a shattered window.

"Yeah, that." Tele-Portal stepped through a portal behind me. "I warned you not to go up here, but here you are. The only option now is surrender."

McHammer cleared his throat. He hadn't stood up when the explosion happened, and he still looked relaxed as he leaned back in Crossbow's seat. "Lady, you're the fifth hero who's told me that today. One of them's over there." He pointed at the wreckage scattered across the room.

I tried my best. "Tele-Portal, it's over. Even if your team's back up and running, we've got the building, Stella-Lunar's out of position, and it's only a matter of time before we lock down control here. I'm asking you, as your intern and auxiliary, to back off. Please."

"Yeah," McHammer said. "Back off before someone gets hurt . . . permanently. Right now, we can call this the Episode. If it keeps going, it'll turn into something else."

"What?" Tele-Portal asked, eyes narrowing and mouth yawning. Boredom or exhaustion, I couldn't tell.

"Your finale."

I stood up. Fursona loomed behind her, but the still-open portal cut off her line of attack. If things happened, we'd be separated, and I'd have to fix that quickly. Somehow, I doubted that Bud Lightbeam and The Underdelver were ready to go again, but I also didn't know what their base's capabilities were—only that they were major-leaguers, so anything was possible.

Including, apparently, a second Underdelver mech that juggernauted its way out of the portal and slammed into McHammer as he stood and swung his maul in a wide arc!

I reacted quickly, putting a full **[Limelight Barrage]** into Tele-Portal before Bud Lightbeam could join the fight. The **[Stellar Ray]** offshoots aimed toward the mech suit, which seemed to shrug them off. Tele-Portal was less fortunate; her exhaustion was showing, and she couldn't get a redirection portal up in time to stop the damage.

[Dramatic Damage! +5 Drama Points]

Then Bud zipped through, firing lasers toward all three of us and heading for the window. Fursona lunged toward him, but she was a touch slow. Her flame breath caught the back of his cape just as he zipped outside.

And just like that, the battle continued. And, in spite of her exhaustion, it quickly became clear that Tele-Portal was still making stuff happen. Bad stuff . . . for us.

I threw myself out the window toward Bud Lightbeam, only for a portal to open right in my path. A moment later, I popped out—right into an Underdelver drill punch that smashed into my face. As I staggered back, another blow came in—this time from Lightbeam, who appeared from the same portal, punched me in the stomach, and then disappeared into a different one.

[HP 0/14]

That last hit had *hurt,* too. I was out of superhero damage, and if I wanted to stay in the fight, I needed some healing right now! I rotated to Rainy Day with **[Quick-Time Change]**, using my seconds of **[Freeze-Frame]** to reposition behind The Underdelver. If I was lucky, I'd be able to use him as cover for a couple of seconds.

[Flashy Fitting-Room! +1 Flamboyance Point]
[Steel Yourself! +1 Grit Point]

Then, before he could turn his mech, I used **[Virga]** to fill the room with rain that mixed with the sprinklers Fursona's flame breath had activated. Bud Lightbeam would heal—but my team would heal *more*.

[Medic! +6 Cunning Points]
[HP 3/14]
[Doctors Without Borders! -3 Cunning Points]

It wasn't much, but it was *something*.

McHammer rushed toward The Underdelver, hammering away with his . . . hammer. Every blow of his maul seemed to shake the Council of Heroes building, but that might also have been the destruction Fursona had caused with her first transformation.

She was busy trying to pin Bud Lightbeam down, but I could tell that was a mismatch. He was too fast and could hit from too far away; my partner didn't have a chance.

I had a choice to make. I could help knock the cloning laser-beamer out of the fight or try to take out Tele-Portal. The only thing I could imagine that was worse than letting Fursona lose her part of the fight was letting my former mentor win the whole thing for her team, so my choice was clear.

I used **[Ride the Lightning]** to hit Tele-Portal before she could warp either herself or me away, then followed it up with a **[Thunderhead]** to knock The Underdelver and McHammer away from me.

[Electric Lightshow! +1 Flamboyance Point]
[Badass Move! +1 Badass Point]

The storm forming outside the Council of Heroes was still building as I back-pedaled for a little extra space, then started up another **[Quick-Time Change]**, this time back into Understudy.

[Flashy Fitting-Room! +1 Flamboyance Point]
[Rejuvenation Activated! HP 8/14]

There. I had more wiggle room. A Lightbeam light beam came in, and I ducked it, then jumped over Tele-Portal's attempt at a portal save. **[Solar Wing]** caught me mid-jump, and I zipped toward the ceiling.

McHammer's maul crashed into The Underdelver with a ripping metal sound, but the mech seemed to shrug off the blow. Fursona was tiring, too, and

I definitely couldn't keep fighting this hard. Most of my best powers were offline, I had no Spotlight Star, and—somehow—both Bud Lightbeam and The Underdelver had arrived fresh and ready to fight after only a couple of minutes out of the Episode.

As it stood, we didn't have a chance, and I had no idea what was happening outside, but if Stella-Lunar won . . .

I didn't want to think about that. She'd mop the floor with us, even if we resolved this fight right now.

McHammer took another swing at the Genius-driven mech suit. This time, the block was too fast—or maybe he'd delayed his hit somehow. A ringing bell sound filled the room, and The Underdelver backed off a step. So did Tele-Portal. "Okay, you've put up a good resistance. Now, let's talk terms for your surrender. I can keep you and Fursona out of the worse parts of Almhurst, Understudy. That's the best I can offer."

"That's a pretty piss-poor offer," McHammer said. He laughed. "I'll show you why in three."

"This is your last chance!" Tele-Portal shouted over him.

"Two."

Tele-Portal opened another portal. This time, it wasn't a member of The Triad that came through. Stella-Lunar's Eclipse Form flew through, solar flares arcing across her arms. She flew straight for McHammer, using **[Total Eclipse]** and **[Dark Side of the Moon]** simultaneously.

But McHammer only laughed. "One."

"And then Stella-Lunar found herself on the other side of town," a familiar voice said.

Stella vanished, her powers disappearing with her, and The Narrator strode in through the main door. All three members of The Triad turned toward her. Powers started, but she just smiled behind her glasses. "The Council of Heroes building's defenses activated and recognized The Triad as enemies."

"Shit," Tele-Portal said, opening another portal as the room suddenly bristled with weapons I hadn't seen before. She threw herself through it as a laser Gatling turret turned her way. It stayed open long enough for The Underdelver to follow her through. Bud Lightbeam was already out the window, disappearing in three separate contrails of color as he faded into the distance.

The Narrator took one look at McHammer. "Bob."

"Mrs. N," he replied.

"It's been a while. You're still causing trouble, just like old times?" She unfolded her newspaper and sat down in one of the remaining chairs.

"Yes, Mrs. N. Hopefully not for much longer."

"Alright. Good kid."

[Episode Finished!]

[Episode: Power War: The Battle of Mid-Town - R]

[Penalties: N/A]

[Episode Finished! +3 of each Style Point]

[Winner Winner! +3 of each Style Point]

[Role Focus: Drama + Flamboyance - Goal Partially Met: +10 to Drama]

[Alias - Understudy] [Archetype - Magical Girl] [Community Rank - 120/523]

[HP 8/14]

[Styles and Skills]

▶ Archetype Skill - Transformation Sequence

▶ Combo Skills - Power-Weaving

▶ Badass (54) (Skill Roll Available)

▶ Cunning (54)

▶ Drama (73) (Skill Roll Available)

▶ Limelight Barrage 2

▶ Starlance 3

▶ Flamboyance (32)

▶ Signature Skill - Adaptive Armoire 3

▶ Stored Costumes: (Rainy Day, Copy Cat, Lab Assistant Panic)

▶ Solar Wing 2

▶ Quick-Time Change 3

▶ Improvised Ovation 2

▶ Grit (45)

▶ Freeze-Frame 2

[50 Badass Credits Used. Rolling Skill!]

[50 Drama Credits Used. Rolling Skill!]

[Rank-Up! Pouncing Panther 2: Additional damage on impact in a small area of effect]

[Rank-Up! Meter's Running 2: +2 power uses]

PART FIVE

36

Tower Defense

WEDNESDAY, FEBRUARY 10

Tonight was our turn on Council of Heroes Tower Defense. We—Honeycomb, Vigilant Vow, Mrs. N, Bee, and I—were supposed to take the shift until eleven, when a couple of heavy hitters would relieve us.

Bee and I were here. But we couldn't see the other three anywhere.

Classes had been going . . . honestly, I had no idea how classes had been the last week. Bee and I hadn't attended anything, and as far as we could tell, neither had most of the other super-students. I wasn't sure the professors were even hosting classes anymore.

So, yeah. Classes had been going. End of sentence. Moving on.

Most of my focus had been on the rebellion, on playing games with Su-Bin as much as I could, and on slowly . . . delicately . . . guiding her toward the understanding that *some* supers were on her side. After the dozenth time playing a spatial tile game and watching her dominate, I thought we were close to that breakthrough. But if Mindstorm needed the local chapter on her side, we'd need a big win—something that showed we cared.

That was why Mindstorm's strategy of repeating our win in other cities was slowly driving me crazy. As far as I could see, it was just getting supers—and Extras—hurt. If it wasn't buying us anything, why was the Pro-Earth League wasting its time with battles in Yorkston, the West Coast, or even freaking Tortuga West?

It didn't make any sense. In fact, it seemed counterproductive to our goal.

The only advantage I could see, other than that we had five similar buildings under our control now, was that it wasn't hard to defend them. Warp Tennyson and the teleporting villain from last semester's run-in with the Student Supervillain Society had both joined the Pro-Earth League, giving us a ton of mobility. That was why, in theory, the five of us could defend the Council of Heroes building by ourselves until help arrived.

In practice, The Narrator should've been able to do it herself. But she wasn't here.

"What do you think is taking them so long?" I asked Fursona as we sat in the first-floor lobby, watching the door.

She shrugged. "No idea, but I'm starting to get—"

[Casting Call]
[Episode: Power War Short: Tower Defense - R]
[Role: Turret! Do you accept the role? (Yes/No)]
[Role Focus: Grit + Drama]
[Power War Short: Tower Defense: Act One in Progress]

"Lemme guess? A bad feeling?" I quipped.

"Yeah. That."

I was definitely getting one, too, especially when a pair of familiar faces stalked out of the evening darkness toward us. One wore a nun's habit over power armor, and the other wore black robes with a staff. "Sister Sly," Fursona muttered.

"And Quick . . . something. Silver, maybe? Remember him from last semester?" I pointed. "He's fast, with those martial arts powers."

"It was Quickstrike. Quicksilver's different. Still." Fursona cracked her knuckles. "Think you can take him? She's gotta be here for me."

"Yeah, I got you." I waved my wand and fired a [**Starlance**] toward the villain— who backflipped over it! I backpedaled as the robed figure kicked off midair, spiraling toward me around his bo staff. He was coming in too fast; I wouldn't have time for another power.

But I didn't need one. I just needed to—there! As I stepped across an invisible line in the floor, a wall of yellowish-white plasma cut down from the ceiling, blocking Quickstrike's progress. He bounced off another invisible patch of air, legs churning in the air like he was running on nothing, and I fired another [**Starlance**]. This one hit, knocking him to the floor.

[Dramatic Damage! +1 Drama Point]

He sprang up, but I was already moving to block the stairs. Across the lobby, Kaiju-sona and Sister Sly were wrecking the few pieces of furniture and corporate art that hadn't been destroyed in the battle last week. The villainous fox-nun's gizmos, power armor, and laser weapons were holding their own—for now—but I didn't see any way Kaiju-sona could lose; even Mindstorm's orders not to go Full Kaiju wouldn't cost her this fight.

The plasma barrier dropped, and Quickstrike rushed me again. This time, he lashed out with his staff, firing a wave of compressed air my way. I'd been hit by those before—my ex, Professor Panic, had used them all the time—but I wasn't ready for it. It knocked me onto the stairs; my elbows sent the funny bone–fuzzy feeling up my arms.

[HP 13/14]

But it wasn't like he'd actually managed to hurt me. Not really. I could handle this guy.

Even as I picked myself up, he was already rushing me. I had to use **[Quick-Time Change]** to stall out the bo staff inches from my forehead, and I reevaluated whether I could handle this guy. Then I switched to Copy Cat, used the **[Freeze-Frame]** time-stop to position behind him, and hit him with a **[Pouncing Panther]** the moment time started again.

[Flashy Fitting-Room! +1 Flamboyance Point]
[Steel Yourself! +1 Grit Point]
[Badass Damage! +1 Badass Point]

In this form, I could 100% hold my own against him in melee; Tails's catlike reflexes gave me the edge, or at least evened it out. As the staff ripped through the air toward me, I ducked it, then landed a **[Cat-Scratch Fever]** into the villain's stomach. He took two steps back, swinging his staff to ward me off, and took a deep, centering breath as his eyes swelled shut.

[Dramatic Damage! +1 Drama Point]

Suddenly, the swelling reversed. "New power?" I asked.
"I have mastered my own body. Every inch of it," Quickstrike said.
I rolled my eyes. "So, no debuffs. Got it." I used **[Pouncing Panther]** again, this time missing on my first bound and getting a staff strike for my trouble. He'd stepped effortlessly out of the first pounce, but my second leap caught the villain by surprise. Even better, **[Fursonal Furcefield]** had taken the blow just fine!

[Tough Kitty! +1 Grit Point]
[Badass Damage! +1 Badass Point]

Before I could follow up with a **[Doom Ball]**, though, Quickstrike spun, swinging his staff like a helicopter blade. I couldn't get out of the way fast enough, and a dozen blows hit me before I got breathing room. None of them individually hurt, but there were so many of them! He landed, eyes closed, and flex-breathed, staff pointing my way as I recovered on the landing. He was pushing me back, and I needed to change the flow of battle.

[HP 9/14]

Instead, before Tails and I could devise a battle plan, Quickstrike pushed again. This time, I focused on blocking or dodging blows; another trap was just around the corner, and if I timed it right, I'd be able to follow up and swing the whole fight. But I couldn't make it obvious. He knew the defenses existed, and he'd be cautious.

I needed him to commit.

Tails counted the steps as I delicately backpedaled up the stairs, dodging his pokes and prods and trying to bait him into an all-out attack. We had three to go. Two. One. I lunged toward the villain again, feigning another [**Pouncing Panther**].

He took the bait, and as he leaped under my abortive jump, I slammed down on top of him. It didn't do much damage, but it pinned him in place while Mrs. N's next piece of narrated-up defenses fired.

[**Badass Move! +1 Badass Point**]

I found myself thrown up toward the ceiling as Quickstrike's body was encased in a forcefield. I couldn't hit him, and that was . . . inconvenient. But he couldn't move a muscle except to breathe. I had a minute. Maybe a little less. But that'd be enough time to shift and start setting up a combo.

I slow-transformed into Rainy Day, starting up a [**Power-Weaving**] combo and using [**Thunderhead**] to start it off. It'd mean finishing on [**Thunderhead**] or transforming, but the setup was potentially really—

WHAM!

Something hit me in the back of my head. It felt like every white van I'd ever encountered. It felt like getting hit by Stella-Lunar's [**Maximum Starlance**].

It felt like getting hit in the back of the head.

[HP 7/14]

As I blinked the stars out of my eyes and whirled, I saw a familiar-looking hero. He stood in a boxer's stance, muscles rippling against a magenta-and-green Costume. "Hi, Punch," I mumbled.

He didn't say anything, instead throwing another rocket-powered punch my way. I rolled, and it hit the stairs. I half expected the concrete to explode, but instead, his fist seemed to bounce off them.

"You know, you really suck," he said, glaring at me.

"I know." I used [**Wind Front**] and threw him down the stairs; I didn't have time to deal with him. Quickstrike would be up any second now, and I wasn't sure I could handle two melee supers working together without using Spotlight Star.

[Badass Move! +1 Badass Point]
[Floating Points: 1 Drama]

I needed to save her for later, especially if it was just Fursona and me defending. I took a quick glance down; she had Sister Sly in a headlock and was breathing ineffectual-looking fire across the fox-nun's power armor. So yeah, she was probably fine.

That left me and the two-on-one I was facing.

I quickly used **[Virga]** before Quickstrike could struggle free from the forcefield; healing one vil was preferable to healing two, after all. As the rain poured down on me, I felt myself toughening up. Yeah, I could handle these two. Water poured down the stairwell as I backed up it.

[Medic! +1 Cunning Point]
[HP 9/14]
[Doctors Without Borders! -1 Cunning Point]
[Floating Points: 3 Drama, 1 Badass]

I was working my way back toward the start of the combo, and even better, **[Thunderhead]** had finished. I had *no* idea what would happen if I empowered a **[Thunderhead]** with another **[Thunderhead]** and a **[Power-Weaving]**. The situation had never come up, but I assumed it'd either fizzle out or be disgustingly powerful.

Either way, I was about to find out. I used **[Thunderhead]**, pouring the finished one into it and finishing my combo.

[Environmental Combo! +1 Cunning Point]
[Thunderstruck! +1 Drama Point]
[Power-Weaving! +6 Drama, +3 Badass, +1 Cunning Point]
[Feedback 1]
[HP 7/14]
[Confirm Combo Continuation?]

I blinked, mind racing. I'd created a feedback loop somehow; the **[Thunderhead]** was feeding off itself, acting as an environmental piece. How long could I sustain the storm overhead, and what would the **[Ride the Lightning]** look like at the end of it? I did a quick head-check. Punch was still at the bottom of the stairs, and while the forcefield around Quickstrike had definitely weakened, I had a few seconds there.

I quickly continued the combo, letting the damage pile up until I sat at an unhealthy-looking **[HP 1/14]**. Then, both because I didn't have a choice and because Quickstrike was free, I stopped the loop. The raging storm overhead howled and spun, with me at the center of the growing tornado that, by now, filled the stairwell. I doubted Punch could get to me if he wanted to.

But I had other plans in mind. As my sixth-grade form braced herself against the raging winds, I used **[Ride the Lightning]**.

[Electric Lightshow! +1 Flamboyance Point]
[Thunderstruck x4! +4 Drama Points]

The building's power went out a split second before the biggest lightning bolt I'd ever created hammered its way down the stairs. Quickstrike, even just out of his forcefield prison, was fast enough to dodge somehow.

Punch wasn't so lucky. The electrical attack slammed into him, throwing him all the way across the lobby. I could *smell* the burning hair as he hit the glass wall on the far side. He tried to get back up, but collapsed in a heap.

Even so, we had other problems. Another pair of supers ran through the door, setting us up for a two-on-four fight. Even with the tower's defenses, I wasn't sure I could handle that.

I pushed my watch button. A moment later, a message appeared on it.

<Dealing with other problems – Mindstorm 10:32>
<Mission Critical. Hold the tower – Mindstorm 10:32>

37

Hold the Tower

I didn't love our odds.

Fursona was still downstairs, destroying the already wrecked lobby with Sister Sly. I had a solid position on the main stairwell, but if any of the progalaxy supers headed for the fire stairs, I wouldn't be able to hold here. And worse, all three other supers—Quickstrike, Punch, and, of course, Iron Fist—seemed intent not on finding another way up, but on going right through me.

This wasn't going to work. Where was Mindstorm? More importantly, where was Mrs. N? We could hold this tower forever with her and the other Tottergarten heroes. Without them?

I didn't have time to think more about it. Quickstrike and Punch, who'd picked himself up from my massive **[Ride the Lightning]**, rushed the stairs, and I spun in place, shifting to Magical Girl Understudy. As the **[Quick-Time Change]** finished, I sprinted up the next flight, abandoning the second floor to the attacking supers. Quickstrike came around the corner, followed by Punch, and I fired a **[Limelight Barrage]** into them from the top of the stairs.

[Flashy Fitting-Room! +1 Flamboyance Point]
[Rejuvenation Activated: HP 6/14]
[Dramatic Damage! +4 Drama Points]

Quickstrike ducked the first shot, which caught Punch in the face. As the others homed in on the temporarily stunned hero, Quickstrike zipped left and right, eating damage and blocking with his staff where he could. When the dust cleared, he looked a little worse for wear, but Punch was still in the fight.

"Goddammit," I swore as the gap closed far too quickly. Quickstrike's staff lunged out, but even as I dodged it, a second, spectral one hit me and knocked me back—right out of range of Punch, whose fist slammed through the white drywall and ripped out, filling the third-floor hall with dust.

[HP 4/14]

As I tried to figure out how to counter my two opponents, Iron Fist ran past. I cursed under my breath—he was heading farther up. "Fursona, I need your help up here!" I yelled.

"I'm a little busy," Fursona said over my headset. "She came ready to deal with me, so it's a fair fight!"

"Fine! I'll do it myself!" I threw myself out the window and used [**Solar Wing**], then angled straight up. As the shattering glass rained down on the street, I headed toward the still-massive gap in the Council of Heroes building where Full Kaiju had ripped the facade off when she'd transformed.

I slid into the Council of Heroes room. If I was right, neither Punch, Quick-strike, or Iron Fist could get up here before I finished what I had to do. I started slow-transforming into Copy Cat, then began a second slow transformation from the cat form into Super Girl Spotlight Star. With enough planning, I'd get all eight of my moves, and since I had time—not to mention a three-on-one fight to look forward to—I was going to take every advantage I could.

"Is it the fuzz?" Lady Lockless asked from the corner, making me jump.

"Oh shit, I forgot you were in here," I said as the transformation finished. "Yeah, it's a bunch of progalaxy supers. Think you can help?"

[**Advanced Accessories: Magical Girl Understudy, Magical Girl Rainy Day, Copy Cat**]
[**Skill Siphon Activated: Style Points Disabled**]
[**Meter's Running: 10/10**]

"I'm no good in a fight," the ballgown-clad supervillain said, leaning on her cane a little. "But I know something you don't about the plan. They're not here for the tower. They're probably here for me."

I rolled my eyes under my hood. "Really?"

"Yeah. Remember, I can pop any lock, right? That means opening a door to the Hot Zone. They barricaded most of them, but the Council of Heroes tower and a few others are still only locked. That means I could open the Hot Zone whenever I wanted to."

This time, there was no eye-roll. Instead, I blinked, my jaw practically on the floor. It was a good thing there weren't any cameras around, because suddenly, the plan would make sense to anyone who'd heard what she just said. Mindstorm attacked other towers because she needed to spread out the pro-Ilneat supers. If all we had was the Tokyexico City door, they could just defend there. The more towers we had, the better our odds were.

But only if we still had Lady Lockless. And someone on their side knew she was important.

I sent another quick message on my watch.

<Mindstorm, Lady L is here - Understudy 10:37>

"Hopefully that'll get her moving," I muttered. "So, any panic rooms or anything like that?"

"You're going to need a panic room when I'm done with you!" Iron Fist shouted from the door.

I whirled. All three stood on the far side of the room, looking ready for a fight. Iron Fist, however, seemed to want to banter. The right thing to do here was stall. To take him up on it and taunt back. But the reality on the ground was that I had a disgustingly strong advantage, and they didn't seem to realize it yet.

The fight from here had three priorities.

First, I couldn't let them get Lady Lockless. If she was really as important as she seemed to think, keeping her safe—and, more importantly, unkidnapped—had to be my main goal. If I had to abandon the tower to protect her, so be it.

Second, I needed to keep the tower under Pro-Earth control. That meant beating the three toughs they'd sent to fight me, getting downstairs, and dealing with Sister Sly—assuming Fursona hadn't won by then. If I could pull off that win, I could probably let Mindstorm know the place was safe.

And last, and least immediately pressing, I needed to figure out why my damn backup wasn't here.

With a rough plan—or at least a priority list—in place, I let loose with a **[Limelight Barrage]**. The **[Maximum Starlances]** slammed into Punch and Quickstrike, driving them back toward the shattered steel door, but Iron Fist tanked the one that had hit him just fine. He was still fresh—and a full Bruiser on top of that.

[Dramatic Damage!]
[Meter's Running: 9/10]

But even with a somewhat disappointing opener, I'd shifted the whole balance of the fight. All three supers split up, unwilling to clump up in case I could do that again. That was fine with me. As Punch and Quickstrike dove in from the sides, I whirled in place. Iron Fist was heading straight in, and all three would hit me at the same time.

Unless . . .

I used **[Wind Front]**.

The hurricane-force blast threw everyone, including Lady Lockless, against the walls. Quickstrike ran against it, ending up outside the building as a few steel plates gave way. Punch slammed into a wall and slumped down. But Iron Fist recovered quickly, charging up his fist and slamming it into Lady Lockless. I winced as she hit the wall a second time, then started convulsing as Iron Fist's . . . iron fist slammed into her repeatedly.

[Badass Move!]
[Meter's Running! 8/10]

I sprinted toward him, readying a [**Pouncing Panther**], but he grabbed the unconscious supervillainess and whirled her around like a shield. "Game over, Understudy! We win!"

"Nah," I said and used [**Set Dressing**]. As I vanished more completely than ever, I leaped to the side with [**Pouncing Panther**], then ran toward the hostage-holding Bruiser.

[Dastardly Plan!]
[Badass Move!]
[Meter's Running! 6/10]

He whirled, flipping Lady Lockless through the air, and I grinned ferally. He'd spun the wrong way! I closed the gap and used [**Doom Ball**], opening wounds across his back, then followed it up with [**Cat-Scratch Fever**]. The damage over time and blind hit almost immediately, and I backed off as he quickly fell to the ground.

[Badass Move!]
[Dramatic Damage!]
[Meter's Running! 4/10]

From here, it should have been easy. But when I turned around to deal with Quickstrike, I got a faceful of bo staff instead. It caught me in the left cheek, and I felt my whole head spin right. My body followed it a moment later, and I tried to roll with it and turn the fall into a graceful spin.

[HP 2/14]

As I recovered into a three-point superhero stance, I looked at my last opponent. He wasn't done—not by a long shot—and I didn't have that many moves left. I needed to play a long game, too; with Lady Lockless already out of superhero damage, getting her really hurt wasn't a risk I could take.

So, instead of going with [**Ride the Lightning**], I used [**Virga**]. Sure, it'd pick up Iron Fist and Punch, but I needed the HP, and so did Lady L.

[Medic!]
[HP 9/14]

[Doctors Without Borders!]
[Meter's Running! 3/10]

Then, before Iron Fist could get too comfortable, I fired a **[Ride the Lightning]** his way. He went right back down, electricity coursing through him. That left me with an almost-out Punch, plus whatever Quickstrike had left in the tank.

Easy.

I stood between the two melee supers and Lady Lockless as I transformed back into Understudy; this was a winnable fight now, and that meant Priority Three might be on the table. Quickstrike split into four colored versions of himself. The four Quickstrikes started swinging toward me, and I **[Quick-Time Changed]** back to Rainy Day.

[Flashy Fitting-Room! +1 Flamboyance Point]
[Steel Yourself! +1 Grit Point]

I could have used my **[Freeze-Frame]** time to dodge, but I couldn't risk getting out of the way and exposing Lady Lockless more. So, I tried something else instead. A **[Thunderhead]** into **[Wind Front]** knocked all four away, with only a handful of hits taken.

[Pause for Effect! +1 Drama Point]
[Badass Move! +1 Badass Point]

That left me with a problem, though; Rainy Day was out of juice. Sure, I could stall all day, but I only had to mess up once to—

Something roared into the room, breathing fire and trailing bits of shredded, flaming plush. Kaiju-sona slammed into Quickstrike before he could react, and the green, red, and blue extra copies disappeared as she wrapped him in a massive hug and vomited flames onto him.

In just a second, the fight was over. All three progalaxy supers lay defeated on the ground. And more importantly, Lady Lockless was alive, unkidnapped, and—if a little grumpy about pain—at least a little grateful for the bailout.

[Episode Finished!]
[Episode: Power War Short: Tower Defense - R]
[Penalties: N/A]
[Episode Finished! +3 of each Style Point]
[Winner Winner! +3 of each Style Point]
[Role Focus: Grit + Drama - Goal Met: +10 to Focused Styles]
[Alias - Understudy] [Archetype - Magical Girl] [Community Rank - 98/523]
[HP 1/14]

[Styles and Skills]
▶Archetype Skill - Transformation Sequence
▶Combo Skills - Power-Weaving
▶Badass (17)
▶Cunning (56) (Skill Roll Available)
▶Drama (56) (Skill Roll Available)
▶Limelight Barrage 2
▶Starlance 3
▶Flamboyance (42)
▶Signature Skill - Adaptive Armoire 3
▶Stored Costumes: (Rainy Day, Copy Cat, Lab Assistant Panic)
▶Solar Wing 2
▶Quick-Time Change 3
▶Improvised Ovation 2
▶Grit (64) (Skill Roll Available)
▶Freeze-Frame 2
[50 Cunning Credits Used. Rolling Skill!]
[50 Drama Credits Used. Rolling Skill!]
[50 Grit Credits Used. Rolling Skill!]
[Rank-Up! Set Dressing 2: Camouflage is significantly stronger, beating some detection devices and powers]
[Rank-Up! Science has Rules? 1: +1 active device]
[Skill Upgrade! Fursonal Furcefield to Nine Lives: Chance to heal damage back on negating damage]

With the fight wrapped up, Fursona and I dragged the semiconscious supers back downstairs and deposited them outside of the Council of Heroes building. Lady Lockless tagged along, breathing hard on the way back up the first flight of stairs, and I raised an eyebrow at her. "I think he dislocated something during the pummeling. I'll be okay—it happens all the time."

"You're sure? I could give you a ride back up to the top," I said. She didn't look good at all; she was pale, with a tight, drawn-looking face. Her ballgown was a little askew, too, but that seemed pretty minor.

For a second, I thought she'd agree. But then she shook her head. "No, I'm fine. After all, I'm going to have to be tough enough for Phase Two."

38

Phase Two

THURSDAY, FEBRUARY 11

"Thank you all for . . . coming. Or for your less . . . personal . . . attendance," Mindstorm said. "I know it's . . . early . . . in Tokyexico, and I appreciate your wakefulness."

She wasn't here, of course. She, McHammer, and all the other heavy hitters were still in Yorkston. But even so, the Pro-Earth League's members had assembled in her lair to hear the next part of the plan.

"Phase Two is simple. All we need to do is break into a Hot Zone, defeat whatever . . . defenders the Ilneats have, and checkmate the studio producers there. If we do that, we can negotiate with them from a position of strength and convince them to either reform their . . . studio system . . . or to leave us alone. However, a simple plan like this has many moving parts, and we're temporarily down a few key elements." Mindstorm's massive eyes closed for a moment on the screen.

I looked around the room. Lady Lockless was here, of course; I hadn't let her out of my sight since last night, except when I dropped her off at her lair in the Roth Arena stands. Lairs seemed pretty safe so far, last semester's 3V1L assault notwithstanding. I'd even picked her up—unthinkable for a villain less than two weeks ago—and flown with her out to Mindstorm's this morning.

Most of the other heroes were here, including four of the five other Magical Girls on our side. Candi Crush, Foamy Flash, Sugar, and Chili Powder stood in a tight knot near the door. They weren't essential to anything, though.

More importantly, Magical Girl Honeycomb was missing. So was Vigilant Vow. Mrs. N hadn't made an appearance, either. I filed that away; it was odd for the three of them to miss not one, but two important Pro-Earth operations. And Mindstorm was both aware and not furious. I didn't think it was because Mrs. N could mop the floor with her, either.

Mrs. N absolutely could. But that wasn't the point.

"Even without those supers, though, we need to start this plan . . . soon. To all outside observers, we appear to have overextended. We currently control hero buildings in Tokyexico City, Yorkston, Tortuga West, Seoul, Mumbai, Sydney, and a half dozen smaller cities. Against a determined progalaxy . . . assault . . . we can currently defend none of them, and their probing attacks learned something of value last night. McHammer, please continue," Mindstorm said as her phone beeped.

The parachute-pants-wearing supervillain nodded. "You got it, boss. Okay, details. First, we're abandoning all but three towers this afternoon. Yorkston, Tortuga West, and Tokyexico City. That'll let us concentrate our forces there, and if we evacuate the others without letting anyone know, the Ilneat sympathizers will have to spread their forces. That'll buy up more time while their teleporters move people around.

"While that's happening, our own teleporters will move our ace in the hole to each of those cities. Lady Lockless will open the doors between the towers and Hot Zones. We'll start in Yorkston, where most of our firepower is concentrated. That should overtax their own mobility as they move people around to defend that door. After that, we'll swing for Tortuga West. It's the least likely target of the three, with no ultrapowerful local supers on their side, so hopefully, we'll be able to break through there."

"And what do we do once we're in there?" a familiar—and terrifying—voice said from the television. The conference call flicked over to a man with a massive handlebar mustache and mullet, holding a beer can in one hand and a bent golf club in the other. His chest was bare except for a tattoo of the state he got his name from.

McHammer nodded slowly. "That's a good question, Florida-Man, and the answer is 'your worst.'"

"Excellent!"

Gourmet's hand was up, but when she didn't get called on, she lowered it and interrupted instead. "And what about Tokyexico City?"

"You're the backup plan. If we can't break through in Yorkston, and Florida-Man loses control—"

"Hey! I resemble that remark!" Florida-Man shouted.

"—then the Tokyexico supers are our best shot. When Lady Lockless opens the door, you pour through and head straight for the studios. We need to capture as many executives as we can if we want them to listen to us. If you get one, *don't* head back to the Council of Heroes building. That'll be abandoned. Get to Mindstorm's lair, then call her. We'll turn on the defenses remotely, but you'll be fine in the central rooms."

A few more questions flew, but there was one pressing one no one else was asking. I slowly raised my hand. "And what if Mays shows up?"

Mindstorm's hand reached into the camera's frame, taking the mic from McHammer. She cleared her throat. "If Dr. Mays shows up on any of your battlefields, you're not getting any help. Your best bet's going to be waiting him out. Without Dr. Jackson, he's missing the half of the combo that *made* them . . . unbeatable. He'll knock out all the other supers around him, too, so the best he can do is stall."

McHammer took a step forward, and Mindstorm nodded to him as she handed the mic back. "If you see him and manage to get clear before he starts an ad, tell us where he is. We'll reposition people to try to deal with him. That's the best we can do with the missing links in our chain."

"And who's missing?" someone from Sydney asked.

Mindstorm paused, composure breaking for the first time since she'd fought on campus last semester. She looked to the floor. "The Narrator."

It wasn't surprising to me that the Tottergarten heroes were missing in action. What did shock me was that Mindstorm was not only okay with it, but willing to make it known. But even more worrying was that she wouldn't tell us why. It seemed like she was content to keep the mystery just that—a mystery.

Well, Honeycomb was a friend, and Vigilant Vow was . . . something. We had almost six hours before we needed to be at the Council of Heroes building. And, most importantly, Fursona and I were veterans of a half dozen Investigative Episodes. If we couldn't solve this puzzle and figure out what had happened to Mrs. N and the Tottergarten heroes, I'd have been shocked. So, after some debate back at the green room, Fursona and I came up with a foolproof plan.

I finished dialing the number, and my phone connected to Magical Girl Honeycomb's.

She didn't pick up on the first several rings, and I looked at Fursona meaningfully. "This was *your* plan."

"Well, it's not like we have a better—"

"Hello! Magical Girl Honeycomb here, sticking it to evil!" Honeycomb's voice came over the speakerphone. Fursona looked at me, her face a vision of arrogant victory. I waited for the message to continue, for us to get sent to her voicemail— anything to wipe the smug smile off her face.

Instead, there was a pause that drew out just a touch too long before Honeycomb continued. "Hello?"

"Uh, hi," I said. "How's it going? Missed you at the Pro-Earth League planning session today."

"Yeah, um . . . about that," Honeycomb said. "We're, um, not going to be at any of the PEL stuff for the next . . ." she trailed off. I could hear a couple of voices talking in the background; it looked like we had all three of them.

Whatever they were discussing, it got more and more animated as I raised an eyebrow at Fursona. Her victory was long since forgotten now that we'd made contact. Instead, I was a little worried. Honeycomb's power had made her a total mess the first time we'd run across her, and even after—finally—beating her rival and finding her place at Tottergarten, I couldn't help but remember that girl.

The one on the phone sounded a lot like her.

"Look, ladies, Mrs. N's dealing with some stuff right now. Some things are more important than PEL." Honeycomb's voice felt a little more confident, but still fragile. And exhausted; the closest comparison I could think of was Tele-Portal after a long Episode. Or Fursona post–Full Kaiju.

Still, we had to push a little. "Well, we thought you guys should know that Mindstorm's—"

"Having us all-in the Hot Zones today. She told us already," Honeycomb interrupted, her voice low. "Look, we already talked to her. She knows what's up, and she fully supports our decision to back out of the attack."

"She does?" Fursona interrupted. "That doesn't sound like her. When she's serious, she gets single-minded."

"Yeah, well, Mrs. N is persuasive," Honeycomb shot back.

She sure was. I remembered when she'd used her powers on us; it had felt like mind control, but she'd just been rewinding the Episode with certain new conditions in place. Still, Mindstorm was . . . *Mindstorm*, and even with Mrs. N throwing her full weight around to eject Stella-Lunar from our tower assault, I couldn't see a world where Mrs. N had persuaded the supervillain that their dropping out of the PEL's plan wasn't a betrayal.

"Can you put Mrs. N on the phone?" Fursona asked. She must've been having the same thought I was. "We get that you can't talk about whatever it is that's got you all worried, but we deserve to know why you weren't there last night."

The other end of the line went silent. I glanced at my girlfriend. "Hopefully you didn't piss them off."

"If I did, I did. We do deserve to know," she replied. "And Mindstorm's not going to tell us. Neither is Honeycomb, but she's obviously stressing about something. So, I figure we go to the source, and either The Narrator throws us back in time by a half hour so she doesn't have to answer, or we get some answers from the person in charge."

"Mindstorm's in charge," I said.

"I know that! But not in this situation, obviously."

"Hi, girls. I don't have long. You want to know what's going on, why we left you out to dry last night?" Mrs. N's voice came over the phone. She didn't sound any better. In fact, there was raw anger in her voice. "Alright, but before I tell you, you need to promise not to get involved. Honeycomb, Vigilant Vow, and I are dealing with it."

"Got it," Fursona said before I could say anything to the contrary.

She shot me a *look*, and I nodded. "Yeah."

"Great. Last night, after the Playpen Patrol went home, someone showed up at the daycare. They didn't take anything, and the kids were gone. They didn't even get inside, so we didn't treat it like an emergency until one of the parents called. Their kid had gone missing right out of her bedroom window, along with her super-suit. So we've been out all night looking."

"You couldn't narrate her back to bed?" I asked. I had a bad feeling I knew which one; at least it couldn't be The Cloud.

"No, because she'd have to be in hearing range. We've been all over the city, and she's not anywhere," Vigilant Vow said, speaking up for the first time. If anything, he sounded more scared than the other two. "I keep telling Mrs. N that I know who did it. The rest of the kids' powers aren't anything special, but hers? Hers is unique. There's only one other person who can turn into a gigantic dinosaur, and Fursona's not trading that power to The Agent anytime soon."

Mrs. N interrupted. "And that, Understudy, is why you have to let us handle this. It's probably bait, but I can handle anything The Agent throws at me. I'm not as sure you can, especially if he's ready for me and gets you instead." Her voice cracked with fury. "I'm going to tear him apart, but promise me, girls, that you won't go after Kaiju Kid. Just focus on your job, and I'll take care of my kids."

39

Kids

As the minutes passed, my fingers started hurting from being clenched into fists. We still had almost an hour before the assault on the Hot Zone started, and nearly an hour and a half before Tokyexico's wave went in. I couldn't stop pacing, though, feeling like a trapped tiger in the green room.

Finally, I couldn't take it anymore. "We should go after her. Screw Mrs. N! Screw The Agent. We need to do something about this!"

Bianca looked up from the Kaiju-sona fursuit she was fixing up in the conversation pit. Her hand held a needle; she'd amateurishly stitched up a gash in the side, making it look like a battle scar instead of torn plush. "Do you think this makes me look more badass?" she asked.

"You're worried about *that* right now? What the hell, Bee?"

She held up her hands like she was trying to calm me down. "Annie, we could get out there and look for Kaiju Kid. It'd be the right thing to do in the immediate term, and it'd make us both feel better. I hate this, too. The Agent's pulling at our heartstrings, and it's only dumb luck that he didn't make a play for The Cloud, or you'd be dragging me out the door, huh?"

I nodded, throat tight and seeing red. "I'd kill him."

"I thought so. But we have another job to do. Too much is riding on us getting into the Hot Zone and capturing Rocko, or Pataki, or any other Ilneats we can find. Mrs. N is capable, powerful, and resourceful, and I trust Honeycomb to give it her all. They'll find Kaiju Kid. So, let's focus on the job at hand."

"But—"

Before I could get a thought out, Bee interrupted me, handing me my phone. "You're not going to listen to me. I can tell. Call your mom and ask her what to do."

That . . . sounded surprisingly reasonable. I hated that it did—I wanted to scream and cry and go fight a supervillain—but Mom probably had insights that Bee didn't. She was someone I could confide in and ask for advice. More importantly, Dad would be at work, and Bee had known it. That left Mom.

I snatched the phone away from my girlfriend, who shook her head and went back to her crude stitch job as I fled the green room.

By the time I collapsed on our bed, staring out the window at the glistening snow that covered Tokyexico University's grounds, I'd calmed down a little. Bee was probably right. We couldn't add much to Mrs. N's search; despite my desire to build a bunch of great, focused Costumes, I didn't have anything that would excel at this kind of job, and we had no leads. It'd take us more than an hour to figure this out. The best thing I could do was play my part.

But I dialed Mom's number anyway. As the phone rang and rang, I thought about what I'd say. Then, Mom picked up. "Hello, Anika. It's been a while."

"I've been, uh, busy," I said, voice cracking a little. Then, all of a sudden, I was crying. "Can we just talk about how things have been at home?"

"Sure," Mom said awkwardly. "Riverside's about the same as it ever was. Your ex was up to his usual stuff, but he's disappeared since that book came out. I read it, and I think Golden Goose saw the same side of the Ilneats that I did."

"Something else, Mom."

"Ah." Mom's voice softened. "No shop talk, huh? Okay. Dad's been busy with work. They're building a new stadium in SeaTac, and the company's handling the drill construction for foundation pilings or something." She launched into a catch-up routine, something we'd done a dozen times before. What the neighbors were up to, how her struggle to quit smoking was going, that three girls had quit the diner in the last month, and she was working overtime again.

Then, she asked me how classes were going.

"I'm thinking about dropping out," I said suddenly. It was the first time I'd thought about it, but the moment it popped into my head, it made complete sense. It really did.

Mom's shocked voice punched a hole in the conversation. "No. You can't."

"Why not? It's all over, anyway. I haven't been to classes in over a week; even the professors aren't showing up, and if we win, the degree's useless. You know which side I'm on, right?"

"Yes, I'm aware of which side my daughter's chosen in the most important Power War we've ever had." Mom's voice had gone icy and cutting, and I winced. "I'm also aware that you've invested a year and a half of your life into this program and that even if you don't use the degree, it'll help you. So, I'm saying no. I'm saying that if you drop out when you're this close, I won't help you find a job back in Riverside."

"You'll cut me off?"

"No. But I won't let you fail when you're this close to something you've wanted. So, take the fight to them, win your war, and then get your butt back in class, Anika."

I winced again as she said my name. "I'll let it slide until you win or lose, but you'd better pass your classes."

"I will, Mom," I said, even though I had no idea how I'd do that. Then I took a deep breath. "Okay. Classes. Last I'd seen, we were studying public relations and social media stuff."

"That sounds fascinating," Mom said. I wasn't sure how honest she was being, but she still let me talk and talk about everything I'd been learning before the shit hit the fan.

At last, Bee cleared her throat from the door. "Sorry to interrupt, but it's time."

I looked at the clock. "It sure is. Sorry, Mom, but I have to go. Love you!"

"Love you too, Annie," Mom said, and the phone went dead.

I'd decided on something dumb for this fight.

Choral music filled the green room, but I'd committed myself to this Costume—the classic Magical Girl Understudy from *Small Town Super*, not the fast, sleek one from *Heroics 101*. My body glowed brighter and brighter as I went through the dance steps, Tails weaving her way through my feet. White thigh-highs sprang up my legs, and elbow-length gloves materialized over my hands.

If I was against Rocko here, I wasn't wearing the Costume that had made *their* show such a success. I was going back to my roots.

When the music finally faded, and my boots touched down on the green room's floor next to the computer monitors, I had poofy off-shoulder sleeves, a ridiculous pink bow on my chest, and star-shaped pupils—just like when I'd first put on the Costume. The lights cut off, and everything went quiet.

I was ready. Almost.

"Don't fear, Magical Girl Understudy is here! I swear to defend the weak against evil, and to uphold truth and love!"

"Alright, alright, let's go," Kaiju-sona said from behind me, and I jumped a little. I'd thought I was alone. "It's a cute Costume, but I'll miss the new one."

"It's just this once," I said. Was it a lie? I didn't know; only time would tell. Flushing red, I summoned my sailboard with [**Solar Wing**], and with Fursona in front of me, we set off for the Tokyexico Council of Heroes building—and for the Hot Zone that awaited us through the locked door.

In the end, after waiting with the rest of the minor-leaguers stacked up in the Council room for something to happen, the beginning of the end happened with a whimper, not a bang.

Warp Tennyson landed next to the door—an unassuming metal one in the wall behind where Crossbow-bot had held his court until last week. With him, he'd brought a tired-looking junior who leaned on her cane. "Okay, last one, Miss Lockless," he said.

"Great. Then we can sit down for a minute, right?"

"Right." The teleporter looked at us. "Okay, good news and bad news. The good news is both the Yorkston and Tortuga West attacks hit major-league resistance right away. We're getting our asses kicked out there, and every super we have is getting sent to Yorkston—Florida-Man is on his own down there. We've counted almost all the major-league threats on those two fronts, though. The bad news is that there are no reserves for you. You either make it in, retreat out, or lose.

"Mindstorm wanted me to tell you to move fast, hit hard, and don't be afraid to sucker punch progalaxy supers to win fights. We're playing for keeps. You ready?"

One by one, we nodded. The Magical Girl squad. A few mixed members of TUSSA and the SSS. Gourmet, The Crumb, and Theseus. And, of course, Fursona and me. The only real firepower we had, and even that was pretty limited.

"Okay, Miss Lockless, open the door."

She nodded, tapped its handle with her cane, and pulled it open without a problem. A rush of hot air blew out, whipping her hair back, and she stepped out of the way. "It's all you now. Signal Dr. Tennyson if you have a problem in there, or if you need my help."

We rushed through into the Hot Zone.

[Casting Call]
[Episode: Power War: In Hot Water - R]
[Role: Invader of Aliens! Do you accept the role? (Yes/No)]
[Role Focus: Drama + Grit]
[Power War: In Hot Water: Act One in Progress]

I'd been here before. But it had always been in Rocko's studio, not outside. The wind blew hard, howling between tall buildings and down empty streets. It felt like stepping out of February in Tokyexico and into July west of Riverside. Nothing grew in the concrete planters that lined the road in front of us. Everything was barren, gray, and hostile.

This wasn't how it had looked from Rocko's studio or the Council of Heroes building. This wasn't how it had looked at all.

A beam of energy rocketed toward me, and I dodged to the left. As I did, I watched a figure duck behind the pillars outside one of the warehouse-looking buildings across the street. "We've got someone!" I shouted.

The street erupted in fire. Beams crisscrossed it from both sides, hitting us as we scattered toward the nearest cover. I saw a familiar-looking helmet—devil horns, an exposed chin, and a red cape—and fired a [**Starlance**] toward the *V*.

[**Dramatic Damage! +1 Drama Point**]

I didn't have time to see what damage it had done. *V*s were pouring out of the buildings; there had to be twenty—no, thirty—of them. Fursona rushed forward, breathing fire into the horde of 3V1L henches-turned-supervillains. They scattered like pinballs, running from her, but when she turned away, they attacked from behind.

Theseus slammed into them, metal tentacles flailing and harpoons firing. "I've gotta *hand* it to them, they really rolled out the welcome wagon!"

"Goddammit shut up," Fursona said through my earpiece. I could hear how hard she had her teeth gritted; it sounded painful. Another *V* leaped toward her, battle-axes in hand, and I blasted him out of the air with a **[Starlance]** before he could make contact.

[Dramatic Damage! +1 Drama Point]

The battle raged all around us, but one thing was clear: The Agent hadn't fixed his problem with having too many temp supers simultaneously. Sure, the *V*s were tougher than a regular hench. And yeah, they had powers. I'd lost a couple of super-hero damage when the fighting finally slowed. But fighting twenty of them wasn't anywhere near as tough as fighting three.

Candi Crush's mace slammed into the stomach of a *V* who looked an awful lot like Flare, and she left it planted there until he surrendered, wriggling on the ground. Then she stretched as her hound tackled the last *V*. "That felt easy."

"Check the buildings. Find anyone you can and get moving," I said, feeling villainous about ordering a mass kidnapping. Ilneat-napping. Whatever. I ordered it. Within a few seconds, the other PEL supers had disappeared, spreading out and rushing for the studio buildings. Once they'd left, I nodded to Fursona. "Okay. Time to find Rocko. Or The Agent. Either is fine."

Something landed in the street behind us before she could say anything, and I whirled. Stella-Lunar stood in her Moon form, arms cradling something. "Magical Girl Understudy, I'm giving you and your scaly friend one chance to surrender. After that, the kid gloves come off."

I squinted under my domino mask. What did she have? Then she started walking toward me, one hand holding a squirming, wriggling kid in a dinosaur Costume. The other fished out a Jolly Rancher from her pocket and started unwrapping it.

She had Kaiju Kid!

40

Kaiju Kid

Stella-Lunar unwrapped the Jolly Rancher even as I fired a [**Starlance**] her way. She ignored the impact, just like our fight in Vigilant Vow's lair, and held out her hand. Fursona was already dashing toward the little girl, but it was too late. Even as the toddler's dino Costume's entire fabric mouth closed around Stella's hand, I knew she wouldn't make it in time.

Lady Lockless was near the door, and the rest of our people were scattered to the winds in the blazing-hot . . . Hot Zone. If either Kaiju Kid or Stella-Lunar got out of control, they'd be in danger.

Sure enough, Kaiju Kid began growing until she towered over the Hot Zone's skyscrapers. She roared, and beneath the roar, I could hear a tiny, high-pitched scream. A gout of fire rippled out from her mouth, her tail thrashed, and an entire intersection worth of stoplights crashed into a building.

"I've got this," Fursona said.

I nodded. "Don't hurt her. Just try to keep her off our people."

"Got it, Understudy. I'll do my best." I heard her knuckles crack from inside her Kaiju suit, and then she started growing, too, her lizard fursuit doubling in size, then doubling again and again until she looked Kaiju Kid in the eye. "COME ON, KID! SPIT OUT THE CANDY!" she roared, almost as loudly as the first giant dinosaur suit.

"NO! RAWR!" Kaiji Kid screamed, and crashed toward my super-sized sidekick.

The battle for the Hot Zone was on.

As the massive lizards crashed into each other, Stella and I both opened fire. I dashed right, rolling into a [**Limelight Barrage**], as she used [**Moonbeam**] and [**Reverse Gravity**] at the same time. The beam zipped my way, while the gravity shift tossed Kaiju-sona a couple of feet to the side and unbalanced her just as Kaiju Kid slammed into her. My light lances peppered the number one superhero but didn't stop her. Worse, her blast chunked me before I could [**Quick-Time Change**] it.

[Dramatic Damage! +4 Drama Points]
[HP 12/15]

She was barely paying attention to me; instead, she was fighting me and interfering with Kaiju-sona! I needed more firepower so I could draw her attention; if Kaiju-sona could handle the kid without being interrupted, we could do this. So, as she fired another **[Moonbeam]** toward me, I **[Quick-Time Changed]** into Spotlight Star.

[Flashy Fitting-Room! +1 Flamboyance Point]
[Advanced Accessories: Magical Girl Understudy, Magical Girl Rainy Day, Lab Assistant Panic]
[Skill Siphon Activated: Style Points Disabled]
[Meter's Running: 9/10]
[Steel Yourself!]

The three spotlights lit up in the sky, drowning out the moonlight as they converged on me, and I struck a pose that felt like Golden Goose's best. Then the hood covered my hair, armor clasped tight around my arms, and the oversized wand with the comedy and tragedy masks on its tip slapped into my hand. I narrowed my eyes at Stella-Lunar as time resumed. Nine powers. I had nine powers to end this, or at least to get such a massive advantage that Stella-Lunar's Eclipse Form wouldn't be enough to turn the tide.

"It's time for your curtain call, Stella-Lunar!"

"Well, your sun's falling, Understudy!" Stella said, voice full of confidence.

It was time to wipe the smugness off her face.

"**[Science Has Rules?]** Not at this power level!" I pointed at the stoplights, and they warped and bent as their particle forces shifted them into the shape I wanted them: two giant metal wings that hovered behind me, each with three holes in them. Electricity sparked across the surface, arcing into the holes as they glowed brighter and brighter. "Quasar Laser Phaser Cannon, using endothermic cooling systems and shock wave-based recharge capabilities."

[Pseudoscientific Mumbo-Jumbo!]
[Meter's Running: 8/10]

BWEEEEEEM!

The Quasar Laser Phaser fired, a beam of energy that rivaled anything Eclipse Form Stella-Lunar could muster tearing down the street toward her. She dodged toward the battling titans' legs, but the beam was too wide. It clipped her, knocking her aside. I was already recharging my beams; hopefully, I'd get a couple of shots off before the traffic light holes melted down.

[**Pseudoscientific Mumbo-Jumbo!**]

Yes! Each shot didn't count as one. I dashed out of the way as a gigantic plushie foot crashed into the asphalt behind me. Its claws punched through the street, and water gushed up from a pipe as Kaiju Kid screamed in surprise. She swung a fist toward me, and it shook the buildings nearby. "Fursona! She's going to hurt our friends!" I shouted.

"I'm . . . doing my best!" Fursona yelled back. Then she screamed. A moment later, I realized why. Stella had fired a [**Maximum Starlance**] into her leg. "Get her off me!"

BWEEEEEEEM!

I fired the Quasar Laser Phaser again, dangerously close to my partner. This time, my steel wings *did* overheat. But the blast also pushed Stella-Lunar back. She jumped into the air, hovering in place fifty feet overhead—near the two Kaijus' hip height.

Fursona needed cover, so I used [**Solar Wing**]—wincing at the lost power—and followed her into the air as she fired another [**Maximum Starlance**] toward Fursona. It hit, and my partner swore.

[**Meter's Running: 7/10**]

As Stella-Lunar spotted me, she dipped toward the asphalt again. I used [**Power-Weaving**], diving after her, but before I could get a good shot with a barrage, the two giant dinosaurs slammed into each other right in front of me. I slowed down, then dipped between their legs as their tails churned the asphalt into gravel and tar.

"Come on! Spit it out!" Kaiju-sona roared again.

Stella-Lunar was waiting on the other side, and a [**Tidal Pull**] ripped me out of the air and sent me crashing toward a warehouse. Both Kaijus staggered, but stayed on their feet. "Jeez, they're big," Stella muttered.

I crashed through a barred window, turning midair and firing a [**Maximum Starlance**] back toward the major-leaguer. It caught her between the shoulder blades, sending her into a spiral that she recovered from even as I surged back out of the window on my [**Solar Wing**].

[**Dramatic Damage!**]
[**Meter's Running 6/10**]

Then, before either of us could stabilize, we were both blasting away.

I used [**Ride the Lightning**] as I dove toward her, and she fired a [**Moonbeam**] my way, slicing through the air and ripping into both Kaijus' plushie armor. One of the Kaijus' tails swung through the air, and I looped around it as it hissed past my head. Stella used [**Reverse Gravity**], throwing everyone into the air and slamming them down again.

[HP 8/15]
[Electric Lightshow!]
[Meter's Running: 5/10]

Then I dropped [**Solar Wing**] and threw myself toward her. As I hit her, I activated [**Wind Front**], catapulting her through the air. She fired another [**Maximum Starlance**], and I barely dodged it. As I disengaged and fell toward the ground, she spun, preparing an attack to pin me to the ground.

[Badass Move!]
[Meter's Running: 4/10]

Before she could fire, I opened up with [**Limelight Barrage**]. She didn't have the angle to dodge, and every combo-enhanced shot hit her; the first stunned her, and the rest of the [**Maximum Starlances**] piled in one after the other.

[Dramatic Damage!]
[Meter's Running: 3/10]
[Power-Weaving!]

A moment later, [**Solar Wing**] activated automatically, and I pulled up a few feet from the ground.

[Meter's Running: 2/10]

Stella didn't. She hit it with what felt like the force of an atomic bomb. Had I knocked her out? I couldn't tell from the dust cloud, but I'd definitely hurt her.

Then, a gigantic foot slammed into the pavement next to her, rocking the nearby buildings, and the sounds of two gigantic plushy fists pummeling each other filled my ears. Kaiju-sona's bobbly eyes rocked on their stalks as she got shoved into a building. Glass shattered behind her, and she roared a gout of flame toward Kaiju Kid, who screamed "NO!" at the top of her lungs and breathed in.

The flames gushed toward her mouth, and a moment later, she breathed them back out at Kaiju-sona, who "dodged" into a warehouse, crushing it and filling the street with scattered bits of superhero Costumes and half disassembled drones.

"I swear, by starlight and new moon, that you're not winning this," Stella-Lunar said.

I whirled. The dust had cleared, and Stella-Lunar was still up. I'd definitely hurt her—her Costume was torn and shredded, and she had the beginning of a bruise on her face—but not enough for the win. I quickly lunged toward the wrecked drones as she fired another [**Moonbeam**] my way.

Two moves left. Could I push Stella further in two moves? More importantly, could I keep her off Kaiju-sona and let my partner win the battle of the titans over our heads? I needed something big. Something powerful. As the **[Moonbeam]** made contact with my arm, I threw myself into the warehouse's wreckage and used **[Science has Rules?]** again.

[HP 5/15]

This time, the thing I made wasn't a cannon. As the drone parts clamped around me, I started rattling off what I imagined the specs might be. "Using subnuclear reactions and reverse-gravity dynamos, and taking Panic principles in mind, Solar-Stabilized HORROR Armor!"

[Science has Rules?]
[Meter's Running: 1/10]

I had no idea if the cobbled-together power armor that encased me would be enough to pull off a win here, but it was better protection than nothing. Plus, if I'd designed it correctly, it'd hold up for one Costume change—maybe two. Two would be ideal.

Its jets started, throwing me wildly into the air toward Stella-Lunar. Before she could react, I'd already caught her in one steel arm and punched her across the jaw with the other. She fired a **[Starlance]**, but I used **[Hometown Heroine]** to accelerate into Speedster territory and landed three more blows before she even got the power off.

[Show-off!]
[Meter's Running: 0/10]

As Spotlight Star faded, I quickly transformed to Understudy, then used **[Quick-Time Change]** to freeze time and transformed right into Rainy Day inside the power armor. **[Hometown Heroine]** was still running, and I kept the pressure up on Stella-Lunar, punching and kicking the moment time started again.

[Flashy Fitting-Room! +1 Flamboyance Point]
[Steel Yourself! +1 Grit Point]

But the blows weren't hitting as hard, even with the Solar-Stabilized HORROR Armor and **[Hometown Heroine]** running. I glanced toward the two titans; Kaiju-sona had almost wrapped things up. I just needed to hold out a little longer until— hopefully—she got the toddler in the other Kaiju suit under control.

Another [**Tidal Pull**] jerked me off Stella and threw me through the air. Then she used [**Reverse Gravity**] and slammed me into a building. The HORROR armor came apart midair, and I [**Quick-Time Changed**] again before I could hit the ground, this time back to Understudy.

[HP 1/15]
[Flashy Fitting-Room! +1 Flamboyance Point]
[Rejuvenation Activated! HP 6/15]

It wasn't much, but it was something. [**Solar Wing**] caught me automatically, and I fired another [**Starlance**] toward the major-league heroine. She took it on the chin, rocking a little as it hit her.

"You did some good work there, Understudy. But now the moon's setting, and the stars rise," Stella said. She whirled in a flash of light, shifting Costumes.

But Kaiju Kid roared before she could hit me with her next form's powers. Her high-pitched scream echoed across the Hot Zone, and both of us spun to face the hulking, toddler-driven plush suit.

She was losing. Kaiju-sona had tackled her onto the asphalt and was wrapping her in a gigantic dino-hug that, no matter how hard she tried, she couldn't escape from. But as the scream went on and on, a boiling, pink light so bright it was almost white filled her massive Costume's mouth. It grew brighter and brighter until I couldn't look at it anymore. Then the scream cut off, and the light concentrated into a beam.

It hit Fursona right in the face.

Chunks of Kaiju-sona suit flew everywhere. A massive eye crashed through a skyscraper's windows, revealing a scared-looking Ilneat who vanished a moment later. Kaiju-sona reeled back, shocked by the hit.

The shock wave blew out every window in the Hot Zone a moment later, raining glass onto the streets, the Ilneats, and the very surprised Pro-Earth League supers attacking the different buildings.

Kaiju Kid started shrinking back down to her normal size. The moment she reached toddler size, she yawned, curling up on the street. "Yuck! Nuc-ular bad breath!" Then she fell asleep, Fursona started shrinking, and I turned my attention back to Stella-Lunar.

41

Stella-Lunar

As Fursona dashed for the door Lady Lockless had opened, Kaiju Kid in hand, I fired another **[Starlance]** toward Stella-Lunar. She ducked it, but the delay let Fursona slip through to safety with the toddler. I sighed in relief, tension boiling off me. Now, the worst that could happen was . . .

Stella getting loose on the other Pro-Earth League supers. I couldn't let that happen, but I needed a moment to get myself back together if I was going to keep fighting her.

In the seconds that it took her to decide her next move, I slipped away, riding my **[Solar Wing]** into the Hot Zone's alleys and back streets.

[End of Act One: Act Two in Three Minutes]

I landed behind a dumpster, taking a deep breath. Okay. New goal. Get back to the fight as soon as I could, start hitting her from cover, and try to play keep-away. Hopefully, I could wear her down before she went Eclipse. If not? I didn't know what I'd do. Probably lose—quickly.

That meant Lab Assistant was probably a trap unless I had time to set up a couple of mid-powered **[Science has Rules?]** weapons. The problem was that, yeah, I'd "won" Act One, but I'd used too much firepower to do it.

Still, the plan came together in my head, even as Fursona reported that she was on her way to Tottergarten. I nodded slowly. "Okay. If you can switch suits to, I don't know, Roo-sona and get back here, great. If not, stay out of it."

"Yeah, that wrecked Kaiju-sona. I'll need some time to put it back together. Pretty sure the cameras caught my face, too. Hopefully, Rocko still feels like editing that kind of thing."

"Yeah, haha," I laughed nervously. The secret identity thing had felt important when I was a kid, until Bee had figured mine out instantly. I'd cared about certain people knowing, too—like Su-Bin. Her figuring it out would be disastrous, even though I'd planned to tell her in hopes of making an alliance. But now that I was an active rebel, literally attacking my boss's business . . .

The secret identity seemed more important.

Something exploded in the distance, and a second later, I got the Act Two message.

[Power War: In Hot Water: Act Two in Progress]

"I've gotta go," I said. Then I headed Fursona off before she could say it herself. "I'll be careful. Let Mrs. N know what's going on, okay?"

"You've got it. Love you."

"Love you, too." I used **[Solar Wing]** and rocketed up until I was near the top of one of the buildings dotting the Hot Zone.

Stella-Lunar was already busy firing a **[Starlance]** into a skyscraper where one of my allies was—I assumed—trying to corner an Ilneat. I'd almost expected the gorilla-otter hybrid aliens to fight back, but they seemed to be both running *and* ignoring the superpowers being thrown at them. As I watched, one vanished into thin air. A second later, Stella's **[Sunbeam]** clipped the Magical Girl who'd been chasing the Ilneat.

I fired a **[Starlance]** and dove down the side of the building, trying to put some distance between myself and the major-league heroine. A moment later, I got the hit message.

[Dramatic Damage! +1 Drama Point]

The grin on my face felt feral and catlike, but a moment later, Stella-Lunar slammed through the building and appeared next to me. "Burn! **[Solar Flare]**!"

I ducked back *into* the building, firing another **[Starlance]** her way. "Nah."

[Dramatic Damage! +1 Drama Point]

The look of fury on her face as the light exploded around her, only to miss me by inches, was super satisfying. She turned midair and zoomed after me, wand extended. A **[Maximum Starlance]** missed me by milliseconds as I switched to Rainy Day midair with **[Quick-Time Change]**. The frozen time worked to my benefit; I got myself turned around and used **[Wind Front]** to knock her off-course as soon as it started again.

[Flashy Fitting-Room! +1 Flamboyance Point]
[Steel Yourself! +1 Grit Point]
[Badass Move! +1 Badass Point]

This time, the building she crashed into creaked ominously, and she didn't come out of it right away. I bounced into an office one floor down from where she'd crash-landed, building a **[Thunderhead]** for the biggest hit I could manage.

But she still didn't appear. When she failed to come back after fifteen seconds, I switched plans to **[Virga]**, letting the healing wash across me. Then, when she *still* didn't show up, I slow-transformed to Understudy.

[Medic! +1 Cunning Point]
[Rejuvenation Activated: HP 12/15]

I was almost full, with all my biggest powers still available. Meanwhile, Stella-Lunar was nowhere to be seen, but I hadn't healed her with **[Virga]**. She was still up, and if she was still up . . . that meant she was after my teammates again!

When I caught up with Earth's strongest hero, she looked a little worse for wear. I'd tattered her Costume pretty well, but the switch to Star Form had reset most of the damage. Still, she'd had the bad luck to run into Theseus, Gourmet, and Foamy Flash, and even though she'd clearly won, they'd hit her pretty hard.

From the burn marks and soot covering her Costume, Gourmet had gone dragon. It hadn't been enough, but I felt like I had a chance now.

"They keep getting away," Theseus muttered from the ground. He'd been disarmed—literally—and he had a look of pure frustration on his face. "We couldn't get any of them."

Stella-Lunar sucked in a breath, turning toward me. "Going to take your shot now?" she asked. "See how it goes."

I nodded, but before I could make a move, the watch Mindstorm had given me buzzed.

<Yorkston is a loss. Holed up in a warehouse. Won't last long – Mindstorm 4:42>
<Good luck, Tokyexico – Mindstorm 4:43>

Well, shit. The feeling of dread that had been building inside me since Stella-Lunar disappeared redoubled. This was bad. Really bad. We couldn't complete our objectives, the other cities were buckling, and Stella had just mopped the floor with three minor-league heroes.

I needed to buy time for us. No one else seemed to be here, other than some 3V1L henches that'd been promoted to *V* by The Agent, and the team had handled those okay. I hadn't seen any around since Stella touched down. It was Stella herself that was the problem.

One big push it was, then.

I used **[Power-Weaving]** and started up a **[Freeze-Frame]**. As I shifted and the world paused, I rotated around to Stella-Lunar's back, throwing myself into position just as the world started moving again. She fired a **[Sunbeam]** at the spot I'd just been, and faux-brick facade melted on an office building across the street.

[Flashy Fitting-Room! +1 Flamboyance Point]
[Steel Yourself! +1 Grit Point]
[Floating Points: 1 Flamboyance]

As I followed up the maneuver with a **[Virga]** that healed her—but healed me and my team more—Stella-Lunar jumped into the air and used **[Solar Flare]**. The damage exploded out, ripping over the whole street like a bomb going off. My healing made up for most of it, but not all. It *did* keep the other PEL supers up, though, so that was something.

[Medic! +4 Cunning Points]
[HP 9/15]
[Floating Points: 3 Flamboyance, 1 Grit]

Not that Theseus was going to be much help without any of his weapons. "You three, leave!" I yelled. Then, before Stella-Lunar could get any more distance, I used **[Ride the Lightning]** and fired the bolt at her as hard as I could. The tendril of electricity ripped into her, knocking her out of the sky.

[Electric Lightshow! +1 Flamboyance Point]
[Power-Weaving! +6 Flamboyance, +3 Grit, +1 Cunning Points]

The hit rocked her, but she recovered with a series of **[Maximum Starlances]** that I couldn't dodge. As they hit me one after another, I ducked for the half melted office building, sliding across the carpet painfully to avoid any more beams coming my way.

[HP 3/15]

I couldn't handle that kind of firepower. If I wanted to win—or even to stall long enough for my friends to get out—I needed to go back to the plan that had pushed her earlier. Another **[Maximum Starlance]** tore through the building, and I ducked under an Ilneat-sized desk. It promptly exploded, showering me in wood shards but absorbing Stella-Lunar's hit.

I crawled under the desks and past cubicles that felt almost human, looking for a window—either one to escape out of or the opportunity kind.

Stella smashed through a wall, and I froze. "Where are you?" she said, walking past the desk I was under as I held my breath. One of the windows was opening up. The others were shattered from all the fighting. And a plan was coming together. I'd give her everything I had in one big burst, see what I could accomplish, and then run. Not skirmish. Not fight. Just run. If she followed me, great.

If not? I'd keep harassing and poking at her until she either turned to deal with me or lost. Either would be fine; Theseus and Gourmet could get out that way. We'd have *someone* to keep up the fight, at least until the Yorkston supers showed up and mopped the floor with them.

One deep breath later, I stood up and shouted, "[**Limelight Barrage**]!" I spun, firing the [**Starlance**] volley into Stella-Lunar's back. They hit in a rippling tide of pink-and-blue energy that knocked her across the office and into a glass-walled executive suite.

[**Dramatic Damage! +5 Drama Points**]

As she rolled to recover, I fired two more [**Starlances**] at her. The first hit, but she waved her wand, and a black hole absorbed the other one. Then, without waiting for her to pop back up—I hadn't done enough damage, and I knew it—I started running.

[**Dramatic Damage! +1 Drama Point**]

When I reached my window—the kind you jumped out of—I did exactly that.

Falling from an office building was a familiar feeling, but this time, [**Solar Wing**] activated and caught me when I was still twenty feet off the ground. I rocketed toward the alleys again. "Chase me, you bitch," I muttered under my breath, both hoping and fearing that she would.

She did.

Overhead, something incredibly bright zipped by, nearly blinding me with its brilliance. It got in front of me, and I fired another [**Starlance**] at it before turning to run the other way.

[**Dramatic Damage! +1 Drama Point**]

But instead of chasing me, Stella-Lunar simply *appeared* in front of me, slightly out of breath. I sucked in a breath myself and fired a [**Starlance**] into a nearby back door, then kicked it as she dashed down the alley toward me. The door swung open, and I ducked through before slamming it shut.

A moment later, it started glowing molten orange. She was melting it! I slipped into a storage room, then out into the convenience store I'd broken into. The windows were all broken, so I hopped through and used [**Solar Wing**] again, playing to escape. Not to win. Just to escape.

All the light seemed to suck out of the world.

Stella-Lunar stalked through the door, the white glow that had covered her Costume almost invisible compared to the ink black shadow covering her. Only an orange halo burning around her body showed me where she was; that glowed brighter and brighter, making my eyes water.

Stella-Lunar cracked her knuckles as the solar flares arced across her shoulders and down her arms. "Understudy, it's time to show you what I should have done to Vigilant Vow. You took your shot. Now it's time for me to take mine."

She swaggered toward me, Iyago the owl spreading his wings behind her and her Costume in full Eclipse.

42

Full Eclipse

With Stella in Eclipse Form, my tactics had to change—a lot.

I knew, for sure, that I couldn't handle her at full power. Maybe—*maybe*—if I'd had Spotlight Star, but I'd already used it. She didn't have much superhero damage left, but I couldn't switch to any build that could take advantage of that.

At the same time, I couldn't just leave. I had no idea if Theseus, Gourmet, and Foamy Flash had escaped yet, and letting this monster get to them would be . . . bad for everyone. So, as she swaggered toward me, I used **[Solar Wing]** again and dove out of the building. This time, I wasn't looking for windows to hit her. I just wanted to avoid Earth's most powerful heroine.

She fired a **[Maximum Starlance]** that punched at least as hard as mine did in Spotlight Star. It slammed into a building, and concrete shards filled the air in front of me. I slid to a halt, landing and sliding across the sidewalk to avoid the worst of it, then switched to the sailboard. A thin barrier against her firepower was better than nothing.

I was almost forty feet up when she started using **[Total Eclipse]**. Right away, I felt the sailboard getting less and less solid under my feet. Below me, twisted traffic lights and broken asphalt faded into blackness as the afternoon gave way to pitch-black night. I fired a **[Starlance]** back toward Stella-Lunar, but as it flew toward her, it grew less and less powerful until, when it finally hit, it seemed weaker than my level one **[Stellar Ray]** had.

[Dramatic Damage! +1 Drama Point]

I threw myself through a shattered window and rolled on the glass shards, coming up with wand ready. Outside, the whole world was black. Then, the silhouetted form of Stella-Lunar rose through the air.

I started running.

Behind me, the darkness blazed suddenly as **[Starflame]** filled the office building. If it could burn, it did. If it couldn't, it started melting. I leaped out of the building's far side as a gush of flame seared my back. **[Solar Wing]** caught me on the way down, and I headed straight down the Hot Zone's main road.

[HP 1/15]

Okay. Resources. I had to have *something* here. One **[Quick-Time Change]**. No heavy hitting powers unless I could cobble together a couple of weapons with **[Science has Rules?]**. Plenty of small moves, but nothing that would shift the flow of battle here.

Running away it was, then.

If I could outmaneuver her, I might be able to get to the door back to the Council of Heroes building. From there, we could . . . I don't know . . . shut it? Or, at the very least, I'd have some allies. And even if I couldn't get there, I'd have a better chance of turning things around against any of her other forms.

I turned around; Stella-Lunar stood on the road. She wasn't pursuing, though.

Instead, tendrils of darkness formed around her. I fired a **[Starlance]** at her in a bid to stop her attack. When that one hit to no effect, I tried again. Another hit, but basically nothing.

[Dramatic Damage! +2 Drama Points]

The tendrils ripped through the air, tearing at me just like they had in Vigilant Vow's lair. I flew through the air, rushing toward the asphalt even as I tried and failed to use **[Solar Wing]**. The impact would definitely knock me out of the Episode. So the real question was whether Stella-Lunar felt merciful.

Based on how hard it had been to change her mind about Vigilant Vow, I doubted it.

But . . . something was wrong. I should have been slammed into the asphalt by now. Instead, I was still midair, suspended by **[Dark Side of the Moon's]** tendrils. I wasn't flying anymore. Now I just hung there.

Stella-Lunar walked up to me, knocking the wand out of my hand. It clattered on the ground, landing near a gutter drain. I braced myself, waiting for her to kick it the rest of the way, but she didn't move. Her brow wrinkled under her mask. "Something's wrong here, Understudy," she said.

I had one chance. One opportunity. I had to convince Stella-Lunar that she was on the wrong side of this war.

It should have been easy. She'd just been involved in kidnapping a child, and she had to know that Golden Goose's situation wasn't *right*. But I couldn't approach her on either of those fronts right now.

"Yeah, there's something wrong. You read the diary, right?" I asked. I didn't bother trying to wiggle free. Any attempt to resist was just going to piss her off.

"No. Not that," Stella said. The orange corona around her body faded a moment later, and a yellow, star-shaped halo appeared behind her head. I could finally see her face—and her eyes. Something felt wrong about them. They weren't the confident eyes I'd seen in all her Episodes, or the vengeful ones I'd stared at when she'd come for Vigilant Vow.

She looked worried.

I hit the ground as **[Dark Side of the Moon]** faded. But before I could attack or run, I got a system message.

[End of Act Two: Act Three in Three Minutes]

I hadn't even realized it *wasn't* Act Three. That meant . . . the beatdown wasn't over. But it also meant I was in for a power reset!

"Listen, Understudy," Stella-Lunar hissed at me, her voice dropping until it was little more than a whisper. "We're not on the same side, but I should have had backup. I haven't seen a single *V* in almost five minutes. So let's slow down and figure this out. Something's *wrong* here."

"Other than kidnapping kids, you mean?" I mumbled, picking myself up and glaring at her. She might be the enemy, but as I replayed the fight so far, she was right. I'd seen essentially no other pro-Ilneat supers since Kaiju Kid went big. "What do you think is up?"

"I don't know. I can't get a hold of my studio to ask, either," Stella said.

"So what do we do?" I asked.

"Nothing's changed," Stella snapped. "You're still my enemy, and I'm still going to beat you. Just . . . let's call our fight postponed until I figure out what The Agent's up to here. Maybe he had to pull his *Vs* for some other reason."

"Like, to kidnap more kids?" My voice dripped with sarcasm, and I held my wand at my side—not exactly ready for battle, but not relaxed, either.

"I'm not going to talk about that right now."

I shook my head. "Of course you're not. But I'm going to. I've been doing this for years, and until last week, I'd only found two real heroes—The Narrator and Tranquility. No one else is doing what's right because it's what's right. They're doing what plays well on TV."

"Not now," Stella-Lunar hissed again.

[Power War: In Hot Water: Act Three in Progress]

Nothing happened. Stella-Lunar and I stood in the middle of the street, ten feet from each other, ready to fight again. I had all my moves back, so I thought maybe I could make a show of it at least. And it *was* Act Three, so anything *could* happen.

But neither of us was expecting a volley of gunfire from across the street.

The first bullets peppered us before Stella-Lunar or I could react. One punched into me, dropping my superhero damage off completely. Others slammed into Stella-Lunar, and I threw myself onto the asphalt. But before I could return fire, another of her black holes appeared in front of me, absorbing the gunfire.

"Get your butt over here!" Stella shouted, and I looked around. She was halfway to the office building I'd leaped out of. "That won't last forever."

I didn't have much time to decide—stick it out against the 3V1L henches that had started moving onto the street or follow a superhero who'd tried to kill me twice? Neither looked like great options, but Stella-Lunar wasn't actively shooting at me.

I ran toward her.

The moment I got inside, Stella-Lunar launched a barrage of beams across the street, collapsing awnings and facades on the henches. I picked off one with a shotgun who'd made it almost across the street.

[Dramatic Damage! +1 Drama Point]

"Okay. Battle plan. You're out of the fight unless you've got something," Stella snapped. She used another power, and the street, already damaged, buckled as gravity twisted and turned.

I nodded, slow-transforming into Rainy Day. As soon as I finished my Itsy Bitsy Spider dance, I used **[Virga]**, this time healing Stella-Lunar. She nodded in appreciation. "Okay, I've got four minutes until my next Eclipse, so let's focus on getting to safety. If we're not there by the time I get back to full strength, I'll finish this."

[Medic! +2 Cunning Points]
[HP 3/15]

"So we're friends now?" I asked.

"No. We're allies of convenience. Those henches didn't care who they shot." She pointed at a bullet hole in her Costume. "That makes them our enemies. Work for you?"

"Absolutely." I started a **[Thunderhead]**, then used **[Virga]** again. The healing rain kept filling our shelter even as the henches pushed harder. "Wonder why he's not using *V*s."

[Pause for Effect! +1 Drama Point]
[Medic! +2 Cunning Points]
[HP 6/15]

"No idea." A blast of starlight filled the whole street, ripping across it like a carpet bombing, and henches flew everywhere. The screams were earsplitting, even over the explosions. "I'm not holding back anymore, though."

I nodded. "I'm going airborne." Then I **[Quick-Time Changed]** back into Understudy. The moment I finished, Stella-Lunar let loose with another **[Sunbeam]**, cutting across the battlefield. I leaped into the air on **[Solar Wing]**, getting enough altitude to avoid her ridiculously strong attacks.

[Flashy Fitting-Room! +1 Flamboyance Point]
[Rejuvenation Activated: HP 11/15]

She was right. She hadn't been going all out until the last minute of our fight. Now she was. The gravity shifts were almost overwhelming to fly in, even aimed well away from me. But even going all out, not all the henches were focused on her.

I fired a **[Limelight Barrage]** into a group that had climbed onto the building's roof with some kind of machine gun. They scattered like bowling pins, leaving the weapon behind, and I blasted it with a **[Starlance]** just in case. Then I circled the building and opened up on another pair of henches trying to flank Stella-Lunar.

[Dramatic Damage! +6 Drama Points]

The henches couldn't possibly beat us both. They probably couldn't even beat me at this point, much less Stella. So what were they thinking? A shot hit me, wobbling me in the air and knocking the air out of my lungs, and I gasped in a fresh breath as I dove.

[HP 9/15]

No matter how many we took out, they just kept coming. A few weren't moving at all—was Stella killing some of them? I couldn't tell, and I didn't have time to find out. Another volley of gunfire ripped across the street.

Then everything went silent. A moment later, gravity reversed, throwing cars, henches, and broken rubble into the air. It slammed down with a crashing sound that filled my ears and a pressure I could feel in my skull.

Stella-Lunar had switched forms again, this time back to Moon Form.

The battlefield went quiet except for a single pair of hands clapping. I landed on the roof next to the machine gun's wreckage as a familiar-looking man in a suit and tie stepped onto the street. "Well done, Magical Girl Understudy. The two of you survived what should have been the perfect ambush."

The Agent rolled up his sleeves. "So now, it's just you, me, and my *Vs*."

43

You, Me, and My Vs

My vision went red.

The Agent was right there. If I swung hard enough, fast enough, I could overwhelm him before he could disappear again. And I wouldn't stop once I had him. Not until he couldn't hurt anyone again. He'd kidnapped *Kaiju Kid*.

My wand went up, aiming at him, but Stella-Lunar cleared her throat beside me. "Understudy, you've got no chance of winning this fight."

Laughter echoed across the street as The Agent slow-clapped. "Good call, Stella-Lunar. Once we clear the board here, it'll be right back to how things were. That's what you want, right? The way things were, the end of the Power War, and you sitting on the laurels of 'most powerful.' And all you have to do to get it is finish off the Magical Girl next to you. It'd be cheapest that way, but I can, of course, pay the cost to get it done without you."

Stella froze, the star behind her head shimmering. Her eyes glanced toward me, and Iyago landed on a piece of broken masonry next to me. The two-headed owl familiar coughed once. "Listen, you've got one shot at getting out of here. You'd better take it."

Then, before I could move, Stella-Lunar **[Reversed Gravity]**, and I got to see how much she'd been holding back.

Every hench in the street below us rose twenty feet, then dropped like a rock. So did the first of three helmeted *V*s who'd just emerged behind The Agent. Only three people didn't move.

The Agent.

Stella-Lunar.

And me.

"Run!' Stella-Lunar shouted. I hesitated—The Agent was right there—but she pushed me off the building, and I fell toward the ground. **[Solar Wing]** caught me, and before I knew it, I was flying for the door out of the Hot Zone as fast as I could.

Behind me, the first two *V*s got airborne—one rode what looked like a dragon, while the other had a jet-pack and some huge cannon that looked like something Professor Panic would have built. The third tried to chase me, but Stella-Lunar hit him with a **[Moonbeam]** and knocked him clean out of the sky.

I rounded the first corner and slowed down, losing altitude. The dragon rider surged around the corner, flames boiling out from her mount's mouth, but I already had a **[Starlance]** in the air. It hit her, and she pulled the reins left, spiraling toward the ground before catching her dive.

[Dramatic Damage! +1 Drama Point]

WHUMP!

The other *V*'s cannon fired—I'd been right; it *was* a lot like my ex's weapons. The hypercompressed air rippled out and buffeted me through a window. I landed in what looked like a break room, complete with a foosball table.

[HP 7/15]

Behind me, a gun fired. Then it fired again. And a third time. Was it a hench opening up on Stella-Lunar? Or was it The Agent? Could he hurt her, too, like Dr. Jackson? I had a bad feeling, but I didn't have time to check; the two *V*s were right back on me, and I had to run.

I'd handled fights like this before, even at half my superhero damage. But I didn't have any heavy hitting powers left, and The Agent had only gone with three *V*s this time. I rocketed toward where the door had been, caromed into the building, and stopped.

It was closed.

I whirled, firing another **[Starlance]** toward the jet-pack user even as his cannon belched out another burst of compressed air. My light lance punched through the airburst, sending it wavering in a dozen directions, then hit the *V*.

[Dramatic Damage! +1 Drama Point]

We traded shots for a second, dodging and ducking next to the closed door as we blasted away at each other. Then, one of the building's walls collapsed, and the dragon rider's steed tore through the rubble. I spun, firing another **[Starlance]**, but before it could hit, the room filled with fire.

[Dramatic Damage! +1 Drama Point]
[HP 4/15]

At least they didn't hit as hard as Stella-Lunar had. So that was something.

Fuck. I couldn't leave anymore. The only way out of the Hot Zone was this one door, and if Lady Lockless didn't open it, I didn't see any way I was getting out of here. And I probably couldn't get to The Agent. He'd just disappear.

There wasn't a good play left here. But if I got lucky, maybe I could make something happen. I could . . . I wasn't sure. Reach The Agent? Maybe hurt him or make him leave? Those both seemed unlikely.

But it was worth a shot.

I ran down the hall toward a shattered wall of windows and used [**Solar Wing**] as I reached them. The dragon's breath roiled out behind me as I erupted from the building, turning back toward the last place I'd seen The Agent. Outside the Hot Zone, thunder boomed.

It was February. We didn't usually get thunderstorms in February—unless a power was causing them.

My wings left trails across the sky as I whipped down the canyon-like buildings, hot wind stinging my eyes. I turned a corner onto the stree—

WHUMP!

The jet-pack *V* fired an airburst, slamming me across the street and bouncing me off a wall. As I hit the ground, my wings vanished, and the huge dragon's feet landed on either side of me a moment later.

[HP 1/15]

I rolled as its jaws closed on empty air, ducking between its legs and using my last [**Quick-Time Change**]. I landed in Lab Assistant Panic this time, letting the villainous impulses wash over me. TA-1LZ appeared, opening fire with her [**New Head-Cannon**] and riddling the monster with rubber bullets and tasers that did little more than annoy it.

But it gave me a second to think. And in that second, I dashed toward a warehouse. Inside was exactly what I was looking for: an old computer. As I tore it apart and the building's wall buckled from a hypercompressed airburst, I muttered to myself. "Electron-repulsive dual-charged defense matrix and screen-shotgun. Relies on, um . . ."

The *V*s pushed into the building. I was out of time.

"Nuclear pro-fission-cy!" I shouted.

[**Pseudoscientific Mumbo-Jumbo! +1 Drama Point**]

The thin wire mesh I'd thrown over me activated, electrifying my Costume and somehow repelling the dragon's flames. A moment later, I fired the screenshot-gun toward both villains. Pixels vomited from the thing's "barrel." They bounced off every surface, tearing into dragon scales and jet-pack alike. A moment later, the computer's screen changed to the moment of impact.

[Pseudoscientific Mumbo-Jumbo! +1 Drama Point]

Everything was coming apart already, though. I'd only get a couple more screen-shots, and the defense matrix wouldn't take another hit like that. Plus, both *V*s were separating.

I fired again. If I had to choose, I'd rather take the dragon rider out. The blast caught the beast on the chin—and everywhere else. This thing was the least accurate weapon I'd ever improvised up! But it was enough.

[Pseudoscientific Mumbo-Jumbo! +1 Drama Point]

It crumpled to the ground in front of me, winged front legs pushing the ground like it was trying to get airborne one last time. The rider herself landed hard but rose to her feet and drew a war hammer. But I'd bought myself an advantage. As another airburst broke my defense matrix apart, I threw the screenshot-gun toward the drag-onless rider and ran.

That left only one super who could chase me. I could take him. Granted, I didn't have much superhero damage, but I could take him. It'd be just like beating Professor Panic.

Except Professor Panic rarely flew, and this guy seemed more comfortable in the air than not.

The storm outside wouldn't stop building. Lightning kept hitting, striking both the Hot Zone's shield and the buildings around it. Three bolts hit the Council of Heroes building, and I hoped the people inside were safe.

Because I had a problem I hadn't realized—I couldn't switch off Lab Assistant Panic. I was out of **[Quick-Time Changes]**, and the jet-pack *V* was too close to slow-transform.

"Villainous breakdown at 94%," TA-1LZ reported from my side as the robotic cat ran along behind me.

I just laughed. I couldn't do much else. Lab Assistant wasn't built to be a primary combatant, and even if I had the space to build a new weapon, it wouldn't have been enough to win. I hadn't knocked out the dragonrider, just pixelated her mount. The fight was over.

When The Agent appeared from around the corner with the third *V* at his side, it only got more over. "Magical Girl Understudy, it looks like you're beaten. Normally, I wouldn't indulge in gloating, but . . . the reality is that I can! Yorkston's been resolved, Florida-Man has to run out of energy eventually, and Stella-Lunar has been taken care of." He tapped the pistol on his hip casually.

"So now you give your speech about world domination?" I asked, heart plummeting. Stella-Lunar had been involved in the kidnapping, yes. But she was also my only ally right now.

"Nonsense." The Agent smiled a joyless smile. "World domination was never my goal. A new world order, with me at its center? Yes. World domination? Absolutely not. There's no profit in that."

He leaned in a little closer as my pursuers caught up. Thunder rolled in the distance. "The trouble with superhero shows is that the Ilneats don't have any control. This mess proved it. But now that I have almost every power ever given by the Style System, I can create that control. Imagine a world where everyone gets a turn to be super. One where no one's at risk of having their neighborhood melted because a villain went rogue and an overpowered heroine had to get involved.

"It'd be paradise, with me keeping it under control. The Ilneats are all on board. They just need it done in a way that'll play well on television, and that's cheap." The Agent's face glowed in the reddish afternoon air. I wanted nothing more than to blast the smug look off his face, but the fact was that Lab Assistant had nothing here. He'd won, and in a way, he'd earned the villainous monologue.

More importantly, the only resource I had left was time.

"So, here's my deal for you. You walk away. Right here, right now. Hand over the cat and wand, leave your Costume behind, and return to whatever podunk town you came from. I won't follow you. You can live a life. Not *this* life, but *a* life."

"Or?"

"Or I kill you here," The Agent said, drawing the pistol. "No one's coming to save you. Stella-Lunar's done, Dr. Mays is on my side, and The Narrator is busy. It's just you, me, and my army. Be smart for once, Understudy."

I looked behind The Agent; a cloud had formed behind him, covering the force-field dome in black smog and reddish lightning that struck faster than it could disappear. I suddenly realized that I'd seen a storm like this before.

"It had been a wonderful day. You'd won. Your enemies were defeated around you, and the path to victory was clear." The voice echoing across the Hot Zone sounded like Mrs. N's, but like she was a chain-smoker instead of a serial coffee drinker. "But a storm was brewing, and as it peaked, you found yourself in a new world. The world of eldritch horror!"

<This is an automated emergency SMS message. The metapowered supervillain Fanfic has launched an Episode in the Mid-Town and Hot Zone Districts. All minor-league and lower supers are required to stay out of the Mid-Town and Hot Zone Districts. Unpowered citizens in the Mid-Town and Hot Zone Districts are urged to shelter in place. All major-league heroes and villains in Tokyexico City not currently on Man vs. Nature duty must respond. Repeat: lower-league supers must stay out of the Mid-Town and Hot Zone Districts. Unpowered citizens, shelter in place - TCoH 3:36>

The forcefield overloaded for a split second. Only a blink of an eye. But it was enough time for the clouds to pour in, covering us in black-and-red fog that made my hair stand on end. In the second where I could see The Agent, I made my decision. Surrender wasn't an option.

I turned and ran headlong into the mist.

44

Into the Mist

Fanfic's voice filled my ears the moment I dove into the mist. It felt nothing like Mrs. N's power, and yet, it was overwhelming, pushing into my head like . . . like narration. I wasn't sure I wanted to play along with whatever her plan was.

"You're walking through the marsh. There's no one around. The black mist swirls around you as you push further through it. Somewhere ahead of you, according to the maps, there should be a village. But there's no sign of one. No roads, no signs, no nothing. The lantern in your hand gutters and flickers as a cold wind brushes against your back."

I looked down. Sure enough, a metal-framed lantern hung where my wand had a second ago. My outfit had changed, too; instead of the pink-and-blue Costume of *Small Town Super* Understudy or Lab Assistant Panic's lab coat, I wore a wool dress, boots that seemed handmade, and a light blue cloak. I waved the . . . lantern . . . seeing if it would act as my wand, but no dice. I was powerless.

Worse, Fanfic's Episodes were all-hands-on-deck. Every major-leaguer usually worked together to stop her, and right now, no one else was around. This whole mess had gone from bad to worse to, somehow, even worse.

Still, if my choices were to flee through the mist, powerless, or to fight The Agent without a chance of winning, one choice felt better than the others. He'd shot Dr. Jackson, after all, and had probably done the same with Stella-Lunar.

The mist *did* swirl around me as I pushed further into it, and the lantern flared as sulfur and rot-smelling wind gusted past me. Then it went out.

"As you walk through the marsh, the skeletal hands of dead trees loom over you. Out of the corner of your eye, you see something. Then, as suddenly as you saw it, it's gone. Was it ever there? You gather your cloak around you and hurry—somewhere up ahead is Craig-head. You'll be safe there, at the lodge."

Well, if Fanfic thought I'd be safe somewhere, the best thing to do was follow her narration. After all, it wasn't like I could go against her narration now. The moment I started walking, though, something flashed in the corner of my eye. It was tall. And short at the same time. I couldn't quite describe it, but it looked metallic and scaly at the same time. Fursona probably could have identified it, or maybe Su-Bin, but they weren't here.

And then, suddenly, it was gone. I looked left and right, but it seemed to have vanished into thin air. Whatever it was, it wasn't anymore.

Now that I thought about it, the lodge in Craighead sounded lovely. It couldn't be more than another mile—or perhaps two. And somewhere in this dreadful bog, there'd be a road leading to it. I simply had to—

Wait. No. Something was *wrong* here. I never thought like that. Was Fanfic in my head? Was she narrating my *thoughts*? How could that be? Was her narration *that* strong? Was that why they always overloaded her Episodes? I had to be careful if I wanted to survive this without losing my mind to her.

"Okay. The Agent and those three *V*s could be in here," I whispered. "If they are, they'll help split Fanfic's attention."

"It takes you an hour of walking, and you never do find the road, but just as the clouds open in a pouring rain that soaks your clothes right down to your skin, the lights of Craighead finally appear through the dark, fetid mist. The thing you saw appears again, this time lasting no longer than a single blink."

As I trudged through the swamp toward the warm, safe lodge in Craighead, I couldn't help thinking about my sister. She'd moved here with her new husband two years ago, and only lasted—

What. The. Hell. I was better than this. This wasn't real; it was all just Fanfic's imagination, and I had to stay focused in case one of The Agent's temps was the thing following me. I stumbled through the swamp until, sure enough, the village's lanterns started pushing weakly against the fog. My thoughts drifted toward my nonexistent sister again, and I slapped myself across the face before I could finish even a single sentence.

And that's when I saw it again.

This time, I held my eyes open as long as I could. The thing might've been dragon-shaped once, but swamp muck had coated it so thickly I couldn't be sure. Was there a person stuck to its back? When my sister had visited, she'd told me tales of the nuckelavee, a horse-and-man abomination that haunted battlefields. Was that . . . this?

"You hurry toward the lights, slipping into Craighead's nearly-empty streets. The village is little more than a handful of homes, a tinker's shack, and the lodge. It looms over the other buildings, its three floors seeming somehow out of place—it's too tall, too thin, to be here in the middle of the marsh. Even so, its windows are lit, and its door's unlocked and open, beckoning you inside."

Sure. Why not?

I followed my sister's advice. She'd always said that the tinker was not to be trusted, and as I passed the man's shack, he shot me a glare that could have bowled me over. The device he was popping dents out of looked like some sort of musket the men in the village must have used to hunt, but three times as large, with a black rubber hose trailing behind it.

I shivered. Something about that man *was* wrong. Why did he despise me? Had I done something to offend him? I bundled my cloak and hurried toward the lodge, where I'd be safe.

I breathed a sigh of relief as I slipped through the door, though I couldn't precisely explain why. The only other occupant of the floor was a man who appeared to be a barkeep, at least by his positioning in the room. However, his clothes were far too fancy to be the inn's proprietor. His bowtie and jacket were impeccable, and his blonde hair parted perfectly.

A name popped into my head unbidden. *The Agent.*

For a second or two, I pushed Fanfic's narration out of my mind to see if I could still do it. It was harder than it had been before; as I approached whatever she wanted me to find, it got harder and harder to fight her. But I could do it. And that meant The Agent could, too.

"Understudy, this is a setback, but it doesn't change anything. Fanfic's already declared her neutrality. She's irrelevant to my plans," The Agent hissed at me. The grin on his face shifted from slick to sinister.

I could feel Fanfic's power pressing in on me, but I glared back. "She seems . . . relevant to me," I hissed through clenched teeth.

"In the immediate term, it would seem so. But not for long. She never stays for long." The Agent winced, and suddenly, his voice shifted from the slick, slimy salesman's tone to something deeper, almost dead inside. "You're in luck, miss. A single room remains unoccupied—the tower chamber. It's twenty pence for the night, and should I assume you'll move on in the morning?"

"Yes, that will do nicely." Whoever The Agent was and whatever he represented, I wanted as little to do with him as possible.

"The journey up the stairs to the tower room taxes you more than you thought possible, but eventually, you slip through the oak door into a room that smells faintly of lye, and less faintly of damp cloth and rot. The bed seems adequate, though, and you settle down for a restful night's sleep. Tomorrow's journey will be longer, with no village at its end."

"You awaken suddenly. Something is in your room."

I jumped from my bed, reaching for the hooded lantern and opening its aperture until I could see—faintly—the silhouette looming over me. It stepped forward. It wore the same suit I'd seen The Agent wear before, but now, it seemed covered in something bright scarlet, and the man's grin had shifted from sinister to empty. Worse, in his hand, he held a pistol. As the gun rose, the man's eyes flickered with a sudden hatred.

"Understudy, this fog-bound hell changes nothing."

My mind cleared. Right. The Episode. As the gun fired, I tore out of my bed and threw myself to the side. The pistol ball slammed into my arm, sending searing pain rippling across the flesh below my bone. I screamed, but some instinct, perhaps, took over, and I lunged at the inn's proprietor before he could finish the job.

We grappled for the gun, though it wouldn't be good as anything but a bludgeon. Still, I needed a weapon. When he threw me off him, I changed plans. The lantern hung from a hook. I grabbed it with my good arm, foot sliding in something sticky and warm on the floor. Then I spun.

The glass-and-iron lantern slammed into his head, shattering and spewing flaming oil across the right side of his face.

I wasted no time. As he roared in agony, I ducked toward the door. My hand closed on the handle.

Locked.

Behind me, the rotten wood burst into flames. I needed a way out—but there was none. The mirror on the door reflected the horrific form of The Agent, standing and ablaze. He staggered toward me, and I screamed as I spun to fight him.

Something grabbed me by the shoulder from behind and pulled me toward the mirror.

I screamed.

[Episode Finished!]
[Episode: Power War: In Hot Water - R]
[Penalties:N/A]
[Episode Finished! +3 of each Style Point]
[The Agony of Defeat! +1 of each Style Point]
[Role Focus: Drama + Grit - Goal Partially Met: +10 Drama Points]
[Alias - Understudy] [Archetype - Magical Girl] [Community Rank - 85/523]
[HP 1/15]
[Styles and Skills]
▶ Archetype Skill - Transformation Sequence
▶ Combo Skills - Power-Weaving
▶ Badass (22)
▶ Cunning (21)
▶ Drama (52) (Skill Roll Available)
▶ Limelight Barrage 2
▶ Starlance 3
▶ Flamboyance (57) (Skill Roll Available)
▶ Signature Skill - Adaptive Armoire 3
▶ Stored Costumes: (Rainy Day, Copy Cat, Lab Assistant Panic)
▶ Solar Wing 2
▶ Quick-Time Change 3
▶ Improvised Ovation 2
▶ Grit (23)
▶ Freeze-Frame 2

The door slammed shut.

"What the hell?" I asked. Everything hurt. But especially my arm. The pain cut through even my fog-filled headache.

I lay on the floor of the Council of Heroes' chamber, a woman who looked super familiar looming over me. My memories felt disjointed, and it took me almost a minute to place her. "Mrs. N?"

"No." The single word sent a chill through my spine, the first clarity I'd had since I stepped into the black mist. Even though the Episode was over, she was the one . . . villain? I wasn't sure. The one super *everyone* feared. "I'm here because she asked me to be here, and because this way, she'll owe me."

I nodded as if it made sense. It didn't. This close, I could see the differences. Mrs. N's hair was a shade grayer, and her face a little more worn. Fanfic's skin was a half-shade darker, a deep brown bordering on black. Her eyes were wilder, too. They looked like something was burning inside of them beneath her glasses.

"She wanted me to get you out of there. I've done that. Now, get out of here. This tower's mine now, until I decide to go somewhere else." In person, Fanfic sounded almost . . . boring. It contrasted with the fire in her eyes. But under that emptiness, there was something else. I knew she'd been in my head and painted a reality that neither The Agent nor I could escape. For all I knew, his henches couldn't get out, either.

As I nodded shakily, my arm sending pulses of pain across my body, she looked away from me. "*Your face burns and melts, but you'll live—so long as you run. The villagers, awoken by the gunshot, swarm into your lodge, torches in hand. As the tower burns, you have no choice but to attempt to flee into the marsh, leaving the life you've built in Craighead behind. It's two days to the next village. If the horrors in the swamp or the angry citizens of Craighead don't find you first; you realize you've left your gun behind.*"

We'd lost.

We'd definitely lost. I checked the watch, but I hadn't gotten a single message on it. My phone had a few—all from Fursona. I sent her a quick one back, letting her know I was on the way. I wanted to call her or Mom. Or someone. But I didn't stop walking until I'd found the gaping hole she'd torn in the Council of Heroes building's side. Then I took a deep, shaky breath and stepped into the air.

I used [**Solar Wing**], tears welling as every flap pulled at the wound in my arm, and flew shakily away from Mid-Town toward the green room. Fursona would be there. She'd know what to do. That wasn't a promise. It was more of a thin hope.

[**Skill Upgrade! Adaptive Armoire 3 to Wondrous Wardrobe: Allows access to all Costumes**]

45

A Thin Hope

The mood in the green room wasn't exactly positive.

My arm still ached, even though Bee had made me go Rainy Day to try healing myself. It had helped. Not much, but at least I wasn't bleeding anymore. The bullet was still in there, though, and I could barely move my arm. Whatever The Agent had hit me with in Fanfic's Craighead, it was real, and I hadn't had superhero damage to protect me. I probably should have gone to a hospital.

Instead, I was moping.

I lay on the conversation pit couch while Bee stood near the static-filled computer monitors. "They've been like this since before I got back. I'm not sure what it means, but it's not a good sign. I think Rocko's finally cut us off. Maybe we went too far for them."

"You think?" I mumbled. My head still felt foggy; as I shook it in a vain attempt to clear it, my face started heating up. "Sorry."

"You're good. What happened after I left?" Bee asked. She was out of her Fursona Costume. Parts of it covered the floor, though the Kaiju head sat on the coffee table, half stitched back together. I winced; that kid was *way* too powerful for a toddler.

The fight was easy to explain, but when I got to the end, Bee asked so many questions about Stella-Lunar and The Agent's betrayal that I couldn't keep my answers straight. Eventually, I cut in with a question of my own. "Do you know who else got out?"

"Theseus, Gourmet, and Foamy Flash did. I haven't heard from Lady Lockless, so I can only assume the worst with her."

"No, she did. Fanfic pulled me through the door, and it was closed earlier. Lady Lockless would have had to open it for her," I speculated.

"Okay, so Lady Lockless is out there somewhere, too. I think a couple of supers got out of Yorkston. They said that it was mostly prisoner-taking. That makes sense; dead supers don't look good for anyone, and if they can convert some of the PEL supes into pro-Ilneat ones, that's a big win for them. Not that they need it. The Pro-Earth League's pretty much done. There's only one super still fighting," Bee said.

"Florida-Man?"

"Florida-Man. The predictions that he'd run out of energy seem unfounded. Every time he slows down, another Red Bull and Vodka appears nearby. His blood alcohol content has to be through the roof, and the news is speculating that he's approaching heart attack levels of caffeine. But he's not *accomplishing* anything, either."

Alright. Okay. This wasn't the worst-case scenario. I still had Bee. We still had the green room—I glanced at the sealed door to Rocko's Studio, half expecting some ridiculously overpowered hero to come surging through it. There were still a few other supers we could rely on. Mrs. N. Our Superpower Ethics partners. Maybe a couple others. But it wouldn't be enough to stop the ebbing tide here.

A dozen questions kept bouncing around in my head. How had the Ilneats all escaped? What was The Agent thinking, going after Stella-Lunar? Had she survived? What exactly went wrong in Yorkston? Would the remaining PEL supers keep fighting, or were they done? I didn't have answers to any of them.

The muted TV changed.

I stared at a set of narrow black eyes that darted from one side of the camera to the other, and to the wide, sharp teeth opened in a fake-looking smile. The gorilla/otter hybrid sat at a desk—not the one I was used to seeing them at, though. Behind them, I could only see a steel wall and stars—brighter and crisper than I'd ever seen them before.

I lunged for the remote and unmuted the television.

"—current Director of the Ilneat Network in the Earth system. In the last four hours, the Network has been forced to pull its Ilneat employees out of the Hot Zones in several major cities due to an employment dispute by several heroes and villains in our employ," Rocko said. The Ilneat stared at the camera woodenly, a single cigar burning in one of their hands.

"Due to this egregious breach of contract, which put several of our Ilneat employees in harm's way, we have no choice but to . . ." They paused for a moment, looking over the camera for the first time, then back down. ". . . terminate the following contracts, effective immediately:

"The Narrator, Harriet Nathans; Fanfic, Halie Nathans; McHammer, Karl O'Brian; Florida-Man, Robert P. Goode; Gourmet, Jessica Andonte; Theseus, Tanner Brown . . ."

The list went on, but I barely heard it. Instead, I looked at Bianca. Her face looked as blank as mine felt. The Ilneats were outing every hero and villain who'd participated in the attacks. That included us. I ran through the list of people who knew either Anika DuPont or Magical Girl Understudy, trying to do some damage control.

"Mindstorm, Rebecca Rogers; Flare; Calvin Bearson; Magical Girl Candi Crush, Sabrina Short; Magical Girl Understudy—"

As Rocko said my name, I hammered out a quick text.

<Sorry. I couldn't let you know. Call when you can - Annie 6:15>

I didn't expect a response from Su-Bin. Not right away; she was probably neck-deep in APPEAL stuff. But she was my friend, and she deserved to know that I at least felt bad about deceiving her.

As for the fight? It was over. Maybe now Mom would let me drop out, and I could go back to Riverside and pretend none of this had ever happened. That didn't seem likely, given that the whole world knew I was Magical Girl Understudy now and that I'd tried to overthrow our alien overlords. But I could dream. I could dream about a lot: being able to go back home, find a job in the diner or as a receptionist at the drill works, and just disappear. That wouldn't be so bad.

I'd had my fifteen minutes of fame. Tranquility could keep fighting for a better world, or Mrs. N, but that didn't mean it was going to happen. Not when so many powerful people wanted to keep things the way they were. And the status quo wasn't so bad, right?

Besides, Bee could come, too. We'd get a double-wide down the street from Mom and Dad's and just . . . be for a while instead of putting the weight of the world on our shoulders. People could survive without Magical Girl Understudy and Fur-sona, especially now. We'd failed, and it was time to move on to whatever we could salvage of our lives.

I was so caught up in my thoughts that I didn't realize the TV was off until Bee tapped my shoulder.

I blinked. She had her backpack stuffed full with the Justice-Roo and Eagle-sona fursuits, a second bag with a few changes of clothes and a toothbrush, and her half fixed Kaiju-sona suit laid out on the green room's floor. "Annie, focus. This place isn't going to be safe in about fifteen minutes. We've gotta move."

"Where?" I asked. "Riverside?"

"I don't know," Bee said. She sounded high-pitched and nervous, like when we first met, and I could smell the anxiety pouring off her sweat. "I've got ideas, but they're not good, and I don't think going to Riverside or Tortuga West is the right plan, but we should tell our families that shit's getting real once we're somewhere safe. I was thinking we would get out of Tokyexico City first and then regroup, maybe in one of the mountain towns we passed on the way to your place, but I'm not really sure. Or we could see Mrs. N. Anything. But we have to leave."

She was right. We couldn't stay here. I shook myself out of my daydream, arm still aching, and jogged out of the green room and into Walnut Tower, Room 1301. I had so much *stuff* here, but what to take and what to leave?

The textbooks were a no-brainer. They stayed. So did the unused make-up stuff; I wouldn't need it if I was on the run. I opened my drawers and grabbed a few changes of underwear, then dumped some T-shirts on top of them without looking at the details. What they looked like didn't matter. Bee was right. We had to go fast. Two sets of jeans, a winter jacket, gloves, hat, done. It wasn't anything like packing to go to school two Augusts ago. Nothing was folded; it just got dumped into the suitcase.

A flash of black, green, and yellow caught my eye from the closet—Mom's Costume. Whether I wanted to wear it or not, Dark Girl Shock and Awe had to come with me. Mom's identity wasn't out, and I needed to keep it that way. Plus, Shock and Awe wasn't associated with Understudy—at least not yet. I dumped the Costume into my suitcase and zipped it up.

Toothbrush, hairbrush, deodorant. Bee hadn't taken her perfumes—not even the green apple one—so I only packed the basics. And *The Diary of Golden Goose*. It felt too important to leave behind.

"Okay, ready," I said, rolling my bag into the kitchen.

"Tunnel elevator!" Bee shouted from the green room.

I dragged my bag one-handed into the green room, transformed back to Understudy, and hurried to catch up with the backpack-wearing Kaiju. "Not your car?"

"Nope. We're gonna have to leave the Civic here. Maybe when things calm down, we can grab it, but too many people know it's Bianca's. The tunnels should be pretty empty. Let's exit at Roth Arena and head toward the Wall from there."

"Sure." I pushed the button, and the elevator arrived, then dropped like a rock as soon as we were inside. Bee white-knuckled her backpack straps the whole way down; I could feel her tension even through her fursuit's plushie scales. When the elevator finally screeched to a stop at the exit to the tunnel network below Tokyexico University, I reached out and squeezed her clawed hand with my good one. "We'll be okay."

"I don't know about that," she said sadly. "We were supposed to play blue tomorrow."

I stared at her for a second as she started power-walking down the tunnel. Then I burst out laughing. A moment later, so did she. "It's so stupid, Annie. That's all I can think about, and it's the least important thing, but I can't get it out of my head."

I didn't have a response, so instead, I just kept walking. She followed, half a step behind, as we pushed through the tunnel we'd taken to get to the job fair last year. That probably wouldn't be happening again—not with half of TUSSA and most of the SSS out of the picture.

When we finally emerged outside of Roth Arena, it was dark out. I looked back at the campus, breathing a sigh of relief. Even though we'd—so far, at least—disappeared, my throat was still tight, and my heart wouldn't stop pounding. I stared back in the direction of Walnut Tower. I'd miss having a proper hideout, and even having access to Rocko's Studio.

A flash of light filled the air as a beam reached out from somewhere in the city. It touched the top of Walnut Tower, then stopped. I braced myself for a shock wave—for anything—but nothing happened. No explosion, no laser sound. Then, another beam arced into another building on campus, and the same thing happened: nothing.

But even so, I couldn't shake the feeling of dread. That something bad would have happened if we'd been there.

"Come on," Bee said. "Whatever that was, we can't stay here, either. We're on the run, so let's run."

She was right. As she hurried off into the darkness, I followed her. Things were moving too fast, but one thing was for sure: we were fugitives—two women driving a car toward the cliff's edge.

PART SIX

46

The Cliff's Edge

We hadn't even gotten off campus when I grabbed Fursona's arm. "This is dumb. Really dumb. You're a giant dinosaur, and I'm a Magical Girl who vomits pink and blue contrails if I fly. There's no world where we're more conspicuous as two college girls than we are as heroes, and we need to be sneaky."

"What am I supposed to do with the suit, then?" Bianca asked.

She had a point; her bags were all but overflowing, and there was no way we'd be able to fit the whole dinosaur suit into a backpack. We couldn't exactly leave the other fursuits behind, either. Who knew what powers we'd need access to in the next day or two? "Okay. Here's the plan. I'll ditch some of my shirts, I guess, and you put on your warm stuff and do the same. We'll make it fit, even if we have to split it up a little."

"Fine," Bee said, and we doubled back to Roth Arena.

It was a simple project to break into one of the main doors, slip into a fan-side bathroom, and quickly change. The painful part was the pile of clothes we had to leave behind. Even with Bee and I overdressing for the February weather, a few of our favorites wouldn't be making the trip to . . .

"Okay, now where?" I asked.

Bee shrugged as we slipped out of the bathroom and toward the edge of campus. I didn't have a better answer, so we picked a direction and walked into the University District.

"I already miss the whiteboard," I mumbled into the darkness, mittened hand in Bee's. Not having a plan sucked.

"Me too." She paused to tie her shoe, which was weird because it was just a sticky fastener, not laces. "Don't look. I think we've got *V*s coming up. Two of them. The Agent's probably going wide, not powerful."

"That's . . . not great for us," I said. Neither of us could use our powers without our Costumes—Bee was a little stronger and faster, but the suits carried a lot of firepower for her. If two *Vs*, even underpowered ones, pegged us as Understudy and Fursona, we were in trouble.

"No. Let's beeline for a diner. That's a normal college thing to do, right?"

"Right."

"We'll think there and try to make a plan," Bee said.

The closest diner sat across the street, but it'd put us right in the villains' path, so instead, I pulled Bee into the art studio we'd . . . saved . . . from Jumper in our first semester. I wrapped an arm around her waist, and we pretended to enjoy the art for about five minutes. It wasn't bad, honestly; lots of landscapes and horses, mostly paintings, but a few sketches. Surely that'd be enough time, right?

I peeked out the window. No *Vs*—at least none that I could see. And the diner was right across the busy street—an easy hop for Understudy or Roo-sona but an undertaking for Bee and me.

The minute waiting at the crosswalk was the most nerve-wracking of the whole evening, especially when some guys from one of the college frats joined us. I smiled nervously; the smell of booze was strong on them. Worse, when the light changed and we crossed, it was clear they were going our way, but at least they weren't *Vs*. They were too loud, too drunk, and too unhelmeted to be henches.

Still, it was a relief when we stepped into the diner. The smell of greasy breakfast food filled my nose. Bacon and sausage, syrup, and not-quite-burned hash browns. The smell of Mom after a shift. My stomach growled, and it wasn't the only one. Neither of us had eaten since a light lunch before the Episode started, and it was close to eight now. The frat guys joked loudly behind us as we waited for the harried-looking waitress to seat us.

Less than a minute after she sat us in the back, near the kitchen, though, I glanced over the top of my menu to see the two *Vs* we'd avoided before. And, worse, they had a third with them this time. "We've gotta go," I whispered to Bianca.

"Why? We just got here," she said.

"We've got company." I nodded my head toward the *Vs*. One of them looked our way, and I pulled the menu back up as casually as I could.

Bianca nodded slowly. "Through the kitchen?"

"Sure."

We slipped through the diner's double doors and into a busy kitchen just as the poor waitress noticed us. She yelled something, but I was already leading Bee through the maze of burners and prep counters and past annoyed-looking line cooks. Someone's dinner overturned behind us, but I didn't even apologize. The door was right there. We just had to get there, and we'd be home free.

Someone burst into the kitchen behind us, and I grabbed Bee's hand as I burst into a full sprint. We crashed through the metal back door and tumbled out in the alley. "Left!" I called.

Then I dragged her right, running until my lungs burned and feeling thankful for the hardcore soccer practices Sierra had put me through. We ducked around the corner just as the door slammed open again, this time accompanied by a chorus of annoyed and angry cooks and the screechy yells of the waitress.

We ran an entire block before I dragged her back into another alley, then looped back the way we'd come. Only then did I slow down, panting and sucking in deep breaths. "Okay, we need a better plan than 'find a diner,'" I muttered.

It had been almost twenty minutes, and we weren't any closer to having a plan.

We were a lot closer to getting caught, though.

The pressure had been intense. So far, Bee had saved our butts twice, including once by ducking across Lincoln Street through oncoming traffic. The *V*s had blasted their way through, but we'd managed to dodge them by doubling right back across. The wild goose chase was leading us toward Tottergarten, and we'd agreed that it'd be our port in the storm.

I didn't like it. But I accepted it. Besides, it wasn't like we could get on a subway and disappear that way, or find a rental car place, do the paperwork, and get out of the city. And the police would only get hurt—if they even helped us. This was super-powered business, after all.

We were only a few blocks from Mrs. N's daycare when a bang filled the air and something flew over my head.

I whirled as the trio of *V*s appeared on the street behind us. One looked familiar; a ridiculously edgy-looking sword hung over his shoulder, and his cloak looked more appropriate to his Costume than the other two. My hand dropped to my wand, only to brush against my jeans. "Shit," I muttered. I hadn't even thought to text Honeycomb that we were coming—we'd been too busy running. That had been a mistake.

"You're in that, yeah," the swordsman said mockingly.

The fight didn't last long; the *V* with the sword didn't even have to get involved. A wave of sound slammed into Bianca, pushing her into the street and knocking her out. And, before I could react, a gun was in my face. My hands went up, and despite my best efforts, I went cross-eyed at the barrel.

He leaned against the wall, spat on the ground, and watched as the other two *V*s tied our wrists with zip ties. "Check their bags, make sure they're who we think they are, and let's take care of things."

I tried to fight back, but without my powers, tied up, and against powered *V*s, all I could really do was flail around on the ground while a lady sat on my back and kept me pinned. When she hit me with the pistol butt, it felt like getting hit by a steel pipe. Then, suddenly, Tails was in front of me, the plushie completely inanimate and yet sympathetic-looking at the same time.

"Yep, that's them. Pack it up and get them to the car. The boss wants to gloat."

Something pressed into my side. Cold, circular, and unyielding. That was enough to convince me to move along with them. Buying time felt like the right play, not going out in a blaze of glory. A small part of me wondered why I wasn't freaking out. Any other Extra would be.

Then again, I was a super, even if I wasn't in-Costume, and I'd been in worse binds.

Okay. There had to be a plan or something here. I could . . . slow-transform to Understudy. That'd take almost a minute. It'd be impossible, even if they gave me access to Tails. And the Fursona suits were even less possible. The *Vs'* car loomed in front of us, a nondescript black one with tinted windows. I braced myself to be put in the trunk; if that was the case, I had a shot.

Instead, the *V* holding my arms shoved me into the passenger's seat, then dumped our bags into the trunk behind us before climbing in herself. I had no way out, no way to transform. Fursona didn't, either; her captor sandwiched us in the middle between them, leaving the front passenger seat empty. For a second, I thought about making a break for it and getting out that way, but the gun was still digging into my side.

The sword *V*—I recognized him from last semester, but his build wasn't quite the same; maybe it was a different hench?—started walking around the car toward the driver's seat.

He never made it.

As the *V* on my side of the car reached for a black bag to put over my head, something slammed into the swordsman's chest, doubling him over. A streak of orangish light no higher than his waist followed the impact, and a moment later, he was on the ground. As he picked himself up, the light streak turned the corner and hit him again, this time knocking him up onto the car's hood. The *V* next to Bianca opened her door, stepped out, and fired her pistol.

Before she could get a second shot off, the streak slammed into her, too.

My eyes went wide as I saw, for the first time, the identity of the *Vs'* attacker.

She was small. Not quite as small as Kaiju Kid, but definitely a preschooler. One of the Playpen Patrol members I hadn't hung out with as much as The Cloud. I winced as she zoomed away, then finished off the last *V*. Then the battlefield was quiet.

Kid Zoomies opened the door. "Okay, civivens, you're safe now!"

"Kid Zoomies, that was really dangerous," I said, extracting myself from the back seat and letting the pint-sized superhero break the zip ties. Bee twitched, opening her eyes and groaning, then shutting them again.

"Nuh-uh. Playpen Patrol, go!" she shouted. "They were being bad, and Mrs. N says we have to stop people from being bad!"

"Okay. You stopped them from being bad," Bianca said. She'd woken up and had already gotten her backpacks and my bags out of the car. "Now, listen, we need to get you back to Tottergarten before you get in trouble."

"Or worse, we do," I added.

Kid Zoomies nodded thoughtfully. "We can go back. Mrs. N and Dad will get mad otherwise. I didn't tell them I was leaving. I just left when Jungle Jim and the others came in!"

"Da . . . er, oh no," Bee said, biting off the swear word. "So no one knows where you are?"

Kid Zoomies shook her head enthusiastically. "Nope! I had hero stuff to do, and they always say no!"

"Come on, let's go." Kid Zoomies hadn't caught on that we knew who she was yet, and she didn't know who we were—hopefully. If we hurried, we could just drop her off, and everything would be fine.

I hefted my bags and started walking. The last place in Tokyexico City I wanted to be at was Tottergarten; there was no way more *V*s weren't waiting there, and Kid Zoomies's attack had only worked because none of the *V*s were ready for her—and because they were underpowered, mass-produced villains, not limited edition ones. Besides, I was done.

Wasn't I?

It was only three blocks to Tottergarten; part of me hoped Kid Zoomies would take off, but no. She kept close, practically vibrating in place and talking a mile a minute about how she'd "saved the day" and "done hero stuff." If it wasn't so embarrassing to need bailing out against a handful of underpowered *V*s, I would have been cheering for her, too. As it was, though . . . it stung a little.

Bee didn't look any better than I felt. She kept eying the bag with the Roo-sona suit in it, like she wanted to spend the time to suit up, but then second-guessing herself. I could sympathize. If Kid Zoomies figured out that not only had she saved two people, but Understuffy and Mouse, we were screwed forever. Might as well die from embarrassment.

My heart stopped as a hand whirled me around to face a wall of muscle. Bianca's feet left the ground a second later as another hand wrapped around her arm and yanked upward.

"I'm going to give you two seconds to explain who you are and where you found this kid," Brick House said, his voice empty of all emotion and his eyes two black pits under the streetlights. "And if your answer's bad, you're both dead. Talk."

47

Talk

For half a second, I let myself feel relief. Kid Zoomies was going to be fine.

Then the fear hit, and it hit hard.

We . . . probably weren't going to be *quite* as fine.

This wasn't Jungle Jim I was looking at, the towering member of the Anti-Naptime League. This was *Brick House*, a serious business villain who—yes—was retired. But he was more than capable of following through on his threat and flattening me. He'd fought a full-grown Florida Maneater, after all. He could snap unpowered me like a twig. His hand wrapped around Bianca's well-muscled arm, engulfing it completely.

And I couldn't do a damn thing about it.

I took a deep breath. "Listen, we found her out here—"

"Nuh-uh! I found you and saved you!" Kid Zoomies interrupted. "I stopped the bad guys from doing bad stuff!"

She sounded so proud of herself that even Brick House's composure broke for a second. Then the glare returned as quickly as it had disappeared. His grip tightened on my shoulder. "Explain. Now."

"Okay, listen," Bee said. She sounded a little fuzzy from getting knocked out, and I didn't blame her for that at all, but she pulled herself together as best she could. "We know you. I'm . . . Fursona. And that's Magical Girl Understudy. If you don't believe us, you can check our bags—the Costumes and cat are in there. We were on the run and got jumped by some villains, and . . . yeah, Kid Zoomies saved us."

Brick House's eyebrow raised a millimeter. Then he let go of me and grabbed a phone. A few button presses later, he was talking into it. "Got her. She was only two blocks out. Yeah, we got lucky. Don't need to tell Mrs. N or the parents. Meet me out front, and we'll sneak her in through the back. I found two other kids, too. No, not ours, but they claim we know 'em. Three minutes."

He hung up. "You're all coming with me."

I nodded slowly. At least he wasn't trying to kill us yet. So that was something.

Brick House's eyes never left the back of my head the whole walk over, even after he carefully handed Kid Zoomies off to an absolutely terrifying Mister Twister, who slipped into Pranky Jones as he led her away toward the playground gate. I started following him, but the massive hand landed on my shoulder again. "No. Not yet."

Then he opened my bag and, for the second time in less than a half hour, someone rooted through my stuff and Bianca's. When he was finally satisfied, he nodded. "Okay. You have the stuff. Inside, bathrooms, and get changed."

"You're not very trusting, are you?" Bianca asked.

"No. Not when Mrs. N calls us saying a kid's gone missing and another one vanishes when she gets her back. When you've proven you are who you say, *then* I'll trust you."

He paraded us through the front door and past a few other members of the Anti-Nap League—Felicia Fire's red hair was missing from the group—and we hurried into the cramped bathroom. It took a few minutes to get the Roo-sona suit on and transform into Magical Girl Understudy, but when we appeared, Brick House finally relaxed, and I could see him slipping into the Jungle Jim persona. I nodded. "Good enough for you?"

"Yeah, good enough for me. You can help Honey and her boy out with the kids while you wait for Mrs. N. She'll be glad to see you, but she's also got parents to manage."

We stepped into the playroom.

"Holy crap," Fursona said through her headset. I nodded in agreement. Tottergarten was a zoo.

Mrs. N must have invited the Playpen Patrol's parents to stay here after Kaiju Kid's disappearance, because the adults not in Costume outnumbered the supers. A harried-looking couple held a kid leash as they stared at their five-year-old hovering near the ceiling, while a single woman desperately tried to corral Kaiju Kid, who was carrying a carrot stick and a carton of milk while roaring at the top of her little lungs.

I tried to be subtle and figure out where the best place for me would be, but before I could maneuver my way toward Honeycomb to ask, Milkbar slammed into Fursona's chest. "It's the mouse! The mouse is back!"

"Still not a mouse," Fursona said. The smile in her voice carried even through her voice modulator as she sat down on the floor, giving in to the superstrong Playpen Patroller's hug. "I'm a kangaroo, remember? It's a marsupial."

"Yeah!" Outlet said. "And you said they all live in Australia, right?"

"I . . . did say that," Fursona admitted. "But sometimes, even adults are wrong. Most of them live in Australia, but *some* live here."

"Like you?" the electricity-powered super-toddler asked.

"Yeah, like me. And like opossums."

I tried to sneak away from the conversation and find Honeycomb. The last thing I wanted to do was get involved in Tottergarten stuff. Getting home was more important. But as I crossed the play place, looking for the bee girl, something hit me from above.

"Understuffy! I love you!" The Cloud said.

"Hi, The Cloud," I answered, grabbing his hand and pulling him to the floor. "What are you learning today?"

"Nothing. Today's a play day! And a sleepover. Mom and Dad get to be here all day and all night!" The Cloud seemed super excited about that; he started dragging me toward his parents. "Mom! Dad! This is Understuffy, and I love her!"

"Hi, Miss Understudy," The Cloud's mom said. She stuck out a hand, and I shook it, trying my best to channel my Extra Relations persona even though I was exhausted. "We met briefly, sort of. He gave you a part of his Costume."

"Yeah, he did." I smiled, remembering how frustrating that day had been. Compared to today, it seemed like a walk in the park.

Fursona was getting swarmed under by preschoolers, but more concerning was the single mom with Kaiju Kid tucked under her arm. She hovered nearby, clearly unsure what to do, as Kaiju Kid roared shrilly at Fursona and raised her arms over her head. Did Kaiju Kid recognize her? And would her mom be pissed at Fursona for the fight? Before I could answer any of those questions, The Cloud took off, his hand slipping from mine. I lunged after him, then looked at his parents apologetically. "Whoops!"

"Oh, don't worry about it. He's learned how to control it a lot better, but we still keep him on the leash outdoors. Mrs. N does excellent work here," his dad said. He waited as his kid reached the top of the play place and lowered himself onto the slide. "We're also thrilled she's taking security seriously, even if seeing the 'villains' Kenny's been fighting in their real personas is . . . kind of a lot."

He glanced nervously at Jungle Jim, who was currently arm wrestling Milkbar. They were both putting their all into it. So far, it was a tie.

"Yeah, I understand that. We just ran into him out of our Costumes, and it was . . . an experience." I shivered, letting myself feel something for the first time since the *Vs* had started tailing us. "Actually, I have a question for you. How do you deal with being a superhero's parent and not having powers yourself?"

The Cloud's dad cleared his throat, but his wife interrupted. "That's not really what you want to ask, is it, Miss DuPont?"

I flushed red; she was right. "No, it's not, but I'm not sure how to ask."

"Rip off the Band-Aid," she suggested. "You and your kangaroo friend saved one of Kenny's classmates, so you're entitled to a dumb question or two."

"Okay. You don't seem to care about The Cloud's secret identity; you just told me he was Kenny twice. But aren't you worried that makes it easier for people to figure out who you are? And who he is? Won't that cause problems later when he's a real superhero?"

She laughed. "My kid is a literal balloon. Sometimes, he even jumps out the car window and rides behind on his leash. Any supervillain who wants to mess with him knows exactly where to find us, so there's never been much point in the secret identity. Maybe when he's older, he'll pick a new one. But just because they know who he is doesn't mean we should panic and run away to a new city. Mrs. N's the best at what she does, and Kenny's only villains are these guys."

"Yeah, his future's worth the risk," Mr. The Cloud added.

"Thanks," I said, disengaging slowly as one of the kids screamed in Fursona's ear. I joined her on the floor, eying the nervous-looking mom. "I'll handle these kids for a little while if you want to talk to her."

"Not really," Bee's voice came over the headset. "I'm terrified. I had to beat the crap out of her daughter earlier today. What if she's pissed?"

"What if she's not?" I whispered. "What if she's happy you got her daughter back? The kid looks fine—I bet you didn't even hurt her."

"Dammit, Annie," Bee said under her breath. Then she stood up, prying Kid Zoomies off her. "Okay, kids, I have to go talk to an adult, but Miss Understudy's going to tell you all about, uh, plays and stuff."

"Gee, thanks," I said. Then I sat down to have a highly improvised conversation.

". . . and so when you're watching movies, everyone in them is pretending," I finished, feeling less and less confident by the second. "None of it's real; they're all acting. It's the same thing as a play."

"Really?" Outlet asked. "Are you sure? My brother always says it's all real, and he knows *everything*."

"Yes, really, really. They all have to play pretend when the movie's getting made, but then they go home, and they're just regular people." Nothing would make me happier than for Mrs. N to interrupt; this whole conversation had gotten out of control—and it had only gotten worse when Kaiju Kid tried to eat my hand midway through.

But at least her mom and Fursona hadn't come to blows yet. In fact, their conversation seemed to be going better than mine was.

"So, they're all lying?" Milkbar's brow furrowed in a glare. "Mrs. N says we're not supposed to lie!"

"No, they're not lying. They're pretending." I sighed. "Look, I'm a superhero, right?"

"Yeah, you're Understuffy!"

"Understuffy's the best!"

The wave of preschool compliments washed over me, and I took a deep breath. I didn't *feel* like the best. "Well, I'm not a superhero all the time. Most of the time, I'm a regular person."

The group of kids was quiet, scratching their heads and staring at the ceiling. Then Milkbar shouted, "Oh! Like how I'm really James!"

And then, all at once, the kids were screaming their real names at me as parents facepalmed in the background. Honeycomb came over with a tray of juice boxes—including one set far away from the others with the words *sugar-free* emblazoned across it—and slowly focused their attention on her. Then, as she passed them out, she leaned over to me. "The Narrator would like to see you and Fursona. She says it's important. 'World-shaking news'—her words, not mine."

I groaned, a mixture of relief and exhaustion filling me up as I pushed off the floor. Fursona and Kaiju Kid's mom were . . . hugging? Yeah, that was an embrace, not a struggle, so that conversation must have ended alright.

Eventually they finished, and I headed down the hall toward Mrs. N's office.

The door hung open, and The Narrator said, "Come in," when we were still halfway down the hall. She looked absolutely drained; a half dozen coffee cups sat on her table, and her computer flicked between different angles of the building's security cameras. The bags under her eyes hung almost to her lips—had she slept in days? Or was this all stress from Kaiju Kid going missing?

"Hi, Mrs. N," I said.

Her eyes met mine, deep brown pools that betrayed an even deeper pain. "Miss DuPont. Miss Marino. Thank you for stopping Maggie from hurting people. I never would have thought that The Agent would resort to kidnapping. I'm also sorry for abandoning you in today's moment of need."

Then she shook herself. "By way of apology and thanks, I want to help you find a path to victory."

48

A Path to Victory

"You have a way to win?" Bianca asked.

Mrs. N shook her head and set down the newspaper she always had. "No. If I had a surefire way to win, I'd make it happen. I think there's a possible path to victory, though.

"After Miss Marino returned Kaiju Kid to me, I drove her back here and phoned her mom. She was beyond happy, and came as quickly as she could. But before she got here, Kaiju Kid talked. You know how kids are—no filter, whatever's on their minds. She told me about where she'd been taken."

"The Hot Zone? We know about that, and unless you've got Lady Lockless hidden away, we're not getting inside. Plus, that doesn't solve the problem of *everyone* teleporting away," I said.

"It might. She wasn't taken to the Hot Zone right away. That took, according to her, 'a long, long time.' But first, they put her in a room underground, somewhere stinky. I asked her what kind of smelly, and she said it was like her friend's house, wet and gross. That gives us a lead—not much of one, since she couldn't tell us where her friend lives. But it's not what's most important. What's most important is that she wasn't the only person stuck there. They had a bunch of empty rooms, and one of them had a lady in it."

I was still trying to wrap my head around something. I'd been close to understanding it when the kids all yelled their names, but even though it was right there, it felt like I needed one more breakthrough to really *get* it. Now, it was fading away, and it took me a minute to refocus.

The Narrator kept talking after sipping some coffee and shivering a little. "Sorry. She said the lady made shimmering bubbles, but they weren't doing anything. And she said one of her arms looked like it didn't work very well. However, they didn't get to talk because Kaiju Kid got moved again. From her description, I think that was Dr. Jackson."

It took me a second. But, no, Dr. Jackson wasn't back as a professor, and . . . Dr. Mays had never been the most financially successful super in terms of Episodes won and money made. Their powers hadn't been "TV good."

Bianca had the same thought. "That explains why he went pro-Ilneat. It was never about what he believed. If The Agent had his partner, he had no choice."

"I agree," The Narrator said. "It means he might be turnable. It also gives us somewhere to look. In fact, I think it gives us a big hint. The Agent's base is somewhere that's falling apart and smells gross and wet. That means Thornton, the Poudre districts, or possibly the Foothills, but they're high up, not near a water source. I'm guessing here."

She typed into her computer, then turned the monitor our way. The map of Thornton was zoomed in on a bunch of lakes and ponds that surrounded the Platte River as it wove its way through the district, but as her finger tapped the screen, I saw what she meant. Three perfectly square ponds and a handful of metal tanks—like the ones we'd fought near at the chemical plant—were clearly visible next to a handful of houses that had once been niceish.

"This is the West Brown Water Treatment Plant," Mrs. N said. "I think it matches everything Kaiju Kid said, and what she described sounds like a prison for supers— like Almhurst, but private and secret. I know we're relying on a toddler, so she could be making things up, but I don't believe she is."

I nodded. "Okay, so the five of us go check it out tomorrow and try to break Dr. Jackson out?"

"No," Mrs. N interrupted. "It'll be you two and you two alone. Vigilant Vow could hold his own with the right familiars, but Honeycomb has no business being in a war zone. And I can't leave the kids here. Not after Kaiju Kid. This plan's entirely on you two."

"What's your endgame, then?" I asked, feeling crushed. It was always on us. Mrs. N had to be the most powerful hero I knew of, and she wouldn't commit herself to battle. There had to be more to it.

"Tranquility is my endgame. I've spent my entire life trying to teach kids the difference between right and wrong, trying to create superheroes who *believe* in right and wrong, who won't follow the Ilneats' studios for a few dollars. Tranquility is my model for success. She's fighting for a better future for everyone, and she has since she was a toddler here. I'm training all these kids to do the same.

"If you win, it'll be easier to move toward a world where heroes do the right thing because it's right, not because it benefits them." She stood up. "But if not, I'll keep teaching the next generation to be better. And, with the Tranquility formula, I'll have less McHammers . . . less Stella-Lunars, and more heroes like her, or like I hope you'll be. By the time I'm old enough to retire, maybe superheroes will act like they're supposed to. I really believe they will, and that on a long enough timeline, we'll win."

"Huh," Bee said.

Bianca and I sat in The Narrator's office alone; she'd left to talk with the Playpen Patrol's parents about long-term arrangements for their children's safety. "I wouldn't have guessed."

My head wouldn't stop spinning. It wasn't just the reveal that Mrs. N had been playing the longest game of any hero. I'd known she was legitimately *good*, so that didn't change anything.

No, I was almost to that breakthrough about identity. And it had . . . something to do with the kids. How comfortable they were being Kenny, James, and Elisabeth, but also The Cloud, Milkbar, and Outlet. They could be both. Why? Our secret identities were so important to all of us that the studios had used them as a weapon. But for the Playpen Patrol, whether they were kids or heroes didn't matter. So why?

The only thing I could think of was that to them, their identities *didn't* matter. They weren't James sometimes and Milkbar others. They were just . . . themselves—all the time.

And there it was. I could resolve the Anika DuPont versus Magical Girl Understudy problem that easily. I wasn't them. I was just *me*.

So, the next question. How committed was *I* to winning this? How competitive was *I*? Could *I* make this path to victory work? I closed my eyes, thinking about myself. Not the domino mask I'd worn as Understudy or the student mask I'd worn as Anika DuPont, but who I was under all that. And eventually, as the seconds of silence turned to minutes, I made my decision.

"I think we can win this," I said.

"You do?" Bee asked. "That's a change."

"Yeah, I do." I reached for my phone. "It's going to take as few moving parts as possible, though. Simple, punchy, and foolproof. That's where Mindstorm went wrong, and that's where we can be better than her. Go see if Honeycomb has a whiteboard around here."

Honeycomb *did* have a whiteboard. It was small—little more than a handheld one—but we didn't need that much space. The plan was simple; there were only two moving parts we had any control over, not counting us.

The Narrator was okay with us using Tottergarten as a springboard and hideout until we started our attack on The Agent's weird prison below Thornton. After that, we could drop off rescued prisoners here, and if it came to fighting, she'd keep the building and the innocents inside it safe. That left some question about whether that included us. She hadn't committed one way or another, instead opening a conversation with Kid Zoomies's dad.

The other moving piece was Su-Bin.

Or, more accurately, the antisuperhero movement in general. I needed an in with them somewhere, because there weren't many supers left that I could rely on. So, I was making a late-night phone call.

It rang three times before Su-Bin picked it up. "One reason not to hang up on you."

"I'll keep calling, and you'll miss your classes tomorrow if you turn the phone alarm off," I said immediately.

Silence. Then Su-Bin snorted. "Fuck you, Annie, you know that?"

"Yeah, I know that. I'm sorry. But how was I supposed to tell you?"

More silence. "Whatever. What do you want?"

"I want to apologize and tell you what's going on." I launched into a massive explanation of the last week or two from the perspective of the Pro-Earth League. What we'd been fighting for, how the fights had gone, and how hopeless it looked now. It took a while, but she listened. Or at least, she didn't hang up.

When I finally finished, the phone stayed quiet. "So, yeah, this is the part where Understudy and Annie are both aligned. I want you to help me, because there's no one else who can."

"You want me to do what?"

"Protest the Ilneats outside of the Hot Zone tomorrow at 11:00 a.m."

"Why?"

I paused. Understudy would have said it was so APPEAL wasn't underfoot. Annie wouldn't have even suggested it, because APPEAL was just a thing her friend did. "Because it's the right thing to do, and it'll help me help people. And because it'll draw attention and let Fursona and I save someone's life."

"And how do I keep my people safe?" she asked.

"Tell them not to try to get inside and keep yourselves as unthreatening as possible, I guess. I think most of the supers on that side will be in a pretty good mood, and they probably won't care much about you. They all but won today, after all. I just need something flashy to draw the eye."

I took a deep breath and kept going before she could interrupt. "I think APPEAL's right about how broken superheroes are right now. I've been talking to The Narrator and a couple of other *real* heroes, and I'm sorry for my part in all this, and I want it to stop."

Even *more* silence. "I don't want your apologies. I want your help fixing it—not just for you heroes but for everyone."

"Okay?" I asked, waiting for the shoe to fall.

It did. "If I'm going to spend the social capital getting APPEAL to show up Mid-Town, midday, on a Friday, you're going to agree—in public—to some principles. First, superheroes and villains need to be cut loose from the Ilneat studio structure. Completely. Not a transfer of control. Not a rebranding. No aliens, no Hot Zones, no unscripted superhero shows, and no more gladiator fights for entertainment."

"Sure, that sounds great. I agree."

"Second," she continued, ignoring me, "you're going to come out in favor of something similar to the New Gotham Accords."

"Absolutely not," I blurted. Bee looked at me funny, and I mouthed the words at her. She rolled her eyes.

"Calm down. We're not pushing to quarantine supers anymore. But, look, people can't keep living in fear that Golden Goose and Lord Destructo could have an all-out brawl in their backyard at any moment, and with no consequences. The current iteration wants superhero shows to be scripted, which you're fine with, and to be in only a few communities."

"That still sounds like a quarantine," I said dryly.

"It's not. It's creating a few 'studio cities' for supers who still want to do for-profit shows, and figuring out a fair tax percentage to go toward people who want to live there as payment for the chaos. If you don't want to play those TV games, you can live where you want, and even fight villains. But if you want the show, you go somewhere where people know the risks."

I wasn't excited about that. "All this is subject to negotiation, right?"

"You can agree, in principle, to the idea. It doesn't have to be the exact wording. But you have to be in favor of something like what we're working on."

"And why do you think my opinion will matter in the grand scheme of things?" I asked.

"I don't. But if you do win, you'll be positioned for people to listen to you, at least a little. If you lose, that doesn't hurt APPEAL at all." Su-Bin paused. "It's a no-lose situation for APPEAL."

"Anything else?" I asked.

"Yes. Annie, I'm not doing any of this for you," she said. That stung a little. "I'm doing this because it has to stop. We're allies right now, not friends. I'll reevaluate whether I want to be friends later, when I've had time to think. But right now, this is business."

"I understand. 11:00 a.m. tomorrow. The Hot Zone," I replied.

"You do your part. I'll do mine." She hung up, and I turned my thoughts toward tomorrow's work.

PART SEVEN

49

3V1L (1)

[Casting Call]
[Episode: Power War: Cell Theory - R]
[Role: Prison-Breaker! Do you accept the role? (Yes/No)]
[Role Focus: Drama + Cunning]
[Power War: Cell Theory: Act One in Progress]

It was 11:15 a.m. when Fursona and I ducked across the border between Mid-Town and Thornton. If I was right, Su-Bin's protest *should* have the pro-Ilneat supers' attention. That left us free to act unchecked. In theory, at least.

The plan was simple—mostly because we didn't know what we were up against. We'd break into The Agent's private prison, fight through the defenses until we got to Dr. Jackson, and rescue her. Bring her to Mrs. N. That was it. Nothing fancy.

So, of course, things went off the rails almost instantly.

Thornton's southern tip wasn't any better off than the rest of it. The feeling of decay and dereliction was almost oppressive, and the half melted snow revealing mud, cracked sidewalks, and weeds didn't help. In the distance, I could hear an engine revving, but I didn't pay much attention to it. "Okay, keep it together," I whispered.

"I'm good," Fursona said behind me. She'd gone Kaiju-sona again. Part of me wondered if she'd ever use the other suits again.

"I know. I'm talking to myself," I retorted. The plan might not have been anything fancy, but a lot was riding on it all the same. Fursona and I had to execute flawlessly, and Su-Bin had to hold attention for as long as she could. Otherwise, this would be the shortest offensive of all time.

The engine drew closer, and I whirled to face the oncoming vehicle.

It wasn't a car. It wasn't even a motorcycle—at least not a street-legal one. The massive dirt bike's spiked wheels ripped into the asphalt, leaving molten gouges in the rider's wake. For a second, I thought it had to be Roadrage, but the devil helmet left me no doubt—this was 3V1L!

The bike zipped forward impossibly quickly, and I threw myself to the side. Fursona slammed a shoulder into the handlebar, and though the rider managed to stay on, the bike's swaying knocked a passenger off her back.

As the second *V* rolled, the first one flipped her bike around and shouted, "This is 3V1L territory now! Leave!"

"Why is it that 3V1L always takes the worst places in town?" Fursona asked through our comms. I shrugged.

The bike rolled a little closer as the other *V* picked herself up and brushed off asphalt that seemed to have melted to her skin. She squinted at us. Then her eyes went wide. "Number Two, that's Understudy! The One *L* wants her, and he wants her alive!"

The dirt biker revved her engines. It shot a cloud of asphalt our way like a huge, never-ending shotgun blast, pushing me back until I fired a **[Starlance]** toward the rider.

[HP 14/15]
[**Dramatic Damage! +1 Drama Point**]

Meanwhile, the tar spiderwebbing in the street had started to boil, filling the air with a sickly petroleum smell. I whirled to attack the other *V*, but her hands were elbow-deep in the road, and a circle of half melted gravel and asphalt ten feet wide had formed around her.

"Outrider and Felsic clones!" Fursona shouted. "Switch!"

I rotated, letting the massive Kaiju lumber after the dirt-bike-riding *V*. The Kaiju suit could probably have tanked the fire damage, but I didn't have to. I hopped into the air with **[Solar Wing]** just as the Felsic clone erupted the street. Cement and streetlights shattered, the street caved in as a massive, orange-glowing sinkhole formed in its center, and the *V* balanced on a pillar as lava surged around her, melting the snow and setting the weeds ablaze.

Somehow, it felt a little underwhelming.

"I don't think it's Felsic," I said. "He'd have taken out the whole district."

"Burn, bitch!" she screamed at me. A gigantic fireball roared my way, exploding against the side of a building and shattering the brickwork. It rained down around me, but I whirled and fired two more **[Starlances]**. Both hit, knocking her off her pillar—but another semimolten tower rocketed out of the ground to catch her!

[**Dramatic Damage! +2 Drama Points**]

Now she was moving, hopping from pillar to half-molten pillar like a pair of gigantic, red-hot stilts. I dove under a stone spear as it erupted from the side of a building; a second later, the whole building collapsed, and a wave of lava surged down the street.

"I'm heading east," Fursona said. "Got a couple of good hits in."

"Understood. Split Ends into Hammertime," I responded, heading east as well, but moving more to the north. The reality was that this Felsic-wannabe—maybe Cinder-Ella's powerset—had the most destructive potential of any *V* I'd ever encountered. But she also posed basically no threat to me as long as I kept her at a distance.

The fight looked flashy, but it was . . . honestly kind of boring. I fired another **[Starlance]**, dodged another pillar, and gained another few feet of distance. Then I repeated. And repeated.

[Dramatic Damage! +3 Drama Points]

"Are you going to do anything else, or should we just keep dancing?" I asked.

"Understudy, pull out!" Fursona shouted in my ear.

"No," the *V* said, lowering herself to the ground and melting the street again. This time, the gooey tar and red-hot gravel spread out around a figure standing in the middle of the street—one with a cane in one hand and a bowler hat in the other. The hat was improbably cut to fit his mask. "He is."

The new *V* locked eyes with me through the mask. Then he raised his heel. "Cover me, One and Two. I'll deal with this."

His shoe touched the ground, and the whole district seemed to shake.

"Tapdance, Tapdance, Tapdance!" Fursona screamed into her mic.

"Oh shit!" I yelled back.

Oh shit was right. Tapdance was a city-destroyer. If left unchecked, it'd be just like that Episode Dr. Jackson had shown us during the first semester of freshman year. There'd be nothing left of Thornton—or The Agent's private prison. Sure, there weren't many people living here. But *some* people did. And his power was indiscriminate, unlike Dark Girl Shock and Awe's. He'd destroy *everything*.

That made my choice pretty clear; we had to drop the dancing *V*, regardless of what the other two did while we weren't countering them.

"Focus on the dancer," I said, toning down a little and letting the mic pick up my voice. "The other two don't matter; we can mop them up after."

"Got it. No ultimate forms, though." Fursona roared and stomped toward the villain, pushing through the shock waves rippling out from the dancing man. His cane spun, and his hat flew into the air.

I used **[Limelight Barrage]**. The first bolt hit, exploding against him in a pink-and-blue light burst, and I breathed a sigh of relief. But somehow, he danced right through the stun. The other lances slammed into him a moment later, and *those* broke his concentration.

[Dramatic Damage! +5 Drama Points]

That let Fursona close the gap—only to take a massive burst of lava to the face as the street erupted. Sweat poured down my face even at my distance, and the black smoke cloud sparked with lightning. At the same moment, the dirt bike leaped through the air, spiked wheels ripping at nothing as the engine screamed. "I'm going the distance!" the rider yelled.

It hit me, and I fell, wings desperately trying to right myself.

Before I could, I hit the molten asphalt.

[HP 10/14]

It burned everywhere all at once, and I squeezed my eyes shut. I rolled, trying to break free of the tar, and pushed myself to my feet even as a wave of lava surged toward me. The heat was unbelievable—the street melted even more as I launched myself skyward again.

But Not-Tapdance was at it again. We had to stop him, or, just like that Episode, he'd break all of Thornton to take us out. Already, Fursona looked wobbly as the earth rippled under her feet, and a nearby building's brickwork was raining into the street below.

I used [**Power-Weaving**] and [**Quick-Time Changed**] into Rainy Day. It was time to lay on the damage as much as I could. My feet touched down on the temporarily frozen street, and I dashed forward, using every second of my [**Freeze-Frame**] to close the gap.

[**Flashy Fitting-Room! +1 Flamboyance Point**]
[**Steel Yourself! +1 Grit Point**]

Everything shook as soon as time moved again, but Rainy Day had the tools to disrupt Not-Tapdance—I hoped. I rolled right to dodge an oncoming dirt bike, then used [**Thunderhead**] at near-point-blank to buffet the dancing villain off his feet.

[**Pause for Effect! +1 Drama Point**]
[**Floating Points: 3 Flamboyance, 1 Grit**]

The world slowed, then stopped . . . shaking, that is. Even as my cloud built overhead, though, the volcanic one from the street behind me rose to meet it, and flames spread along the weed-choked gutters. Steam poured off the quickly melting snow.

Another ball of lava exploded, this time on Fursona's armored plush, and she rolled on the ground to put out the fire. I wanted to help her—to use [**Virga**] to quell the blaze.

But Not-Tapdance was getting back to his feet. "I said *cover me*," he said. His shoes clicked again, and the rocking started. This time, when Kaiju-sona lunged toward him, he tip-tapped away, whacking her with his cane. I nodded; he was *good*.

Then I used [**Ride the Lightning**].

[Electric Lightshow! +1 Flamboyance Point]
[Thunderstruck! +1 Drama Point]
[Power-Weaving! +6 Flamboyance, +3 Grit, +1 Drama Points]

But even as the storm broke overhead, I could tell it wouldn't be enough. Worse, a volley of gravel and molten asphalt arced through the air and shattered against me, and yet another fireball burst overhead a moment later. I screamed as hot shards of sharp stone rained down on me.

[HP 7/14]

Still, we'd made progress. A little more, and—
CRASH!
The first building came down. Bricks and steel screamed as it twisted, collapsing into the fiery sinkhole below. I desperately tried to dodge the stones, but even as I did, someone screamed.
Someone was riding the building down.
I used [**Quick-Time Change**] and rocketed toward the building as soon as the Understudy transformation was finished. Fighting Not-Tapdance didn't matter; I'd said the whole thing was wrong, and we should be helping people, not just fighting.

[Flashy Fitting-Room! +1 Flamboyance Point]
[Rejuvenation Activated: HP 11/15]

The whole building was coming apart. I only had one shot at getting the resident out, so I aimed for the window where I saw a man's silhouette. Then I crashed through it, wrapping one arm around his waist and hoisting him clean off his feet. There wouldn't be time to turn around; instead, I blasted his apartment's door open with a [**Starlance**] and zoomed out into the hall.

[Dramatic Rescue! +1 Drama Point]

A moment later, we were back outside, breathing dusty air. "You should be safe here," I said, depositing him on the ground. "Was anyone else in there?"
"N-no. I lived alone. Last tenant in the building. Hell, last tenant on the block."

I breathed a sigh of relief even as the tension left my shoulders. Thank god Thornton sucked so much. "Okay. Stay here, or run away. Either is fine, but *don't* follow me."

Fursona roared, an earsplitting shriek accompanied by crackling flames, and the ground rolled again. I jumped back into the air, leaving pink and blue contrails behind me. Not-Tapdance needed to be stopped.

So this time, when I got to the battlefield—dodging a dirt bike in the process—I shot straight for the villain. Instead of using any of my powers, I lowered my head and led with it, right into his gut. If I could keep him off his feet, he'd be powerless.

It'd be just like the Outrider vs. Tapdance Episode.

And it was working. Fursona stomped toward us, shrugging off another fireball as the volcanic *V* struggled to stop her. If she got to us, she could finish off Not-Tapdance. It'd be easy to mop up the other two villains from there.

But something grabbed *me* by my collar and pulled. Hard.

Gravel shot up next to me. I kicked and thrashed, trying to break my attacker's grip even as she yelled, "Get off him!" in my ear. We bumped along the road. Asphalt and gravel gouged into me, and my whole body felt stretched. I needed a plan. Something had to change before the dirt bike *V* pulled us too far from Fursona.

[**HP 10/15**]

The solution was simple. I couldn't fight while holding Not-Tapdance. And Fursona couldn't catch up. So I needed to get rid of Not-Tapdance.

I let go. Then, as he hit the road behind us, I kicked with both feet.

[**Badass Damage! +1 Badass Point**]

He rolled, arms flailing as the rough road chewed through his superhero damage. I used [**Quick-Time Change**], switching to Copy Cat. And Fursona leaped into the air, then crashed down on Not-Tapdance before he could regain his feet. They disappeared in a cloud of debris as another fireball exploded on her back.

[**Flashy Fitting-Room! +1 Flamboyance Point**]
[**Steel Yourself! +1 Grit Point**]

When the dust around them cleared, she was standing, and he wasn't.

50

3V1L (2)

With Not-Tapdance down, victory was inevitable. Most of the *V*s we'd fought didn't have the superhero damage to hang with us—especially not as we got stronger. All we had to do was mop up, and the first target was pretty clear. The First *V*'s skin was red-hot, and she had the potential to hurt us on the way out. By contrast, the Second *V* was little more than a BMX bandit—or an underpowered white van.

And as annoying as white vans were, the right play was simple. Take out Lava Girl, then the bike rider.

Fursona agreed with me. She stomped across the molten, tire-tracked street, roaring her own flames as she closed the gap with the First *V*. I was still Copy-Cat, and Tails's reflexes worked perfectly as I dodged the Second *V*'s wheels and **[Pouncing Panther'd]** off a wall and toward the lava-spewing villain.

[Badass Move! +1 Badass Point]

She looked like she was about to blow her top. Both her hands were glowing orange lava that slowly hardened into black stone, and she ran toward Fursona. The Kaiju vomited even more flames onto the already molten street, and I had to bounce off another building to avoid the inferno. I ricocheted off the street, claws outstretched, and slammed into the First *V*.

[Badass Damage! +1 Badass Point]
[Tough Kitty! +1 Grit Point]

It *hurt*. She had to be three or four hundred degrees, and her temperature was only rising—I was lucky **[Fursonal Furcefield]** had taken the flames instead of my superhero damage. I whirled, firing off a quick **[Cat-Scratch Fever]** and thanking Past Understudy that I'd gone combat cat instead of stealth cat.

[Dramatic Damage! +1 Drama Point]

Then something massive hit us.

I stumbled across the street, falling off the First *V* as a roaring sound filled my ears. Was it Fursona or the Second *V*'s bike? I couldn't tell, but right now, my main goal was to get away from the massive heat source in the middle of the street. It was already burning through my superhero damage, and I needed distance.

[HP 5/15]

Preferably before it blew up.

I looked over my shoulder; sure enough, Fursona had wrapped the First *V* in a massive embrace—but the temp villain wasn't out of the fight yet. Her skin had cracked in a hundred places, and as I watched, her Costume burst into flames. Her eyes were red, and she'd clenched her jaw like she was trying to hold something back.

Then, all of a sudden, she relaxed. So did I; Fursona had done enough damage to stop her.

The street exploded.

[HP 2/15]
[Tough Kitty! +1 Grit Point]

It felt like a bomb going off. Like the tanks exploding at the MoonTech chemical plant. A giant hand shoved me into an apartment—then *through* the apartment's wall. The heat rippled out a moment later, bathing me in pure fire. And a moment after *that*, fragments of brick and gravel rained down like mortar shells, peppering the space the building had just been.

I picked myself up, glad no one lived around here anymore. Then I took stock of the battlefield.

The Second *V* was picking up her blackened bike, and Fursona stood at the blast's epicenter, her suit burning in a half dozen places as she held a thin woman in a dancer's leotard. The poor girl was out, and for a second, I had a ton of sympathy for her. She'd used everything she had to try to turn the tables, and it showed.

The neighborhood was little more than a crater surrounded by a war zone.

Fursona shook her massive head, eyestalks waving back and forth. Then she dropped the woman to the still-steaming road and roared at the top of her lungs. "Come on! Who else do you have!? I'll fight them all!"

The dirt bike's engine revved, and I whirled, dodging the outstretched Second *V*'s hand. She took a single swipe at Fursona, but the Kaiju suit tanked it. "No, thanks," she said. "I've had enough." Then she spun around in a donut, peppering my partner with gravel, and took off down the street for the water treatment plant.

I tried to keep up. [**Pouncing Panther**] threw me from wall to fence as I burned powers trying to catch the *V*. But in the end, I couldn't keep up with her machine. I had to give up the chase and wait for Fursona's lumbering form to catch up.

[**End of Act One: Act Two in Three Minutes**]

Losing the Second *V* hurt, and not only because we hadn't gotten the full mop-up we'd wanted. She'd tell the prison guards we were coming.

"Okay, stealth was never an option, right?" Fursona asked, shrugging her shoulders. Neither of us had planned on this being a stealth mission; the combat cat Costume had been a nod to that reality. Right now, what mattered most was the hope that Su-Bin had pinned down enough pro-Ilneat heroes with her protest, and that they'd take a few minutes to get here.

Which meant it was time to move fast and break things.

I shifted into Rainy Day, using a charge of [**Virga**] to top Fursona off—and to put out her flaming fursuit. Then I switched back to Understudy. "Right. Let's do Hannibal."

[**Medic! +2 Cunning Points**]
[**Rejuvenation Activated: HP 9/15**]

Fursona stared at me. "We've never done Hannibal. You're sure?"

"Yeah, I'm sure. It'll be great, and it's not like we can get help here."

"I hate the idea of Hannibal." She shook her head; the eyestalks bounced, and I laughed.

[**Power War: Cell Theory: Act Two in Progress**]

"RAWR!" Fursona yelled.

She might've hated the idea of the Hannibal plan, but by the time we crashed through the water treatment plant's gates and stomped over the Second *V*'s bike like a war horse on an ancient battlefield, she was roaring and shouting just like me.

She wasn't Full Kaiju, but even her normal form was big enough to ride—I stood with my legs on her tail, waving my wand and firing [**Starlances**] like a mounted archer. Her fursuit gave me plenty of cover, and the silly-looking eyestalks acted like a set of reins—except I had no control over where Fursona went. She roared again and clomped her way between the three huge settling ponds.

The whole place was built around a pair of enormous water tanks, an enclosed building covered in rust and vents that shot foul-smelling air into the sky, and the settling ponds—a pretty typical treatment plant layout, if a little old. And when I said foul-smelling, I meant it; even though the treatment process was entirely enclosed, thousands of gallons of raw sewage ran through its pipes every day.

It reeked.

The first bullets started bouncing off Fursona's suit, and I ducked reflexively behind her head before returning fire. At the same time, her flame breath shot out— mixed with the faint scent of freshly mixed Tang. But even though my [**Starlances**] aimed toward the muzzle flashes inside the plant, Fursona's target was different.

[**Dramatic Damage! +1 Drama Point**]
[**Good Thinking! +1 Cunning Point**]

She breathed right on the water around us. The water turned to vapor that hung in the air around us like a smoke screen. When I couldn't see the flashes in the distance, I thumped Fursona's head and pulled on her eyestalk. "Okay, let's get moving!"

"I'm your partner, not your noble steed," she grumped, but she started moving forward and to the left. A few bullets hit her, but her [**Fursonal Furcefield**] was ridiculous, and most of them just bounced off, flattened.

The smoke screen was even blowing the right way; I couldn't see the sheet metal walls until they loomed in front of us less than ten feet away. "Now!" I shouted.

"RAWR!" Fursona yelled, rushing forward as I grabbed both eyestalks and swung down and to her left. She led with her right shoulder, slamming through the thin tin metal and into the maze of pipes and chemical containers inside.

But unlike my fight against Polar Vortex in the plant near Confluence Park, we didn't care about the individual villains in the plant. For all we knew, there weren't any yet; we'd only seen a few henches with guns. One turned and pulled the trigger, and I blasted him away with a [**Starlance**].

[**Dramatic Damage! +1 Drama Point**]

Then Fursona shook me off, and I rolled right, firing another two [**Starlances**] into the hall toward two henches—mostly to keep them behind cover, but also hoping for a hit. No such luck. "Fursona, try that way!"

"Got it!" She stomped toward the defenders, roaring and spewing spurts of flame at them as she closed the gap. I followed her like a soldier following a tank, watching her tear into the two henches until their hands went up and they started whining about being forced into the job.

I didn't have time to give them orders. A door loomed up ahead, and I pointed; it was chrome, unlike the rest of the building around it. "That's a trap!"

A second later, it opened, and a gun turret dropped from the ceiling behind it. Fursona dodged left, and I went right—a perfect Split Ends. The turret looked like a Tesla coil, and a second later, lightning filled the hall where we'd just been standing. "You deal with it!" Fursona shouted.

"On it!" I started volleying [**Starlances**] toward it, but it took four to break through its armor. When it finally exploded, sending a ripple of shrapnel across the room, Fursona lumbered toward the door.

[**Dramatic Damage! +1 Drama Point**]

"Empty," she said a moment later. "Just a trap. Keep your eyes open for more."

A second later, the floor opened under her, and she fell through it, screaming, only to get cut off with a splash. As she resurfaced, she sputtered into the mic. "Annie, maneaters!"

I popped onto my sailboard and dove through the hole after her, then skimmed across the massive, foul-smelling lake until I found her. Sure enough, she and a Florida Maneater were death-rolling each other through the water, flames, and droplets of . . . stuff . . . filling the air. "Break off and get ready!" I yelled, "Pickup's coming in!"

I dipped below the water until it was rushing against my chest, struggling to keep flying forward. My speed dropped, and a maneater took a chomp at me. Its teeth didn't get purchase, but they ripped my arm open in a cut that went from elbow to wrist, and I screamed.

[**HP 6/15**]

Then I screamed again as I hit something massive in front of me. It was Fursona, and she clambered on board as a half dozen of the massive, overgrown reptiles closed in around us. I rocketed for the square of light overhead before she was really on the board.

We burst through it, dripping with disgusting, half-treated water. Neither of us could stop laughing as we lay on the tile next to the trapdoor. "You . . . you really stink," I said after a second.

"You're not exactly rosy either, you know?" she shot back. Then she stood up. "Okay. Traps everywhere. Got it. Let's keep moving."

Things happened fast after that. We worked our way through the mazelike treatment plant, being careful where we had to and moving fast when we could. A few henches took shots at us until we beat them up, but nothing felt like a threat. More dangerously, pit traps, acid-sprayers, and even a massive blade that fell from the ceiling greeted us around every turn—a sure sign that we were closing in on The Agent's hiding place.

But eventually, we reached a simple, nondescript door. It had exactly the right amount of rust, and its keypad had clearly been pushed thousands of times—a four-digit code with four buttons worn down so far I couldn't read the numbers anymore. I pushed the numbers in order—2, 5, 6, 7—and the door popped open to reveal an elevator.

The small space had no obvious traps, and after a moment, I switched to Lab Assistant Panic. A quick [**Speed-Hacker**] didn't show anything worth messing with, which was weird—an elevator was the perfect place for a lethal trap. Then again, every person coming in and out might use it. "I'm not seeing anything weird, just an ultra-low-powered laser grid. It's for decontamination. I think."

"Well, I feel contaminated as hell right now," Fursona complained. She stepped into the elevator, which creaked ominously. "You coming?"

I didn't really want to; even though it wasn't a trap, it was so *obviously* a trap I couldn't shake the bad feeling. But I *did* stink, and it *was* the only way to wherever The Agent was keeping Dr. Jackson. So, after a second, I stepped inside and closed the door.

"Attention! Decontamination in progress!"

The laser grid fired, and I flinched as the elevator descended.

51

3V1L (3)

Luckily, the laser grid wasn't lethal.

It did sting a little, but it burned off everything that could stink. By the time the elevator reached full speed, it smelled less like body odor and half-treated sewage water and more like . . . stale. Like air that'd been treated too many times, and a hint of bleach or chlorine.

As the elevator crept downward, I slow-transformed to Rainy Day and used **[Virga]** to top Fursona and myself off a little, so when the door did open, we'd be more ready to face whatever was coming. The plan at this point was pretty simple. We'd find Dr. Jackson, grab her, and leave the way we'd come in. Simple, for the most part, meant foolproof. And if something went wrong? Either one of our battle strategies would help, or we'd have to do some improvisation.

[Medic! +2 Cunning Points]
[HP 8/15]

Besides, what could go wrong? The Agent probably wasn't here, and we'd already beaten three low-powered *V*s. Chances were good we'd just have more henches, and maybe a big fight on the way out. Easy-peasy.

I'd just switched back to Understudy when the door opened, and Fursona and I dashed out into The Agent's prison.

The hall looked like any other secret underground hall—nothing special, just fluorescent lights hanging from the ceiling and bare concrete walls. I'd seen it all before, even the traps that popped out of the floor and walls to slow us down. I even blasted a couple of turrets with **[Starlance]** for good measure, but most just . . . weren't a threat.

[Dramatic Damage! +2 Drama Points]

"Where's the challenge?" Fursona bellowed from inside her Kaiju suit. She kicked a bomb away, and it exploded against the concrete wall, showering the whole hallway in dust. I couldn't help but agree with her. If these were the best defenses keeping Dr. Jackson imprisoned, we practically had her freed already.

The cement dust swirled and coalesced into a man-shaped figure with a rough approximation of the 3V1L devil helmet on his head. "I'm afraid you're about to find out, unless you'd be so kind as to surrender. We've got cells just for the two of you."

"No thanks," I said, firing a **[Starlance]** toward the V's chest. It passed through him, though the rest of the dust shivered like static on a TV.

[Dramatic Damage! +1 Drama Point]

"Very well. I can do this the hard way. As Second *V*, I will—"

I never got a chance to figure out what he'd do, though. Fursona crashed into him, and the dust scattered across the hallway floor. "Let's go!" she shouted, lumbering toward where the prison had to be. But even as we ran down the hall, the Second *V* formed in front of us again—this time spraying out of a drain on the floor in a burst of water.

"An Elementalist!" I said.

"No. *The* Elementalist," he replied. Two huge, watery arms crashed into the floor, filling the hall in front of us with a wall of water. It hovered overhead as Fursona roared into battle. Then, just before she made contact, the Second *V* released the flood, washing us down the hallway in a localized, directed tsunami. "Time to put out your spark of resistance!"

[HP 6/15]

Even as the waves receded, though, the water was already heating up around us. He'd shifted again, this time to fire. "I will boil away your will to fight!" The lake spread out, covering the entire floor. But it vaporized even faster. The steam exploded down the hallway, ripping chunks of concrete off the wall and exploding lightbulbs.

I took cover behind Fursona's bulk, and the heat washed over us. Then she was charging again. This time, I fired **[Limelight Barrage]** into the flaming supervillain's body, punching holes in the blaze. He was still stunned when Fursona hit him like the tidal wave that had just hit us.

[Dramatic Damage! +5 Drama Points]

Then he vanished, only to appear down the hall in concrete dust form. "You two are persistent, aren't you? We'll see how much fight you have when I go after the prisoners!"

"Fuck," I muttered under my breath. "We've gotta move fast!"

But no matter how fast we moved, the Second *V* was faster—and he knew where he was going. All we could do was follow him deeper into The Agent's prison.

In a way, fighting the Second *V* was a lot like fighting Waterspout in classes last year. Most of his powers were easy to avoid—waves of water, or dust clouds that choked the air but that we could dash through without taking damage. But his matter-switch forms only seemed to take a fraction of the damage we needed to be doing.

So even though Fursona and I had cornered him near a door with a keypad and retina scanner, we couldn't actually bring him down. And worse, he was determined to get that door open.

I **[Quick-Time Changed]** to Rainy Day as the Second *V* transformed into his watery form. There wouldn't be time for a full-on combo, so instead, I fired off a **[Ride the Lightning]**, hoping for the extra damage from the water to matter. It did, but not enough. Even as the bolt hit him and coursed through his liquid body, one hand reached for the keypad.

[Flashy Fitting-Room! +1 Flamboyance Point]
[Steel Yourself! +1 Grit Point]
[Electric Lightshow! +1 Flamboyance Point]

Fursona charged him, and I knocked him away from the door and into her arms with **[Wind Front]**. But even as she wrapped him in a bear hug, he turned into a wisp of wind and rematerialized in front of the retina scanner—this time looking like a person. We both lunged for him.

[Badass Move! +1 Badass Point]

The door popped open, and my hands closed on grains of sand as he slid through. A second later, Fursona threw herself into the already closing door. It crunched shut on her waist, then started slowly grinding open as her massive plushie limbs shoved against it. "Go!" she grunted.

I didn't waste any time—I was already halfway through the door, stepping on her plushie stomach to get by, when she said it. Behind me, Fursona roared, and the door kept screeching and grinding as she forced it off its hinges. Then it toppled to the floor, and she picked herself up.

We stood in a nearly standard prison block, built just like the ones I'd seen in Almhurst, or on old police dramas. Only two things were different. First, only a handful of cells were full—all on the same side. And second, the air was all but choked with dust.

"Surrender, or the prisoners die," the Second *V* yelled. He was everywhere: on the catwalks, in the common space, and inside the cells. The air grew thicker with dust every second, and it was only a matter of time before the prisoners couldn't handle it anymore. Already, someone was coughing and choking in a cell next to me.

I [**Quick-Time Changed**] again, this time into Rescue Girl Lucky Star. "Can you get the cells open?" I shouted over the whirlwind that had engulfed the entire prison.

[**Flashy Fitting-Room! +1 Flamboyance Point**]
[**Rejuvenation Activated: HP 9/15**]

"Yeah!" Fursona's claws wrapped around one of the cell doors, and she grunted. Then she roared and leaped onto the common area floor. Then, she started growing.

Part of me wanted to scream at her to stop; we needed to save our big powers as long as possible. But the rest of me knew this was the only way. As Lucky Star, I couldn't fight the Second *V*, and I couldn't switch off her quickly either. It was all on Fursona to fight—and to open the door.

So, as Full Kaiju Fursona filled the prison and started prying doors open, I hurried inside. None of the prisoners in their individual cells looked anything like supers; they weren't in Costume, and they had defeated, beaten looks to them. But even so, I reached out to the first one and used [**Noncombatant Teleport**].

A moment later, he vanished.

[**Dramatic Rescue! +1 Drama Point**]

"Stop that!" the Second *V* yelled. He switched to fire, and suddenly, the whole prison's temperature skyrocketed. I hurried to the second cell, repeating my [**Noncombatant Teleport**] trick and getting those [**Rescue Re-Arm!**] activations, but there were still three more. Even though I'd be able to handle the heat—barely—the prisoners wouldn't.

[**Dramatic Rescue! +1 Drama Point**]

"Fursona, you have to stop him!" I yelled.

She roared in response, slamming into the pillar of flame that'd once been the Second *V*. They crashed into the wall right above the prison's entrance, her fire breath piercing into the villain's chest.

Suddenly, the heat cut off.

I didn't have time to figure out what was going on. My hand snaked through the third cell's bars and grabbed the skinny-looking man's hand. A second later, he, too, had vanished.

[**Dramatic Rescue! +1 Drama Point**]

As I ran to the next cell, though, a sudden burst of wind knocked me off the catwalk and to the ground. The Second *V* had vanished, or he'd gone Wind Form. Something was collapsing near the entrance, too; the whole tunnel sounded like it was falling, and the rumbling even shook my teeth. I looked for a set of stairs, but couldn't find any that weren't destroyed.

Fursona. Fursona was a set of stairs.

[Good Thinking! +1 Cunning Point]

As she stomped toward the re-forming *V*, I ran headlong toward her tail and started climbing the spines and fins that ran along her back. She didn't even notice me; a gout of flame burst forth, covering the Second *V*, whose sandy body broke into shards of glass. At the same time, I leaped back onto the catwalk and sprinted toward the next cell.

"Annie, look out!" Fursona thundered. I ducked and wrapped my hands around the bars.

A second later, the tidal wave hit.

[HP 6/15]

It knocked me into the prison's wall, driving the air from my lungs, but even as the deluge filled up the cell in front of me, I got a hand free and touched the prisoner. And that was all it took; she disappeared into thin air a moment later as **[Noncombatant Teleport]** activated.

[Dramatic Rescue! +1 Drama Point]

That left one more.

The Second *V* formed in front of me. This time, the dust compacted into something like clay, with two huge fists. He swung at me, and I ducked a second too late. The blow rang my head like a bell.

[HP 3/15]

But he didn't get a chance to swing again.

Fursona's fiery breath blew over him as I threw myself to safety. I could see the clay man's skin hardening even as he tried to switch to another form; the freshly fired clay spread across his body, and when she was done, only the *V*'s face could move. He couldn't shift, either. We had him beaten.

"Surrender!" I said. "Otherwise, I'll let the dinosaur do what it wants with you."

Fursona roared.

"Alright. You win. I'm done," the *V* said. He strained against his porcelain prison, but couldn't move a muscle except to blink.

"We'll be back for you," Fursona said, shrinking back to a reasonable size. A juice box crumpled in my earpiece, and I winced at the sound. But, hopefully, she hadn't been Full Kaiju for long enough to compromise her regular powers.

As the *V* complained and whined, we hurried to the second to last cell on the row. And there, with her arm in a sling, was Dr. Jackson.

52

3V1L (4)

[End of Act Two: Act Three in Three Minutes]

It took Fursona all of ten seconds to bend, then snap, the cell's bars. Dr. Jackson's eyes opened for the first time. She seemed to pop into awareness as the steel bars bent. Her arm was definitely still injured, and something like anger filled me up for a second before Lucky Star forced it back down. There'd be time for that soon. First, the job we had to do.

Dr. Jackson blinked, staring at me like she couldn't quite recognize me. "Who? What?"

I ignored her for a moment, using **[Jinx-Bearer]** to pick up some of her pain. As my arm started aching—especially around my shoulder, but also where I'd gotten shot—her face cleared. I could handle her pain for a while, at least for as long as I was Lucky Star. And after I **[Noncombatant Teleported]** her out of here, I'd be able to switch around.

[Gritty Sacrifice! +2 Grit Points]

It was such a relief to have had *something* go right. My jaw and throat relaxed, even as the pain hit me. We had Dr. Jackson. With two metapowered supers, we might actually have a chance. Now I just had to figure out how to tell Dr. Jackson everything that had happened. But how best to do it?

"Understudy and Fursona? *That* team? Really?" she said, shaking her head. She'd gotten to her feet while I pondered my plan, and she looked a *lot* better than she had just a minute ago. All of a sudden, she was giving orders. "There's a vil in the next cell over. She's been here less than a day, but she told me what she could from outside. See if you can break her out, Fursona."

"Sure," Fursona yawned and started walking away.

"Wait. Are you good to keep fighting?" I asked. She'd just been Full Kaiju, and that always took so much out of her.

"Do I have a choice? I stole a few extra drinks from the Playpen Patrol. Guess I'm a villain now!" Fursona quipped. Then she stomped away, and a second later, the air filled with grunting and screeching steel.

"Who is it?" I asked.

"No idea," Fursona called back. "She's in worse shape than Dr. Jackson, though."

"Lady Lockless," Dr. Jackson said. "She doesn't take a punch well—never has. Almost failed Combat Styles two years ago. Without that cane, she would have for sure."

I cracked my neck, wanting to take the fight to any 3V1L henches or *Vs* still in this jail. They'd deserve it, and I still had Super Girl Spotlight Star in reserve for them. They wouldn't know what hit them. But I couldn't—not until we had both Dr. Jackson and Lady Lockless out of here. So instead, Dr. Jackson and I waited until Fursona stomped up, carrying a girl in leggings and a baggy T-shirt on her back.

"Alright, ladies," Dr. Jackson said, finally stepping out of her cell. "We need a battle plan."

"The plan's simple," I interrupted. "I **[Noncombatant Teleport]** you two to safety, then Fursona and I fight our way out. We regroup at Tottergarten."

"No." Lady Lockless slid off Fursona's back, leaning on my partner's shoulder and breathing heavily.

"No?" I asked. She was covered in bruises and wobbly, even with the dinosaur suit's support. If she wanted to fight, the odds of a win only went down—a lot. And Dr. Jackson wasn't in any better shape.

"We're not leaving, because you won't get out of here without us," Dr. Jackson said. She started walking toward the prison's far side, away from where we'd come in. There, in bright neon letters, was an Exit sign. A door sat below it, with a key card reader. "Miss Callum, would you mind?"

Lady Lockless reached out and pushed a couple of random buttons, and the door beeped green. A second later, it opened, and I sat, flabbergasted, as Dr. Jackson and Lady Lockless strolled out into the hall. "Wait, you could have opened your cell any time?" I asked.

"No. They welded it shut," Lady Lockless shot back. "They're vils, not idiots, sadly."

"Uh, if this prison break's turning into something else, would you mind telling us what's going on? Because I'm *confused*," Fursona said.

"Okay, listen, past this room's where they've been keeping Dr. Mays. He's in charge of keeping this whole lair running—in theory. In practice, he's pretty powerless without me. That's why they put him in charge, I think."

I stopped and put a hand on Dr. Jackson's shoulder. "Lair? Whose lair?"

"The Agent's."

So, that was a shocker.

I'd thought 3V1L's lair had been under a house in the Poudre districts, not here. But, as Dr. Jackson led us down the hall, I started to believe it. The walls gradually changed past the prison until the underground tunnel felt less like a prison and more like an office.

And if this was The Agent's lair, he'd be on his way to defend it. Could we really turn this thing around and beat The Agent here?

Maybe. Yes. Yes, we definitely could. We just had to solve a bunch of problems:

1. How to find The Agent? He'd come here, yes, but he'd come with the best Temp Supers he could muster, and he'd come ready to finish us off. So finding him wouldn't be a problem. Beating the *V*s would be, though.
2. Could we neutralize Dr. Mays? Granted, without Jackson, his powers were pretty minimal—all he could do was stall out fights. But if we ran into him before The Agent, stalling would be enough—and any henches or *V*s with him would go for Dr. Jackson to stop her from countering him.
3. Could we stop The Agent from simply teleporting away? And where did he teleport to, exactly? If he always teleported to his lair, we had him cornered. But if not? If not, we needed a plan to pin him down—otherwise, beating him would be impossible.
4. How the hell could we keep Dr. Jackson and Lady Lockless safe?

Luckily, Dr. Jackson took over before I could start voicing my concerns. She pulled us into an empty office room with a simulated view of a shoreline somewhere. "Up ahead is the loop station. He always comes in from there, and he always goes to the same place first. His 'office.'"

"How do you know?" I asked.

"I've been here for a while. He uses henches with guns when he wants to gloat at me about . . . whatever. And he likes to gloat—a lot. Listen up. Important need-to-know information. First, he's going to show up there. We can ambush him, but it might be better to set up somewhere else—like his main lair. If we can set up a trap, things might go better for us; he'll get off that loop ready to fight.

"Second, he's working with the Ilneats," Jackson finished.

"Yeah, we know he's on their team," Fursona said.

"No. Not like that. He's got a deal worked out with the Network that gives him producers' powers. That's how he teleported away after he shot me," Dr. Jackson said.

Well, that was a complication. It also meant this probably *wasn't* where he was going when he emergency teleported. "So, we're not beating him here?" I asked.

"I think we can," Dr. Jackson said. Then she dropped her voice almost to a whisper as we put our heads together over the office desk. And when she got to the core part of her plan, I nodded, a smile spreading slowly across my face. It was bold, and risky, and it relied on some weird conceptual language, but we had all the pieces right here.

It just might work.

[Power War: Cell Theory: Act Three in Progress]

Fursona and I ran down the office-like hall past cubicles and computers, barreling headlong deeper into The Agent's lair. We'd passed the loop station a while back, and the plan required us to move fast and break stuff. Fursona, for her part, was a half step slow, and her suit had to be half-full of spent Hi-Cs and Capri Suns. But she kept trucking along.

A camera swiveled to follow us, and I took a second to make sure it saw me clearly before blasting it with a **[Starlance]**. The plan required that The Agent know exactly where we were; he knew my powerset, so if he saw the two of us, he'd assume I'd done what I'd wanted to do and teleported Lady Lockless and Dr. Jackson out.

[Dramatic Damage! +1 Drama Point]

Hopefully he'd assume that, at least.

We hit another door—this one wooden and formal-looking—and Fursona breathed a line of flames that chewed through it before slamming through the weakened, charred wood shoulder-first.

"About time you got here," The Agent said smoothly.

He sat on a chair that reminded me of an office chair if you crossed it with a king's throne, at the end of a wide, circular room. Tapestries covered every possible wall, and behind him, a pair of flags hung from their poles. It looked a little like the pictures of the president's office from old textbooks about Pre-Launch America. And he wasn't alone.

Flanking him were three supers. The first, to his left, was a hulking man every bit the match for McHammer, but with a mace that felt more medieval and armor that covered his whole body—except for the 3V1L helmet. One glance confirmed that The Agent's Temp Super had to be copying Lord Destructo. On the far side, another familiar-looking villain stood ready; the tight racing suit and helmet design looked a lot like Springlock's setup.

But the last Temp Super was worse.

They wore a kangaroo fursuit and an orange suit with blue racing stripes that looked like it was designed for speed. Fursona's original suit. So . . . that was going to get confusing.

And, as a cherry on top, The Agent wasn't the only metapowered super in the room. In the corner, a defeated-looking Dr. Mays sat at a much smaller desk, his polo shirt wrinkled and beard disheveled. He glanced up at us and shook his head, then lowered it. "You shouldn't have come here. I'm sorry," he said softly.

"So, I'm assuming you and Marino are here to surrender, DuPont? That's the only reason I can see for you two walking into my lair, strolling into my office, and presenting yourselves so perfectly. So, how about it? I'll take your familiar and your fursuit, have the First *V* hop you back to my prison, and wrap this whole pointless storyline up for the Network," The Agent said.

"Or I could blast you right here," I countered, feeling a lot braver than I should. "[**Starlance**]!"

"Dr. Mays here for . . ." Before I could finish my power, the metapowered professor stood as a tube of something materialized in his hand. He stared at it for a second. "Professor Beavis's Top-Tier Topical Solutions."

The room froze. Even my power stalled midair, hovering there like a pink-and-blue ray of death midway across the office. Only two people could move. Dr. Mays desperately shouted out his advertisement for whatever weird alien product he was pitching as the Episode rolled into an impromptu commercial break. He looked at us with eyes wide and full of something like fear and remorse.

And The Agent stood up slowly, pulling out his briefcase—where I knew he kept his pistol. This was it. The moment we'd been waiting for and dreading. But even though The Agent could easily kill us both right here, I wasn't worried at all. Far from it. I was thrilled.

So far, everything had gone exactly as Dr. Jackson predicted. We'd destroyed the cameras all along our path. The Agent had been right where we'd thought he'd be. And, even better, Dr. Mays was there, along with three *V*s impersonating Bruisers. And, most importantly, our two aces in the hole *weren't* in the room. But they would be soon. The trap was set.

It was time to spring Phase One.

The door opened, and Dr. Jackson walked in.

53

3V1L (5)

Dr. Mays's advertisement sputtered to a stop, and for a split second, nothing moved except my [**Starlance**]—which slammed into a wall and fizzled out—and Dr. Jackson. She walked toward Dr. Mays, grabbed the hand he reached out toward her, and slammed him into the ground face-first.

The First *V* moved immediately, hopping toward Kaiju-sona as my partner roared and rushed The Agent. A pair of shots rang out, but the bullets bounced off her plushie hide. Not-Springlock was already pulling back for a self-sling into the battle, and Fake Lord Destructo slid between The Agent and me like a bodyguard blocking his VIP.

Under normal circumstances, that'd be too much to handle, but I had a trick up my sleeve. Activating [**Power-Weaving**] and [**Quick-Time Change**], I moved out of Not-Springlock's way and shifted to Super Girl Spotlight Star.

[Flashy Fitting-Room! +1 Flamboyance Point]
[Steel Yourself!]
[Meter's Running: 9/10]

The trap's second part was closing around The Agent, but he didn't realize it yet.

I unloaded on Fake Lord Destructo with everything I had, using [**Limelight Barrage**] at point-blank even as Not-Springlock hit the wall behind me with a surprised whump. The [**Maximum Starlances**] shredded the Temp Super's armor and whirled him around—and a second later, he turned that spin into a massive hit with his mace!

[Dramatic Damage!]
[Meter's Running: 8/10]
[HP 1/15]

That was the last move Fake Lord Destructo made for a bit. I fired a combo-empowered **[Ride the Lightning]**, and the massive lightning bolt threw him into the wall. He wasn't out, but he was definitely down. When the thunder stopped rocking across the room, I used **[Virga]** to top my team off.

[Electric Lightshow!]
[Power-Weaving!]
[Medic!]
[HP 6/15]
[Meter's Running: 6/10]

Fursona was handling the First *V* just fine; she didn't need my help. Another shot rang out, and something pressed against my head, but **[Fursonal Furcefield]** took the hit instead of my superhero damage. Still, The Agent wasn't my problem yet; we had a plan for him.

Instead, I leaped forward with **[Pouncing Panther]** and slammed into Not-Springlock midair. She tried to redirect herself, but she wasn't Springlock, and we crashed into The Agent's desk even as he whirled and pulled the trigger again. The desperate shot went wide.

[Badass Damage!]
[Meter's Running: 5/10]

I hit her with a **[Doom Ball]**, scratching the hell out of her back and arms with cat claws that materialized, then disappeared. When she didn't go down, I followed it up with **[Cat-Scratch Fever]** and disengaged. With blurry vision and a brutal damage over time effect, Not-Springlock wasn't going to be making any—

WHAM!

[Badass Damage!]
[Meter's Running: 4/10]
[HP 4/15]

"Ooof!" Fake Lord Destructo's mace crashed into my ribs and I buckled around it. Then it smashed me into the floor. He raised it over his head, bellowing a war cry.

"Not her! Take out Jackson!" The Agent screamed from the middle of the chaos.

The mace spun around as Fake Lord Destructo turned to follow his boss's orders. I never gave him a chance, though; a **[Maximum Starlance]** hit him between the shoulders and lower back, and he went down again.

[Dramatic Damage!]
[Meter's Running: 3/10]

That left Not-Springlock, who couldn't see anything and wasn't much of a threat, and the First *V*. Fursona could handle that; my job was simple now: pressure The Agent.

He pulled the trigger again, and a bullet hit me. This time, it punched into my superhero damage, knocking me to dangerously low levels—thankfully, it didn't affect me the same way it did Dr. Jackson—but I kept on my feet and rushed the metapowered villain.

[HP 1/15]

If he shot again, I'd be out of the fight—if I survived. So many ifs and no way to tell what'd happen. Fursona vomited fire across the room, and tapestries burst into flames as she panned it over the First *V* and The Agent. At the same time, I fired another [**Maximum Starlance**] his way.

[**Dramatic Damage!**]
[**Meter's Running! 2/10**]

"Emergency teleport for Thornberry, now!" The Agent shouted.
Time seemed to stand still again.

A dozen things could have gone wrong. Things we hadn't thought about, or that Dr. Jackson hadn't seen. But so far, everything had gone according to plan—and that made me even more worried as The Agent shimmered and started vanishing.

We'd perfectly executed the trap, cornering him in the same place as Dr. Mays before springing Dr. Jackson on them to counter his first ace in the hole. Then, the fight had gone perfectly; Fursona countered her double and then some, and two fresh-ish Temp Supers couldn't stop Super Girl Spotlight Star.

But at the end of the day, the whole plan came down to whether we could trust a villain to do what she had to do—and even though we'd trusted her before, I couldn't quite shake that feeling of panic as The Agent grew more and more transparent in what felt like slow motion. His evil smile was the only thing still fully there—that and his hand pressed against the name tag on his chest.

Then another hand darted up to join it, and he solidified suddenly.

The trap's final step was sprung.

Lady Lockless's power could open any door—that made her one of the best supervillain thieves out there, and made keeping her locked up an almost impossible challenge. The power was tailor-made for a villain, and especially a less combat-oriented one. But a lesser-known side effect was that she could *lock* any door, too.

Just like she'd locked The Agent's teleporter.

A teleporter was a door if you thought hard enough about it. Or didn't think too hard—I wasn't sure. The point was that Lady Lockless thought it was, and that was good enough.

He looked at her, dumbfounded, and batted her away with the pistol; the impact knocked her across the room, and she crumpled into a corner. The gun clicked in his hand, and the sinister smile disappeared from his face, but I knew exactly where it had gone. It was plastered on mine.

"Agent, it's time for us to renegotiate our contract." I cracked my knuckles.

He knelt and grabbed something from his abandoned briefcase—a pair of magazines for the pistol. "I think you'll find my terms disagreeable," he said, but there was a hint of discomfort there. I had him off-balance, and I had a couple more tricks up my sleeve.

"Fursona, Hannibal for Lady L, cover Dr. Jackson," I said. She moved instantly, scooping up the busted-up supervillain and waiting for Dr. Jackson to get to the door. The plan was still running, and I still had exactly the right number of moves left. "Get the henches out if you can. I've got The Agent."

I used **[Grounding]**, letting the electrical bindings root me to the shattered concrete floor, and started charging **[Wallshocker]**. The power coursed through me—the *full* power of a top-tier major-league's **[Wallshocker]**, not the mid-minor power my mom had used to flatten a bank. As the lightning rippled through me, building in my heart, my stomach, my *brain*, I focused almost entirely on it—and on holding the charge.

[**True Grit!**]
[**Meter's Running: 1/10**]

Someone ran out of the room, following Fursona. Then another one. But I couldn't spare an ounce of focus for them. My allies were clear—that was what mattered.

That and the bullets bouncing off me, their energy either dissipating down the **[Grounding]** wires or getting absorbed by **[Fursonal Furcefield]**. The Super Girl Spotlight Star Costume was coming apart—I'd maxed out my powers and then some—but I had to hold on to the **[Wallshocker]**. Just a few seconds more . . .

No. The Costume wasn't going to hold. I felt the electricity slipping away as bullets hit me—now, one of them hit me through the fraying Grit powers, knocking my last point of superhero damage away.

I used **[Quick-Time Change]** and switched into Dark Girl Shock and Awe. As time started again, the maxed-out **[Wallshocker]** exploded outward, rippling out and shaking the lair's concrete tunnels. Stone and dirt collapsed around me, and The Agent dropped his gun and lunged for the only safe spot in what, a second ago, had been his lair—the few inches around my feet that **[Grounding]** protected.

The air filled with dust and rubble—worse than the Elementalist *V*'s dust—and everything went dark.

[Meter's Running: 0/10]
[Flashy Fitting-Room!]
[Devastating Damage! +5 Flamboyance Points]
[True Grit! +1 Grit Point]

[Episode Finished!]
[Episode: Power War: Cell Theory- R]
[Penalties: N/A]
[Episode Finished! +3 of each Style Point]
[Winner Winner! +3 of each Style Point]
[Role Focus: Drama + Cunning - Goal Partially Met: +10 Drama Points]
[Alias - Understudy] [Archetype - Magical Girl] [Community Rank - 49/523]
[HP 1/15]
[Styles and Skills]
▶ Archetype Skill - Transformation Sequence
▶ Combo Skills - Power-Weaving
▶ Badass (32)
▶ Cunning (33)
▶ Drama (98) (Skill Roll Available)
▶ Limelight Barrage 2
▶ Starlance 3
▶ Flamboyance (30)
▶ Signature Skill - Wondrous Wardrobe
▶ Stored Costumes: (Rainy Day, Copy Cat, Lab Assistant Panic, Lucky Star, Shock and Awe)
▶ Solar Wing 2
▶ Quick-Time Change 3
▶ Improvised Ovation 2
▶ Grit (39)
▶ Freeze-Frame 2

Water poured down around us as my **[Grounding]** wires retracted and the dust cleared enough to see. **[Quick-Time Change]** threw me back into Understudy, and I activated **[Solar Wing]**.

The fight was over; The Agent's suit jacket was torn and shredded, his leg was twisted in a way legs shouldn't go, and his neck lolled awkwardly as I dragged him up and onto my sailboard. The whole tunnel was filling with water from the damage I'd done to The Agent's inner sanctum, but I couldn't worry about any of the henches, the *V*s we'd beaten, or even Fursona.

I took off into the sky, gaining altitude even as the fetid, half-treated water rose under us. Part of me—a *huge* part of me, probably most of me—wanted to drop him. For all I knew, he was dead already, and if anyone was going to be my first kill as a superhero, The Agent was the best villain I could think of.

But I didn't drop him, even though every fiber of my being wanted to. He was an attempted murderer, a toddler kidnapper, and probably a dozen worse crimes, too. But I'd beaten him. *We'd* beaten him.

"Fursona, are you okay?" I asked into comms for the dozenth time. Hopefully she'd gotten the henches out, but more importantly, hopefully she'd gotten out herself. If she didn't answer—if I didn't catch up to her by the time I got to Tottergarten—I was dropping him off from the fiftieth floor and going looking—screw the consequences.

"Understudy, we're okay. Just got out of the subway," Fursona said a minute later. "You must've won, because we got the end of Episode that we were winners. Did you kill him?"

"Not yet. I haven't decided whether it's a good idea or not," I replied. "And I'm not even sure he's still alive."

"He has to be. Dr. Jackson says that if he's been working with the Ilneats, he'll know how to get to them—and where they are. So *don't* kill him. Mrs. N can get something out of him for sure. And if not, there's always the Anti-Nap League."

"That's vil shit," I said, echoing something Sara-N-Dipity had told me a long time ago. Then I looked at the battered, broken Agent sprawled across my sailboard. He'd deserve it, but dammit, I wanted to make the world a better place, and killing him or letting the toddlers—or worse, the retired villains—have him? That wouldn't help anyone. "We'll let Mrs. N have him, but not Kaiju Kid, and definitely not the Anti-Nap League."

"Got it. Dr. Jackson's working on getting us a car. We'll meet you at Tottergarten in an hour. Love you," Bianca said, letting herself come through the mic for a second instead of Fursona.

"Love you, too," I said back. And, with that, I pressed the sailboard to fly faster. The Agent's limp arms waved in the wind, a wad of paper blew out of his pocket and floated away, and I squeezed the name tag in my hand as tight as I could—so tight I could feel the name *Thornberry* pushing into my palm.

PART EIGHT

54

The Agent Takes a Nap

I almost couldn't hear Su-Bin telling me about the protest over the hum of a hundred thousand bees buzzing and the shouts of five superpowered children at the Honey Hive's door. But from what I *could* hear, it had gone shockingly well. "We showed up, protested for an hour, and left. Easy-peasy," Su-Bin said.

"That's great." My hand was cupped over my phone's receiver so she couldn't hear the whining kids or Honeycomb's attempts to hold them back. Kaiju Kid had recognized The Agent, and now we were under siege in Honeycomb's hideout. "So, when do I need to follow up on my part of the agreement?"

"You're not going to try to worm your way out of it?" Su-Bin asked. She sounded a little disbelieving.

"No. I said I'd do it. If you don't have a time, how about mid-March? This will all be over one way or another by then, and if we win, maybe people will be ready to think about the future."

Su-Bin went quiet. "Mid-March. That works, unless there's a window for you to do it sooner. I'll keep an eye out for one, and I'll send you what the national wing is thinking for the Accords so you can know what you're agreeing to. We can negotiate the details later."

"I'd appreciate that. The fight's not over. I have to go help interrogate a top-tier villain now, but I'll be in touch when I have some time."

"Understood." Su-Bin paused again, then continued. "Annie, be careful. You've been a good friend, even if you lied. I'm not sure if I want to continue that friendship yet, but if you get hurt or killed, I won't have that option, so don't do that to me."

"Okay." It should have hurt that she wasn't sure, but all I could feel was relief—that she was safe, and that she wanted *anything* to do with me after my year-and-a-half-long lie. "Talk to you later."

"Make him take a nap!" Milkbar yelled from the door as I—finally—rolled my Drama roll.

[**50 Drama Credits Used. Rolling Skill!**]

[**Rank-Up! Science has Rules? 2: Weapons and armor last longer before physics reasserts itself**]

I ignored the pint-sized strongman and slipped back inside. Honeycomb and Vigilant Vow could manage the kids—or their parents could. What mattered to me were the four supers sitting inside Honeycomb's hive with The Agent.

Mrs. N was there, as were Dr. Jackson and Fursona. I'd expected them, and even though none of them looked *happy* about the unconscious villain flopped in a hexagon-shaped chair in the corner, they didn't look *murderous*.

Brick House did, though.

I was legitimately terrified in a way I hadn't even been when the supervillain's hand was on my shoulder. He'd looked angry then, but the amount of hate pouring off him now? If it weren't for The Narrator, The Agent would probably be in a dozen pieces right now.

"So no, we're not killing him," Dr. Jackson said, "even if he deserves it. He's a prisoner, and *most* of us are heroes. We need information, though, and he has that. So feel free to intimidate him—"

Brick House cracked his knuckles. "Yes!"

"—*without* hurting him," she finished.

"No!"

"Mrs. N, would you wake him up?" Dr. Jackson said, ignoring the hulking supervillain's protests.

"And then The Agent was awake," The Narrator said.

The Agent glared at me through blackened, swollen eyes. "I'm still . . . willing to cut a deal, Understudy. How about this one—"

"I've got a deal for you!" Brick House shouted in his face. "How about you tell us everything you know, and I don't tear you limb from limb? You know I can do it—you've got my power contracted—so think it over. Take your time. Three! Two! One!"

Dr. Jackson interrupted, a hand on the big man's shoulder. "There's no way for you to worm your way out of this. We'd prefer you cooperate because it'll look better for you when they're deciding which part of Almhurst to stick you in."

"You think you're going to win this? Listen, Catherine, the odds are still stacked against you, and no amount of cooperation is going to change that, so no, I'm going to clam up. You're heroes, and you won't let your trained gorilla rip me apart with those kids nearby, so I'm totally fine. And if Mrs. N tries any of her tricks—"

"And then The Agent wanted to talk instead of argue," Mrs. N interrupted.

It felt . . . wrong . . . to watch The Agent spill his guts onto the Honey Hive's floor—metaphorically, though Brick House *wished* it'd been literal. He obviously didn't want to, but Mrs. N's power wasn't mind control, and it wasn't hurting him. It was just . . . narrating what was happening, and everyone went along with it. I'd never seen it used like this—at least, not by Mrs. N. This felt less like her and more like Fanfic. It churned my stomach; this was vil shit.

But it *was* effective.

He told us *everything*. How he'd killed Thornberry and taken their place as a producer for the Network. How he'd been in a power struggle with Rocko—*Rocko!*—for weeks, and how he'd all but won. How he effectively owned the Network now, how they moved to *his* orders, and about their meetings, goals, and how fragile their grip on Earth really was. That the Greater Ilneat Prosperity Community wouldn't intervene in this conflict.

But most importantly, he told us one crucial bit of information.

"The Thornberry emergency teleport works anywhere, but it'll only move one person to the Network's cruiser at a time. But there *is* a better way in. It's in the Hot Zone, in one of the studio building's conference rooms, and if you use it, you could get four or five superheroes into space all at once," he said, glaring at The Narrator.

Behind him, Brick House ground his teeth, fury pouring off him in waves.

"Which building?" I asked.

"I could show you on a map, but none of them are named."

"Good enough," Mrs. N said. "Do you know what their ship's defenses are like?"

"No. As far as they're concerned, I'm an Ilneat. None of their security systems activate when I'm around, and I haven't cared enough to ask them about it. If you were to put me through to Rocko or someone, I'd be happy to ask, though," The Agent said, voice smooth and snakelike.

"No, that's okay. And then the Agent took a nap," Mrs. N said.

The Agent snored on his wax throne as Brick House bound him to it. "Honeycomb can lock him in place when I'm done, but you're gonna let me do this."

"We sure are," I said. I had no sympathy for the beaten, bound, and utterly defeated villain; he'd long ago stopped being even remotely heroic in my book, and his long, rambling confession had only solidified that. He'd been planning this for years? For a decade? And, for all intents and purposes, he'd *won*? It was almost unbelievable, but I forced myself to believe it.

"Brick House, if you'd take over guarding the door, that would be appreciated," Dr. Jackson said. She looked tired—no, exhausted. "We don't want one of the kids getting in there and being manipulated. Or worse, having a tantrum and killing The Agent."

"Why not?" Brick House grumbled, but he stomped over to take Honeycomb's place as we left the Honey Hive.

Mrs. N took us back to her office; as the three of us jammed ourselves into plastic chairs, she collapsed into her own. "Thoughts?"

"None of that can be used in a court of law, can it?" Dr. Jackson asked.

"No." Mrs. N took off her glasses and rubbed her eyes. "But we're a little beyond that at this point, aren't we? More importantly, we need to figure out whether to chase the Ilneats into space, and if we do, who's going."

"We'll do it," Bianca said immediately from inside her fursuit.

I blinked. "We'll go to space?"

"Absolutely. Mrs. N, you said you wanted to help us find a path to victory. This is it. The Ilneats go to their cruiser whenever they feel threatened. If they have time, they do a full evacuation. That's what they did when Golden Goose got murdered. But if they don't, they emergency teleport. This is our best chance to checkmate the Network—just like Mindstorm was trying to do, but without all the information."

I nodded slowly. "And you think that since we took The Agent off the battlefield down here, we have a window to make something happen?"

"Yes," Bee said. She pointed up at the sky. "It's like soccer, okay? If someone on the other team gets a red card, they get kicked out, and they have to play a man down. You don't ignore that advantage. You push—hard. That's how you win. Right now, the pro-Ilneat supers' keeper's out of the game, and we can see the goal clearly."

"So, we go for it, then? Who's going? The Agent said only five people," I said.

"You and me are in," Bee said immediately. "And we need Lady Lockless at least as far as the teleporter in the Hot Zone. So that leaves two."

"I'd say Drs. Jackson and Mays," Mrs. N said, "but they'll be useless up there. You need someone who can handle themselves against the Ilneats. They're going to ignore most of your powers, but if you punch them in the face, they'll still fold."

"I fought Iron Fist last year after he kidnapped an Ilneat, and they didn't disappear," I said. "And Iron Fist could still grab them and carry them around."

"Must've felt pretty safe, then, if they chose to stick around," Mrs. N said. "But once you're up there, the Ilneats won't have anywhere to go. Hopefully."

I thought about it. We needed someone like Iron Fist—and we had access to a villain every bit as big and tough as the metal-fisted super. "What about Brick House?"

"No, he's staying here. I'm not letting that monster out of his cage until I'm sure he won't tear the whole ship apart the moment he gets there. And I'll never be sure about that."

Who else could we ask? Did we even know where anyone was? Gourmet was around, maybe, and so was Theseus, but they'd both just gotten destroyed by Stella-Lunar, and they might not want to get back out there and fight. I sent them both a quick text, though, just in case.

None of the Pro-Earth major-leaguers were available. The Anti-Nap League wouldn't work, either, and even though the Playpen Patrol was ridiculously strong, neither Mrs. N nor their parents would let us borrow Milkbar and Kaiju Kid.

"There's gotta be a plan that could work," Bee said, taking off her fursuit's head. "Where's the whiteboard?"

In the end, we came up with something simple.

That seemed to be working the best so far.

Mrs. N was on the phone talking to her sister about letting five of us through the door in the Tokyexico Council of Heroes tower. If Fanfic was willing, we'd try the stealth approach until we got caught. Then, Dr. Mays would lock down any heroes who came to fight us, and Jackson would . . . make them not fight us anymore.

That'd be enough to get Fursona, Lady Lockless, Gourmet, and Theseus—if they showed up—and myself to the teleporter. And from there, we'd . . .

We'd . . .

"We'll think of something," I said. All of us were stuck on that last part. We didn't know what was inside the space cruiser. Sure, we had a good idea of what it looked like, but The Agent hadn't seen any of its defenses. We'd be going in blind— assuming we made it that far.

The two of us would . . . I wasn't sure. Find Rocko? Try to destroy the ship? It was all way too up in the air, and as good as improvisation was, sometimes I needed a script to stick to. Keeping Lady Lockless safe was a definite, but beyond that, there were a lot of options. Probably too many.

"Yeah. We just need to know what we're up against. I'll backpack up all the suits, and . . . I'll probably start out as Eagle-sona, because that Costume's the stealthiest I've got," Bee said.

"Sure," I said. "So, tomorrow morning, as early as possible?"

"We'll end this then," Bee said. "For a better world. It's time."

55

Time

FRIDAY, FEBRUARY 12

Lady Lockless slipped into the Council of Heroes' conference room, where the door to the Hot Zone lay closed and sealed shut. Outside, Mrs. N and Fanfic were having a heated argument about . . . something I couldn't follow, honestly. The butterflies in my stomach felt more like ravens, they were so big, and I could barely focus on what we'd have to do.

The only good news was that Theseus and Gourmet had both turned up—the limb-swapping supervillain with a quartet of arm-transport drones and so many appendages that he looked less like a person and more like a squid, and Gourmet with a bag of candies and snacks. Both had fire in their eyes, as well as fear. But even with them, it was us seven against whatever pro-Ilneat supers were packed into the Hot Zone, and from what Su-Bin had said, it wasn't exactly empty.

"Okay. First contact with a super you four can't overpower, and we're locking down the zone. Dr. Jackson will take them out if she can, but if not, she'll move you five out of my range," Dr. Mays said. He looked a lot better; he'd shaved, showered, and the despair and lack of any motivation were gone. He still looked haunted, but now it was mixed with determination.

"Got it. I've gotta *hand* it to you, Understudy, I think this might work," Theseus said. A chorus of groans covered up the rest of whatever he was trying to say.

"Door's open, everyone," Lady Lockless said. She leaned on her cane and pointed to the door, where hot air once again rushed into the room. "If we're going, let's go."

I was already halfway through; the best way to deal with stage fright was to commit, and I was *feeling* the pressure like a hand squishing me into the ground.

[Casting Call]
[Episode: Power War: The Last Power War - R]
[Role: Superhero! Do you accept the role? (Yes/No)]

[Role Focus: Drama + Cunning]
[Power War: The Last Power War: Act One in Progress]

The funny thing was that even though my role was superhero, Lady Lockless was obviously fiddling with the villain settings in the Style System. I breathed a sigh of relief as Fursona stepped through in her eagle Costume and Lady L shut the door. If she had control over the system settings like vils did, we could maneuver for a little while before the pro-Ilneat supers caught on.

Still, it was only a matter of time, and we had to cross most of the Hot Zone. Sweat was already pouring down my face as we started filing down the street between office buildings' shattered windows and broken warehouses. According to The Agent—who hadn't been able to lie—the teleporter was in the main studio tower on the far end of New Colfax Street.

We were less than halfway there when a pair of supers swooped down on us.

The first impacted the street with a massive crash, wielding a mace that was too familiar—but this wasn't Fake Lord Destructo. This was the real deal. And the second gracefully landed a moment later, pure white energy pouring from her hands. I didn't recognize the woman—probably a major-leaguer from Yorkston or something—but I didn't need to.

"Dr. Mays here for . . ." Dr. Mays said softly.

I didn't pay attention to the rest. The world stopped, and so did both supers. For a second, I expected Dr. Jackson to grab my hand and hurry us toward our goal, but that's not what happened. Instead, she walked calmly toward Fake Lord Destructo, unstrapped the big man's helmet, and punched him in the throat before zip-tying his wrists. A moment later, the other woman was similarly restrained but with added tinfoil mittens covering her hands.

"That's standard for Elementalists. Works well on about 60% of them," she said, smiling. "Thanks, Dr. Mays."

"No problem, Cathy," he replied, letting the commercial drop. "Happy to help."

"I know it's not your fault," Dr. Jackson said.

"Not now. Later. Let's get the job done." Dr. Mays looked away and walked hurriedly down the street, and after a moment, Dr. Jackson followed him, shaking her head. I stared at the two pro-Ilneat supers; I hadn't even figured out who the one was, and now she was helpless on the ground.

Golden Goose might've been scary, but the metapowereds? They were terrifying.

Unfortunately, the next time we ran into more supers, things weren't so easy.

Dr. Mays locked them down just as quickly, but one look at the product in his hands, and he shook his head. There were eight supers, plus us, and Dr. Jackson didn't bother attacking any of them. Instead, she grabbed Theseus's fourth left arm and my right wrist. As the shimmering silvery bubble extended over me, I grabbed Fursona, and within a couple of seconds, the person chain was complete, with Theseus picking up Lady Lockless.

Then we left Dr. Mays behind.

"He can't keep them locked down long enough for a fight with that commercial," Dr. Jackson explained as we ran. "So, we're going to move you five out of range, then I'll go back and he'll try for a new one. If we win, we'll head back to the door and hold it for you in case you need to retreat. If not—"

"We should go back and save Dr. Mays," Fursona said.

Dr. Jackson shook her head. "No! The most important thing isn't Dr. Mays. He can hold his own there for a minute or two. The most important thing is getting you to the teleporter."

One of Theseus's right arms pulled on Fursona's wing, and she screeched. I cleared my throat. "Dr. Jackson's right. We have one shot at this, so let's *go.*"

It only took ten more seconds for Dr. Mays's power to stop. The second it did, Dr. Jackson pointed. "Run!" she said, and turned back toward her fellow professor.

I didn't need any encouragement. My hand slipped out of Gourmet's as she reached for a candy—a Reese's Fast Break. Fursona got airborne, and I summoned my sailboard and pulled Lady Lockless on board. We rocketed toward the skyscraper in front of us just as Dr. Jackson disappeared around the corner.

Five minutes later, things were falling apart.

An alarm blared across the Hot Zone. Already, a half dozen supers had rallied to the warning, and we had our hands full. It wasn't just quantity, either. The Triad was here, fighting in the chaotic streets.

"[**Starlance**]!" I shouted, firing a pink-and-blue bolt at The Underdelver.

[Dramatic Damage! +1 Drama Point]

Next to me, Theseus had grabbed two Bud Lightbeams and was tearing into them with oscillating blades and claws, but the third had sliced off two of his arms. They thrashed on the ground like worms, molten ends melting the asphalt.

Meanwhile, Gourmet had two minor-leaguers on her, and even with the Fast Break giving her an improbable amount of superspeed, she was hard-pressed. Worse, I couldn't *really* engage—not with Lady Lockless. I had to keep her safe; she was the key to winning.

Eagle-sona strafed the battlefield, shrieking at The Underdelver, only to fly face-first into a portal that appeared suddenly and, a moment later, fly *out* of its pair and faceplant into the sidewalk. We could mop this fight up easily—all I had to do was switch to Spotlight Star—but doing that felt like the wrong call. And it wasn't a total disaster yet. We were on the right side of the fight. All we had to do was retreat.

BWEEEEEM!

[HP 13/15]

Bud Lightbeam's laser vision ripped across me, and I almost dropped Lady Lockless as my sailboard rocked. "Guys, we need to keep moving!" she called, clinging to the steering bar just like Fursona had. Could *no one* handle this?

I turned and volleyed a **[Limelight Barrage]** into the replicating superhero as he turned a wide arc for another pass. The shots hit him, knocking him off-course and into a wall. "We've got a window! Disengage!"

[Dramatic Damage! +5 Drama Points]

Theseus finished tearing apart the two clones and stomped down the street, arms waving and disconnecting as one of his drones reloaded him with saw-blade limbs and a laser cannon of his own. A box-shaped arm fired a dozen grenades out into the street, filling it with a curtain of orange smoke that stung my eyes even from way over here. But The Underdelver didn't care about the corrosive gas.

Gourmet took a bite from one of the minor-leaguers' Costumes, then spat it out before she could absorb his powers. Instead, she ran toward us, and we started our retreat into the Network's main building. If The Agent was right, we'd find the teleporter on the fifteenth floor.

Another super threw himself through a window, but Theseus's blades and grabber arms savaged him before tossing him out the window. "I've gotta hand it to these guys, they're not giving u—oof!"

The Underdelver's drill cut off his boring, repeated joke as the hulking mech surged through a suddenly-open portal. I still hadn't seen Tele-Portal, but this whole situation felt like a repeat of our battle to take the Council of Heroes building.

Then it wasn't.

As soon as we ran to the third floor, the entire building seemed to vanish around us. One second, we had cover, and the next, the whole skyscraper above us was gone, cut off perfectly where the ceiling met the wall. I fired another **[Starlance]** toward Bud Lightbeam, whose three bodies were already strafing us even as Fursona rocketed up toward him, screeching a sound wave that hit him, him, and him clean in the face.

[Dramatic Damage! +1 Drama Point]

Then I saw what had happened. Tele-Portal had grabbed the entire top of the building in a single, massive portal and dropped it somewhere else. My heart sank; she'd known what we were trying for, and she'd stopped us in our . . .

Something glimmered a hundred feet up.

It was small compared to the building Tele-Portal had just moved. We could probably fit the five of us if we tried, but it'd be tight. More importantly, it was still *there*. I stared at it for a moment until something hit me from the side, knocking me toward the truncated building's edge.

[HP 11/15]

But the way was open. I grabbed Lady Lockless and surged into the air on [**Solar Wing**]. Fursona was already airborne, and Theseus activated a quartet of massive rockets attached to his hips, taking flight in a cloud of dust and exhaust. The three of us pushed toward the teleporter, then stopped.

Gourmet was still on the ground. She opened her bag, dodging one of the minor-leaguer's attacks, and popped out a buffalo wing. As she ate it, she turned into a Gourmet-sized dragon, belching fire across the battlefield.

But another flying super joined the fray, cutting her off. Worse, Bud Lightbeam was angling in toward the Ilneats' teleporter. I realized what was happening too late; even as my [**Starlance**] headed toward him, I knew it wouldn't be enough. He was going to try to destroy it!

[Dramatic Damage! +1 Drama Point]

Then, Theseus opened fire with everything he had. Missile launchers, lasers, and grenades filled the air, exploding all around the attacking superhero and choking the air with smoke and shrapnel. One of the Buds fell back toward the ground, then another.

But the last Bud surged through the explosions—at least until Gourmet's draconic jaws clamped down on his legs and threw him back toward the street below. He recovered, and a moment later, his lasers hit her dead center. A gout of flame filled the air as they rocketed toward each other.

"Girls, unless you want this all to fail, we've gotta go!" Theseus yelled.

I turned away from Gourmet's battle. Sure enough, he hovered at the edge of the teleporter—and a dozen supers were closing in. "I don't want to leave her," I shouted back.

"Just go, Snack! I'll be fine!" Gourmet said over our headsets. I looked at her, heart sinking; against all those supers, she wouldn't be fine. "I'm just gonna surrender once you guys make it through."

I nodded and turned the sailboard up toward the teleporter. There was nothing in the way. The moment I got there, Fursona landed next to me, and Lady Lockless opened the door. We fell through the suddenly shimmering floor, and the last thing I saw was Gourmet rocketing toward us, Bud Lightbeam and four other supers on her tail. Her flame breath filled the air around us.

Then we vanished into space.

56

Space (1)

[End of Act One: Act Two in Three Minutes]

Space wasn't anything like I thought it'd be.

Every movie I'd watched about space fell into one of two categories. Sometimes, ships all had onboard gravity, and it was just like being on board a real ship on Earth, with everyone walking and oriented the same way. The rest of the time, it was more "realistic." People floated in zero-G or climbed ladders and oriented their bodies however they wanted. I'd always thought artificial gravity was a myth.

I'd been wrong about so much before that it didn't shock me to be wrong about this, either.

Still, the view from the massive windows in the circular room we'd landed in was breathtaking. I could see the Moon *and* all of North America at the same time; from here, the Earth looked like a tiny marble I could almost reach out to touch.

A computerized voice said something I couldn't quite understand, even though I'd taken some Ilnean. "I think it said it was equalizing pressure, and that we had like five minutes," I said. "But I'm not sure."

"Great. Help me get changed," Fursona said. She was already halfway out of her Eagle-sona fursuit, wearing a one-piece swimsuit underneath and pulling out the Kaiju-sona suit from her backpack. I was jealous—she could dress for the temperatures inside that thing, while I still had my winter jacket on—at least as Anika.

My stomach wouldn't stop rolling as I worked, though; were Gourmet and the professors alright? There was no way we had cell phone service up here, right? I checked my phone—sure enough, no bars.

I strapped her into her helmet, working quickly while Lady Lockless sealed the teleporter behind her. Then I thumped the plushie dinosaur on the back of the head. Her eyestalks wobbled a little. "You're good to go," I said.

"Thanks." Bee got ready and faced the teleporter room's hatch as a bar of light slowly filled up.

[Power War: The Last Power War: Act Two in Progress]

The door opened into a shockingly wide corridor with slightly rounded walls; I had no idea what the Ilneats' cruiser looked like from the outside, but it almost seemed like a thin neck between the teleporter room and the rest of the vessel. A flashing red light silently spun in alarm, but aside from that and the hint of smoke in the recycled air, I couldn't find so much as a hint that an Ilneat was on board.

Theseus was already halfway down the hall—he was really hoofing it on the half dozen multijointed legs he'd equipped, and his rearming drones were struggling to keep up. Fursona gestured for me to go, then hurried along behind, with Lady Lockless riding piggyback.

The hall stretched on and on, but after a disturbingly long time, we burst through the door into the biggest conference room I'd ever seen. There had to be a hundred empty seats around the massive table, and the stench of cigars stung my nose. I coughed once, and the moment I did, a gigantic Rocko appeared in the center of the table from the shoulders up.

"DuPont, Marino, Brown, and . . . um, Callum. I see Andonte didn't make it, and neither did Mays and Jackson," Rocko said. "You've put on a great performance, one for the ages! Do you have any idea what this has done to our bottom line?"

Theseus narrowed his eyes, leveling a laser cannon arm and putting a shot into the receptor. But Rocko only laughed and waved a virtual cigar the size of my arm in the air. "You think you can hurt this ship? It's got the same protections we do! Don't worry your little head over it, though; I'll let your producers talk to you two when we're done with our chat, and you've remembered whose side you're really on. DuPont, Rocko Studios is the best-selling studio in the whole Network right now. Your rebellion storyline's been *gold*. Pure *gold*! And I didn't even have to coach you on it!

"Now, listen up. I'm prepared to offer you a raise of half a percent. That's unprecedented for Earth supers. And I'll throw in a nonbinding veto clause on three Episode ideas a year."

"No," I said.

"No? Listen up, DuPont!" Rocko's teeth bared, and they lowered the cigar out of the hologram. "You and me—and Marino, of course—we're going places. The sky's the limit! What are you, mid-minors? And you're handling major-league threats like it's no problem. I told you **[Adaptive Armoire]** was an investment. A slow-burn investment. That you'd have to work on it, and you *have*!

"You're gonna be a star, kid. Number one! We'll strap one of Marino's eyestalks onto a Costume, and you'll be fifty feet tall. Get Stella-Lunar to give you one piece of her halo, and that pulsing power's all yours! The possibilities are endless, and you want to say no?"

"Yeah, I *do* want to say no." My eyes narrowed, and my throat felt tight. This alien—this *scumbag*—had been using me as a profit engine, and the whole time, their coworkers were abusing Jasmine Saxton, my mom, Vigilant Vow; the list went on and on. Stella-Lunar had taken bullets because of the Ilneats' greed. Golden Goose—and Haze-Matt, and who knew how many other people, Extras and supers alike—had died to make them a profit. And now they wanted me to forget all that—for half a percent?

"You don't know what you're throwing away, kid," Rocko said.

"Actually, we do," Lady Lockless interrupted, sliding off Fursona's back and sitting in one of the undersized chairs. "We've put together a pretty good idea of how much money the Ilneat Network makes from Earth, and half a percent of one studio's average income is the same amount as North America's GDP. It's an unfathomable amount of money."

"But the cost is too high," Bianca said. She wasn't using her modulator—in fact, I realized that her modulator had been off since last Episode. "You did a great job of cleaning up Earth after Launch Day, but according to Pennyworth, we paid that cost back in the first three years of shows. It's time to renegotiate."

Rocko blinked, their black eyes locked on us. Their cigar dipped up to their mouth, and a cloud formed around their head. The hologram flickered, and Rocko cleared their throat and clapped a pair of their hands. "Alright, now we're getting somewhere! Let's negotiate, already! What do you want?"

"We want you gone," I said.

"Well, that's on the table, DuPont! We can do our jobs from somewhere else. It'll be more complicated, and the extra cost would come out of your salaries, but we could do it."

"No, not working from somewhere else," Theseus said, aiming a rocket pod toward Rocko's hologram. "Gone as in not controlling what we do. Gone as in no more Episodes, at least not produced by Ilneats. That's what we mean by gone."

"Ah. That's not negotiable," Rocko said. "A shame. But if you can't work with us, then we're at an impasse. And when impasses happen, and strikes drag on too long, they need to be broken. Callum, Brown, Marino, and DuPont, we'll talk again real soon, yeah?"

The hologram shut off, and red lights flicked on all around the room. At the same time, the conference table and chairs started to retract, dumping Lady Lockless onto the steel floor. "Shit," she said, rubbing a shoulder.

"Yep. That went well," Fursona said. "I expected Rocko to throw security measures at us right away. If they're negotiating, it can only be for two reasons."

"Either they've got the weaker hand and they know it, or they don't understand how you could turn down that kind of money," Theseus interrupted.

I groaned at the limb joke, but Theseus was right. Rocko had never cared about anything but money, and they probably couldn't understand how we'd turned down their offer. That felt right. But it didn't feel like the truth. Not the whole truth, anyway. "They were stalling. Get ready."

A second later, the doors on the room's far side blew inward like massive steel bullets, and two robots stomped in, boots clanging magnetically on the ground. They stood in the doorways as smoke billowed into the room behind them, identical red capes waving in the breeze. Then the first one's eyes glowed a brilliant red, and a second later, a laser swept across the room—and across us!

[HP 9/15]

Theseus was already returning fire with his own laser, and a split second later, Fursona hurled toward the second robot—whose arm swelled to an incredible size. When the two met, it was like watching two icebergs hit. Neither moved for a moment. Then Kaiju-sona went flying back.

I didn't waste any time, starting up a **[Power-Weaving]** combo and firing a **[Limelight Barrage]** right into the second robot. The first shot hit, but it didn't stop moving; the thing shrugged off my stun and started weaving back and forth on its hip joints to dodge the rest of the rays.

[**Dramatic Damage! +1 Drama Point**]

"You were always replaceable," Rocko's voice echoed over the ship's loudspeakers as the first bot fired a rocket out of its fist. The shrapnel rained down onto Theseus, shredding arms and legs alike. A rearming drone dipped in as Rocko continued, "You were just the cheaper option. We've been studying what the System did to you, and we haven't just replicated it. We've *improved* on it—controlled it, even!"

I **[Quick-Time Changed]** to dodge the second bot's punch, but even as **[Freeze-Frame]** activated and the bot's fist froze in place, I watched its soulless eyes follow my movement. The moment time sped up, its fist changed direction and hit Lab Assistant Panic right in the chest. I felt something crunch, and hoped it was just superhero damage.

It didn't feel like just superhero damage.

[**Flashy Fitting-Room! +1 Flamboyance Point**]
[**Steel Yourself! +1 Grit Point**
[**Floating Points: 3 Drama, 1 Flamboyance**]
[HP 6/15]

My vision went black, even though the blow had hit me in the chest. TA-1LZ opened up with her **[New Head-Cannon]**, tasers streaming from the Gatling gun like a party streamer going off. And the shocks to the bot's system saved me; the bot's blow went just an inch wide, and I rolled behind it.

I needed something—anything—to use as a weapon. The bot whirled, and Fursona slammed into it, roaring flame across its still-twitching frame. As they fought, I ran toward Theseus's pile of destroyed arms; they'd have to do.

As I slid into the mess of molten limbs, I realized that not only would they do, but they'd be perfect. "Using Alkirk's proprietary prosthetic plans and fissile-reductive material, I am become Her-seus, destroyer of bots!"

[Pseudoscientific Mumbo-Jumbo! +1 Drama Point.]
[Power-Weaving! +6 Drama, +3 Flamboyance, and +1 Grit Point]

"I told you the extra arms would give you a *leg* up!" Theseus yelled. And this time, I didn't groan. Instead, I flexed the extra two arms I'd slapped together for myself. The first spun like a circular saw with three massive blades that beat the air with a whumping, humming sound. The second looked a lot like Theseus's laser cannon arms, but bigger. Much, much bigger. Unrealistically large.

I fired the unrealistically large cannon.

BWEEEEEEEEEEEEEEEEEEEEEEEEEEEM!

BOOM!

The cannon vaporized. So did all the air between me and the bot. As the air collapsed inward, a shock wave rippled out, and every window in the conference room shattered. For a moment, the room was airless, and I started panicking as the air got sucked out of my lungs. It burned like fire in my chest, and my ears popped painfully.

[Pseudoscientific Mumbo-Jumbo! +1 Drama Point]
[HP 5/15]

Then, the ship's emergency systems took over, sealing the room off and pumping air back in. I took a desperate breath to refill my suddenly empty lungs, thanking the system for superhero damage, and I looked at the damage I'd done.

The laser hadn't even scratched the ship's hull. There was a little black spot where something had been smudged on the shiny, curved wall, but aside from that, it looked as good as new.

But the bot was gone from the waist up. Its legs toppled over, one to the left, the other to the right.

"I've gotta get me one of those," Theseus said.

Fursona snorted. "In your dreams, Theseu-ass. She's all mine."

57

Space (2)

My three-bladed heavy saw arm lasted just long enough to join the *real* Theseus in tearing apart the other super bot. When it finally collapsed in a heap of scrap metal and wires, I breathed a sigh of relief and disconnected his arms from my shoulders; they didn't fit quite right, and they were a temporary weapon by **[Science has Rules?]** very nature. Besides, I needed to get back to Rainy Day.

I used **[Virga]** to top off the whole team the second I finished transforming.

[Medic! +4 Cunning Points]
[HP 7/15]

It wasn't much, but it was something.

"Well, that was messy!" Fursona said. She'd shifted plans to cover Lady Lockless—without her, we weren't going home—and hadn't gotten in on the fighting.

"Uh, ladies?" Theseus said from one of the doors. "I don't think it's over."

My gaze shifted to the shattered door, and even though I couldn't see much through the haze of smoke, the metal stomping sound made what he meant obvious. "Fursona, check the other door!"

"Don't bother," Rocko's voice filtered into the room. "I've got a squad going that way, too. But in the interest of ratings, I'll let you know what you're up against. The first type's a Bruiser/Speedster, able to switch forms in about three seconds for maximum aggression. We're talking superspeed, superstrength, laser eyes, and a solid frame for taking punishment. Not whatever *that* was, but a *lot* of punishment."

We didn't bother listening to the rest of his speech. Theseus was already halfway down his hallway, and we piled in behind him. We hadn't come this far to lose—no way! And the win condition was pretty clear. Rocko was on board somewhere, probably in a smoke-filled office with the thermometer at a hundred fifty degrees. If we cornered him, we could force him to shut down the bots and negotiate—this time in good faith!

The wave of super-bots came around the corner, and Theseus hit them like a tsunami of limbs. Saw blades and drills revved, bots started falling apart, and severed arms crashed to the ground. I fired a **[Wind Front]** into the clustered bots, and Fursona breathed fire into the hall behind us to stall the other wave.

[Badass Move! +1 Badass Point]

Then a door opened up next to us, and a different bot soared out. Rocko laughed over the intercom. "We've also got Elementalist bots, of course. Right now, they're focused on four elements or on support mode. You'll see what I'm talking about soon!"

This bot had a blue cape, and was a lot slimmer than the Bruiser bots. It moved fluidly between Theseus and the bots he was fighting, then raised its hands before bringing them down in an arc—a shimmering shield formed in the air, twinkling like a fragile pane of ice. Theseus slammed a saw against it. A horrible screech filled the air. When he pulled it back, the blade was dull and notched.

"Shit," he said, disconnecting the arm and waving for a replacement. Then he ducked for the side passage. "In here!"

I grabbed Lady Lockless and pulled her in, then made room for Fursona as she vomited even more fire. Battered, shattered, and half melted super-bots filled the hall behind us, firing lasers and blasts of energy into the hall as we retreated down it.

The passage opened into another wide room, this one filled with smaller tables. It smelled different, too—more like food and less like tobacco. As the super-bots poured in behind us, I couldn't help but admire them. "You got this idea from Peter, didn't you?"

"No. But his LABRAT bot experimentation solved a few problems for us," Rocko said. "We also took cues from someone with an AI Magical Girl robot. You'll see that soon. Super-bots, get them!"

I was already Rainy Day, so I started a **[Power-Weaving]** into a **[Thunderhead]**. The shock wave from the power starting rippled out, knocking bots off their feet before the supports could get shields up. "I'm on crowd control for a minute. You two pick off any stragglers."

[Pause for Effect! +1 Drama Point]

The bots were still recovering when I rolled into my next move, another **[Wind Front]** that pushed several of them back and let Fursona and Theseus quickly dismantle one caught on the wrong side of the burst. Theseus's arm setup was disgustingly lethal, but even so, he was losing two or three for every bot, and he was down to just one rearming drone. Fursona's fursuit had gouges in the plush, and they weren't going to hold much longer.

[Badass Move! +1 Badass Point]
[Floating Points: 1 Drama]

But they didn't have to. I used another **[Virga]** to fill in the gaps as the bots rushed my teammates, topping them off and fixing their damaged Costumes. Another bot exploded in the back, and then the Elementalists and ranged Bruisers started opening up with their lasers again.

[Medic! +4 Cunning Points]
[HP 9/15]
[Floating Points: 3 Drama, 1 Badass]

Then I used **[Thunderhead]** again. I'd used this technique before to create a massive, self-feeding cloud, and I was confident it'd work again here. The feedback loop filled the thin storm cloud clinging to the ceiling with so much static that my hair stood on end.

[Environmental Combo! +1 Cunning Point]
[Thunderstruck! +1 Drama Point]
[Power-Weaving! +6 Drama, +3 Badass, +1 Cunning Point]
[Feedback 1]
[HP 8/15]
[Confirm Combo Continuation?]

Fursona and Theseus were getting the shit kicked out of them, but I figured I could ride the combo one more time before they outright lost, so I let the electricity build and build overhead until it looked like a full-on monsoon and tornado all at once.

[Environmental Combo! +1 Cunning Point]
[Thunderstruck! +1 Drama Point]
[Feedback 2]
[HP 7/15]
[Confirm Combo Continuation?]

Then I poured the comboed-up **[Thunderheads]** into a massive **[Ride the Lightning]**. It ripped across the bots, overloading circuits and triggering an enormous chain reaction. Metal arms and legs flew every which way, and Lady Lockless screamed as the ship's power went off and tables, bots, and the four of us went weightless.

[Electric Lightshow! +1 Flamboyance Point]

Fursona couldn't move. She doggy-paddled in the air and tried using her fire breath—but nothing worked. Theseus's rocket legs propelled him toward the ceiling, and a moment later, he was spider-walking on it and wrapping Lady Lockless in a multilimbed embrace.

As for me? I used **[Quick-Time Change]** to switch to Understudy. She had the best kit for weightlessness, and some of the surviving bots seemed to be struggling. As I finished transforming and scooted toward Fursona on **[Starlight Sail]**, Theseus was already most of the way to the exit.

[Flashy Fitting-Room! +1 Flamboyance Point]
[Rejuvenation Activated! HP 11/15]

We pushed through it into a massive airlock.

The entryway looked less like something to move people through and more like where two ships would connect if they needed to move supplies between them. A huge door covered the outside, with reinforced glass windows revealing . . . nothing. No planet, no other ships, just empty space as far as I could see—and probably a *lot* farther than that. On the far side, another door was open, with a flashing red emergency light overhead. Theseus fired his thrusters and zoomed toward it, and I followed.

WHAM!

[HP 10/15]

Something hit me from the side. Fursona screamed as the impact knocked her off my sailboard, only to go cartwheeling off into zero-G. I banked the sailboard and rocketed toward her. Theseus shredded the Bruiser bot a moment later.

Then the main lights went on, and Rocko's voice filled the airlock. "Okay. Okay, ladies and gentlemen, this has been fun, but it's time to stop before someone important gets hurt."

The small doors on either side of the huge airlock started to close.

Another Ilneat's voice filled the air, sounding slightly synthetic. I couldn't catch it all, but what I heard gave me chills. Rocko was going to open the outside airlock! I had to get to Fursona and get out of here!

I rocketed past her, looped around, and picked her up—just as the doors slammed shut.

"Okay, that's bad," I said.

The digital Ilneat's voice filled the airlock again as I looked around. We had two minutes. Maybe three—I hadn't done great on numbers. Theseus and Lady Lockless were nowhere to be seen. I let out a sigh of relief; they must've gotten out in time!

"Sorry," Fursona said, "but you shouldn't have come back for me."

I shook my head. "Of course, I was coming back for you. I have a plan." Then I **[Quick-Time Changed]** into Lucky Star.

She looked at me, and even though I couldn't see them, I knew her eyes were either wide or glaring. "No. You'd better not," she said. But she didn't have any leverage. There was nowhere for her to go.

"I'm switching back to Understudy as soon as I do. Babe, Lady Lockless will have the door open in just a second, and I'll be fine. But just in case she *doesn't*, I'm getting you out of here."

The fuzzy dinosaur started flailing around, and I pulled her in close to avoid the worst of the thrashing. She couldn't get away. There was nowhere to go. "Love you, Bee," I said.

Then I activated [**Noncombatant Teleport**], and Fursona vanished.

[**Dramatic Rescue! +1 Drama Point**]

"This is perfect," Rocko's voice said over the intercom. "I hadn't introduced the Magical Girl bots yet, and now that you're not with your friends, they'll need a couple to remind them of you. I'll let you play with one or two as well. And as for the door? Well, let's just say Callum and Brown have their hands full. They won't be saving you."

They were lying. Theseus and Lady Lockless would come through. They had to. I started the slow shift into Magical Girl Understudy. Choral music and flashing lights filled the room as the Rescue Girl Lucky Star Costume disappeared and my body went bright white. The dress formed over my torso, and tights and gloves worked their way from my fingers and toes up my limbs.

And the whole time, Rocko wouldn't stop talking. "You can save them, and yourself. All you have to do is agree to some simple terms. Sign back on with Rocko Studios, same contract as before. We'll choose the Episodes, create a more controlled schedule and persona for you, and together, you and I can rule the superhero show galaxy. And I'll make sure Fursona gets a show somewhere far away from you, so you both stay under *control*."

I couldn't respond. Bows were tying themselves into my hair and across my chest as I transformed. The music swelled, and for a minute, I couldn't hear what he was saying. Then, as it slowly faded to a reasonable volume and the boots laced themselves all the way to my knees, I heard him say, "That's a no, then? That's fine. We'll test out the MG bots for a minute."

The music stopped. The lights faded. I hovered midair, gravity completely cut in the room as [**Solar Wing**] activated like it thought I was falling. Then two hatches opened, and a pair of bots entered the room.

These ones had no capes. Instead, pink dresses covered their metal skin, and two steel staffs hung from their grips. And behind them came two familiars. I couldn't quite make out what they were supposed to be, but they were definitely animals of some kind.

I raised my wand. One of the Magical Girl bots fired a beam of energy my way before I could even get my **[Starlance]** off, and I had to spiral toward the floor. At the same moment, the digital Ilneat gave a warning; I had fifteen seconds.

I opened up with everything I had, zooming toward the exit door. Lady Lockless would get it open. She had to. **[Starlance]** after **[Starlance]** poured into the MG bots, and they returned fire with rays and beams of their own. For a few seconds, the room was an apocalypse of bright, flashing lights and color vomit.

[Dramatic Damage! +4 Drama Points]

But the door wasn't opening.

The voice counted down. Five. I ducked a massive beam that swung across the room like a scythe. Four. Two more **[Starlances]**, then a roll—I had to keep my distance or I'd get torn apart.

[Dramatic Damage! +2 Drama Points]

Two seconds. Where had three gone? I looked at the door one last time. Still closed, still locked. Then I took a deep breath.

One.

The massive airlock opened, and I lost control of my **[Solar Wing]** as every scrap of air vented from the room—and from my lungs.

58

Space (3)

It was good to be CEO.

Rocko leaned back in the oversized chair in their office. From here, they could watch the ship's bridge below them, or any of the three big-screen monitors on their desk. Right now, one showed Marino, Callum, and Brown fighting a tide of super-bots—mostly Bruisers and Supports, but with a pair of the brand-new Magical Girl variants in there. They were making a good show of it, and as Rocko watched, their mind raced with thoughts about the marketing.

This would be huge. It'd probably move the Network past the space opera films in the average weekly ratings. And all that would be good for Rocko Studios.

"Pataki, see if you can salvage any of their Costumes. We'll recycle them later on new heroes, or dress the bots in them," Rocko said over the intercom.

"You've got it," Pataki replied. Rocko bared their teeth in a smile. Their subordinate was always on top of things, always willing to do the dirty work when needed.

The second monitor showed the Network's stock value. It was a black line shooting straight up, as vertical as Rocko had ever seen in their career. A quintupling of value was unheard of—even from the other show-makers. Forget buying moons—Rocko Productions and the Network were gonna be picking up planets by the dozen!

And, on the last monitor, a single figure drifted through space, arms flailing more and more slowly as she froze over. Rocko barely spared that screen a glance. The two Magical Girl bots would make sure nothing was left of DuPont.

It had been tight, and some luck *had* been involved, but Rocko had led the Network down the exact right course to outmaneuver The Agent, reassert control over Earth, and even put this last-ditch rebellion down. They'd even managed to get rid of Snowball and Thornberry, cementing them as the sole power in the Network.

Sure, DuPont and Marino might not have been the most powerful heroes in the Network, but they were rising meteorically. Everyone knew it was only a matter of time before DuPont was number one, with Marino in the top ten—worldwide, not locally. If any other studio had lost its two best supers like this, it'd be finished. Look what had happened to Snowball and Cartman.

But Rocko Studios? No way. The Ilneat had invested too much into every possible future to lose just because some humans died, got bored, or retired. They had their fingers in every possible pie, to use the human phrase. When DuPont and Marino lost in their poor, rebellious teenaged attack on the Ilneats' cruiser, none of it would be shown on Earth.

Everywhere else, but not Earth.

It'd position Rocko's hero bots as the next big thing in Ilneat space, though. It might even replace the superhero genre completely. Then they could leave this frigid, backwater planet behind, and every studio that wanted to make superhero shows would use *their* bots. Eliminate the competition and raise your own product. That was the way.

Yep. It was good to be—

Something flashed on the third monitor.

"DuPont's trying Spotlight Star," Rocko said under their breath. They pushed a button, and the feed appeared on all three screens. The flashing lights—without choral music in the void of space. The Costume working its way up her light-colored body in ultra-fast-forward as the rest of the battle froze for a second. And then, the hood.

Rocko watched. It wouldn't matter. The hood wasn't a helmet, and they *knew* DuPont's Costume choices, her powers, her upgrades—everything. She had nothing that could possibly save her. Nothing.

The hood sealed over DuPont's head, and two bright pink, star-shaped eyes started glowing where her eyes had been a moment before.

[HP 9/15]
[HP 8/15]

I spun out of control through space, the freezing cold competing with the scorching lack of air in my lungs. It was quiet—so quiet. The Ilneats' cruiser was already fading into the distance, a hulking, reverse rubber-chicken shape half eclipsing the Earth and Moon.

[HP 7/15]

My superhero damage couldn't take much more of this. No, *I* couldn't take much more of this. Even though my HP was keeping me alive—barely—my vision was already going black. It was getting hard to think. Hard to feel. Just . . . hard . . . in general.

[HP 6/15]

Bee was on the ship. That was . . . good. She'd . . . be okay for now. And Mom and Dad. They'd miss me, but they'd understand. They'd have to; they . . . made me this way. And Mom . . . she'd especially get why I'd had to fight this . . . fight.

I didn't want this to be the end. But . . . my brain felt slow. Like . . . trying to swim through butter . . . or something. That wasn't quite right . . . but I couldn't think of what was.

The pressure was getting to be a lot. At some point, it'd be too much. But I could . . . do something.

[HP 5/15]

Couldn't I?

Sure. I started . . . going through my Costumes. Which one could save my life here? Lab Assistant, maybe . . . or Rainy Day?

[HP 4/15]

Then, as two metallic figures rocketed toward me, I realized . . . I didn't have time, and I only had one transformation left for this act. I needed to use Spotlight Star. Even if I . . . needed it later. There wouldn't be . . . a *later* if I didn't use it now.

I used **[Quick-Time Change]** before another point of HP could disappear. The quick fanfare of jubilant choral music was strangely missing in the silence of space, though the quick light show happened just like normal as my Understudy Costume traded up for the medieval-inspired Spotlight Star one. The hood buckled over my head, covering me from scalp to chin.

Then—miraculously—it closed over my face.

[Flashy Fitting-Room! +1 Flamboyance Point]
[Steel Yourself!]
[Meter's Running: 9/10]

I took a deep breath of cool, crisp air, screaming in my head as my deflated lungs filled painfully. I still had hope! More than that, I had nine of the most powerful powers I'd ever used to destroy these bots, get back on the ship, and reunite with Bee.

She had to be worried sick.

The two Magical Girl robots were surging toward me, picking up speed, but I had whole seconds to think through my battle plan. Every power had just reset and been maxed out. If Rocko was watching, I was about to give them some fireworks. And then I was getting back on that ship and kicking their ass!

I activated **[Solar Wing]**.

[Meter's Running: 8/10]

As my spinning stopped and I slowed down mid-space, I took a second to figure out the two robo-girls' powersets. They'd already used big, sweeping beams, so I had them pegged for something like a Stella-Lunar clone, with **[Stellar Rays]** and **[Maximum Starlances]**. That meant the most dangerous part of the fight would be closing the gap.

Luckily, I could do that quickly. Without any friction, **[Solar Wing]** was pushing me toward them faster than I'd ever been. The pink and blue contrails didn't fade, either—they hung there behind me, painting speed lines in space. A beam of pure white energy sprang across the void. I ducked reflexively, even though it was already past and on its way to Pluto or something.

At least we'd be giving a good show.

Then I returned fire, screeching to a stop a few dozen yards from the first robo-girl. I used **[Power-Weaving]**—none of the other bots had thought to **[Combo-Break]**, so I figured Rocko hadn't programmed that in yet. Then I whipped a single **[Maximum Starlance]** toward the first robo-girl as she tried to evade.

But in space, no one could hear her thruster's scream. And the **[Maximum Starlance]** bore down way too fast to dodge. It punched a hole in her chest, and for half a second, I saw flames. Then, just as quickly, they died down. Her metallic familiar landed on her shoulder and started repairing the damage.

[Dramatic Damage!]
[Meter's Running: 7/10]

That was fine, though. I unloaded a **[Thunderhead]** into space over our heads. But that's not what came out. Instead, a whirling miasma of darkness filled the sky, sucking light into it as it swelled. The bright halo around it left no doubt in my mind that I'd copied a Stella-Lunar move on accident—especially when it ate one of the robo-girls' beams, warping it into a spiral before consuming it.

[Pause for Effect!]
[Meter's Running: 6/10]

Then, as the first robo-girl's familiar finished her repairs, I rocketed at the second one, leaping toward her and using **[Doom Ball]**. I didn't expect big results. But I got them. The bot's casing parted as my claws punched into her chest and ripped through wires and tubes inside.

[Badass Damage!]
[Meter's Running: 5/10]

Both girls were still up, though, and before I could finish my **[Power-Weaving]** combo, they lined up their staves with the moon between their circular ornaments. They both shouted the same word into the silent void, though I couldn't hear it.

A moment later, a silent ray of moonlight a dozen feet across engulfed me.

[HP 2/15]
[Tough Kitty!]

The light burned. I could barely see, and only [**Fursona Furcefield's**] passive defense kept me up and running. But when I flew out the other side, both robo-girls were lined up perfectly for a [**Limelight Barrage**]. I waved my wand, and the volley of [**Maximum Starlances**] bore down on the bots.

[Dramatic Damage!]
[Power-Weaving!]
[Meter's Running: 4/10]

Every shot hit *something*, but when the flaring light and bursts of flame cleared, one bot sported two holes in its torso, while the other's staff arm had been blown off by a single shot. They glanced around, almost as if looking for their familiars.

I grinned a sharklike grin. Their familiars had both vaporized. I'd targeted them first.

So, three moves. Could I finish off both robo-girls in three moves, then get inside the ship in one? The airlock's door had finally finished its long, grinding opening, and now it was starting to cycle closed. One robo-girl was all but out of the fight, and the other had taken critical damage that her familiar had only half repaired.

But they both still had some tricks up their sleeves. The one-armed robo-girl rocketed toward me, grabbing me by the arm and hurling me away from the airlock. At the same moment, another beam cut through the air. This time, it only clipped me, but it was still a hit, and I *couldn't* take more of them.

[HP 1/15]

I grappled with the one-armed robo-girl, trying to get her off me. Then I realized that wasn't the solution. Instead, I pulled her in close, then started charging a [**Wallshocker**].

She realized what was happening almost immediately, and started fighting like crazy to get away, but with only one arm, she *couldn't* escape. She just didn't have the leverage, and I didn't have to charge for long.

[Devastating Demolition!]
[Meter's Running: 3/10]

Two powers, plus one to get inside. That'd be enough—more than enough. I already had it all planned out. As the first robo-girl disintegrated into a cloud of scrap behind me, I turned in midair. **[Solar Wing]** was gone; the grappling had taken care of that. But I only needed two powers.

The robo-girl charged up another beam, but I **[Blitzed]** through space, ramming into her before even her digital reflexes could react.

[Badass Damage!]
[Meter's Running: 2/10]

The beam fired off a moment later, slicing into the rapidly closing airlock door. I had to finish this *now*. If the robo-girl got away, she'd keep me from getting inside to my friends. And to Bee.

And I couldn't rely on **[Wallshocker]**. This close, and with both arms, she'd get away. So instead, I used **[Shock and Awww]**. The shock wave wasn't anywhere near as big. The bot didn't disintegrate this time. But as her eyes stopped glowing, I could feel stuff rattling inside her metal frame.

[Dramatic Damage!]
[Meter's Running: 1/10]

The door was almost half closed. I kicked off from the broken, shattered wreckage of Rocko's robotic superhero, propelling myself toward it.

Then, just before the metal touched, I used **[Blitz]**.

I popped into the wide room. Air was already venting into it, filling it up even as I slow-transformed back into Understudy. The Ilneat's digital voice filled the air, letting me know that the airlock would be fully cycled in three minutes.

And, at the same time, the second act ended.

[End of Act Two: Act Three in Three Minutes]

59

Space (4)

[Power War: The Last Power War: Act Three in Progress]

The second the door opened, I slipped through it and into a scene of utter devastation.

Robot parts and Theseus's arms lay everywhere, along with a thin layer of Kaiju-colored fur that blanketed the ground. Lady Lockless leaned against the ship's bulkhead, breathing heavily as the door closed behind me and rubbing her shoulder. Other than that, she looked fine.

Theseus didn't look quite as fine. He was down to four arms on his left shoulder, one on his right, and a tripod of beaten, bent legs holding him up. When I stared at him, he laughed and raised his right arm. It bent, screeching as it gave out. "Could you give me a hand? I'm out of rearming drones."

"*You* need to wait," Bee interrupted. She was halfway into her kangaroo suit; the Kaiju-sona fursuit was completely out of commission. Pataki could probably fix it, but without the Ilneat's help, it'd be a while before Bee went Full Kaiju again. She half hopped to me and wrapped me in a gigantic hug. "You made it."

"Of course I made it," I said nonchalantly. Then I kissed her. It wasn't a big, romantic kiss. There wasn't time for that. But I needed it—bad. And so did she, by how insistently she returned it. I pulled back way too soon, but we *were* still mid-Episode, and we needed to focus. "What happened here?"

"Your girlfriend went turbo-lizard, and Theseus buzz-sawed the survivors," Lady Lockless said. She pressed her hand to the door's control, and a second later, every light went red. "That's not opening until I give it permission."

"So, what's left?" I asked, disengaging from the hug and slow-transforming into Rainy Day.

"Not much. We had a leg up on the bots—choke points, superior firepower, and better powers. Whatever Rocko designed, we think he threw everything he had at us," Theseus said. "But we *handled* it."

While I finished the transformation, Fursona finished gearing up, and Lady Lockless removed Theseus's broken arm and replaced it with one of his less-damaged left arms. He wiggled it around. "Ugh, it's backwards. That's going to take some getting used to."

A pair of **[Virga]** uses later, we were in as good a shape as we were going to get. Fursona took point, and we followed, pushing down the chrome-and-glass hallway toward what—we hoped—was the bridge. Or wherever Rocko was.

[Medic! +8 Cunning Points]
[HP 7/15]

The halls were quiet. Nothing moved. Theseus was right; they'd destroyed almost every bot on the ship—at least on this side of the airlock. And with Lady Lockless's power, the ones on the far side couldn't get to us. Here and there, an Ilneat stared at us from inside a locked door, peering through the windows with wide, black eyes. They looked curious, not angry or scared.

We ignored them for now. Only one Ilneat mattered: the one in charge.

Locked doors weren't a problem. Lady Lockless navigated them within seconds, and between the three of us, the occasional stray bot went down too fast to do much damage. By the time we reached what *had* to be the fancy executive wing of the ship, we were practically sprinting.

As we sped around a corner, a pure white **[Moonbeam]** fired into Fursona, throwing her against the wall. Two Magical Girl bots flanked a closed and locked door, staves ready to use their powers again. I used **[Limelight Barrage]** to pin one down long enough for Fursona to land a brutal **[Double-Kick]**.

[Dramatic Damage! +5 Drama Points]

As the two of us hammered away at her steel armor, the other danced away from Theseus and fired a beam his way. Another arm hit the deck, thrashing and sparking. His last laser arm activated, and a moment later, one of *her* arms was off.

Fursona had her hands full with the first bot, and I couldn't get a clean shot on either of the two without hurting my friends. Beams and laser blasts surged every which way, and I ducked around the corner a second too late. A ray of moonlight sliced across me and knocked me to the ground.

[HP 4/15]

But the robo-girls couldn't cover us all. Lady Lockless pressed her hand to the door. It popped open, and there, smoking four cigars, fur sticking every which way, and tie hanging loosely from their neck, sat Rocko.

I **[Quick-Time Changed]** into Copy Cat, ducked through the frozen fight, and used **[Pouncing Panther]** to get right next to the alien executive. Then I extended my claws. "Stand them down, Rocko!"

[Flashy Fitting-Room! +1 Flamboyance Point]
[Steel Yourself! +1 Grit Point]
[Badass Move! +1 Badass Point]

Rocko didn't stand them down.

Instead, a forcefield shimmered into existence, throwing me out of the door. Behind me, one of the bots exploded as Fursona tore it limb from limb. But the fighting didn't matter. Only one thing mattered.

The smug grin on Rocko's face.

"DuPont, you're acting like an idiot," they said as I picked myself up and glared at the shining barrier. "You can't get through this with any of your powers, and it's only a matter of time until more hero bots get here. But I'm willing to make a deal here. 3%. Take out Brown and Callum, and convince Marino to cooperate. Easy."

I slammed into the barrier with a **[Pouncing Panther]**. It didn't hurt. It was more like landing in Jell-O. But I couldn't get to Rocko—not like that. And if I couldn't get to them, and they weren't bluffing about the other bots . . .

Were they bluffing? It was getting hard to tell through the smoke filling up their office.

"I just told you, DuPont, you can't get to me. Now, listen. I've always had *your* best interests in mind. Every scrap of power Pataki and I scrounged up for you, every rule we bent for that death-defying Costume, every theft we committed? They were all for you, kiddo. Not us. You. You're our golden . . . well, that's a bad comparison. You're an investment, and you've paid off so well."

"That's why you threw me out of the airlock?" I asked. Something inside of me felt cold. No, not cold. My heart felt frozen.

"Showbiz, just showbiz!" Rocko said, their grasping hands waving cigars in the air. "You needed a moment alone in the spotlight. I got that for you. It was all about setting you up for success, and you should see what it did to the ratings!"

They touched one of the three screens hanging behind their head. A moment later, it enlarged until I could see it clearly, even through the shining barrier between us. I didn't have a degree in economics, but the general idea was pretty clear. This Episode was popular.

Really popular.

That sickened me, and my cheeks burned. Everything we did played into Rocko's hands somehow. They'd had years to watch me, over a year to figure out Bee—they'd probably even predicted *this*. I wanted to break through that shield and tear them apart. I wanted to end this.

But even as the heat rose in my throat, my heart was still ice-cold. And the cold was winning.

"Listen up, now. Marino? She's near her cap. There's not much further we can push her. She'll be in the top ten—not counting the metapowereds. But you? Your potential is almost limitless. You're a number one–caliber hero. Always have been. I saw it when you were just a kid. That's why I invested in you for so long." Rocko smiled and put out one of their cigars.

"Now, you want Stella-Lunar's powerset? We can do that. Dr. Jackson's? Tricky, but doable. The Agent? Why not? Just say the word and take out Brown and Callum."

"No." The cold place in my heart had solidified. It felt like a diamond, not ice, and it had pushed the angry heat back to almost nothing. Rocko was playing with me. They thought they were in control of this whole scene. But if they were right, and I was a number one–caliber hero with no limits, then I had to have a Costume for this. Right? I just needed to think through it.

"No? Alright, how about this? I've got another dozen bots on the way. You just sit back and watch. Don't need to raise a hand to help them, they'll take care of the other three. Then it won't be on you. We can get back to negotiations once they're taken care of. Oh, and I'll throw 5% your way for your trouble. It's a better deal than any super has ever gotten. What do you say to that?"

There was only one answer.

I was halfway through my [**Transformation Sequence**] when the first explosion filled the air behind me. Every turn, every musical trill, I'd tried to lock eyes with Rocko— to keep them focused on my face, not on the Costume I was transforming into.

So far, it had worked. But as the second bot exploded, Rocko's eyes glanced across the Costume piecing itself together over my glowing body.

A pink T-shirt, ripped jeans, and tennis shoes. A puffer jacket. And nothing else. No sign that I was Magical Girl Understudy, except for the plushie, two-tailed cat in my arms.

The music stopped.

I dropped Tails to the floor. She bounced, then flopped over, the system not powering her anymore. But her star-button eyes were locked on Rocko.

The reason the Hot Zone's shield worked . . . what Rocko had said about my powers not being able to hurt them . . . it all made sense.

I stepped toward the Jell-O-esque forcefield. If I was right about what they'd said, none of my powers could get through. So I'd dropped my powers. They wouldn't hurt the Ilneat anyway.

"DuPont, listen up. That's not going to work. The forcefield's designed to keep supers out; I tested it myself, on the bots and with The Agent's Temp Heroes. You can't hurt me. Now sit down, let the inevitable happen, and we'll talk. Seven percent, no oversight, no comms in-Episode."

People who'd outplayed their enemies didn't need to negotiate. The Agent never had, and we hadn't once we'd won. One offer, then business. If Rocko really thought they were winning, they'd . . . do what they always did. Make me do what they wanted with wordplay and by keeping me ignorant.

They weren't doing that. My eyes narrowed, and I lunged toward the gorilla/otter alien.

The Jell-O resisted for a second. Then, slowly, I started pushing through it. Behind me, the sounds of fire and fighting grew muffled.

"Whoa, whoa, whoa! Wait a second! DuPont, you don't know what you're doing. The whole Greater Ilneat Prosperity Community's going to be after you. ProsComm's not gonna be happy. So how about you spare everyone on Earth and settle down, huh?"

They were lying. ProsComm wasn't coming. The Agent had told us they were sitting this one out.

Everything inside me felt cold. The icy diamond crystal was growing, and it couldn't be stopped. Neither could I; my arm broke through the forcefield, and I grabbed Rocko by the collar. This close, they were so small. "I don't want your money, and I don't care about your threats. I want you all *gone*."

Both the Ilneat's squeezing hands reached for my arm, grabbing and twisting as cigar ashes covered their office's floor. My other arm broke through, and a moment later, so did the rest of me. But even then, Rocko wouldn't. Stop. Talking. They leaned in close, close enough to smell the smoke on their breath. "Well, that's not going to happen, DuPont. Listen up. I'm the best thing that's ever happened to you, including your stupid girlfriend back there."

My other hand slammed into Rocko's face—palm open. A tooth—wide and sharp like a gorilla's—flew out of their mouth, and their narrow black eyes went wide. For a second, in the hot, smoke-filled office, everything was quiet. Not silent—I could hear Bee, Theseus, and Lady Lockless fighting hard behind me.

But I could only do one thing to help them. I raised my hand again, and this time, I balled it into a fist. "Stand. Your bots. Down. Give up, and we'll get in touch with ProsComm so they can take you away. That's the only deal I'll accept. Think fast."

Rocko froze, their grasping hand touching their cheek gingerly. I reeled my fist back.

Then, with a shaking grasping hand, Rocko slowly pressed a button. The fighting outside tapered off as the bots stopped moving. The Ilneat's squeezing hands let go of my arm, and all four of their hands rose, their last cigar ashing onto the carpet. "Fine, DuPont. You win."

[Episode Finished!]
[Episode: Power War: The Last Power War - R]

[Penalties: N/A

[Episode Finished! +3 of each Style Point]

[Series Finished! +10 of each Style Point]

[Winner Winner! +3 of each Style Point]

[Role Focus: Drama + Cunning - Goal Met: +10 to Focused Styles]

[Alias - Understudy] [Archetype - Magical Girl] [Community Rank - 3/523]

[HP 4/15]

[Styles and Skills]

▶Archetype Skill - Transformation Sequence

▶Combo Skills - Power-Weaving

▶Badass (57) (Skill Roll Available)

▶Cunning (73) (Skill Roll Available)

▶Drama (108) (Skill Rolls Available)

▶Limelight Barrage 2

▶Starlance 3

▶Flamboyance (52) (Skill Roll Available)

▶Signature Skill - Wondrous Wardrobe

▶Stored Costumes: (Rainy Day, Copy Cat, Lab Assistant Panic, Lucky Star, Shock and Awe)

▶Solar Wing 2

▶Quick-Time Change 3

▶Improvised Ovation 2

▶Grit (57) (Skill Roll Available)

▶Freeze-Frame 2

[50 Badass Credits Used. Rolling Skill!]

[50 Cunning Credits Used. Rolling Skill!]

[50 Drama Credits Used. Rolling Skill!]

[50 Drama Credits Used. Rolling Skill!]

[50 Flamboyance Credits Used. Rolling Skill!]

[50 Grit Credits Used. Rolling Skill!]

[Skill Upgrade: Doom Ball 2 to Cat Trap: A scratching, biting whirlwind that slows the victim and adds a damage over time effect.]

[Skill Upgrade! Virga 2 to Misty Downpour: A healing rain that sticks around for up to a minute]

[Skill Upgrade! Limelight Barrage 2 to Spotlight Surge: A single beam of energy instantly hits the target area, with no time to dodge the spotlight]

[Skill Upgrade! Starlance 3 to Maximum Starlance: The big one. Increased damage, tracking, and speed]

[Skill Upgrade! Quick-Time Change 3 to Tear-Off Costume: Allows free switches between Costumes up to six times per Act.]

[Skill Upgrade! Rejuvenation 2 to Trance Heal: A large baseline heal, then more as long as you avoid taking damage]

60

The New Gotham Accords

SATURDAY, FEBRUARY 20

So much could change in a couple of months. But it's even more amazing how much stayed the same.

Two months ago, I'd been giving a press conference in the December cold, wincing as flashbulbs went off and reporters shouted questions my way. Now, I was an hour away from giving another one in the February chill, but I'd be giving it as the victor. As the winner. As the *hero*—the most famous hero on Earth.

Negotiations had begun to figure out how to pull all the Ilneat Network's stuff off Earth. Almhurst had been processing heroes and villains nonstop, with The Warden working overtime to determine who needed to be held and who needed to be released after the Ilneats' surrender. And, of course, my email and phone had both been blowing up nonstop with interview requests and invitations to appear on shows I'd never heard of.

But Mom and Dad were still angry with me for cutting classes.

"What do you mean you haven't been to class all week, Anika?" Mom asked over video chat.

I sighed. She just didn't *get* it. "Mom, I'm literally the most famous superhero in the world right now."

"And finishing your degree is even more important because of it. You said you were taking classes on public relations and how to keep your image up, right? Those are going to matter *more* now, not less. Sure, you could hire someone to help you and Bianca manage your public image or something, but there's no way of knowing what kind of money will be in superhero work in the future. You might be working the diner with me and being a superhero in your free time."

"Wouldn't be much of a change from now, then," I muttered.

"What was that?" Mom asked sharply.

"Nothing." I'd been working and doing college full-time. What would the difference be?

"Your mom's right, Dot. You don't know what the world's going to look like in three months. We're both proud of you for what you did, but you can't expect to ride that fame into the future," Dad said.

Half the professors weren't even in class yet. Drs. Jackson and Mays were recovering from their last two months, and it didn't look like they'd be back until next week at the earliest. And there wasn't a clear timeline for Dr. Mindstorm's return; she'd only been released from the Ultra-Max wing at Almhurst yesterday, and her statement included phrases like "find the truth about Launch Day" and "Ilneat interference in everyday Earth life."

That didn't sound like someone eager to return to teaching.

Besides, most of my classes weren't *relevant* anymore. Who cared about manipulating Episodes when the Network was on its way out? Rocko themself was stuck in Almhurst, too, until negotiations started, and everything about the system was canceled except the system itself.

Classes had taken a back seat for another reason, too. Bianca had been . . . extra affectionate . . . since my little space mishap. I'd spent a lot of time stuck next to her, unable—and, frankly, unwilling—to escape. As far as being kidnapped by a super went, it was the most fun I'd ever had.

Not that Mom and Dad would believe any of those reasons—or that I could *tell* them some.

"Alright. I'll start going to the classes I can on Monday. It's been a busy few weeks, though, so I might need to ease back into it," I said, crossing my fingers off-screen.

"Just as long as you don't fall behind," Dad said before Mom could cut in. "We know you can do this. It's been a rocky semester, but we believe in you."

"Thanks, guys," I said, sniffling a little. "I've got a press conference I have to be at in an hour, and I've been having nightmares about it all week, so I need to get ready, but I love you both."

"A press conference? You can't go to classes, but you can go to a press conference?" Mom said.

"Claire, it's okay. It's the weekend, and she's going to do better next week. That's all we can ask, right?" Dad interrupted. "You *are* going to do better next week, right, Dot?"

"Yes, Dad. I'm going to do better," I said. "I'll talk to you tomorrow, okay?"

"Alright. Good luck with the media. Let us know how it went. Love you, Anika. Bye," Mom said, and the video feed cut off.

The nightmare I'd been having was so *stupid*.

I'd find myself giving the press conference. At first, it'd go well. Lots of questions about the battles in the Hot Zone, a focus on what being on the Ilneats' cruiser was like, and all that. Easy-peasy. But then, I'd look out at the sea of reporters, and they'd all be the woman in the blue jacket from my press conference in December.

And that's when it'd get weird. They'd all ask me the same questions in unison, and no matter what I answered, they'd just keep asking for more. More answers, more elaboration, more details. I couldn't leave the mic either; as soon as I went to move, I'd realize I was in my undies. In front of the Tokyexico Council of Heroes building. In February. With a million cameras on me. Then I'd die of embarrassment and wake up.

I'd woken up sweaty and warm-cheeked the last three nights. Sometimes several times a night.

So, even though I desperately wanted a fifteen-minute catnap to catch up just a little bit on sleep, I did my make-up, picked out a nice outfit to wear, and did everything a normal person getting ready to meet the press might do.

Then I transformed into Magical Girl Understudy.

All that work at looking pretty, covered up in a fanfare of choral music and lights. But it *had* distracted me, so it was worth it. Probably. I waited for Bee to climb aboard my sailboard and rocketed toward the Council of Heroes building.

The conference was scheduled for 10:45 a.m., so when we landed at 10:40 a.m., Bee and I took a minute to get ourselves in order after the flight. I had to double-check that my Costume was on, just in case.

Then I took the podium and cleared my throat. "Hello, everyone. I'm Magical Girl Understudy, and this is Fursona. We've got a prepared statement before we get to the question-and-answer part of the conference."

Su-Bin and I had talked a *lot* in the last week. And I'd been paying attention to the other supers; a few of the pro-Ilneat ones had already started putting together the pieces for a post-Ilneat Network, run by supers instead of by the aliens. That sounded appealing in almost every way—but from everything Su-Bin could see, it still didn't take the Extras' safety and livelihoods into account.

I'd also reread the intro to Golden Goose's diary a couple of times, and I had to agree with my friend. If we picked up the Ilneats' shows right where they'd left off, nothing would really change for most people. She wanted me to start putting a stop to that.

And, thanks to the very public knowledge of my win over Rocko, I had a *lot* of social capital to spend—and that was a superpower all its own.

"I've been a superhero since I was thirteen—the same age as Golden Goose was when she got picked up by the Style System. This has been my entire life, and I love what I do. But so much of it isn't real. It's been a game for me my whole career—climb the leaderboard, do the Episode, use this city or that building as set dressing."

I paused to take a sip of ice-cold water. The winter sun shone brightly on the street beneath the half-destroyed CoH building. "I've worked with a few heroes who are true believers. People like Tranquility and The Narrator, who think they can make a difference—a real difference—in people's lives. They're not in it for the Episode wins or the power-ups. They're trying to do better.

"I don't think there's anything wrong with anyone who wants to make a career out of this. I've been a fan of superhero shows since I was five. I have a Stella-Lunar poster on my bedroom wall back home and everything. I want to keep doing this myself, but I've seen us at our best and worst, and I think we can do better."

My lips were already dry, but I powered on. "I'm announcing my support, in principle, for a negotiated version of the New Gotham Accords. We need an agreement that takes into account people's safety and their right to live a normal life without worrying about two superpowereds blowing up their living room. But it also needs to take into account superpowereds' rights. I'm not sure what that looks like. I'm not the most qualified person to figure that out. But I do know that if we put our minds to it, we can make it happen."

There. My obligations to Su-Bin were done. I took a deep breath. "Fursona and I will take questions now."

Someone shouted, "Are you done being a superhero?"

"No," Fursona said. "We're taking the semester off to focus on our last semester at TU, and waiting for the future to be more clear. Annie and I have done enough for now. This is our last act as heroes until graduation—unless there's an emergency. We'll still be ready, but neither of us want to participate in the Network's Episodes—or what's being built to replace them—anymore."

"What role do you think superpowered people will play in the future?" a woman further back in the crowd yelled.

I took a deep breath as Fursona looked my way. Somewhere, Su-Bin was watching. I'd done what she asked me to do, but this was a chance to show I believed it. And I did believe it. "I'm not sure. I think that, as long as people have powers, there will be people who use them for evil and people who use them for good. I don't see a world where heroes aren't necessary. But I do see one where heroes aren't automatically moneymakers for someone—where they do good because it's good, not for money or points. What that will look like is up to the people trying to negotiate that future."

The next question came in, and the next one. And, to my relief, almost all of them were about my statement. It was just like Su-Bin had said. If you took control of the press conference, the media would follow along. Fursona and I took turns answering them until, at last, an alarm went off silently on my phone. "I've got time for one more question, and then we have to get back to TU and study."

"What's it like being spaced?" a man shouted from the front row.

I laughed. "It sucks. A lot. I don't recommend it, and I hope I don't have to do it again." Then I walked away from the podium and ducked into the Council of Heroes building.

An hour later, I shut off the lights in the green room, walked to the maintenance door, and pulled it shut. Tails was on my bed, and the Roo-sona fursuit was in our closet, but neither of us had any plans to be Fursona or Magical Girl Understudy for a while. The politics and negotiation that were about to happen would happen with or without us, so it might as well be without.

Not that we had anonymity. The Pro-Earth supers had all been outed, and there was talk about naming the rest to even the playing field. But even with our secret identities thrust into the spotlight, we had a model for how to act. I couldn't help laughing at that; the models were all under five. But even so, they were comfortable being themselves, no matter what Costume they wore.

We could do the same.

61

What of the Future?

FRIDAY, APRIL 29

Gourmet and Theseus—Jessica and Tanner—dropped Bianca and me off at Walnut Tower. Jessica drove her Corvette, while Tanner white-knuckled the panic bar in the shotgun seat. I had no idea when they'd gotten together; if someone had told me the unserious, fun-loving girl would fall for Theseu-ass in our first semester, I wouldn't have believed it.

But they *were* great as a double date, and we hadn't caught up in so long. Not since February. And none of us had homework—not homework we wanted to do, anyway. So an evening out was perfect.

"Thanks," I said, heart racing almost as fast as Gourmet's—*Jessica's*—driving. Bianca was already wobbling back toward Walnut Tower. "I'd catch that movie with you, but we've already got a plan for the rest of the night."

"I can't quite put my finger on what," Tanner said. It was a lot easier to think of him as a Tanner than Gourmet as a Jessica.

"It's no biggie. I'm sure *We Dance in Dying Moonlight* will be playing next week, too," Jessica said.

"And I'm sure I'll want to see it even less the second time around," Tanner complained.

"Bye, guys," I said, leaving them both to their bickering as I hurried to catch up with Bianca. It hadn't *just* been a double date, either. Today was a special day for a bunch of reasons.

The Ilneat Imperial delegation had arrived in Yorkston to negotiate for Rocko and the rest of the Network Ilneats' release. They'd been stuck in Almhurst, New Riker's, and a half dozen other prisons since February. Finally, after weeks of talks, the Network's cruiser was moving out of our solar system—with all the Network's producers and employees on board, plus a handful of Ilneat guards.

Frankly, I didn't care what happened to Rocko once they returned to the Greater Ilneat Prosperity Community. There'd been something about legal issues the Network might be facing back home, and they'd lost so much money they probably couldn't pay their investors, but what mattered to me was that they, and all the other producers, were gone.

So, tonight's dinner had been about celebrating that.

They'd also started negotiations for the New Gotham Accords.

Right now, there were some . . . disagreements . . . about the status of powered and unpowered people, the Episode Cities, and . . . well, just about everything else. But with Mindstorm, Stella-Lunar, and a dozen of the heaviest-hitting major-leaguers at the table, along with delegations of unpowered diplomats from the largest cities and countries on Earth, disagreements were inevitable.

The most optimistic timeline for an agreement was two years. Most of the talking heads said four to five.

But it was a start. And it was worth celebrating.

We'd also been invited. Some of the heads of state didn't care that I was a sophomore in college; they only cared that I was a world-famous hero now. But I didn't want to suit up again until the future was a little clearer—or at least until Bee and I knew what the possibilities might be. Theseus was working again, and Gourmet was shooting her first *Gourmet's Glutton Hour* Episode since January next week. But Bee and I weren't ready yet.

We didn't want to go back to the way things were.

I didn't know what future I wanted to make yet, but I knew it had to be different. And until I knew, Magical Girl Understudy was staying in my head. And in Tails's.

My hand slipped into Bee's, and we hurried upstairs. We had an hour until 7:30 p.m., when Su-Bin and Cam would come over. And I had just the game for them.

But first, I needed some Bee time.

The doorbell rang at 7:36, and Bee climbed off my lap, flushed red. We'd gotten a little, uh, distracted. Just making out, but from the way she looked at me, there'd be more later.

Bee's lipstick was smudged, and she looked sweaty as she grabbed her shirt and fled for the bathroom. "You get it. I've gotta get decent."

"Dammit, Bee," I cursed under my breath, buttoning my own shirt up. I checked my hair—tousled and messy but acceptable—and sprayed deodorant under my arms, then hurried to the door. They were late, but we'd been so busy we hadn't bothered getting ready. They'd understand, though. They'd have to understand.

Cam—all two-fifty-plus of him, stuck out his hand. "Thanks for having us over for this. What's the game?"

I winced. The game was still in my room, still in its plastic wrap. I'd watched a video of it, but it wasn't exactly a two-player game, so we hadn't played it. "It's about finding connections between words. Come on in—booze can go on the counter, and I've got snack bowls somewhere. Thanks for supplying tonight. We had some other stuff come up."

Cam stepped inside, and I backpedaled to give the big guy some space. He nodded and headed for the kitchen, where we'd—thankfully—gotten the table set up before distraction set in.

That left me with Su-Bin.

I hadn't talked to her since the day we'd raided The Agent's lair. We'd texted a lot while I was coming up with my press conference speech, but she hadn't called me, and I hadn't wanted to push it. But then the texts had dried up . . . until earlier this month. I remembered the first one.

<You never did virtual game night - Su-Bin 2:31>

I'd offered to have her over, and after some discussion, she'd accepted. And now, here she was, in all her tiny glory—with soda cup in hand.

"Uh, hi," I said to the first person I'd talked to—probably my first friend—at TU.

"Hi. Show me the game."

I slipped away to our bedroom, taking care to keep the door shut so Cam and Su-Bin wouldn't see Bee's mess, and dug around until I found it. It featured a man in a suit and a professionally dressed woman silhouetted against a wildly orange-and-purple background. I retrieved it, tucking it under my arm and carrying it to the coffee table. Cam had already occupied the couch, claiming it for him and Su-bin, so I shrugged and pulled up a spot on the floor.

"Okay, this is *Code Names*. I've never played it, it's still in the wrapper, but I watched a little bit of it. It looks fun and goofy, so I'm thinking us versus you, in a battle of the word association game!" I said, peeling the wrapping off the box as Bee flopped down beside me, her knee bumping mine.

"You're on," Su-Bin said. We set up the words in a five-by-five grid, and I grabbed the first code card. "Alright, let's see . . . uh, Propeller, 2."

Bee rolled over, staring at the board. "Plane."

"Yep."

"And, uh . . ." She paused. "Uh, Wind?"

"No, that's one of theirs. Sorry, babe." I leaned over to kiss her, but she was already pushing herself up.

"I'm going to get a drinky drink. If I'm going to play this with Annie's word choice, I'm gonna need it. Anyone else?"

All our hands went up. She stared at us for a second, then rolled her eyes. "Cam, help me out here. This girl's only got two hands."

"So . . . are we okay?" I asked Su-Bin three minutes later, staring at the kitchen. Cam and Bee had been gone for a long time—way too long for a quick drink run. Even if she'd been mixing something, it shouldn't have taken this long. Which meant she and Cam had abandoned us on purpose. "I don't mean to be blunt, but—"

"I don't know, Annie," Su-Bin said. "You lied to me for a year and a half. That's pretty tough to get over."

"Su-Bin, I didn't lie to *you*. I lied to everyone. The secret identity thing felt important. Like, Rocko really stressed how important it was, how I needed my secret identity to keep my personal life separate from my superhero one. It all made sense when I was a teen, and I didn't have any reason to question it until really recently."

Su-Bin shook her head. "Who knew you were a superhero? Before the announcement, I mean."

"My parents, my ex-boyfriend, Bee, and her parents. Plus the Superpower Studies program professors, the TU administrators, and Rocko and Pataki. That's it. And that was too many, to be honest. I was horrified when Bee told me she knew." I stood up and started pacing the living room, tapping my hand against my hip.

"That's it, you're sure. No one else?"

I paused. "I don't think so. And I only told the TU people and Peter. Everyone else figured it out on their own. But you see why I couldn't tell you, right? You were—are—in charge of APPEAL. I was a super you were targeting. There was no way you wouldn't out me."

"That's true," Su-Bin admitted. "We actually tried to run an information-finding campaign on you, but it didn't work well. Everything about Magical Girl Understudy and Tokyexico University led to the same public-facing page and nothing else. Same for every other super. Eventually, we gave up."

"Well, that's . . . concerning," I said.

"I guess." Su-Bin shrugged. "We needed a win. Never thought we'd get one from allying with Magical Girl Understudy, though. You know, if the New Gotham Accords work out, it'll be your fault."

"Yeah, I've thought about that. They wanted me to be part of their talks, but I'd rather be a college kid for a while. I also declined all the medals, but they keep offering them, so I might have to accept," I said.

"They're giving you medals!?" Su-Bin asked. "Screw the game! Tell me about *that!*"

"So, we're okay?" I asked.

"Sure, just spill it!"

Cam and Bianca chose that moment to come back, and I shot my girlfriend a glare. She rolled her eyes and smirked, then chugged from a bottle of something clear. "Yeah, spill it. Why *did* we decline those medals? They'd be such a bragging point, and I know for sure that *Theseus* accepted his."

"Because I'm trying to be a better hero, and so are you. We shouldn't be fighting evil for prizes—we should be fighting it to help people. *Right*, Bee?" I said.

She laughed. "Sure, Understudy, whatever you say. Now, I think it's Su-Bin's turn to pick a word."

I poked my partner and girlfriend in the side and went for my own bottle. It turned out to be an IPA, but I didn't mind the bitterness. I needed to get drunk if I wanted to deal with *her* for the next couple of hours.

"How about Arrow, Four," Su-Bin said, smiling deviously.

By the time Su-Bin and Cam packed up their snacks and left, Bianca was so drunk she didn't care that we'd lost, and I was pleasantly tipsy. I held her hair for a minute, helped her strip down and put on pajamas, and tucked her into our bed. This wasn't the first time I'd be the big spoon to keep her propped up sideways, and it wouldn't be the last.

As I lay in bed with my hand around her chest, feeling her breathing, I couldn't help but think about the negotiations in Yorkston and about why I'd *really* declined the medals a half dozen governments had offered me.

They felt cheap, like prizes for a job half done.

None of this was over yet. It wouldn't be over until the New Gotham Accords were signed and the Ilneats agreed to leave Earth alone. Even then, there'd be studios—human-run, but still studios—making money off the Style System. And where that happened, there'd be abuses. Unless we built Mrs. N's better world, or Tranquility's, we could be right back to where we were.

So, as Bee breathed alcohol breath on my hand, I started planning out what Magical Girl Understudy would become. What she'd look like, what she'd fight for, and how I'd use her to build that world.

By the time I felt okay with Bee's level of drunk and fell asleep myself, I'd thought for a long time. The Costume was coming together, and so was her goal. I had a month to set her up before the best moment for a big reveal.

Epilogue

SATURDAY, MAY 21

Roth Arena was packed. There had to be ten thousand people in the stadium, and they'd filled the entire basketball court with chairs for the graduating class of 2044. But even though I couldn't stop sweating under the black-and-gold graduation robe I wore, I also couldn't stop shivering.

And it wasn't from the air conditioning.

My parents were out there, somewhere. So were Mrs. N and some of the Anti-Nap League, the professors—all four of them—and even, probably, Tele-Portal. I'd invited her, and I hoped she'd show up. We'd never been enemies. Not really. Just on opposite sides.

The nerves were getting to me. They'd been getting to me for weeks.

This would be my first public appearance as both Anika DuPont and Magical Girl Understudy, and even though Bianca and I had stayed up all night working through my speech, I had no idea how it'd be received. I slipped my hand into hers and squeezed. She squeezed back as the band played "Pomp and Circumstance" and more and more graduates filed in to fill the seats behind us.

"You've got this, Annie," Bee whispered.

"I know. But what if I don't?"

"Then you'll get it some other way. We've been doing that for two years, so you should be pretty good at it."

"Har har," I muttered as the music stopped.

"Hello, and welcome to . . ." the TU president said. I tuned him out. My speech was right after his introduction, and I couldn't focus. I could barely breathe. Even three months after the end of the Third Power War, I was still a celebrity. The keynote was mine, whether I wanted it or not.

I didn't. But that didn't matter.

"Our first speaker is a student in the first graduating class of the Super-power Studies associates program. She's been more trouble for the university than she's worth at times, but in the end, she's proof that our program produces the finest heroes in the world, and that our students are more than capable of changing it. Anika DuPont, more famously known as Magical Girl Understudy," the president said.

"That's your cue," Bianca whispered, poking me in the side.

I was already standing, walking automatically toward the podium and the lectern. The crowd went quiet as I tapped the mute button on the microphone and set Tails down in front of me. Then, I started my [**Transformation Sequence**].

I hadn't put the Costume on in public in . . . ever. On camera, sure, but not in front of ten thousand people. And I hadn't put it on at all since February. But I *had* been working on its design, in secret, with Tails.

The skirt was mid-thigh this time, silvery, with pink and blue highlights and *none* of the frills and bows that'd been staples of my previous Costumes. The tights were still white, but more see-through, and the boots only went up my calves. They were flats, too—none of the high-heeled stereotypical Magical Girl look for me. I wanted to look like I could run in my Costume.

I included only a single pink bow on the dress across my chest; the rest of the outfit's top was sleek and had silver cloth and dark lace paneling, with the same highlight tones. And instead of being festooned with comedy and tragedy buttons, I'd opted for a single one in the center of the bow. I'd spent a long time modeling the outfit and even longer convincing a cosplayer on campus to make it for me in a rush, but it was perfect. Even the tiara felt more mature—more adult—than either of the Costumes Rocko had designed for me, and the bow behind it in my hair didn't feel like *too* much.

The Costume felt sexy, powerful, and confident.

But it also felt like me. I'd foregone the ubiquitous domino mask; everyone could see my face, and even if my pupils went star-shaped as the music faded and the light show stopped, they could clearly see Anika DuPont under the tiara.

I turned the microphone back on. "Hello. It's an incredible honor to give this speech. I even picked out a new outfit for it."

I waited for the polite laughter to stop, heart in my throat. So far, so good. "But I didn't make a new oath. Every Magical Girl has one, from Stella-Lunar's Starlight and New Moon to Foamy Flash's Cleaning up Crime. Right now, I'm the only one who doesn't. And I didn't make one for two reasons. First, as my girlfriend knows, I'm really, *really* bad at them."

More polite laughter. I took a drink from the provided plastic bottle. It looked just like the ones Rocko had offered me at their studio in the Hot Zone. There was something poetic about their bottles lasting longer on Earth than they had, but I didn't dwell on it. "The other reason is that the world's changing, and I want my oath to reflect that. It's been focused on justice, and standing against evil, and all of that stuff.

"But the future will be different, and I want my new oath to focus on hope, transformation, and how I can affect that future. And not just me. All of us." I used [**Quick-Time Change**] to pop out of my Costume and back into my black-and-gold graduation robes.

"It's easy to think only those with great power can change the world. We see it on TV, in the news, everywhere. Stella-Lunar and Mindstorm are negotiating with world leaders and the Ilneat Empire's representative. Or the powers that be are hashing out the New Gotham Accords, figuring out the first steps of that future. You see that, and it's all people with great powers. You think they're not like you. But they are.

"I fought the Ilneats in space. I stood up to The Agent when no one else could. But I didn't do it alone. Other people—people without great powers—stepped up and took responsibility to help me all the way from when I was a kid until today. My parents, teachers, and professors all invested in me with no expectation that they'd benefit directly. They helped me build my future and made me who I am today. Not the hero, but the person. And as we, the 2044 Tokyexico University graduating class, step into the world, we're all going to have to step up to build ours."

Was I bobbling the speech? Maybe. I couldn't be sure. The only thing I could do was power on toward its end.

"I know we can all shape our futures and our world." The corny line was coming up. I'd fought with Bee for so long about it. She thought it was dumb. I *also* thought it was dumb, but every commencement speech had some bad lines, right?

"Just remember, we don't know what the future will hold, but I swear to meet it with hopeful eyes and a pure heart. To do the best I can for everyone, and make that future a better, more just place. I hope you all do, too. Remember, you're all heroes to someone, and you can all make the world better. Thank you."

I headed back to my seat, leaving the podium behind. I'd come back for my degree later, but for now, I just wanted to sit down next to Bianca and let myself relax. Tails was tucked under my arm; she looked smugly out at the audience as they cheered and clapped.

When I finally sat down, a wave of relief crashed over me. Bee's fingers wove between mine, and I squeezed her hand and tried to melt into my chair. The next speaker walked onto the podium, but I couldn't pay attention to him. All I could think about was that future.

There were *so* many questions. Would the modified New Gotham Accords work for the supers who wanted to keep making shows? How would their contract with the Ilneats work, and would everyone get a fair deal there? And what about the rest of us? I knew I didn't want to go back to the shows. I'd had enough of semiscripted hero work, and Fursona and I were strong enough to not need the leagues anymore.

I could be a hero anywhere. But what would that look like? It wouldn't be a career—not like acting in the Episodes had been. But it would be infinitely more fulfilling. So much more meaningful. This semester, we'd opened the door to a new future.

That future held so many questions, and so few of them had answers right now. But that was okay. Magical Girl Understudy and Fursona could handle the future. So could Annie and Bianca.

So could we.

Author's Note

Hello, Aest here! Thanks for reading Magical Girl Undergrad. My debut series is finished, but if you enjoyed it, I'm always writing and have two new series coming up. The Halcyon System is a thriller/supernatural LitRPG dealing with the end of the world and one girl's quest to grow strong enough to both protect her family and friends *and* uncover the mystery of why her reality's merging with so many others. Apocalypse Engineering is a crafting-based LitRPG apocalypse focusing on Hal as he tries to survive Earth's Integration into the Universal Order through engineering and mechanics. Check out https://aestbelequa.com/ for more of my work, and follow my author page on Amazon.

Please leave a review; it means a lot to me.

I'm usually on Discord (discord.gg/xvkfnNMzfe). Come say hello, tell me your favorite superpowers, and meet the fantastic community!

You can find the work of several talented authors at https://linktr.ee/coteh.

If Discord isn't your favorite, you can keep up with LitRPG through these Facebook groups:

LitRPG Books
LitRPG Forum
GameLit Society

About the Author

Aest Belequa is a LitRPG and progression fantasy author, play-by-post RPG game master, and former teacher from Colorado. He grew up loving fantasy and science fiction and tries to bring that same energy to his writing.

RESPAWN YOUR CURIOSITY

follow us on our socials

podiumentertainment.com

@podiumentertainment

/podiumentertainment

@podium_ent

@podiumentertainment